M000110660

# The Keepers of Alba

## Jordan Bernal

DRAGON WING PUBLISHING

Danville, California, USA

ISBN: 978-0-9910134-6-3
ISBN: 978-0-9910134-7-0 (ebook)

THE KEEPERS OF ALBA



Cover Design: Christine McCall, Christine McCall Designs

Library of Congress Control Number: 2020909680



United States * United Kingdom * Australia

To my family and friends who encourage
me to spread my wings and take flight.

"Life isn't about finding yourself.
Life's about creating yourself."
—George Bernard Shaw

# The Keepers of Alba

Jordan Bernal

# One

*Beltaine, Present Day—Hill of Tara, Ireland*

Devan Fraser ran her hand over *Lia Fáil*—the Stone of Destiny where ancient Irish kings had once been crowned—and thanked the gods above that she and those she considered family were still alive. For though no kings were coroneted today, a battle had been fought. A murderer stopped.

Since she'd first arrived in Ireland searching for her heritage, Devan's boring life had erupted into one of intrigue, magic, and heart-pounding terror. She'd met Christian Riley, and together they'd learned of the secret clan of dragons and riders and discovered they both possessed magical talents and talismans. They'd also rescued GRAYSON, a bullied wingless dragonet.

Now, after thwarting a murderous madman, Devan and Christian had sworn an oath to protect and nurture Ireland as the newest members of the Tuatha Dragon Clan. Devan had partnered with DOCHAS, a blue and silver dragon, and Christian with green ROARKE.

Tears of joy blurred Devan's vision as Christian wrapped his arms around her. She held tight to the man she loved, the infuriating, yet charming Irishman who'd nearly died earlier tonight. And she couldn't forget about GRAYSON who'd saved her life by taking a poisoned dagger meant for her. *Thankfully, both of them are now safe.*

The pebbled surface of Lia Fáil reminded Devan that life could be rough, that her destiny was not set in stone. In the time it took for the reciting of her oath, Devan had gone from being recently orphaned to having her most secret desire realized—being a vital member of a group. She finally belonged.

*"The poison continues in the Wingless One. He is dying."* DOCHAS's frantic voice interrupted Devan's thoughts. *"Ye must hurry, the Wingless One is dying."*

The telepathic litany from the dragon hammered Devan. Her knees buckled and darkness clouded her vision. "No. I can't lose anyone else I love," she mumbled as she slid to the grass.

"Devan, *a ghra*. What is it?" Christian's lilting voice anchored her. "Come now, my love. Breathe." He gently pulled her to her feet. "Tell me."

"It's GRAYSON. DOCHAS says he's dying. The poison from that murdering bastard's dagger is still in him. How can that be? We have to help." Devan stumbled but Christian grabbed her hand to steady her as they ran.

They tore past the bonfire toward a large white tent where the clan members and dozens of dragons had gathered to celebrate Beltaine and the new dragon and rider pairings.

"Let us through," Christian shouted as they approached.

Niall, the ten-year-old grandson of the clan healer, knelt beside the wingless gray dragonet. The boy rubbed his dragon scale pendant and chanted GRAYSON's name over and over, fear lacing his tone.

Devan dropped to her knees and lightly stroked the dragonet's snout. *"Speak to me."* GRAYSON's silence terrified her. *"Please."* She swiped at her tears. *"Stay with us."*

"I can't hear him," Devan said aloud, whirling in all directions until she spotted Sean, the clan leader. "What should we do?"

Sean clasped Devan's shoulder. "The poison must have reached his heart. I'm afraid there's nothing any of us can do."

"It's imperative we do something. For God's sake, he saved my life." Devan wrenched free of Sean's hold. She bent over the dragonet's neck injury. "What if FIONN flushed GRAYSON's wound with his flame, would that burn out the poison?"

*"GRAYSON, hang on. We'll help you,"* Devan bespoke the gray drake before calling to her compeer. *"DOCHAS, my sweet, call to GRAYSON. Urge him to fight."*

Devan lifted her teary gaze to Sean. "I know I'm grasping for any wisp of a solution, but we have to try something. He can't die."

*"The Wingless One struggles against the poison,"* DOCHAS bespoke.

"You must have some idea if the dragons can use their magic to purge the poison," Devan begged Sean.

"I'm not sure." Sean's voice wavered. "We've never used the magic to heal one of our own."

"No time like the present," Padrick, Sean's second-in-command, interjected. Then he pitched his voice so all could hear. "Quickly, gather in a circle as we did for the Chosen Ceremony."

The dragonriders clustered around and joined hands. Their dragon compeers formed up behind them.

"*Mo Caras*, my clan family," Sean began, "gather the *draíocht*, the magic. Hold it close to your heart and pray for the healing of GRAYSON." He scanned the dragonriders, then nodded to Devan.

"Dragons and dragonriders of Éire," Devan said. "I beseech you on GRAYSON's behalf to bond with him, allow your magic to flow through him. Use your strength and power to flush the toxins from his blood."

The only sound was the crackle of the Beltaine fire.

"*Ni neart go cur le cheile*. There is no strength without unity." Sean's voice rose. "And GRAYSON is one of the mighty Tuatha Dragon Clan."

The clan members repeated the motto, then released hands. They pressed their right fist to their hearts and recited the clan oath, "*Dilseacht. Fáil. Saoirse*. Loyalty. Destiny. Freedom."

Over two-dozen melodic dragon voices chanted the Gaelic words in Devan's mind, then she heard their vow. *"We share our cumhacht, our power, with the Wingless One so he might be healed. He is brave. He is our brother. He will live."*

At first, nothing seemed to happen, then GRAYSON stirred as a black viscous sludge pushed its way out of the gaping wound in his neck. *"It burns, it burns,"* his weak whisper tore at Devan's heart.

Niall whimpered and scrambled back as the poison emerged.

*"It sears me. Please make it stop."* GRAYSON's tail twitched and his sapphire blue eyes whirled at a frantic pace.

*"Lie still and let the magic work. Just a bit longer. We must get it all out,"* Devan soothed as she knelt again beside Niall and the young drake.

The poisonous sludge lightened in color until the rich red of clean blood flowed. Sulfur overtook the sweet scent of spring as the grass turned the color of peat under the growing puddle.

GRAYSON's scaled body relaxed. He nuzzled Niall, then Devan.

*"My blood is as cool as the water in the lough,"* GRAYSON said. His voice drifted. *"I am so tired."*

*"Don't sleep yet. We need to make sure your blood is poison-free before we close the wound,"* Devan crooned.

Christian knelt beside her. He wrapped his arms around her and kissed her cheek.

"I don't think I could handle it if he died. He took the dagger meant for me." Devan leaned her head on Christian's shoulder and wept, exhausted. The sounds of the other clan members slowly filtered to her, so she fought back fresh tears.

Christian lifted his shoulder, directing her gaze to GRAYSON's neck. "His blood runs red now, free of the poison. Thanks to you."

*"The Wingless One is purged,"* DOCHAS bespoke Devan. *"It is time to flame the wound. FIONN, as dragon leader, is ready. Warn GRAYSON. Then move away."*

*"I can hear FIONN. There is no need to warn me,"* GRAYSON said, his tone filled with uncertainty and wonder.

Devan scratched GRAYSON's eye ridges. "We'll be right over here," she told the drake. Devan and Christian rose, pulled Niall with them, and the trio moved to stand next to Sean.

"How can we be sure the poison is all out?" Devan asked Sean.

"We need to rely on what the dragons tell us. FIONN says GRAYSON is clean. Never before has so much dragon power been infused into anyone, let alone a dragon so young."

Devan looked at Christian but spoke to Sean. "We must make sure all the poison is out of Christian's blood as well."

"Are you crazy? I'm fine." Christian rotated his shoulder, wincing as beads of sweat formed above his upper lip.

"We thought GRAYSON was fine. Look what happened. He almost died." Devan lifted a palm to Christian's cheek. "Do this for me. For your dragon, ROARKE. Please. I love you."

Christian stared into her eyes for so long that Devan was sure he would decline her plea. Finally, he gave a short nod. "If it will ease your worry."

Devan lifted to her toes and pressed a light kiss to his lips. "It will, a ghra." She was getting better at speaking the few Gaelic words she knew.

Christian turned to Sean. "Then let's get this done."

While Healer Timothy and Niall attended GRAYSON, Sean led Devan and Christian away from the crowd. Padrick followed.

"Padrick, get the dragonriders and their compeers together," Sean said. "We'll repeat the purging for Christian. Just as a precaution."

Christian removed his coat and shirt. His stomach muscles bunched as he lowered himself onto an empty table. Devan peeled the bandage away from his collarbone, revealing the angry red laceration.

Christian hissed when Padrick used the tip of the scalpel Timothy had given him to reopen the wound.

Devan brushed Christian's black hair from his forehead and leaned close. Her warm breath feathered over his skin as she whispered her love into his ear. He turned his head and captured her lips in a searing, intimate kiss. Before she fell too far into the kiss, she ended it and joined the circle of dragonriders around the table.

Sean once again spoke the plea for healing.

Devan silently said her own prayer, then she joined the dragonriders and the dragons in the clan oath. *Sweet Lord! How could I demand he do this? What if the dragon fire kills him? But if the poison's still in there, he'll die anyway. I just found him. He can't die!*

The clan oath chanted from the clan members intensified, taking over Christian's thoughts.

*"Stay with me. I will no' let ye die,"* Christian's dragon, ROARKE, bespoke him.

A boiling, searing pain started in Christian's chest and flowed outward with every beat of his heart. He bit down on his lower lip to keep from crying out, yet inside his head, he screamed.

The clawing agony provoked tumultuous thoughts. *Is this what dying feels like? Must be hell. It's certainly not heaven. In my reckless youth, I never considered I might die. And now, a nick—a poisoned dagger—might seal my fate.*

With his heartbeat pounding in his ears, Christian writhed and let out a ragged breath as dark, muddy red blood flowed from the wound and ran down his neck and arm. "Christ Jesus." He closed his eyes, then clenched and unclenched his fists.

When the blood changed to a bright red, Sean spoke aloud. "Enough. FIONN, please cauterize it."

Christian's eyes popped open.

The red dragon raised his triangular-shaped head above the circle of humans. His sapphire blue, multifaceted eyes whirled faster as he sent a tight stream of red-orange flame directly toward Christian's open wound.

Christian's back arched off the table as the jagged tear in his skin closed. He moaned as Devan's cool fingers soothed the throbbing of his seared flesh. He hadn't realized he'd squeezed his eyes shut again, but he left them closed to savor his lover's caress.

"It's done," Devan whispered as she finished applying a fresh bandage. "Just lie back. You're quite pale."

"You would be as well if you'd just been flamed by a dragon. And I can't even begin to describe how the magic felt burning through my veins." Christian opened his eyes and tried to sit up. Dizziness overtook him. He slumped back down on the table. "Bloody ifrinn."

# Two

*Beltaine—Lochbuie Standing Stones, Scotland*

Liam MacLean bristled when The MacLean, leader of the two-dozen MacLean dragons and riders now gathered on the Isle of Mull, strode toward him and his mates. The clan chieftain's stormy expression didn't bode well for anyone who got in his way. Damnation, what did I do now? Liam thought as he took another sip of whiskey.

"Liam." The MacLean zeroed in on him. "Ye are no' a novice rider. I expect ye tae ken yer duties, no' pass them off tae others whilst ye tap the whiskey casks." The MacLean indicated the untouched pallet of foodstuffs stacked next to the opening of a white tent. "Yer da would be disappointed."

Liam's mates made rude gestures and snickered behind the chieftain's back. When The MacLean shifted to glare over his tartan-clad shoulder, Liam's mates scattered.

"Leave my da out of this." Liam slammed his glass down. "You never understood him. At least he wasn't a bastard to his own family."

The MacLean scowled but didn't respond to the jab. "Since ye 'ave so much time on yer hands, ye can build the Beltaine bonfire."

"But . . ." Liam balled his hands into fists. "That means I'll miss most of the *cèilidh*. All the food and drink'll be gone. That's not fair."

The MacLean tucked his thumbs into his kilt belt. "Ye might've thought o' that afore ye started drinking when ye were tasked with set up." The burly chieftain tilted his head as if contemplating more punishment, then his features softened. "Ye ken the young riders look tae ye for leadership. I expect more from ye."

Liam watched through a red haze of anger and embarrassment as the chieftain strode away. *Who made him God? The unloading of provisions would've gotten done. Eventually.*

With none of his mates in sight, Liam stormed to the clearing north of the standing stones where the bonfire was to be lit. Piles of firewood were scattered where the dragons had dropped their pallets. *Great. This'll take forever.*

Under the shadow of the nearly 2,400-foot grassy hill known as Ben Buie, Liam began his task. He spotted several of his mates with his brother-in-law, Graeme Fraser. *I thought that kiss-arse left after bringing my wife back from her visit with her mum. Is he staying to spy on me?*

Graeme joined him at the wood stack. "What did The MacLean want with you?"

"What he always wants—to berate me in front of everyone. I'm not allowed to enjoy myself. It's supposed to be a damn cèilidh, for feck's sake." Liam stood hipshot with his arms crossed. "I'm to miss all the fun because I'm to build the bonfire—all alone."

"I know you're angry with The MacLean, but don't do anything stupid that would reflect badly on your family, especially my sister," Graeme said. "Being pregnant with twins is hard enough on Merida. I won't see her unhappy because her husband is impulsive."

"I'm not impulsive. I'm just not as complacent as my da was. He should have been clan leader. Look where that got him. Dead." Liam jerked his head in the direction of the standing stones where The MacLean was talking animatedly with an elder. "That bastard's the only family I have left, and I'm not even allowed to call him Uncle Brian."

"Merida is your family now. And the bairns soon." Graeme cocked his head. "I can't do anything to change your relationship with your clan chieftain, but I can help with building the bonfire."

"Nah. Wouldn't want The MacLean to say I wasn't doing my job." Liam watched as the mist rolled in from the sea, obscuring the nearby cottages. *Damn wood'll be too damp to burn properly.* He gazed longingly at the large, white tent that held the food and drink. Inspiration struck. "What I could use is one of the small casks of whiskey. What do you say? Bring one over, since I'm not welcome in the tent until I've finished building this bonfire." When Graeme hesitated, Liam smiled. "Please."

"All right. But don't get blootered. Remember, Merida needs you sober for the Beltaine Ceremony."

"Don't fash. I'll only have a wee dram."

When Graeme left for the tent, Liam searched the stacks for tree stumps. He found three that were two feet in diameter to serve at the fire's center. He'd rolled each of them into the center of the dirt circle by the time Graeme returned.

"Thanks, mate." Liam took the whiskey cask. "I've got it from here. Why don't you check on Merida? She's to help serve up the food."

Graeme nodded. "I'll make sure she remembers to take an occasional break. And since it's getting late, I've decided to stay tonight. Give a shout if you need help."

*As if.* Liam waved his pesky brother-in-law away. *Now for some oomph.* He was warming to his idea. He shifted one of the stumps and set the cask in the middle. Piling small logs on top of the stumps to hide the cask, he stacked logs and branches into a large pyramid. He was careful to keep his thoughts closed off from his dragon, KENNETH, as he didn't want any grief from his compeer. Liam continued building the wooden byre until it was over thirty feet in diameter and over half that in height.

He looked over his handiwork and grinned. *The MacLean won't have anything to complain about. Best Beltaine bonfire ever built.*

When Liam strolled back to the white tent, he was pleased to see there was still plenty of food and drink. He filled a plate, poured himself a mug of beer, then went in search of his mates. No way did he want to eat and drink under the judgmental eyes of his wife and brother-in-law. That ballbuster The MacLean on his arse was enough for one night.

Liam found his mates listening to music at the far corner of the tent. He grabbed a seat and wolfed down his food as though he'd not had a meal in days. He'd barely finished when The MacLean's booming voice called the dragons and riders to the stone circle.

As the sun slipped to the edge of the horizon, twenty-four dragons gathered amongst the standing stones of Lochbuie. The riders took their designated places next to their dragons.

"MacLean dragons of Alba, prepare for yer oath." The MacLean placed his left hand on the tallest stone while his right hand clasped the MacLean crest pinned to the tartan draped over his left shoulder. He bowed his head and spoke the clan motto: "*Biochas. Mianach. Onóir.* Virtue. Mine. Honor."

Each dragonrider in turn repeated the words. When all had sworn their oath to the clan, The MacLean led them to their places around the byre Liam had erected. In unison, the riders chanted, "*Glóir go Alba.* Glory to Scotland." At a signal from the chieftain, each dragon spewed fire at the stacked wood.

Flames backlashed and the ground trembled. The sound wave roared like a Chunnel train speeding past. An invisible hand shoved Liam hard into KENNETH. Liam lost his breath as he smashed into the diamond-hard, yellow scales of his dragon's chest. Wind swirled in a vortex and the conflagration swept toward The MacLean and several other dragons and their riders. Chunks of wood spewed in all directions, reminding Liam of javelins. Riders and dragons scattered.

Screams mixed with the roar of the immense heat. The stench of burning flesh assaulted Liam's nostrils.

"No! No!" Liam pushed away from his dragon and frantically searched for Merida. Ghostly images of dragons and riders swayed in the flickering flames. "It wasn't supposed to explode."

Shoved from behind, Liam fell and skinned his hands. Smoke blinded him. Tears streamed from his eyes. "Merida! Merida! Where are you?"

When Liam regained his feet, riders had clustered around a burning hulk.

Graeme spun him around. "What the bloody hell have you done? You've near killed The MacLean."

Liam pulled his arm free of Graeme's tight grasp. "All I did was add some punch to get the fire ablaze." Merida appeared out of the smoke, covered in soot with blood pouring from her nose. Liam threw his arms around her. "Thank heavens you're alive."

"What happened?" Merida pointed helplessly toward the raging inferno.

"You used the whiskey cask, didn't you?" Graeme accused. At Merida's confused look, he continued. "Your eejit of a husband wanted to impress The MacLean by building the largest fire ever." Graeme rounded on Liam. "Congratulations. Auld Alain's dragon is scorched dead. Alain might be as well."

"You lie. A dragon can't be flamed by a simple fire." Liam gazed over Merida's shoulder toward The MacLean.

The man's skin was red and blistered, clumps of hair singed. The shoulder tartan he'd worn lay smoking on the ground near Alain's curled body. When his uncle's dark gaze pierced Liam, it wasn't his uncle Liam saw, but an enraged chieftain out for blood.

"Liam!" The MacLean bellowed just before he charged.

Liam gently pulled Merida behind him, keeping his hand rested on her extended stomach.

Graeme and two other riders grappled with The MacLean, holding him back.

"Ye built the bonfire." The MacLean spit the words at Liam. "What did ye do?"

At the chieftain's growl, Liam rushed to explain. "I just added a bit of whiskey to help get the fire started. I've done the same in my griller a thousand times when the drizzle won't let the flame catch."

The MacLean glanced at the fully engulfed bonfire, then back to Liam. "But ye never spoke words of power afore lighting yer griller, aye?" Liam shook his head. "Nor has yer dragon ever flamed the fuel?"

Liam's eyes widened as he finally understood what he'd done.

*"Ye killed NESBIT and his rider,"* KENNETH condemned Liam telepathically.

"But . . . I didn't think—"

The MacLean grabbed Liam's shirtfront in his meaty fist. "Nae, ye never do. Now a dragon and his rider are dead. Whether intentional or no', ye abused the magic bestowed on the dragons tae kill one o' our own." His brogue thickened with his rage. "'Tis shame ye 'ave brought on the MacLean clan. Shame on yer family. Shame on yerself."

The MacLean swept his arm to encompass the whole area. "As clan chieftain, 'tis my duty tae see Alain and his dragon honored in death." He bowed his head. "*At dheis Dé raibh a anum.* May his soul be in God's right hand."

Then he turned on his nephew. "And ye punished." The MacLean, his tone rough with anguish, raised his voice for all to hear. "Ye, Liam MacLean, are hereby exiled until ye prove yerself worthy o' being a member o' the clan. And if it 'twas within my control, I'd strip ye o' yer dragon as well."

Merida gasped.

Liam felt her slide away and turned to find his pregnant wife lying crumpled at his feet, unconscious.

# Three

*Summer Solstice, Lough Gur, Ireland*

Devan rolled her aching shoulders as she finished oiling the joints on DOCHAS's outstretched silver wing, then spoke aloud. "You grow so fast I can't keep up with the dry and cracked patches, my sweet."

*"Thank ye. It was itching fiercely,"* DOCHAS bespoke as she folded her wing and settled onto her cushioned platform.

"ROARKE grows as well," Christian said as he leaned against the lair opening and wiped his fingers on a rag. "I swear he's doubled in size since we partnered at the Chosen Ceremony."

Devan shuddered at the reminder of the night six weeks ago she almost lost Christian and GRAYSON, the wingless dragon who saved her life.

"Can you believe it? I've been in Ireland three months. I need to go back to America." She closed the jar of ointment and grabbed a fresh rag to clean the residue off her fingers.

"What?" Christian approached her. "I thought you were staying."

Devan scratched DOCHAS's eye ridges. "Of course I'm staying in Ireland. But in a very real sense, I ran away from my life. I found the ring and the letter and embarked on this journey without forethought. I've things to wrap up before I can move here permanently. I'll need to put my parents' house on the market, sell the furniture, the cars. I'm thinking it will probably take two or three weeks to cull through their things and find a reliable estate agent. Then I'll still have my belongings to sort through."

She glanced at a silent Christian. *Is he mad at me? Dare I ask?* She hesitated. "Will you come with me, if Sean and Padrick and the clan can manage without the two of us for that long?"

Christian shook his head, his shoulder-length black hair swaying. "I should head back to Dublin as I've things of my own to handle." He took a step away. "Besides, I've no passport."

Devan reached for his hand, held him in place. "I'm sure Padrick could assist with that. He helped pave the way for me on my dual citizenship. A passport should be much easier, especially since he's your father."

"There's no need. I've never left Ireland before. I'm not in any hurry to now. Besides, I could tie up my own loose ends and be back here while you're in America."

"You're sure?" She waited until he nodded. "Then let's talk to Padrick about when would be a good time for us to be away." *I hope Christian's not tired of me already.* Devan forced a smile through her insecurities and searched for a lighter subject as they left DOCHAS's lair. "Maybe he'll tell us which dragons Sean has chosen for tonight's mating flight. I wouldn't miss that for anything." She grinned, then her smile faded. "Do you think Sean's nervous about this flight?"

"Why would he be?"

"It's the first one not on one of the four main Celtic holidays," Devan explained. "I still can't believe Sean had FIANNA and KIERAN mate after everything that happened on Beltaine. FIANNA should drop her clutch of eggs around the middle of September. I can't wait. It'll be our first hatching."

Christian didn't respond. He seemed lost in his thoughts.

A brilliant blue sky and a cool breeze greeted them as they emerged from the underground hill that housed the dragons at Lough Gur. Hearty flowers poked their heads up through the rocky landscape. Devan wanted to spend some time researching all the flora and fauna of her new surroundings, but her curiosity would need to wait, especially since she invariably got lost in any of her research projects.

Devan and Christian continued toward Padrick's office before she spoke again. "I'll need to book a flight. The sooner I go, the sooner I can get back. But I want to be in San Francisco for July fourth—Independence Day. It's my favorite holiday, the last one I'll get to celebrate in America."

Christian grunted. "There'll still be a long time before the clan is at full strength—no thanks to Kiely's ruthless treachery—grandmother or not."

"Right. But her misplaced actions hatched GRAYSON. He saved my life by taking that dagger meant for me, so I'll forgive Kiely, at least on that issue."

"On that, I'll agree." Christian lifted their joined hands and kissed the back of her hand before tapping on Padrick's office door.

Padrick ushered them into comfortable chairs, then he leaned against his desk and crossed his booted feet. Devan explained her need to return to America and Christian added his desire for several days in Dublin. Padrick agreed to block out the requested number of days on the flying schedule, then mention it to Sean after the solstice ritual and *céilí* that evening at the Hill of Tara.

Devan and Christian left to get ready for the celebration.

While Devan bathed, she pondered over Christian's quietness. *What's the real reason he doesn't want to accompany me? Does he want his freedom? Maybe Rick was right. I'm not good at relationships.* Stop it, she chided herself. *Christian also has a past life that he needs to deal with. Don't go inserting your insecurities into every interaction with him. He's not Rick. Don't be needy. That would surely drive anyone away.*

A knock on the bathroom door broke into Devan's self-destructive thoughts.

"Are you almost finished?" Christian opened the door. "I think the whole contingent of Lough Gur dragons are harnessed and ready to go in the time it takes you to get ready," he teased.

"I'm not one of those women who take hours to get ready.

Besides, I've only my back to wash. You could help—"

"Then we would be late." His sexy grin flashed and his deep blue eyes twinkled. "I'm heading over to harness ROARKE. Thought I'd let you know."

Devan nodded. "I'll be there shortly." When Christian left, she resolved not to borrow trouble and was determined to enjoy every minute she had with him before she left for America.

*After all, it might be all that's left to me.* And just like that, her fickle self-doubts crept in again. She scowled at her reflection in the mirror: short, spiky brown hair, plain brown eyes, and an oval face that wasn't beautiful, yet wasn't homely either. Devan threw up her hands in frustration. "Don't be an idiot. Remember what Mom and Dad always said, 'Be yourself and you'll find the right person. The one who loves you and only you.'" She stormed out of the bathroom. "If it's not to be Christian, then so be it."

Thirty minutes later as she and Christian joined the rest of the riders in preparing for the flight, she tried not to overthink every comment or motion from Christian. She noticed the strain lines near his eyes and could tell he was forcing a jovial mood.

Padrick approached Christian as he climbed aboard ROARKE. "Everything okay?"

"Yes," Christian answered, his tone sharp.

"You're tense, son. Relax. There's nothing special required of either of you or your dragons," Padrick said. "You'll both be fine tonight. Enjoy the céilí."

Devan answered for Christian. "We're both a bit nervous. It's the first time back to the Hill of Tara since . . ."

Padrick shifted his gaze to Devan. "Right. Well . . . there's no killer to deal with tonight. Though my mother will be there. My hope is that my father will keep her in line." Padrick grimaced, then waved away any possible concerns. "And the sooner we have mating flights, the sooner dragons hatch and grow, the sooner Sean can retire Kiely and Ronan and their dragons." Padrick patted ROARKE's gleaming green chest scales.

"I can take care of Devan and myself." Christian snapped out. "Your job is to keep Kiely away from us."

Devan gasped at Christian's vehemence, but Padrick just nodded.

"Understood." Padrick turned to where his dragon, DECLAN, waited. *"Gaothchothrom agus eitilt sábháilte."*

"Fair winds and a safe flight," Devan replied in English since she still had not quite mastered the Gaelic phrase the clan members used as the newest incantation before flying adragonback. She and Christian climbed aboard their dragons.

DOCHAS swooped over the rows of bundled items to be taken to the celebration. Wrapped pallets full of folding tables and chairs, food and drink, plates and cups, and all the other items that went into throwing a party awaited transportation.

Devan marveled at her dragon's dexterity as DOCHAS picked up the bundle assigned to her. Here was a dragon that nearly filled a baseball diamond from wingtip to wingtip, snout to horned tail, yet the dragon's front claws could grip something without ripping it to bits. Devan guided her compeer into formation next to ROARKE. The Lough Gur dragons circled the clan compound once, then turned northeast and headed away from the billowing white clouds that built against the deep blue of the late afternoon sky.

The cool breeze warred with the summer sun much the same way as Devan's turbulent emotions as the Lough Gur dragon contingent winged their way toward their destination. She carefully shielded her thoughts from her dragon—after all, there was no point in infecting DOCHAS with all the ridiculous self-doubts that plagued her. *Is Christian really upset over Kiely's past actions? Or is it something else?* Various possible scenarios circled in Devan's mind. None of them were good.

*"What has ye distracted?"* DOCHAS bespoke Devan. *"Ye are tense. No' enjoying the flight as ye normally do."*

*"Just have a lot on my mind. You know I have to go back to America for a short time, don't you?"*

*"Aye. I believe ye should demand we fly together to the land of yer birth. I am strong. I can fly forever without tiring."*

Devan leaned forward and stroked her compeer's neck. *"Your abilities aren't in question, my sweet. But where I need to go wouldn't suit you. It's a huge city—"*

*"Did no' black* DECLAN *fly into Dublin to save ye?"* DOCHAS snorted. *"I am as agile as he is. I have been practicing my magic-gathering flight patterns."*

*"I know you have and I love you all the more for wanting to go with me, but Dublin is small compared to where I'll be going. There is nowhere you can stay that wouldn't put you in jeopardy of exposure. And there are no stone circles for us to regenerate the magic. Without that, you would not remain hidden."*

DOCHAS sulked.

*"I won't be away too long. I promise,"* Devan said. *"I'll ask Sean if you can visit* GRAYSON *and Niall while I'm away. Would you like that?"*

*"Aye. And I shall fly with* ROARKE. *Perhaps I shall even challenge him to complete the Drombeg stone dance pattern for best time."*

*"Sure. And you could help me by keeping an eye on Christian while I'm away."*

During the flight, Christian wrestled with his doubts about Devan returning from America. There was no question she was fully bonded with DOCHAS, but would she stay for him? No one in his life had ever stuck around for him. *Am I setting myself up to be left again? Maybe I should hold back how I feel about her.*

He constantly checked his surroundings, making sure he and ROARKE kept in the designated flight formation. Not so much because the formation was new, but Christian still felt out of place with the dragon clan. He had not only joined the clan with Devan in the Chosen Ceremony, but he had found family. Padrick, his father, hadn't known that Erin, the girl he'd loved long ago, had been pregnant with Christian and had run from the manipulative Kiely—Padrick's mother. The shocking reunion had taken place after he and Devan had been found by the dragon clan and he'd experienced one of his visions.

Together, he and Devan had rescued GRAYSON from abuse. While Devan had heard the frightened cries for help, he had seen the bloodied wingless dragon imprisoned in a dark barn-like structure.

He had been angry with the abuser, but that hadn't been the weirdest emotion. No, that had been when he'd come face-to-face with his birth father—a man he'd never met, yet resembled so much.

Christian scanned the dragons and riders in front of him. He saw his father sitting tall in the riding saddle atop his dragon, DECLAN, leading the formation. *I shouldn't be so hard on Padrick. He's adjusting to our situation just as I am.*

His gaze strayed to Devan atop DOCHAS. *And I should trust Devan to stick to her word. After all, she's the one person who's never lied to me. Or abandoned me.*

DOCHAS banked to the right as the dragon formation reached the western border of the Hill of Tara.

Devan berated herself for being too absorbed in her thoughts to pay attention to the flight.

*"Nonsense. I am able to fly in formation and bespeak with ye at the same time. I will always keep ye safe. We are compeers."*

*"You are the cleverest of all dragons."* Devan praised DOCHAS. *"I would fly you to America if it was possible, my sweet. I shall call every day to see how you are faring. We can even try bespeaking, though the distance might be too great."*

Devan glanced around just as DOCHAS backwinged and slowly lowered her bundle into the clearing to the south of the church where the killer had hidden six weeks ago.

A shiver ran over Devan's neck as DOCHAS landed. She twisted her dragon ring around her finger and searched for Christian until she found him amongst the crowd of riders disembarking from their dragons. He slid from ROARKE's back and met her silent gaze.

"Keep him safe for me," Devan whispered aloud as she slid to the ground.

*"ROARKE will no' allow harm to befall his compeer, yer Christian,"* DOCHAS bespoke, then blew a warm burst of air over Devan's spiky brown hair. *"Do no' fash."*

Devan held a shaky grin as she scratched DOCHAS's eye ridges. *"I know. I'm just being silly."*

*"What is silly? Ye have no' bespoke a joke."*

Devan shook her head. *"No. I meant that I was worried about the depth of my relationship with Christian and that I shouldn't worry over things that aren't true."*

*"Aye. Tonight we celebrate and strengthen the magic. And our bond."*

Devan hurried to catch up with Christian and the others who were unloading the carnival-sized white tent, chairs, tables, food, and beverages. She glanced over at Meara who was helping Braeden unpack his guitar and *bodhrán* for the céilí later in the evening.

*"Braeden sure has come a long way since he attacked us when he thought Christian killed his wife,"* Devan bespoke DOCHAS.

*"Aye. His heart is lighter when he and FAOLAN pair with Meara and CARRIGAN."*

*"Interesting . . . I wonder if Padrick knows."* Devan searched for the clan's second-in-command and found Padrick directing the setting up of the enormous tent and food tables. *"Very interesting."*

# Four

*Summer Solstice—Scotland*

Liam paced the tiny, two-room stone bothy he had been exiled to for the past six weeks. He'd been awake since before dawn, watching the rolling fog shred through the rocky crevices of the skerry, feeling as torn asunder as the grayish-white wisps creeping ever nearer. His stomach growled, but he was too wired to eat. "Today. Today should be the day that Merida gives birth. I should be there. Not stuck on this spit of rock. It's not fair."

Of course, The MacLean hadn't been a complete bastard on Beltaine when Merida had collapsed. He had allowed Liam to accompany her and his brother-in-law to the hospital in Inverness. The doctor had said that the stress she'd been under was taking its toll on both Merida and the bairns. It was dangerous. If they couldn't get her blood pressure down, then she'd have to be admitted to the hospital until after the bairns were born. Liam had been too shocked and guilt-ridden to say anything at all. It was Graeme who had assured the doctor he would take care of his sister. In the end, Liam had had no choice but to leave his wife in the care of her brother.

He glared at his primitive surroundings. The skerry didn't have electricity, save for a generator, and Liam needed to be frugal in its use as the fuel had to last until one of the MacLean dragonriders could bring supplies. So far, that had been once. He and his dragon, KENNETH, ate the fish KENNETH caught, the vegetables in the sparse garden, and the provisions provided by the clan. Definitely not an environment for a wife, especially one ready to give birth to twins.

"Why haven't I heard anything?" Liam kicked a wooden bookcase in frustration. His booted foot caught in the splintered wood and books spilled onto the stone floor. Liam cursed.

After disentangling himself, he noticed a small hole hidden at the foot of the stone wall behind the dusty bookcase. He knelt, reached in, and was surprised when his fingers brushed against a roll of paper. Unrolling it, Liam rushed to the window and tried to read the faded, spidery script.

The Keltoi Prophecy

On the eve when the veil between the worlds 'tis thinnest,
When the darkness 'tis deepest and the tempest 'tis most fierce,
Seek The One who comes from the land across the sea.

For in the age when The One Who Hears All
Unites The Seer, The Wronged, and The Exiled,
Long sacrificed bonds shall be forged anew.

Loyal tae one another, their destinies interwoven.
Each bares a talisman tae harness gifts of the soul.
Through these gifts, truths shall be unveiled.

With faith, grace, insight, and respect,
The One must heal a fractured nation
magic extinction.

"Does *Keltoi* mean Celtic? How old is this prophecy?" He scrutinized the aged parchment, rubbing it between his thumb and index finger. The brittleness told him it was quite old. "Who is The One? Or The Seer, or The Wronged? I am clearly The Exiled. What talisman?" He squinted at the smudges where words were missing in the last line, but could only make out parts of it. And the words he could read frightened him.

"Could the magic go extinct?" He supposed so since this rocky spit of land he'd been exiled to no longer held any magic. Liam had discovered that fact his first week here when he'd taken his dragon on what should have been their normal, twice-a-week magic sharing flight. For the first time since Liam had paired with KENNETH, neither of them had felt the magic surge within their blood as they flew the Celtic pattern over the standing stones at the south end of the skerry. Liam had worried about it and had meant to mention the lack when the MacLean dragonrider had made his delivery weeks later, but he had been so relieved to have the new supplies and someone to talk to—even if only for the short time it took to unload the provisions—that the loss of magic slipped his mind. KENNETH had been content to fly solo either west to Colonsay or back to Mull, and Liam couldn't deny his compeer the magic sustaining ritual.

Liam glanced once more at the words written on the parchment, felt a shudder scuttle down his spine. He hastily put the books back into the case and placed the prophecy on top of the bookcase so he'd remember the next time someone came.

He shifted his thoughts to Merida and the bairns. *Had she given birth yet? Was she all right? What about the bairns? Would someone even be sent to tell me? Oh God, what if something had gone wrong?*

Liam picked up his pacing. He was muttering to himself, frantic with terrible possibilities when KENNETH's baritone voice broke into his thoughts.

*"A dragon and rider approach."*

Liam dashed outside and stood rooted in place as Graeme and his dragon circled the skerry, banked into the wind, and landed on the grassy hillock next to the garden.

Liam studied his brother-in-law for any signs that might indicate how Merida fared, but Graeme's features didn't show any emotion. In agony, Liam silently prayed for Merida's safety, then stumbled in his haste to meet Graeme. "Is it Merida? Is she all right? The bairns?"

Graeme held up his hands to stop the questions. "Let's go inside. I'll tell you everything."

Fear pierced Liam's heart. He grabbed Graeme's arm and held him in place. "Just tell me."

Graeme's dragon roared. Liam released his hold on his brother-in-law. "Please."

"Merida is fine, now." Graeme ushered Liam into the bothy.

"What do you mean 'now'?"

Graeme glanced around the room with its sleeping alcove in one corner, the makeshift cooking area near the open fireplace, and the sparse furnishings scattered about. He chose to lean against the stone fireplace and indicated Liam should sit.

"The last month was hard on Merida. She had to stay in the hospital for the final two weeks. The bairns were born early this morning—by cesarean. Merida was exhausted and had some complications. The doctor was finally able to stop the bleeding. Our parents are with her now."

"What of the bairns?" Liam felt the blood drain from his face. "Are they . . .?"

"Your sons are holding their own."

Liam let out a shaky breath. "Do you think The MacLean . . .?"

"I'm here to take you to see your family. The MacLean has granted you two days reprieve. Then I'm to bring you back here."

Liam scrambled out of the chair and rushed toward his brother-in-law.

"Hold on." Graeme clasped a hand over his nose. "You'll need to clean up before I take you. You can't go to the hospital looking and smelling like a deep-sea fisherman or an oil rigger that's just off a six-month job. Where's your pride, man?"

"You'd be the same if you didn't have hot water except for what you could boil." Liam waved his arm to indicate the rough state of his living conditions. "No creature comforts, that's for sure. KENNETH might not mind a bath in the ocean, but I don't want to die from hypothermia serving my penance. Speaking of which, has The MacLean said how much longer I have to stay here? Or what task would prove my worthiness?"

"Sorry, no. I got the feeling he wanted you to understand that being a dragonrider is a privilege, not just a role you're owed." Graeme stuck his hands in his pockets. "Go ahead and grab some clothes, then we'll go. You can clean up at my place before I take you to the hospital."

Liam tossed a few things into a duffle and nodded to Graeme. "Ready. I'll saddle KENNETH."

"No. Today you ride with me."

"But . . ."

"I put my honor and reputation and that of the Fraser clan on the line when I got you this visit, so we'll do it my way." Graeme glanced at his watch. "Time's a-wasting. I'm sure KENNETH will be fine." Graeme guided Liam outside.

Liam gazed forlornly at his dragon. *"I'll be gone for a couple of days. Merida's had the bairns."*

*"Aye. Ye need to see yer mate and the wee ones. I shall be fine here. Make haste,"* KENNETH bespoke in a gentle yet excited tone.

With his dragon's blessing and his heart racing, Liam mounted Graeme's dragon and once again failed to remember about the loss of magic and the prophecy.

# Five

*Summer Solstice, Hill of Tara, Ireland*

Devan heard the murmurs change to greetings as dragons and clan members arrived from the clan compound of Beaghmore in Northern Ireland.

She searched the sky. Maggie's dragon, FIANNA, unencumbered with baggage, flew beside brown KIERAN, Matthew's dragon. Matthew was Sean's and Aisling's son.

When FIANNA landed at the edge of the clearing, Devan saw the expanse of the buttercup yellow dragon's belly that signaled she was in the middle of her gestation period.

Maggie waved as she carefully slid off her dragon's back.

*"DOCHAS, my sweet, can you inquire with FIANNA as to how she is feeling? I'm a bit concerned about the flight in her condition,"* Devan bespoke her dragon.

*"FIANNA is strong. She is ravenous much of the time, yet otherwise well. KIERAN watches her every move. She wishes he would no' fash. When I mate with ROARKE, I shall fly until the day I drop my clutch. I will no' be a burden on the clan."*

Devan choked at her dragon's self-assured declaration of mating, even though DOCHAS and ROARKE were at least four years away from being old enough. Maturity is surely another reason the dragons must be at least five, Devan thought, besides the more technical aspects of fertility cycles and whatnot. She hesitated on her way to greet Maggie. *"Did someone make FIANNA feel like a burden?"*

*"No' directly. Yet TULLIA, compeer to Kiely, shuns FIANNA and KIERAN. That is no' correct."* DOCHAS's tone was tinged with anger.

*"No, that isn't right."* Devan continued toward Maggie as FIANNA lumbered toward the other dragons. *"I'll have a word with Padrick and Sean."*

*"I shall greet FIANNA. And stay close to her."*

*"Thank you, my sweet."*

Devan clasped hands with the approaching Maggie. "You are looking lovely today. I take it all is well with Matthew and FIANNA?"

"Yes," Maggie said. "And you know how my dragon is doing as she told me you had DOCHAS ask. You can always ask my dragon yourself."

"I know, but I wasn't sure how detailed FIANNA would be and figured communicating through DOCHAS might be better." Devan led Maggie toward the white tent. "You're a bit flushed. Perhaps you should sit down."

Maggie laughed. "Did DOCHAS say something?"

"No. Why would she?" Devan scrutinized the young woman, then slapped her hand over her mouth. When she lowered her hand, she whispered, "Are you? Of course you are. How far along?"

"Since our dragons' mating flight, so Beltaine. It was . . . intense."

"Are you happy?" Devan wrapped her arm around Maggie's shoulder. They pulled a couple of chairs from a pile and sat in a secluded corner of the tent, away from the food and drink tables.

"Yes. Matthew and I were dancing around each other when Sean decided to experiment with the timing of mating flights. We talked about it. It forced us to come clean about our feelings for each other. We spoke to Sean. He and Aisling were thrilled.

"You're the only other person who knows," Maggie said. "We wanted to wait until I was farther along."

"I won't tell a soul." Devan crossed her heart. "Are you going to get married?"

Maggie glanced around before she spoke. "Well—"

"Don't tell me Matthew doesn't want to," Devan interrupted, a bit testy on her newfound friend's behalf.

"Of course he does," Maggie said. "We're going to have the handfasting ceremony today. Here, next to Lia Fáil. Before LORCAN's and REGAN's mating flight."

Devan squealed, then composed herself. "Wow. Well, there's not much time to get ready. Do you need anything? I'm not sure what all is involved in a handfasting ceremony."

"I've everything I need, as the only requirement is both Matthew and I be present. It's a commitment ceremony that can be used in place of, or before, the more formal marriage ceremony. We decided it would be our formal marriage. Padrick is going to officiate since Sean is standing for Matthew." Maggie clasped Devan's right hand. "I know it's a lot to ask, but will you stand for me?"

Devan swallowed the lump in her throat. "What about your mom?" Maggie shook her head. "Or other girlfriends? Don't get me wrong, I'd be honored, but we've known each other just a short time. Surely there's someone you've been friends with longer."

"I have several friends within the clan, but I felt a strong connection to you. First, when you rescued GRAYSON. Then when you thwarted Kiely. Please say yes."

"Yes." Devan grinned. *Is this what belonging to a family feels like? If so, I'm never leaving this clan.* "But I'm not exactly dressed for the occasion." She indicated her brown trousers and blue shirt.

"Don't fash. I happen to think you look amazing." Maggie stood and pulled Devan up with her. "But I could use some help changing into my handfasting dress. Come with me?"

"Lead the way." Devan followed as Maggie retrieved a satchel from the pile of things Matthew had unloaded from his dragon.

"Sean made sure I could use the antechamber here at St. Patrick's Church," Maggie said.

The two women made their way past the cemetery and into St. Patrick's and its antechamber. Devan shuddered, remembering the dragon killer who had hidden himself and his dead wife and baby behind several headstones just six weeks ago. She pushed that memory aside and let Maggie's joy infuse her. Her friend was committing herself to the love of her life, and even though Devan hadn't had the best of luck with Rick, her ex-fiancée, she was still a romantic at heart.

When Devan left Maggie to notify Padrick that the bride was ready, she found chairs set in rows facing Lia Fáil—the upright stone that was purported to roar when the rightful High King placed his hand upon it.

Clan members were milling about, murmuring excitedly.

Devan tapped Padrick's shoulder. As he turned toward her, she saw Matthew with his father, waiting anxiously. She smiled. "Maggie's ready."

"Thank you," Matthew said. "I knew she'd convince you to stand for her, for us."

"It didn't take much convincing," Devan said. She looked around but couldn't find Christian, and sighed.

"Don't worry," Padrick said, apparently taking a good guess as to her feelings. "Christian's around. I think he's with young Niall and the dragons." He pointed to the northern grassy hill known as the Mound of the Hostages as Christian led FIANNA and KIERAN toward them.

Braeden, sitting off to one side, strummed a soft ballad on his guitar, and the clan members took their seats.

"I better go get Maggie. Don't want her to be late for her special day." Devan rushed back to the church.

The handfasting ceremony began with a blessing., then Maggie handed her flowers to Devan. Matthew took both of Maggie's hands in his. Braeden played a sweet melody as one-by-one each dragon rider rose, selected a colorful ribbon from a nearby basket, and draped it over Maggie's and Matthew's clasped hands. Padrick laid a final white ribbon over them all. The music stopped right on time.

Matthew spoke his own words for vows. Maggie followed, sniffling into a lace handkerchief.

Devan smiled at Christian seated in the first row. He grinned back.

Padrick closed the ceremony by tying the ribbons together with his ribbon and announcing the new couple, to raucous cheering.

FIANNA and KIERAN leaned past Padrick's shoulder and blew warm puffs of air on the couple's joined hands.

Matthew kissed his bride and, still holding hands, they walked around the Stone of Destiny—Lia Fáil. After the circuit, they made their way to the enormous white tent, where a feast was laid out.

The rest of the clan followed suit.

Devan hung back near Lia Fáil and waited for Christian to join her. "I've never been to a handfasting before. That was beautiful, don't you think?"

"Aye. Simple yet it involved the whole clan."

"I think it helps bond everyone together into a family." Devan sighed. "Being dragonriders, keeping the dragons a secret, has some downsides. Friendships are limited. Trust of outsiders is scarce." *I don't make friends easily anyway, so no great sacrifice.* "Shall we give our congratulations?"

Christian skimmed a hand over her hair and kissed her temple. "Aye." Together they joined their new family, the clan.

After supper, the remaining food was packed away and the tent rearranged for the céilí. The musicians gathered at one corner, tuning their instruments.

Devan remembered what DOCHAS had told her earlier about Braeden. She easily found him fine-tuning his guitar and talking with Meara. He smiled at something Meara said.

"Very interesting indeed," Devan said.

From behind her, Christian asked, "What's interesting?"

Devan jumped and clutched at her chest. "Don't sneak up on me like that. You scared the bejesus out of me."

"I wasn't sneaking. Anyway . . . what's interesting?"

"Braeden." Devan tilted her head toward the corner of the tent where she heard the discordant notes of instruments being tuned. "DOCHAS tells me he's coping well after his wife's death."

Christian stroked his throat, rubbing at the spot where Braeden's hands nearly choked him two months ago. "So?"

"Coping better when he's around Meara. When he and FAOLAN fly patrols with Meara and CARRIGAN."

"So?" Christian repeated.

*Were all men so clueless? Was it a genetic deficiency that men couldn't see the emotions that swirled around them? Or maybe it was just love they couldn't accept.*

"I'm wondering about Padrick's and Meara's relationship," Devan explained. "Padrick's been alone more lately. Especially since he and I have begun researching where your mother might be if she's still alive."

As the bottom edge of the mid-summer sun dipped below the western horizon and the sky took on orange and red streaks, thirty Tuatha dragons and riders gathered around Lia Fáil with humans in an inner circle and dragons in a larger outer circle.

Clan leader Sean raised his voice. "Tuatha Dragon Clan, prepare for your *geall*, your promise." He placed his right hand on Lia Fáil, held his pendant in his left hand, bowed his head and spoke the three words on the back of the clan pendant. "Dilseacht. Fáil. Saoirse." He dropped his hands and stepped back into his place in the circle.

Aisling stepped forward and repeated the oath. Each dragonrider followed. After Christian, Devan intoned her promise. DOCHAS's exuberant tone echoed in her mind. Padrick completed the oath.

When all had promised, Sean led the riders and dragons east to their places around the pile of wood at the center of the nearly 150-foot circumference of the grassy hill fort known as Teach Cormaic. He stepped forward as a hush came over the crowd. Placing their right hands over their hearts, they chanted in unison, "Ni neart go cur le cheile. There is no strength without unity."

At Sean's signal, each dragon spewed forth a burst of fire at the stacked wood. The fire leapt into the deepening red sky, casting an eerie glow over the surrounding hills. A whoop went up from inside the white tent as several children and adults ran across the uneven grass toward the bonfire.

Sean's voice once again rang out. "Tonight, as we celebrate the summer solstice—the longest day of the year—and the handfasting of Maggie and Matthew, we are also present to witness the mating flight of REGAN and LORCAN. We call upon our draíocht to guide the dragon pair in a safe and fertile flight."

Devan cheered with the rest of the clan as REGAN and LORCAN were led by their riders, Shea and Daniel, back to the Stone of Destiny.

As the upper tip of the sun disappeared, maroon-colored REGAN leapt into the twilight. She bugled a challenge to mate.

Devan squeezed her eyes closed and clapped her hands over her ears, but it wasn't only the mating call that reverberated in her head. Dozens of female dragon voices urged REGAN on. *"Fly higher." "Fly faster." "The longer ye mate, the stronger the hatchlings."*

Even though Devan never saw LORCAN take flight, she knew the moment the taupe-colored dragon left Earth. Husky male dragons telepathically encouraged LORCAN toward his goal.

Over two-dozen voices blended into a cacophony. Devan dropped to her knees and lifted her head. She tracked the two ever-smaller, dark bat-like shapes amongst the deepening twilight.

The dragonriders stood, gazes transfixed on the aerial acrobatics as REGAN led her enamored pursuer spiraling and weaving through an invisible obstacle course.

*"Must fly. Must mate. Now. Now. Now!"*

Suddenly Devan realized the chorus in her mind wasn't the two mating dragons but her own DOCHAS. Devan tore her gaze from the spectacle in the sky and searched frantically for her blue and silver compeer. She staggered to her feet and bolted toward Lia Fáil. *Was that DOCHAS? And ROARKE?*

Just before DOCHAS launched into the sky, Devan screamed. "No! It's not your time. You'll die!"

# Six

Devan raced up the hill, one step ahead of Christian. Together, they managed to grab DOCHAS's riding harness and lead shank to keep her grounded.

DOCHAS screeched and thrashed. Her blue eyes whirled like a pinwheel caught in a hurricane. *"The ancestors are calling me. I must fly. I must mate."*

Afraid her dragon would break free, Devan leapt up and yanked DOCHAS's triangular head down to hold her attention. *"You can't. You're too young. Please, I can't lose you,"* Devan implored her dragon.

While Devan was busy pleading with DOCHAS, Sean and Padrick arrived and helped control the young dragon. FLYNN and DECLAN flew in and hovered over both DOCHAS and ROARKE, preventing them from attempting flight.

"What's going on?" Sean asked. "I heard FLYNN shouting to stop the yearlings."

Christian answered. "One minute Devan had her hands over her ears and was falling to the ground. The next, she's running. ROARKE was . . . keening. It's the only word that comes to mind." Christian loosened Devan's grip from the lead shank and pulled her into his arms, soothing her.

"She . . ." Devan gazed up at DOCHAS. The dragon's blue multifaceted eyes still whirled too fast. Devan cleared the tears from her throat and began again. "She started to launch for a mating flight."

"What?" Sean stepped closer to DOCHAS, taking up the lead that Devan relinquished. "That's impossible. Well, obviously not impossible. But female dragons don't hit their mating cycle until they're at least five years old."

"DOCHAS kept saying she must fly, she must mate," Devan said. "I couldn't let her take flight. Something urged me to stop her, or she'd die." Tears streamed down Devan's cheeks.

Christian pulled her closer and kissed the top of her head. "Shh. She's okay. You stopped her. She's not going to die. Hush now."

"Tell me everything. All that you remember," Sean said.

Devan lifted her head from Christian's chest and wiped her cheeks. "When REGAN took flight, I heard female voices. I assumed they were Tuatha dragons giving words of encouragement. There were so many kinds of chanting. Then, male dragon voices mixed in and I knew LORCAN had taken off." Devan took a steadying breath. "The voices were so loud, excited. I . . . I could feel the heat . . . the sexual energy of the dragons. And between . . . between their riders." She ducked her head to hide the blush on her cheeks. Several moments passed before she lifted her gaze.

"I didn't even realize it was DOCHAS I was hearing at first. When her words finally penetrated, I panicked. I just knew if she tried to mate, she'd die." Devan grabbed Sean's arm. "She would die, right? That's why you restrict the mating to dragons of a certain age?"

Padrick spoke for the first time. "There are stories in some of the clan histories that hint at disastrous mating flights—all with young dragons. That was long ago, but we've never had the need to test the issue of age before."

"DOCHAS said that the ancestors told her to fly, to mate. Could she have mistaken the voices and emotions because of her youth?" Devan moved to stroke her now trembling dragon.

*"I did no' recognize the voices that spoke to me,"* DOCHAS bespoke Devan. *"They were insistent. I do no' understand what I did that made ye angry."* She lowered her head to nuzzle Devan.

*"I wasn't angry, my sweet. I was terrified. My instincts screamed that you'd*

*die if you tried to mate."* Devan wrapped her arms around her dragon's neck. *"I can't lose you. Not now. Not ever. You're mine."*

*"As ye are mine. I shall no' fly without ye."*

Devan realized the men were staring at her. "Sorry. Just a little re-bonding time. No worries." It was then that Devan noticed the other dragon voices in her head had stopped. "Perhaps we should get back to the céili before others wonder what we're doing over here. DOCHAS has assured me she won't take flight without me."

Darkness had fully descended while Christian listened as Devan explained her communication with her dragon to the clan leaders.

*"Were you going to fly after DOCHAS?"* Christian asked ROARKE.

*"Aye. I would have kept her safe, even though I was unsure what she was doing."* ROARKE answered.

*"Can you feel if she will try to fly now?"*

*"I do no' get a sense of her driving need to fly anymore. I shall keep watch."*

Christian pointed toward the dragonriders and other clan members milling about the bonfire. "We should head back."

Sean and Padrick agreed, so they started back, in deep discussion of doing more research in the clan histories. Christian slowed his pace to allow Devan to control her emotions before anyone could question her. *Bloody ifrinn, that could have been disastrous.*

"Did you have a vision about what might happen tonight?" Devan asked.

"No. It was a complete surprise. Believe me, if I'd had any idea, I'd have mentioned it." Christian rubbed her hands between his. "You're cold. I think the shock of being so scared is hitting you. Let's get you something hot to drink. Maybe cut the celebration short. Fly back to Lough Gur before people start asking questions."

Devan nodded. "Perhaps Padrick and DECLAN should come with us. In case . . ."

"I'll ask Padrick. Do you want something warm here, or do you want to wait until we get home?" *Home? Yes, Lough Gur was now home.*

"Let's go back to Lough Gur now. I don't want to leave DOCHAS for too long. I think she's just as shaken as I am." Devan stopped. Her whiskey-colored eyes still held shimmering moisture. "I'll wait for you and Padrick at DOCHAS's side." She turned and headed toward the group of dragons lounging in sleep circles nearby.

Christian called out to the two men walking ahead of him. "Wait up." Sean and Padrick stopped and turned around.

"Devan's knackered," Christian said. "I want to take her back home, but she's nervous about flying on DOCHAS and not being able to control her."

"I'll come with you," Padrick said. "Start researching tonight."

Christian nodded. "Thanks. That would ease Devan's mind."

"No problem. There's nothing that's required as far as clan rituals, just enjoying the céili, so I'm ready to go back," Padrick said.

"What about Meara?" Christian asked.

"I don't want to interrupt her fun." Padrick glanced toward the white tent, where the sound of music drifted to them. "She'll be fine leading the rest of the Lough Gur dragons and riders home."

"I'll fill her in," Sean said, then he left Christian and Padrick.

"You're sure?" Christian persisted.

"Yes. Why wouldn't I be?"

"Devan mentioned you've been alone lately. She was worried about your relationship with Meara." Christian started back toward the dragons. "I didn't want to know all the details, but Devan mentioned Braeden and Meara working together a lot."

Padrick caught up to Christian. "We've both been a bit preoccupied. But no matter what, Meara and I will be fine. We promised to be friends, always. Devan shouldn't worry. You either."

"I'm not concerned. But Devan's a champion worrier. Perhaps the trip back to America will be a blessing for her. Perfect timing. It will keep her busy worrying about her parents' estate. And it'll let her get her affairs abroad cleared up."

"I'll get that cleared with Sean tomorrow. And for you to head back to Dublin for a few days as well," Padrick said. "Will you go when Devan leaves for America?"

"Yes, if that's okay. I don't want to leave the clan in a bind, but I want to see her off. I should be back here within a week." Christian stole a glance at his father. "Thanks for doing this."

"I'll keep both ROARKE and DOCHAS current with their magic rejuvenating flights. You and Devan have been thrust into a new world unexpectedly. And you've done a terrific job adapting. I'm not sure I'd do as well, given the same circumstances. I'll do my best to give you both time to adjust—not just because you're family." Padrick stopped Christian with a brief touch on his arm. "I know it's a bit late to be your da, but I'd at least like to be your friend."

"I've accepted you're my father and my clan leader, the rest . . .? Can you understand I need time?" Padrick nodded. Christian stared at the face of his father—nearly the same features he saw in the mirror every morning. He wondered if he'd get a chance to compare his features with those of his mother. "Being aware of Devan's vulnerabilities is a plus. Let's get her back to the safety of Lough Gur. And figure out what happened to DOCHAS tonight."

Late that night, with Devan asleep, Christian slipped his hand into hers, weaving his fingers with hers.

She whimpered softly, then tossed her head from side to side and called out, "No."

Christian pressed a gentle kiss to her forehead, then her soft lips. She responded in kind. He deepened the kiss, then groaned as Devan's hand roamed down his bare chest to the waistband of his boxer briefs.

When he pulled back from the kiss, she was fully awake and her desire for him made her eyes glitter.

"I need you. Make love to me. America is far away, and I'll be gone for a couple of weeks." Her need-roughened voice aroused him further.

He deliberately kept the pace of their lovemaking slow. He wanted to savor every ragged breath, every tingle, every moment. As she clenched around him, he could no longer stop the freight train that was his love for her, so together they soared.

# Seven

*Scotland*

Liam's gaze softened as he rocked wee Riordan in the crook of his arm while Merida nursed a fussy Rhys. *My boys. Oh man. I'm a father. They're perfect. And my Merida's so beautiful.* He wiped a stray tear from the corner of his eye with his shoulder. *I love them even more than flying adragonback.* His thoughts of KENNETH and the dragon clan veered to why he'd missed the birth of his sons. He brushed Merida's soft cheek. "Maybe I can ask The MacLean to defer the remainder of my exile until the bairns are older."

Merida shook her head, her strawberry blond curls bouncing. "Nae. We need to take advantage that I'll be staying with my parents. Maither can't wait to help. And I made Graeme promise to go to bat for you with The MacLean. So I'm sure your exile will be short."

"I just don't want to be away from you and the wee ones for too long. I wish there was a set timetable from The MacLean. Then I'd be able to handle the separation better. The unknown is driving me radge. How am I to know what I must do to prove myself worthy?" Liam dragged a hand through his newly shorn mud-brown hair. "I can't even describe the loneliness I've felt over the last six weeks. And now that I've gotten to spend these two days with you, I'm not sure how I'll not go completely radge on that isolated spit of rock."

Merida rested her free hand on Liam's arm. "You'll concentrate extra hard on ways to prove yourself to The MacLean. And Graeme will keep you up-to-date as much as he can on me and the bairns. Speaking of—"

Graeme knocked on the open door and swept into the maternity suite. He kissed Merida's cheek, then averted his gaze when she removed Rhys from her breast. "How're my nephews getting on today?" He reached for Riordan.

"Hungry." Merida chuckled as Rhys burped, then she handed him to Liam. "Go ahead and lay him down. They both should be ready for a nap."

Liam brushed a kiss on Rhys's forehead before gently placing him into the bassinet. Graeme followed suit with Riordan.

"And what of you?" Graeme asked Merida. "Will you nap with them?"

"Is that your way of saying I look the hag?"

"No, no," Graeme stuttered. "It's just you've had twins. I read somewhere that new maithers should rest when the bairns do."

"Have you been reading my new maithers book?" Merida lifted one eyebrow.

Graeme's face turned ruddy.

Merida winked at both men. "Slagging you." She pulled the covers away and got out of the bed.

Liam rushed to her side. "What are you doing?"

"Using the loo."

"But—"

"It's another thing new maithers do when the bairns are asleep." Merida closed the door behind her.

Liam shuffled back to his sons. He couldn't believe how full his heart was at seeing two healthy bairns. Nor how scared he'd been. "I'll be the best da ever. I promise. And you'll be spoilt in no time with your granny and pop-pop to care for you." He ran a finger lightly over each of their cheeks. "I love you so much. I didn't know I could love anyone like this, even your mum or my dragon, KENNETH. You'll get to meet him when you're older. Don't grow too much until I come home." His voice caught on the last word.

Graeme clasped Liam's shoulder. "We should get you back. Show The MacLean that you aren't pushing the boundaries he set."

Liam nodded and kissed his boys. He tried to be strong, but when he turned around he had to wipe the tears from his cheeks. Merida came out of the loo and hugged him.

"Oh God, I . . . I can't," Liam blubbered as he held tight to his wife.

"You can. You must." Merida pulled her face away from Liam's shoulder. "You're the strongest man I know. You can do this."

Liam shook his head, heedless of the tears that continued to fall. "How do you know?"

"Because I need you to. The bairns need you to. And I'm not raising our boys without you. So you'll do whatever The MacLean commands, then you'll redeem yourself to the whole clan, to the whole of Scotland. The MacLean knows this. It's why he's so tough on you. I have faith you'll make him proud. You'll make all of us proud. But most of all, you'll make yourself proud." Merida pressed a soft kiss to Liam's lips. "For all you know, this could be a test to see if you're ready to rejoin the clan."

"And if it's not?" Liam used the sleeve of his shirt to dry his tears.

"Then you'll find another way."

Liam pulled her tight once more. "I love you more than life itself. You and the bairns. Promise me you'll do everything the doctor says. And if there's any problem, you'll send Graeme for me." When Merida didn't answer right away, Liam growled. "Promise me."

"I promise," Merida conceded. "But we'll be fine. I love you too."

Liam looked at Graeme, then back to the sleeping bairns in their shared bassinet.

His in-laws tiptoed into the room.

Liam lowered his head. He couldn't face Merida's parents' scrutiny, their disgust. Liam tucked a folded, handwritten note into Merida's hand. "It's for the wee ones. A bedtime story from their da, until I can be home to hold them and read to them." He hurried from the room before he crumbled.

Graeme met him at the lift. "I'll make sure Merida and the boys—"

"You better. I'm counting on you." Liam entered the lift with his brother-in-law. "Otherwise, I'd leave the clan right now and to hell with The MacLean and the consequences. The police couldn't charge me with murdering auld Alain and his dragon. It was an accident." He stalked out of the hospital.

After Liam collected his duffle from Graeme's house, the two men mounted REED, Graeme's rust-colored dragon. Liam brooded for the entire flight back to his exile.

As the desolate skerry came into view, Liam's black mood increased. *God. How am I to get through this? I'm not sure I can live up to Merida's faith in me.*

REED circled the bothy and garden, dumped the air from his wings, and landed on the hillock with a slight bounce.

*"Ye have returned,"* KENNETH bespoke as he exited his cave lair. *"How does yer mate fair? And the bairns?"*

*"Merida gave me two healthy sons, Riordan and Rhys."*

*"Then why are ye no' happy?"*

*"Because I can't be with them. We've spent six weeks in this hell hole, all because of an accident."* Liam climbed down from REED. *"And I've sentenced you to my exile. I'm sorry."*

*"Dinnae fash. I am enjoying this place and our time together."* KENNETH dipped his yellow, triangular head and nudged his rider.

Liam rubbed his dragon's snout, lost in thought.

Graeme cleared his throat from atop REED. "I'm heading out. I'll come back when I'm able." He reached into his breast pocket, leaned down, and handed Liam two snaps of Merida and the bairns. "Don't do anything impulsive. Remember what you're working toward. Merida and your bairns need you."

Liam didn't respond. He couldn't take his gaze from the glossy snaps of his family. *I'll find a way to get back to you quickly. Whatever it takes. I swear.*

# Eight

*Dublin, Ireland*

Three days after the summer solstice, Christian drove Devan to Dublin Airport for her journey back to America. Unusually quiet over the last few days, she'd spent hours scouring the clan histories with Padrick, looking for any clues that might explain why young dragons were lost on mating flights. As far as Christian knew it had all been for naught.

"I'll call when I get home . . . I mean, to my parents' place," Devan said. "Wait. That'll be like three o'clock in the morning here."

"Doesn't matter. Call my mobile. I'll still be awake." Christian held her close for a long time. Finally, he kissed her and guided her to the security gate. "Gaothchothrum agus eitilt sábháilte."

Devan tried to repeat the Gaelic words but butchered them, so she said the phrase in English. "Fair winds and a safe flight." Christian grinned. However, she managed, "*Is breá liom tú I gcónaí.* I shall love you always."

"*Agus mé, tú.* And I, you," He replied. "Don't worry about DOCHAS. ROARKE and I will keep her safe. Go now, or you'll miss your flight." He squeezed her fingers, then let go, shoving his hands into his pockets lest he drag her back and never let her leave. As she passed from his sight, he muttered, "Hurry back, *mo chroí.*"

*"The Ring Wearer loves ye. And is torn about leaving so soon after partnering with DOCHAS. And with ye."* ROARKE's voice was soft with

the distance between Lough Gur and Dublin, yet his wistfulness was clear.

*"And I love her. Which is a first for me."*

*"What of me?"* ROARKE's uncertainty bled through.

*"Our partnership is different. The love is different, but aye, I love you too,"* Christian bespoke his compeer. *"Are you sticking close to DOCHAS?"*

*"Aye. She is resting, though no' peaceful. It will be good when ye return. Soon, aye?"*

*"As soon as I can, but probably at least three days. You and DOCHAS will fly with DECLAN to visit GRAYSON tomorrow. Give the little guy a nudge for me."*

*"I think I understand. The nudge is affection. Be safe."* ROARKE ended the mental contact.

Christian made his way out of the airport and back into Dublin proper. He parked down the block from his flat and sat in his unwashed cobalt blue Audi sedan surveying the comings and goings from each building, like a thief.

"Old habits die hard," he muttered as he finally exited the vehicle. Inside, he skirted the elevator and took the stairs, two at a time. At his door, he checked his security and found the small strand of hair he'd placed between the door and jamb missing. He backtracked and silently climbed another flight of stairs.

At the front door of the flat directly above his, he placed his ear against the painted wood. No noise, no voices. He picked the lock and went in fast and low. No movement. He closed and locked the front door then exited onto the balcony. A quick scan of the lone plastic chair and small table, and he felt too exposed to the occupants of the opposite building to wait until nightfall. *Either go now or come back later. The owner'll probably be home by then. It's a risk either way.*

Decision made, Christian scrambled over the side railing. He lowered himself until only his fingers gripped the upstairs balcony. *Do it. Fast.* He let go and dropped into a crouch in the corner of his balcony. He took a series of slow breaths. *Getting lax, boyo.*

A peek through the one-inch cutout at the bottom of his blinds revealed his living area was empty—at least of people. The sofa cushions were on the floor, the stuffing ripped out and strewn everywhere. Books, lamps, and other odds and ends added to the mountainous pile. His brand new telly lay shattered amongst the carnage.

Unable to see the rest of the flat from his vantage point, he unlocked the balcony door and moved inside with his knife drawn. He scanned the kitchen nook, found broken crockery thrown in the sink and the icebox door ajar. The ice was melted and the contents were warm to the touch *Bastards are long gone.*

Nonetheless, he remained cautious as he made his way to his bedroom. Knife extended, he pushed open the door and found towels and bedsheets trampled on the floor. His bedroom was tossed, just like the rest of the flat. Slashed clothing strewn amongst the destruction pointed to more than a simple burglary. No, this was personal.

"Well, at least this won't take too long." He scooped up a couple of pillowcases and stuffed any clothes and shoes that weren't destroyed into the makeshift suitcases.

The nightstand drawers were empty and dumped upside down on the cut-up mattress. "Feck. I liked that bed." He left the pile of chaos alone. He tapped a complicated design on the checkerboard-patterned bedpost. A door popped open in the oak headboard. He pulled a metal box from the hidden compartment, stuffed the contents in various pockets, and resecured his hidey-hole.

He gathered his belongings. As he headed back to the living area, he heard the distinct click of his front door being picked. As much as he was itching for a fight, he'd be smarter to find out who he was about to be dealing with. He hurried onto the balcony and closed the door just as Logan Walsh, his boyhood mate, walked into the flat.

"When did that blighter get out of gaol?" Christian muttered.

# Nine

*America*

Devan fretted for the first hour aboard the jumbo jet. She communicated with DOCHAS to help soothe herself as much as her dragon. After she was too far away to continue talking with her compeer, Devan began a list of tasks ahead of her for when she reached her destination. She needed the distraction to keep from missing Christian too much.

Somewhere over the Atlantic, as the aircraft followed the sun westward, Devan dropped into an emotionally exhausted sleep.

The flight attendant roused her when they approached San Francisco. Devan accepted the warm washcloth and bathed the sleep away. She gathered her lists and readied for landing. *Here's a bonus of flying in an aircraft instead of adragonback—I don't fall to my death if I take a bit of a nap.*

After landing, Devan collected her suitcase and hailed a cab to her parents' home. She didn't want to disturb Christian with a phone call in case he was asleep, so she texted instead.

"Flight was fine. Slept for most of it. Heading to my parents' place. Hope you're asleep. Text when you wake up. Miss you already."

Christian's reply came just as the cab dropped her off. "Call me when you're settled." She let herself in and left her suitcase by the front door before she called Ireland.

"Hey. I'm here, safe and sound," Devan said when Christian

answered. "I'm going to grab a bite to eat and go to bed early. I want to hit the ground running first thing tomorrow."

"That sounds like a plan." Christian's voice sounded gravelly.

"I'll call you in the morning . . . afternoon your time." Devan yawned. "Tell everyone that I arrived. I love you." She was too tired to think of the Gaelic words.

"Okay. Love you too, a ghra. Good night."

Devan grabbed one of her mother's lightweight jackets from the entry closet. Chanel No. 5 wafted into the stale air. Devan wrapped the jacket around her and closed her eyes to refresh the memory of the last time she saw her mother wearing it.

Devan and her mother had met for lunch on one of San Francisco's beautiful, summer-like days right after the New Year. Following a particularly nasty December that included spitting rain nearly every day and a cold snap that frayed at the nerves of the city's residents, the sunlight and balmy conditions were like a breath of fresh air. And Devan needed a fresh start to her life, especially after learning her research position at the university might be cut. And her discovery that the man she thought she would marry turned out to be a controlling son of a bitch.

Over seafood salads at a favorite out-of-the-way bistro, Devan had relayed her work and relationship troubles—though without listing the litany of her faults, at least according to Rick.

"If the funding at the university runs out, you'll find another job. One more suitable to your research skills," her mother said as she buttered a slice of San Francisco's finest sourdough. "And your father and I never liked Rick anyway."

Devan stared open-mouthed. "But you never—"

"Of course not. You've a bit of your father's Scottish stubbornness. We didn't want you to dig your heels in, so to speak." Her mother took a delicate bite of bread and chewed carefully, as though she debated how much more to say.

"Funny you should mention my stubbornness," Devan said. "Rick thought I was a doormat. His personal one."

"That man is a jackass. He may be a persistent reporter, but with little to no scruples. He'd sooner sell his mother for a story than work hard to report the truth." Her mother nibbled on shrimp from the salad. "No. Your father and I are glad that you've broken off the relationship—no matter how it ended."

"Or how much he hurt me?" Devan asked before she thought better of it.

"No, of course not." Her mother looked chagrined. "What did that sorry excuse for a man say to you anyway?"

"Never mind. It's not important now." Devan sipped her iced tea. "He's out of my life. For good."

Six short weeks later, both her parents were gone and Devan had embarked on a life-altering journey. And she'd found her true calling—as a dragonrider in Ireland.

As the memory faded, Devan snatched her keys from the entry table and headed out for an early supper at the same hole-in-the-wall bistro. A seafood salad and perhaps a glass of wine this time, she decided.

An hour later, as Devan savored the last sip of her wine, a shadow fell over her table. Thinking it was the server with the tab, she reached for her purse.

"Well, well. Look who's finally surfaced," a deep male voice said.

Devan stilled her hands and looked up into the twisted smirk of Rick Hunter. Her gut clutched in a painful knot. She breathed deeply.

"I wasn't aware I'd been missing." She wiped her suddenly dry mouth with her napkin, wishing for another sip of wine. "What are you doing here?"

"I figured you to run home like a child who needs her mommy." Rick curled his upper lip. "Oh wait . . . both your parents have been dead for months."

Devan's eyes narrowed at the intentional cruelty.

"I couldn't reach you. Your cell phone's been disconnected. So, dearest, I repeat where have you been?" His tone demanded an answer.

"I don't answer to you. You ended things, remember?"

Rick seated himself at her table—uninvited. "I voiced my displeasure at your inadequacies. That's my right as your fiancé."

Devan shook her head. "Is that what you call your aggressive tirade? No, you didn't have the right to yell and throw things at me. My things. You don't own me. You never did." Devan exhaled slowly, trying to remain calm, and met his gaze. "In retrospect, I realize I may have been far too passive in our relationship to stick up for myself, but you cured me of that." Looking away, she caught the attention of the server and signaled for the tab. "Now, if you'll excuse me, I'm done. I don't have to listen to your diatribes any longer, we aren't engaged anymore." She stood.

Rick grabbed her arm, squeezing tight. "We're not through."

"Yes, we are." Devan's free hand closed in a fist. She didn't pull away, but stared daggers into Rick's lifeless brown eyes and wondered how she could have ever found this obnoxious heathen attractive. "I'm not the same submissive doormat you once knew, so let go of me, or I swear, I'll cause a scene."

"This isn't over, *dear.* Not by a long shot." Rick growled and tightened his grip. When Devan winced, his smile grew cruel. "You owe me. I lifted you out of obscurity. You're nothing without me." Slowly, one finger at a time, he opened his hand.

Drawing a shaky breath, Devan's hatred for the man swelled as he sauntered out of the bistro. He paused at the door and used his thumb and forefinger to mime pointing a gun at her.

Devan shivered and grasped her throbbing arm. She knew she'd have a nasty bruise.

The server brought her tab. While she found her credit card, he glanced toward the door and whispered, "Are you all right? I think he left, but I've called the police."

"I'm fine. Really. I don't want to cause a fuss." Devan handed him her credit card.

"Knew there was something off with that dude." The server left to process her payment.

When he returned, Devan asked, "Has he been in before?"

"Many times, starting in early March. Hangs out for an hour or two. Picks at the food on his plate, then he complains to the owner. Never tips, either. None of the staff want to have him in their section."

Devan figured the tip in her head, then added an extra amount and signed the receipt. "I'm sorry. Maybe after this, he'll stay away."

"No need to apologize for his rotten behavior. But, you need to stay away from him. He's got a mean streak." The server walked her toward the front door as two uniformed police entered.

"You called about an altercation?" The older officer directed his question to the server. The second officer, a young man with a high-and-tight haircut and looking fresh from the academy, glanced around.

"A man came in and harassed this customer." The server indicated Devan. "The guy was belligerent, threatening. He grabbed her arm when she tried to walk away."

"Ms.? I'm Officer Jennings. Can you tell me what happened?"

Devan wanted to get home and climb into bed, but she figured the officer couldn't leave without taking a report, so she explained about her ex-fiancé tracking her down and getting a bit rough attempting to keep her from escaping.

"Do you want to press charges?" Officer Jennings asked as he wrote notes in a small notebook he took from his chest pocket.

She didn't want any trouble that would delay her return to Ireland, so she declined.

Officer Jennings handed her a business card. "If you change your mind or have another run-in with your ex, don't hesitate to call." He nodded to the server before he and his partner left.

"Thank you again." Devan smiled at the server, then checked the street before exiting. *The faster I can get my tasks done, the better. San Francisco's no longer my home anyway.*

# Ten

*Dublin, Ireland*

Christian tossed and turned most of the night. When sunlight burned bright on his eyelids, he knew he'd finally slept. A glance at the desk clock in his hotel room told him it was ten o'clock.

*What the bloody ifrinn happened? Why was Logan free?* That thought brought him fully awake.

Christian climbed out of bed and showered. By the time he was done, he had a plan. He'd need to call in a few favors, but he wasn't leaving Dublin until he had the answer to three questions. Who had ransacked his flat? Why wasn't Logan still in gaol? And what was he doing at Christian's place last night?

He placed a phone call before leaving his room, then paid cash at the desk for two more nights. After driving his car to the long-term parking at the airport, he caught the shuttle bus back into town. He bought a Guinness ball cap and a touristy-looking Ireland green windbreaker from one of the many shops near Trinity College. He also purchased an aerosol spray that guaranteed blond hair—at least until he washed it out.

His transformation took less than an hour. By sacrificing a toothbrush, he even managed to change the color of his eyebrows.

With his ball cap pulled low and mirrored sunglasses covering his blue eyes, he looked like an awestruck tourist. Several times he stopped to take a few snaps of the scenery. Of course, he also managed to capture Logan's crew of pickpockets and buskers working the crowd.

At noon, he strolled into Kehoe's—a typical Irish pub and a tourist draw. He spied Sergeant Finley at the end of the highly polished oak bar. Christian sat on the stool next to the garda.

"Howdy," Christian said in his best American accent. Finley glanced at him, tapped the brim of his uniform hat, then returned to chatting with the publican.

"Nice place you've got here," Christian spoke to the publican. "Can I get a Black and Tan?" At his words, all conversation stopped. The publican scooped up a bar towel and twisted it until his fingers turned white.

"I don't serve that in me pub. Nor any who are bloody eejit enough to ask for it."

Out of the corner of his eye, Christian saw Finley scrutinize him. Then the sergeant's mouth gaped open.

"Well, geez," Christian continued his spiel. "This is Ireland, ain't it? What's wrong with a Black and Tan?"

Finley put his hand up between Christian and the publican. "I've got this, Jimmy. I'll straighten this boyo out. Don't you fash."

The publican threw the twisted towel on the bar top in front of Christian. "You do that, Sergeant. Or I will." He scowled.

"We'll just borrow that back booth." Sergeant Finley yanked Christian off the stool and shoved him toward the back wall.

"Hey. Watch the threads, or I'll have you up on police brutality charges." Christian straightened his windbreaker. He muttered for Finley's ears only, "Don't relish your role too much."

Christian slid into the booth and sunk down, acting as though he was sulking.

"That's a fine disguise. You had me fooled." Finley glared at Christian. "Well, I'm here. What's so secret you couldn't say over the telephone? Had to drag me all the way to Dublin."

"I need a favor." Christian raised a hand to prevent Finley from asking any questions. "I can't tell you why. But I will say that it has to do with Devan Fraser's safety. I'm trusting that you still care about her."

The sergeant perked up at the mention of Devan. "How is she? No lasting pain from her injuries?"

"Devan's fine, for now. She's in America, handling some things so she can immigrate here." Christian glanced toward the publican and saw the man frowning. "I'll make this quick. Can you find out why Logan Walsh is out of gaol?"

"What do you know of Mr. Walsh?"

"He was picked up about two months ago for extortion and money laundering. He's out. I saw him last night. I need to know why."

"I'll ask again, how did you know about Mr. Walsh?"

Christian stared blank-faced at the sergeant's question.

Finley sighed. "Fine. How's Devan involved? I'll help if you tell me that."

Christian studied the garda who had helped Devan back when she'd been brutally attacked in Galway. The man's inscrutable gaze held steady. Christian shrugged. "The man who attacked Devan was hired by Logan. Now with Logan free . . ."

"Christ." Finley rubbed his clean-shaven chin. "I'll see what I can find out—"

"On the quiet," Christian interrupted.

Finley nodded. "I'll be in contact." Christian rose when Finley did. The sergeant briefly touched Christian's shoulder. "When this is over, I'd like the whole story. I think I've proven you can trust me."

Christian slapped Finley on the back and pitched his voice to be heard over the din in the pub. "Thanks for setting me straight on the history, Officer . . ."

"That's Sergeant."

Christian slid his sunglasses in place and strolled out to continue his tourist charade. He stopped in another pub and ordered a bookmaker sandwich and pint of Guinness.

After lunch, he made his way to Logan's favorite hangout but didn't see him. On the way back toward Grafton Street, a young girl picking the pocket of an ancient gentleman with his frail wife caught Christian's attention. He strolled parallel to the street urchin, heading on an intercept path. Once he was close enough, he bumped into the thief—neatly re-stealing the old man's wallet and sticking a tracker on the girl's back collar.

"Sorry. Guess I wasn't watching where I was going," Christian said, continuing his American accent. "There's so much to see, isn't there?" He lifted his camera as though to take a snap of the girl.

The pickpocket backed up, then turned and bolted down a side street.

Christian laughed and headed for the elderly couple. Three steps away, the elderly couple stopped in front of a busker playing folk tunes. The old man started to reach for his back pocket. Christian stepped up and casually leaned over the man's shoulder.

"Good, isn't he?" Christian said as he slid the man's wallet into his back pocket, then tossed a couple euro coins in the open guitar case. His mobile rang, so he walked away.

Christian glanced at the caller ID, then scurried away from any prying ears. "Good morning, a ghra. How did you sleep?" He moved farther down the side street.

"I dropped like a stone after dinner. How about you?" Devan replied.

"Good," Christian lied. "Have you been in touch with your solicitor—um, lawyer?"

"I just got off the phone with her receptionist. I'm meeting her today. That'll give me time to list all the assets and gather some paperwork."

"Don't wear yourself out on your first day." Christian entered a small courtyard with a scattering of wrought iron tables and chairs for café patrons. He sat with his back against a wall at a table that afforded him the best view of anyone entering the area.

"I won't. My attorney has a realtor friend, one less thing I'll have to deal with. I should have a better idea of how long I'll need to be here after the meeting."

"You'll call me later?" Christian pantomimed sipping from a cup and mouthed the word coffee to a server who came outside to take his order.

"I will," Devan said. "How's it going for you?"

"Mostly done at my flat. There really isn't much I want to take. It'll all fit in the Audi's boot." Christian grimaced, thinking about things he'd probably need to leave behind. "Nowhere near the task you're dealing with."

"Have you communicated with ROARKE and DOCHAS? I miss them terribly, and I've only been gone a day." Devan gave a shaky laugh.

"They're fine. Padrick took them to visit GRAYSON today. I was just about to check in with ROARKE when you called." Christian accepted the steaming cup of coffee and thanked the server.

"That will perk up DOCHAS's spirit. Did I tell you we communicated for almost an hour during my flight? I'm not sure exactly how far away we were, but that's got to be quite a distance. Are you heading back to Lough Gur today?"

"Not yet. I've a few more things to take care of first. Maybe tomorrow, or the day after." He sipped his coffee and watched a group of teenagers arrange themselves at two nearby tables. "I better let you go, mo chroí."

"Okay. Touch base with ROARKE and DOCHAS. Let her know—"

"Don't fash. She knows you love her. You take care of my Yank."

"I love you too. It'll be late your time, but I'll call."

Christian smiled, then lowered his voice to a whisper, "Love you too, a ghra." He disconnected the call as heat rose in his cheeks.

*"ROARKE?"* Christian bespoke his dragon. The teenagers paid no attention, but he was immensely grateful that he and his dragon's communication was telepathic. He remembered his disguise and pretended to take snaps of the patio. He couldn't switch his accent back to American, but he could act like he was from another part of Ireland. *"ROARKE. Are you hearing me?"*

*"Aye. DOCHAS and I are swimming in the lough. The Wingless One is*

*wading, bemoaning that he can no' dive into the middle of the lough from on high."*

*"Sounds like you're having a good visit. How's DOCHAS handling being without Devan?"*

*"She fares well. The Wingless One fills her time, keeps her from missing the Ring Wearer."*

*"I just talked to Devan. She misses everyone. Tell DOCHAS that Devan is hurrying as fast as possible so she can come home."*

*"What of ye? Will ye be back at Lough Gur when we arrive tonight?"*

*"No. I've a few things still to handle. I told you I'd probably be a couple of days."* Christian drained the rest of his coffee, pulled out a five euro note and several coins and dropped them on the table. Then he left the gaggle of teenagers.

*"I thought ye had less to deal with than the Ring Wearer."* ROARKE sounded upset.

*"I do. My business will be quick compared to Devan's, but even I need some time."* His mobile rang. *"I've got to go. I'll check in later. Be good."* He broke the telepathic communication and answered the call. "You have information?"

"Yes, but you're not going to like it. Where do you want to meet?" Sergeant Finley said. "And not Kehoe's."

Christian thought a moment, then said, "Trinity. Meet me at the Campanile. Do you have clothing other than your uniform?"

"No, I'm still on duty. I can be there in twenty minutes."

"See you there." Christian sighed and ended the call.

He zigzagged through Phoenix Park as well as Grafton Street, watching for a tail or any of Logan's crew. He wandered around the Trinity College grounds. The Campanile stood tall in the center of the main square. People milled about as a tour guide herded his charges into a cluster and began his talk.

Christian made his way along the edge of the group, then wandered to the opposite side, keeping his eyes and ears open for anyone suspicious.

Sergeant Finley arrived, took one look at the tourists, and directed Christian toward the buildings farthest from the Old Library, where the *Book of Kells* drew throngs from all over the world.

The two men strolled along as though the sergeant was pointing out historical details to a tourist.

"Not exactly private," Finley said.

"No, but Logan wouldn't dare send his crew here. No easy escape, like on the streets. Besides, the students here don't make the best marks for pickpockets." Christian scanned the campus. No one stood out to his trained eye. "Logan's more lucrative business dealings are done in a few pubs in the Liberties. So . . . ?"

"Logan Walsh was indeed let out a few days ago."

Christian swore. "How? What about all the criminal charges?"

"He cut a deal. The scuttlebutt is Walsh had some very incriminating evidence against the director of public prosecutions. Some even say Walsh owned someone at CAB."

"What's that?"

"Criminal Assets Bureau. An independent agency that focuses on the illegally acquired assets of criminals involved in the types of crimes Walsh is accused of." Finley rubbed his chin. "Walsh had a 'Get out of gaol free card,' and he used it."

"Bloody ifrinn. All that work. Shite." Christian paced away from Finley.

"You said you saw Walsh last night. Where?" The sergeant stood perfectly still, one eyebrow raised.

Christian looked back at Finley. "In my flat." At the sergeant's unwavering gaze, Christian continued. "I got back into town yesterday. After I took Devan to catch her flight, I went to my flat. I knew someone had been inside." *Remember, he's gardaí.* "The whole place had been tossed. Things ripped to shreds or broken."

"Did you file a report?" Finley nodded at Christian's inscrutable look. "Never mind. Was anything taken?"

"I don't leave valuables there. The place was a mess, but nothing was missing. Anyway, I grabbed some clothes and stuff and started to leave when I heard someone trying to pick the lock. I escaped out the balcony door just as Logan entered."

"Did he see you?" Christian gave Finley an incredulous look. "So, no. And you're not in cahoots with Walsh, or you wouldn't need my help. What now, then?" Finley raised his hands, palms facing out. "No, don't tell me. What I don't know, I'm not required to report. Why was Walsh after Ms. Fraser?"

"He took a surveillance job from someone. Logan hired Kelly to keep a close eye on Devan. Kelly botched the job, the one that the Dublin Gardaí brought you in on."

"Who is the contract with?" Finley was growing impatient.

"A dead guy."

"What?"

"Robert Smyth. He died on Beltaine."

"Why does that name sound familiar? Never mind. It'll come to me." Finley said. "Anyway, with the guy bankrolling the surveillance dead, why are you worried about Walsh? There's no more job."

"Devan got Logan's muscle locked up," Christian said. "Kelly is still locked up, right?"

Sergeant Finley nodded. "In the mental ward in gaol. Wait a minute. You said you'd come back into Dublin yesterday. Where have you been? Last time I saw you was weeks ago here in Dublin."

*Feck*. "Devan and I were visiting my father—near Limerick."

"Right. Padrick Nolan. I remember now. His name is familiar too." Finley tapped his temple. "I'm sure it'll come to me. So Walsh holds a grudge, does he? Maybe Ms. Fraser should reconsider immigrating."

"That's not going to happen. I'll just have to find another way to deal with Logan." Christian reached out to shake Finley's hand. "Thanks for looking into this for me. I'll have Devan give you a call when she gets back. I'm sure she'd like to thank you again for your help a few months ago." He strode away as quickly as he could. He needed to leave before the sergeant could ask more questions or connect Smyth with Padrick or himself. Christian had no idea if Finley knew of the Tuatha Dragon Clan, but he sure wasn't going to tell the secret.

# Eleven

Christian brooded while waiting for his pint of Guinness. If Logan owned members of the gardaí, then Christian would need to tread carefully. For now, at least, Devan was safe in America. And when she returned, he'd make sure she stayed away from Dublin.

His pint arrived and he took a deep drink. *I should find out exactly who in the gardaí knows about the dragon clan. If Logan gets his hands on that secret, what kind of damage would he wreak?*

Christian reached for his mobile to call Sean but smiled when it vibrated and Devan's name crossed the screen. "Hello, a ghra. Are you finished with your attorney, then?"

"Yes, for today. I'm meeting with an accountant next week to work on all the taxes. There are other legalities the attorney is assisting me with. And her realtor friend is coming to see the property later this week."

A thumping sound helped him imagine Devan unloading mounds of paperwork. "Sounds like you've accomplished quite a bit today. How've you handled being back in your parents' home?" Christian sipped from his pint.

"To be honest . . ." Devan started, "it's been a bit surreal. Intellectually I know they're no longer here, but my heart expects to see them relaxing with a cocktail or strolling through the front door. The house is too quiet, too big without them." She sniffled. "I've completed an inventory of all the large pieces, but most of that's just ordinary things—they don't hold much significance for me. The real test will be tomorrow when I start on Dad's tools and Mom's boxes of handmade holiday decorations."

"Maybe you should crate up everything, ship it over here. I could help you with all that."

"Are you joking? That would cost a fortune." Devan chuckled. "No, I'll wade through. As it is, I'll be shipping plenty. My parents' armoire and Dad's desk are the lone pieces of furniture I want."

Christian sipped his stout. *Closest thing I've got like that is my specially made bedframe. Guess I should take that apart and bring it back to Lough Gur.*

Devan interrupted his thoughts. "But the best news is, I might be able to wrap this up and head home by the end of next week. I'll still stay here for my last Independence Day in America."

"That's great news. You should have led with that." He grinned.

"Gotta make you work some. You've got it easy over there," Devan teased. "I've a whole house to sort through. Speaking of . . . are you finished with packing up your flat?"

"Aye. I'm done there." He drained his pint and decided a change of subject was in order. "It's a record."

"What is?"

Christian narrowed his eyes in the dim lighting of the pub. "At least three minutes and you haven't asked after DOCHAS. She and ROARKE went swimming with GRAYSON."

"I wish I was there to see that."

"ROARKE was a bit smug that he and DOCHAS could dive into the lough from on high, while GRAYSON could only wade in." Christian signaled the publican for another pint. "GRAYSON is keeping DOCHAS occupied."

"I'm glad. I miss you all. I'll give you a call tomorrow. I'm sure I'll need a break. That garage is tightly packed."

"Take your time. If it gets to be too much, I've money enough to cover the shipping."

Devan was silent for a moment. "Thanks. Did I mention I love you?"

"No, but you can never say it enough." Christian kept the light banter going, but he was missing Devan. "I love you too."

"Take care of my sexy Irishman."

"Ha, ha. Call me anytime, a ghra."

"Good night, my love."

Christian ended the call as the publican set a fresh pint in front of him. A trio of musicians began to warm up, so Christian decided to call Sean after he got back to his room. For now, he'd enjoy his pint and some lively music.

The pub was soon hopping as the bodhrán player kept the crowd cheering.

Christian sipped his stout. At the publican's sudden gasp, Christian tracked the man's gaze to the front door as Logan, his boyhood mate and now nemesis, strode into the pub and right up to the bar. Christian choked.

A worn-out looking Logan slapped him on the back. "Careful there, boyo. You're supposed to drink the Guinness, not wear it." He pointed to Christian's head. "Ha! I crack myself up. Get it? You're wearing a Guinness cap."

Christian faked another cough and ducked his head away from Logan. *He doesn't recognize me.* Before Christian could form a response, Logan turned away and rapped on the bar. Christian kept his head down but kept Logan in sight in case he suddenly realized who he was standing next to.

"O'Malley, O'Malley, O'Malley," Logan called the publican over. "I hear you're late."

"I—I told your associate I needed more time. Pop has been in hospital. I'll get what I owe you. I just need a wee bit more time," O'Malley pleaded.

Logan nodded. One of the no-neck brutes that stood by the pub entrance joined him. "Young O'Malley here needs some incentive." Logan cracked his knuckles.

O'Malley backed up with his hands out in front of him. "No, no. Give me a moment. I'll be right back." He hurried to the other end of the bar, ducked under and headed to the back. No-neck followed.

*Christ.* Christian coughed again, then stood.

"You okay?" Logan turned to face him.

Christian ducked his head, coughed, and pointed in the direction of the loo.

Logan nodded.

Christian, adjusting his normal gait, made his way toward the back. He slowed as he passed the loo and saw the open door at the end of the narrow hall.

"How much?" O'Malley pleaded with Logan's muscle.

"Five hundred euros."

"Then I'd be square?"

"Until next month."

"That's extortion."

"No, that's security. What the boss calls the installment plan."

Christian crept closer. No-neck stood just inside the office door with his back to Christian.

*If I take him out, then what? Logan would just have his other goon mess up O'Malley. Or Logan would do it himself.* Christian whipped off his cap, tucked it into his back pocket, and raked his hands through his freshly-dyed blond hair to mess it up. He took bills from his wallet and folded them in half.

"Hey, boss," Christian called. No-neck lumbered to turn around and glared at him. "Your uncle came by, said you needed this." Christian handed O'Malley the euros.

"My uncle?" The publican looked at the euros in his hand.

Christian nodded. "He was wearing his commander's uniform. Perhaps a special ceremony with the Assistant Commissioner?"

"Commander?" O'Malley shook his head as if to clear it.

Christian winked when No-neck glanced at O'Malley. "Yes, and the Commander said to make sure Mr. Walsh understands his security services are no longer needed—as per orders from the A.C." Christian poked No-neck in the shoulder. "You'll relay the Gardaí Commander's words, won't you?"

No-neck grunted, then indicated O'Malley should precede him

back to the bar where Logan waited.

Christian hung back, then mingled with the crowd listening to the music. He watched as O'Malley went behind the bar and handed the money to Logan. Then No-neck leaned in and said something to his boss.

Logan slammed his fists onto the bar. His face was redder than a basket full of raspberries.

Christian grinned, then lowered his head when Logan pushed No-neck and his other goon out the front door. He glared at O'Malley, then strode out.

When Christian was sure Logan was truly gone, he returned to his stool at the bar.

"I don't know who you are or why you did what you did, but thank you." O'Malley reached out to shake Christian's hand. "I'll pay you back. It might take a week or so. I wasn't blowing smoke when I said Pop is in hospital. What's your name, mate?"

"My name's not important. You can pay me back with some information."

"Whatever I can tell you, I will, but I don't know very much. Pop ran the pub until a month or so ago." O'Malley poured Christian's flat Guinness down the drain and pulled a fresh pint.

"When did you first meet Mr. Walsh?"

"His goons came by about a week after I took over for Pop. Told me how I owed scratch to the big boss, Mr. Walsh. I hadn't met Walsh until tonight, but I knew of him. You don't have a pub near the Liberties, even blocks away, without knowing of the local mobster."

"How long has he been extorting money?"

"I don't know exactly. I didn't want to embarrass or pressure Pop—he's recovering from a heart attack—so I haven't brought it up." O'Malley finished building the Guinness. He set it in front of Christian. "That's on the house." He wiped his hands on a bar towel. "I honestly don't know how I was going to come up with the money. We run on a fairly slim profit margin here."

"I might not have helped too much. Maybe bought you some time." Christian took a long drink of his stout. *Maybe I can use Logan's greed against him.* "Do you know if Walsh is shaking down other businesses?"

"He must be. He needs the money. I heard he was scooped up by the gardaí several months back. Heard they froze his assets and didn't give any back when he was freed."

Christian laughed. "What else have you heard?" He surveyed the crowd over the rim of his glass and noted most of them enjoying the band. One or two boyos stood out for their surreptitious glances toward the bar. Logan's men, Christian thought. He didn't recognize them and figured if Logan hadn't seen through his disguise, then these two certainly wouldn't know him.

O'Malley continued. "Just that Walsh is seriously pissed with an old schoolmate by the name of Riley. Seems Riley got Walsh picked up and put in gaol." O'Malley's eyes widened. "Shite. You're him, aren't you? You fit the description, excepting the hair color and tourist get up."

"Shh. Keep your voice down." Christian took another sip of his Guinness.

"But you're him, right? Riley? I won't tell a soul."

Christian nodded. A plan was forming on another way to neutralize Logan, but he'd have to work it all out—and some contingencies—before he'd set it in motion.

"Forget you saw me." Christian put his Guinness cap back on and took one last drink of the black stout. *"Sláinte."* Then he headed out. Now he'd definitely require the names of the gardaí that knew of the Tuatha Dragon Clan. He hoped Sergeant Finley was among the chosen few. For the first time in his life, Christian genuinely liked a garda.

# Twelve

*America*

After an emotionally draining day of sorting through her family's keepsakes, Devan treated herself to a luxurious bubble bath in the master bedroom's large claw-foot tub. She dozed to thoughts of Christian and the time she'd spent in Ireland. When next she opened her eyes, the water had cooled. Shivering, she quickly toweled off. She slipped into her pajamas, curled up in her own bed, and fell into a dreamless sleep.

Devan awoke disoriented to a pitch-black room and the distinct sound of breaking glass. She reached for her cell phone on the nightstand. Something fell to the floor and she held her breath—listening. She didn't dare turn on the light, so she fumbled around in the dark until she found her cell phone and called 9-1-1.

"Someone has broken into my house," Devan whispered when the emergency operator answered. She strained to hear if the intruder was climbing the stairs but couldn't hear anything over her thudding heartbeat and the rasp of each terrified breath she drew.

"The police are en route," the calm voice on the other end of the phone said after Devan confirmed her name and address. "I'll stay on the line with you until they arrive. Is there any way you can make it to the front door safely?"

"No. I'm upstairs. I can't tell if someone's inside or not." *Was that a footstep?* She climbed out of bed as quietly as she could, then searched for a handy weapon. Her gaze settled on one of her glass dragon globes that sat atop her dresser. She switched the phone to her other hand, hefted the globe, then waited with one ear pressed to the closed bedroom door.

The sole light came from the cell phone, and Devan was careful to keep that pressed to her ear.

In what seemed like hours, but probably less than five minutes, she heard the wailing of sirens growing closer. *Should I make a run for it?* Before she could get her feet to move, she heard a loud knock on the front door.

"San Francisco Police. Open up."

The heavy glass globe still clutched in her hand, Devan clicked on the light and pulled open her bedroom door. The light seeped out and down the hall. No one was there. She hastened downstairs and unlocked the front door.

"Ms. Fraser?" A middle-aged police officer took a step backward and glanced at his partner on his left. "Officer Jennings and Officer Vance."

Devan nodded, then remembered her phone and told the 9-1-1 operator that the police had arrived. She disconnected. "I remember you from the other evening . . . at the bistro."

"We'll have a look around," Jennings said. "Please stay out here on the porch."

The two officers drew their weapons and went inside.

Devan stood on the porch, suddenly cold and aware she wore only her pajamas, her feet bare.

She heard the officers calling out, "Clear. Clear." The voices faded as they made their way to the back of the house and up the stairs.

A few minutes later, Officer Jennings waved her in. He guided her into the living room. "What happened?"

"I was asleep. I woke up when I heard glass breaking. I called 9-1-1. When I thought I heard footsteps, I grabbed something to hit the intruder." She held up her makeshift weapon, then set it down on the table. "You showed up, and I figured I was safe to open the door."

"Is this your home? Do you live alone?" Again, Officer Jennings led the questioning.

Devan's throat tightened and she had to clear it before she could speak. "This was my parents' home. They died in February."

"I'm sorry," Officer Jennings said.

"I've been out of the country until a couple of days ago. I'm back to sell the house and finish settling the estate." Devan took a deep breath.

Officer Vance spoke for the first time. "Whoever it was made it inside but isn't here now."

"How do you know they were inside?" Devan asked as she clasped her hands together to keep them from shaking.

"The little window in the kitchen door was broken, there's blood on the floor and the door lock." Officer Vance glanced at his partner.

"I'll get my kit. Collect a blood sample and check for prints. Might get lucky." He grinned like a kid with a new toy as he headed for the police cruiser.

Officer Jennings interrupted Devan's scattered thoughts. "Ms. Fraser, let's have you check if anything's missing." She nodded.

They made their way to the kitchen and laundry room at the back of the house.

Devan shuddered at the drops of blood on the floor and trailing to the counter where paper towels had obviously been ripped from the holder. Her dishes were in the drainer. The half-filled bottle of wine stood on the counter next to her tote.

The blood drained from her face. She stumbled forward.

"What is it?" Officer Jennings asked.

Devan reached for the tote, but the officer intercepted her.

"The tote . . ." Devan's voice trembled. She began again. "I left it in my father's study. It has all the estate documents inside. Yesterday—" She glanced at the clock above the kitchen table and noticed it was after three in the morning. "Now the day before. Anyway, when I finished with my attorney, I left everything in the bag and placed it on my father's desk in his study." She waved helplessly in the direction of the study.

Jennings pulled a pen from his shirt pocket and carefully lifted the tote open. "There's a binder and several folders inside. Was there anything else?"

Devan tried to think exactly how many folders she brought to the attorney's office but was flustered and couldn't remember. "There were various papers in each folder. I'm just not sure exactly how many folders. Can I have a look?"

"We'll let the Rookie get prints first." Jennings motioned for her to head back toward the foyer. "Let's have a look in your father's study. See if anything else was disturbed."

Devan led the way, stopping when Officer Vance reappeared with a black briefcase.

"There's a bag on the counter that Ms. Fraser says was in the study," Jennings said. "There's blood on the top folder. We'll be in the study."

Vance nodded then made his way to the kitchen.

Devan could find nothing obviously out of place in the study, so she and Officer Jennings returned to the kitchen.

The back doorknob and frame had black dust coating them and showed smudges. The tote was still on the counter, but the binder and folders were spread out on the table. Again, black smudges could be seen, but this time Devan recognized prints as well. And more of the red smears of blood.

"I've found several prints on these." Vance indicated the binder and folders. "I'll need to take a set of your prints to rule yours out. Anyone else touch these?"

"Just my attorney."

"I'll need your attorney's name and contact info." Jennings stood poised to write in his notebook.

Devan rattled off the information, then reached a shaky hand toward the papers on the kitchen table. "Can I see if all the paperwork is still here?"

"Sorry, no. But I can lift the cover," Vance said.

The bloodied folder held her dual citizenship application.

"Did your parents have any enemies? Someone they might have owed money?" Jennings asked as he indicated Devan should sit at the table.

"No. Dad always paid his bills on time, usually early. Besides, they've been gone over four months now. No one's ever broken in. This has always been a safe neighborhood." The shock of the break-in was taking its toll. Her brain clouded over.

"Is there anyone who would want to hurt you?" Jennings flipped through his notebook. "What about your ex from the bistro the other evening?"

"Rick Hunter?" Devan inclined her head.

"The reporter?" Vance asked as he bagged and labeled the collected evidence.

"Investigative journalist." Devan winced as the automatic correction that stemmed from Rick's constant refrain of the perceived slight. Apprehension filled her. *Was the officer a fan? Would he mock her? What if the intruder was Rick? He'd know she was filing for dual citizenship. He'd ferret out that she was moving to Ireland. Oh God! The dragon clan. I've put the secrecy of the dragons in danger.*

She reached for her phone to call Ireland and nearly missed Officer Vance's mutterings. "That's one untrustworthy waste of humanity."

"Sorry. What'd you say?"

"Nothing." Jennings glared at his partner, then concentrated on writing on his notepad.

Devan stared at the two officers. "Do . . . do you think it was Rick?"

"Can't get ahead of ourselves," Jennings said. "Could have been bored kids looking for easy money."

"I'll process the blood and prints and check to see if Hunter's prints are on file, but B and E isn't the department's priority," Vance said.

"No, of course not." Devan dropped her gaze to her cell phone. *Should I call Ireland? Warn them? What if it isn't Rick, but some kid just rifling through the tote looking for a laptop or cash? No, better wait until I know more. No reason to put everyone on alert for no reason.*

Devan escorted the two officers out the front door as pre-dawn lightened the summer sky. The streets were still quiet of cars, only the birds chirping to signal the start of another day.

"You'll let me know . . ." Devan shuddered in the cool breeze.

"Someone will follow up," Jennings said as he climbed into the patrol car. Vance quirked a smile and thumbed his chest, indicating he would be in touch.

She'd have to rely on the police to do their job, but she'd work faster so she could get out of town early. *And watch my back.*

# Thirteen

With another two days of hard work, Devan was ready to turn the property over to the realtor her attorney had recommended. The realtor would list the house, furniture included, next week. Arranging shipping for the items she couldn't part with, donating her parents' personal effects, and selling the vehicles would put an end to what had been an emotional process. With that realization, the true depth of her grief, held at bay over these last few days of frenzied activity, hit her hard. She doubled over and began to sob.

When her cellphone rang, she composed herself as best she could and answered with a shaky, "Hello."

"Ms. Fraser? Officer Vance. Rick Hunter's prints were on the paperwork in your kitchen."

"That bastard." All remaining sadness evaporated from Devan.

"Had he ever been inside your parents' home before? Could he have thumbed through any of that before your parents died?"

Devan hesitated, thinking over the past year. How often had Rick been with her for dinner at her parents'? *Had he ever been inside Dad's study? Maybe . . .*

"Ms. Fraser?"

"Rick came to the house several times. I suppose he could have paged through the binder, but all the other folders and my immigration paperwork have been recently added. Some of it I brought with me from Ireland. Why?"

"I brought him in for questioning."

Devan's stomach roiled and she pressed her hand against it.

"He gave me some story about helping you collect papers that had fallen out of your bag."

"No way," Devan said. "Ask the waiter. He can verify my version."

"I will. I just wanted to confirm everything in case Hunter changes his story. I can book him on breaking and entering, but since it's not a violent crime, he'll probably be released on OR until his trial."

"What's OR?"

"Own recognizance—no bail money."

Devan shuddered. "When will the trial be? Will I have to attend?"

"The judge determines the date. You might not need to testify in person. Maybe a deposition would suffice, especially if you add in the episode at the bistro," Vance said. "Come in anytime. Ask for me."

"Okay." Devan disconnected and slumped in her chair, resting her head on her folded arms on the kitchen table. *When am I going to be free of that bastard?* She allowed herself to wallow in self-pity until her phone rang again. Upon seeing Christian's number on the phone screen, she dried her eyes and blew her nose before answering.

"Hello, my love." Devan heard the melancholy in her voice and forced a smile. She'd read somewhere that if you smiled, it was impossible to sound sad. "How are you? Back in Lough Gur yet?"

"I'm heading there tomorrow. What's wrong?" Christian's voice sharpened.

"Nothing's wrong."

"Devan, I can hear it in your voice. Something happened since we last talked. You *are* coming back, aren't you?"

"Of course I am. I've got the shipper coming tomorrow. There will be any number of crates delivered in the near future. I've got another few days to arrange for selling or donating what's not being sold with the house. Then the realtor will start showing it. I'm on schedule to fly home late next week."

"So, what's the problem? Don't say nothing and don't shut me out."

Devan debated about mentioning the break-in and her fears that her ex would track her down in Ireland. She didn't want to worry Christian needlessly. Would he even understand her fear of Rick? She shook her head and decided that was a conversation better done face to face. "Nothing. Really. I'm just a bit . . . out of sorts. This whole trip has been more exhausting than I thought possible. Going through everything, I wasn't prepared for all the memories. I miss my parents so much," her voice broke.

"Ah, mo chroí," his tone softened. "Maybe it's too soon for you to sell the house."

Devan sniffled. "No. The house is just a place. They're not here anymore. Besides, I'm keeping a few things from each of them to hold them close to me." She straightened in her chair. "New topic. What have you been doing in Dublin all this time?"

"Wrapping up on some business of my own." Christian yawned.

"That exciting, huh?" Devan teased.

"Not much to keep me up late, what with you clear across the pond," he bantered back. "Talk tomorrow?"

"I'll call earlier, so you're more awake. Love you." Devan hung up.

Too exhausted to climb the stairs, she lay on the couch with a light throw over her and fell into a fitful sleep. She dreamed of the night her parents were killed.

New York City pulsed to the beat of the city. Billboards lit up the mid-February night sky with ads that hawked diamonds, blood-red roses, or romantic date packages that included a Broadway show.

Yellow cabs jockeyed for position, horns blaring, shuttling patrons from luxury hotels to swanky dinner houses. Rain splattered between black umbrellas, creating puddles. The Empire State Building reflected in the largest of these pools as Joseph opened the cab door for his wife, Meghann. They had enjoyed celebrating their thirtieth anniversary too much and were running late for their dinner reservation.

Meghann giggled like a schoolgirl when Joseph told the cabbie there was an extra ten dollars if he could make the restaurant in time.

The truck came barreling out of the alleyway, oblivious to the cross-traffic and weather conditions. Horns screeched. Pedestrians dashed for safety. As the cabbie swerved madly, there was no time to scream. Breaking glass and tearing metal overwhelmed the city sounds as the cab rolled over and over, throwing Meghann into Joseph. Together, they bounced around inside until the last sickening crunch of the vehicle coming to a stop—upside down. Bloodied glass lay scattered everywhere as the puddles slowly turned red.

A face appeared in the shattered back window—Rick Hunter, laughing. "Devan's all mine now. She won't get away from me again."

Devan bolted awake, gasping for air, her lungs locked up, as she reached out in a vain attempt to stop what was too late to change—her parents' deaths. She wrapped her arms around her middle to slow the shudders that racked her body. Once she was sure her legs could hold her, she went to the kitchen and filled the kettle for a cup of tea. As she waited for the water to boil, she sat and rested her head on the kitchen table.

The NYC police hadn't told her the awful details of the accident. Those she had read from the report and the witness statements.

*Had Rick really been there? No, that's my subconscious trying to deal with his scary behavior these last few days.*

The kettle whistled. She wiped her cheeks on the sleeve of her long-sleeve T-shirt, then fixed her tea. She leaned against the counter, sipping tea and reflecting on her dream and her uneasy feelings about Rick.

"You haven't slowed down enough since they died to allow for the grief, the mourning," she said aloud. "No wonder you're a wreck."

A brisk knock on the front door brought Devan to peer out the Judas hole. No one was there. The hair on the back of Devan's neck stood up and a shiver raced down her spine.

"That's it. I'm changing my flight. I'm leaving tomorrow. I'll stop at the police station on my way out of town." She double-checked that all the locks were engaged and raced back into the kitchen to do the same. Luckily she'd had the little window repaired yesterday.

*No way am I sticking around for Rick to get to me. He's deranged.*

# Fourteen

*Ireland*

Christian cleaned out his safe deposit box at the bank then finalized the plan he'd worked diligently on for the past two days. He had learned long ago not to divulge all he knew at one time. So he'd kept incriminating information on Logan, more damaging than the one incident of extortion that had the gardaí locking Logan away weeks ago. Armed with ironclad proof of identity theft, blackmail, and extortion, Christian could finger Logan as the gang leader running the local protection racket. And thanks to the willingness of publican O'Malley and the other local merchants to testify that they were being threatened, Logan should be back in gaol and out of Christian's and Devan's lives for a long time.

When he returned to his flat, he waded through the mess to his bedroom and stripped the bed. *No way am I leaving my specially constructed bedframe.* It took three trips to transfer the bedframe downstairs and secure it to the top of his Audi. He made one last sweep through the flat he'd called home for the past five years. There was nothing more worth taking.

Someone rapped twice on the door. Christian peered through the Judas hole, then opened the door to the cleaner he had hired.

"Christ. What happened here?" The beefy man in coveralls set down a box filled with refuse bags and cleaning paraphernalia. "You surely pissed off someone." He whistled as he stepped inside.

"Right." Christian gave the man the front door key. "It all goes. I expect pictures of each room once you're done cleaning. The landlady's in One-A. She gets the key when you're done. I'm friends with her, so she knows to expect you later today."

"No worries, mate. You confirmed use of the rubbish bin?"

Christian nodded, shook the cleaner's hand, then left.

More than an hour later, he had just exited the M7 heading south when his mobile rang.

"Hey," Devan greeted him with her clipped American accent. "Are you in Lough Gur?"

"On my way. What's up?"

"I'm booked on a flight into Shannon Airport early tomorrow morning. I figured Shannon would be closer to Lough Gur." Devan spoke rapidly.

"What?" Christian pulled off the roadway. "I thought you'd need another week. What about you celebrating America's independence? Did something happen?"

"No. The shipper picked up everything yesterday, and the realtor doesn't need me underfoot while she preps the house for selling. And I realized there's no one to celebrate with. It's kind of depressing—no one to share a barbecue and fireworks. It's better for me to . . . I'm looking forward to my new country. There's no reason to stick around here." Devan paused. "I have a few leads to check on about your mother, but I can do that there. Besides, I miss you and DOCHAS."

"That's great. Text me your flight information and I'll pick you up." Christian grinned like a madman, even though his gut twisted at thoughts of something causing his Yank more grief.

"Will do. Let DOCHAS know."

"Safe flight, mo chroí. See you soon." Christian disconnected, then spent the rest of his journey suspicious about what could have happened to change her plans so drastically—especially her leaving before America's Independence Day. All his possible scenarios spelled trouble.

He arrived in Lough Gur to find Padrick waiting for him. As Christian stepped from his loaded down Audi, Sean emerged from Padrick's office—with Sergeant Finley close behind.

*Feck! Now what?*

Christian didn't hesitate. He strode toward the three men, but before he reached them, ROARKE's triumphant bugle tore through the warm breeze. Christian halted. ROARKE's green neck ridges bristled as the ever-growing dragon trundled out of the opening in the hillock that camouflaged the Lough Gur dragons' lair complex.

*"Finally, ye have returned,"* ROARKE bespoke, then opened his wings. *"I have a mighty itch and no one to scratch it."*

Christian barked out a laugh. *"Being a little dramatic, no?"* As the green dragon folded his translucent wings, Christian continued, *"I know for a fact you've been well cared for while I've been away."*

DOCHAS ambled up next to ROARKE and stretched her scaled neck forward. Her eyes whirled fast.

Christian reached up to rub both dragons' chins and to soothe the anxiety he felt coming from DOCHAS in waves. "Devan is coming home tomorrow. Not to worry. She's missed you terribly." DOCHAS rumbled low in her throat. Christian took that as thanks. He faced ROARKE. *"I've got to meet with Sean, Padrick, and Sergeant Finley, then I'll be in to give you a proper oiling. DOCHAS as well."*

*"I shall permit this, but do no' tarry. We must fly today to rejuvenate the magic. It has been longer than is wise."*

*"Right. We'll fly after my meeting. DOCHAS can come with us."* Christian tapped ROARKE's snout with affection then turned back to the three men waiting for him. He noticed Sergeant Finley staring in awe at the dragon pair and wondered if the garda had ever seen a dragon up close.

Sergeant Finley may have been struck mute with the emergence of the dragons, but he quickly found his voice once everyone sat in Padrick's office.

"You're playing a dangerous game with Mr. Walsh. I hope you know what you're doing."

"Who's Mr. Walsh?" Sean asked.

"Logan Walsh is a bloke I used to run with a long time ago," Christian said. "He's the man the killer hired to find Devan and the boss of that eejit Kelly that accosted Devan. Twice." Christian leapt to his feet. He couldn't sit still while reliving the near abduction of his Yank. *And by God, she is mine.*

"Okay," Sean said. "What's that have to do with now? The killer's dead. Devan's safe." He turned to Padrick and Finley. "Didn't Devan's attacker land in gaol?"

"Aye," Finley said. "But your boyo here had unfinished business with Mr. Walsh."

All three men stared at Christian. He pushed a hand through his too-long black hair, mimicking Devan when she was frustrated. He nearly laughed aloud at the realization that they were picking up each other's idiosyncrasies. He sobered at the shocked look on Padrick's face. *Christ. Does he believe I'm still tight with Logan?*

Christian sighed then returned to his chair. He leaned forward, elbows on knees, and told the three men the details of what he had implemented back in April that landed Logan in gaol. Christian explained he had done it because his childhood friend had still been after Devan. Christian would do whatever it took to protect her. He lifted his chin, daring each man to criticize his decision.

"So, what happened?" Padrick asked.

"The blighter was released," Christian said. "All my hard work for naught."

"I don't understand." Padrick looked from Christian to Finley.

"Mr. Walsh had someone in his back pocket." Finley shook his head. "The charges were dropped and he was released."

Christian then explained what had happened over the last several days while he was in Dublin, starting with his realization that finding Logan in his flat meant that Logan knew Christian had snitched to the gardaí.

"What dangerous game are you playing now?" Padrick asked.

"I'm protecting Devan and myself. And the dragon clan. Believe me, if Logan gets wind of a secret society of dragons and riders, he'll stop at nothing to use that information for personal profit."

"What's your play?" Sean asked. There wasn't condemnation in his tone, just curiosity.

"I have other evidence of Logan's criminal organization that I didn't use before. More damning." Christian shrugged when he saw Padrick's eyes widen. "I also organized the business owners Logan has been shaking down to call his bluff. I put them all in touch with a guy I've done security jobs for in the past. He's going to see them through the criminal complaints. I figured the authorities—even corrupt ones—can't turn a blind eye when over two dozen upstanding, tax-paying, business owners band together and show what Logan has been doing."

"That's risky," Padrick said. "And costly for the business owners."

Christian tilted his head in the sergeant's direction. "Finley told me what Logan did to get released. What I gave to the gardaí months ago was very damning, so I think Logan used up all his leverage. He never was one to hold anything back, plan for the next shoe to drop." Christian straightened his shoulders. "I gave my contact enough money for any losses the business owners might incur as long as they file the complaint in the next month or so." Padrick gasped, but Christian ignored him. Instead, he looked at Finley. "I'm guessing they didn't waste any time if you're here."

"Your solicitor friend filed earlier today. He specifically asked that I be informed when Mr. Walsh was taken into custody. He also requested the commissioner assign me as lead investigator on the case, to avoid any political backlash after the fiasco of Mr. Walsh's previous release. You, sir, have a powerful ally." Finley shook his head. "Mr. Walsh and a dozen others were apprehended and charged. I was told he went stark raving mad. He threatened everyone from the patrol officers to the commissioner. And shown the mountain of evidence and sworn statements, he insisted he took his orders directly from one Christian Riley."

"Christ." Padrick groaned and rubbed his forehead. "What are the chances of someone high up believing this eejit?"

"Not likely. Especially since the commissioner has over twenty signed affidavits from leading business owners stating the contrary. And that Mr. Riley is the single person who has bothered to listen and do something about their ongoing complaints. It's true, politics often make for interesting bedfellows." When no one spoke, Finley continued. "The commissioner has never had to take orders from anyone beneath him, but he knows it would be career suicide to dismiss the solicitor. No, Christian is safe."

Christian breathed out a sigh of relief. He hadn't thought he'd be caught up in Logan's takedown, but it was nice to hear Sergeant Finley's confirmation. And to know he had placed his trust in the right garda. He glanced at the uniformed sergeant as another thought crossed his mind. "Did you know about the dragon clan all along?"

Finley nodded. "Once I made sergeant and was assigned to lead the Galway office. Though I've never actually seen one of the dragons until today."

"How did you know where to find me?" Christian caught Sean's attention. "I never mentioned the clan, I swear."

"I finally remembered where I'd heard your father's name before—he's the leader at Lough Gur. The rest was easy. You said you were staying near your father. I put it all together."

Christian rose. "I need to take ROARKE and DOCHAS for a flight. ROARKE's mine and DOCHAS is Devan's. She'll be home tomorrow, but the dragons need to fly today. If you stick around, I'll introduce you to them both."

"I'd like that." Finley rose with Sean and Padrick. "I'll need to check in with my office. Do you have a phone I can use? Seems my mobile doesn't have reception here."

Christian heard Sean begin to explain about the limitations of technology with the dragon magic as he headed outside.

ROARKE and DOCHAS were waiting in the smaller courtyard. Christian was grateful someone had saddled ROARKE. He didn't bother with riding gear. He swung up into the riding harness atop

ROARKE and gave the signal to take flight. His dragon bunched his powerful hind legs and leapt into the late afternoon sky, beating his wings to gain altitude. DOCHAS followed a moment later. Once both dragons were clear of the houses and grazing cattle, Christian directed his dragon southwest toward County Cork and the Drombeg Stone Circle.

As the warm summer air blew against his face, Christian relaxed one muscle group at a time until his whole body felt like liquid mercury. He hadn't realized until this moment how much tension he'd held while in Dublin.

When the stone circle came into view, he cleared his mind and linked with ROARKE. They flew the complicated Celtic knot magic rejuvenating pattern above the tightly packed standing stones, then hovered to the south and watched DOCHAS repeat the pattern.

Christian knew he had Finley waiting for his return to Lough Gur but wasn't eager for the euphoria of flying adragonback to end.

*"Take us west to the ocean, then we'll make our way along the coastline to Ardmore and northward back to Lough Gur,"* Christian bespoke his dragon. *"I've missed the fresh air of flying. And the freedom."*

*"And I have missed ye."* ROARKE banked left and headed toward the fiery orange ball making its way to the edge of the landscape.

Christian tightened his legs around ROARKE's girth, then threw his arms in the air and gave a shout of exhilaration. *My plan worked. Finley is on our side. And my Yank is coming home.*

# Fifteen

Christian drove to Shannon Airport half expecting a text from Devan saying she'd changed her mind about coming home early. He'd gone over her words from yesterday for a hint of why she'd abruptly changed her plans but couldn't find a reason. "She's scared, but why?"

Inside the terminal, he waited with the meager crowd for the arriving passengers to exit through customs. Once again, he mentally reviewed the conversations they'd had over the past week to see if he could pinpoint what made him so uneasy. *It was all so innocuous. Nothing of any real substance. So whatever is wrong can't be on my end.*

Devan finally emerged within a group of travelers. Christian almost didn't recognize her. She wore a rumpled jumper and jeans, her hair in disarray. Dark smudges bruised the delicate skin under her whiskey-colored eyes. She looked exhausted. But more than that, she looked defeated. Her shoulders slumped, not just from the weight of the rucksack and tote bag she carried. When she spotted him, her smile broke free. She rushed to him, dropping her tote and throwing herself into his arms. Her eyes filled with unshed tears.

*What the bloody ifrinn happened? I should have gone to America with her. Then I could have stopped whoever frightened her. What a damn bloody fool I am.*

Christian gently framed her face with his hands. He inhaled her unique scent that reminded him of the ocean with a hint of forest. His eyes lingered on her soft, unpainted lips before he kissed her tenderly. "God, I've missed you."

"I've only been gone a week. Less than I had planned." Devan ran her fingers through his hair. "I missed you too."

Christian took a small step back and carefully brushed the pads of his thumbs under her eyes. "Rough flight?"

Devan shook her head. "Not really. Long story and I desperately want to see DOCHAS, soak in a tub, and cuddle with my sexy Irish lover. Not necessarily in that order." She winked.

Some of the tightness in Christian's chest loosened. "Glad to hear it." He kissed her temple, hefted her tote bag, and guided her outside the terminal, her hand gripped tightly in his own.

Inside his car, Devan leaned back and her eyes took on the dreamy gaze of a dragonrider bespeaking a dragon.

Despite his burning need to understand what happened in America, Christian didn't disturb her. *Let her tell her story in her own time. Besides, I've kept a few things from her as well. Things I'll need to divulge before she hears about Sergeant Finley's visit from someone else.* Christian took the scenic route back to Lough Gur to give himself time to figure out the best approach to explain the Logan situation.

When he realized he'd unconsciously headed away from the clan compound and toward the lough instead, he decided it was fortuitous and slowed to take a side road. "I saw a rocky formation on my flight with ROARKE and DOCHAS yesterday. I want to check it out."

He leaned forward, scanning the view past the stacked stone walls that bordered the road. At a narrow pullover, he eased the Audi between a thicket of blackthorn and piles of boulders. "I think this is the place." He exited the vehicle and helped Devan from the passenger's side.

They climbed over the low stone wall, made their way across a hillock, and skirted around several trees in full bloom. Less than ten steps past the copse of trees stood a wedge tomb made up of four large roof stones staggered over two virtually intact outer walls.

Devan still hadn't said a word since they'd exited the airport terminal.

Christian led her back to the low stone wall. He leaned against the trunk of the largest tree and shoved his hands into his pockets. "Tell me."

Devan glanced at the wedge tomb before setting her gaze on him. "Tell you what?"

"What has you so spooked that you'd change your plans so drastically?"

"Nothing." Devan bit down on her lower lip. "It was just time I left."

"Bollocks!" Christian pushed away from the tree and pointed to the wall, indicating Devan should sit. "Look, I know something happened to frighten you. I can feel it. How can I help if you don't trust me enough to tell me?"

"Trust is a two-way street, Christian." Devan sat on the stone wall. She pulled her knees to her chest and wrapped her arms around them. "DOCHAS told me Sergeant Finley was at the clan compound yesterday. So what happened that had the good garda out to speak to you?"

*Feck.* Frustration roiled through Christian. *I'm the one pushing her. I've got to trust someone. Should be the woman I love. Maybe coming clean needs to start with me.* Decision made, Christian straddled the stone wall and turned Devan so she faced him. He took a steadying breath, then stole a quick peek at the Neolithic wedge tomb standing as a silent witness.

"Let me start by saying I've never felt about anyone else the way I feel about you." He waited for the usual unease he felt whenever he talked about his past to tighten his chest, but it didn't happen. "Growing up in the orphanage encouraged me to keep my feelings to myself. The lone person I confided in—I trusted—was Logan. I found out pretty quick that he would have sold out his mother if he'd known who she was. After one time too many that he'd left me holding the proverbial and literal bag, I left his gang. I was a bit of a chancer myself but decided to get out of that life. Afterward, I trusted no one. Committed to no one. That worked for me . . . until I met you.

"I've been on my own for a long time now. Used to doing things my way without consulting anyone or worrying about anyone else. And that worked well too . . . until you.

"When you were in America, when I sensed something was going on with you, when you wouldn't tell me . . ." He took a shaky breath before he continued. "I figured you didn't trust me. That maybe you didn't feel the same way I did. Maybe because I didn't go with you to America, you were done with me."

Devan looked stricken. "No." She laid her hand on his forearm. "It's just that—"

"I know I need to open up more, learn to trust more. I'm doing the best I can." Christian rubbed his chin. He continued before Devan could interrupt. "I love you. And that isn't a casual thing for me—"

"You think it is for me?"

"I have no way of knowing," Christian said, exasperated. "Because you won't tell me what's wrong."

Devan twisted her dragon ring on her right middle finger, then took Christian's hand, linking their fingers. "I ran into my ex-fiancé shortly after my arrival in San Francisco. It wasn't pleasant." She shook her head. "No, it was downright unnerving."

Shock stole Christian's breath. There was so much he didn't know about Devan. Before he could get control of his emotions, he sputtered, "You were engaged?"

"The engagement, if you could call it that, lasted about six months. Rick was a controlling bastard. He thought he owned me, and I guess I didn't disabuse him of that notion. Last Christmas, he basically said I wasn't important enough, smart enough, sexy enough for him. That no man would want me. He really messed with my head. Made me question myself." She shrugged as though her insecurities didn't matter. "Then after my parents died, I didn't have the energy to deal with Rick and his mercurial moods. I believed it was over. Apparently, he had other ideas and accosted me at a small bistro."

Christian shoved to his feet, his fingers still entwined with Devan's. "That bloody gobshite. No one hits—"

"He didn't hit me, just grabbed my arm hard enough to bruise. Lobbed insults. When I threatened to cause a scene, he left. You see, Rick's an investigative journalist. I knew he wouldn't want his reputation sullied if the police were called."

"But, he could have jumped you when you left." Christian's blood still boiled. A red haze clouded his vision. Devan squeezed his hand, and he realized she was still talking.

"The waiter called the police anyway. They took statements. I thought that confrontation settled the whole sordid affair, but the next night the house was broken into." She told Christian the details of the intrusion and about her fears that Rick may have found out she was moving to Ireland. How she was afraid that he would keep digging until he uncovered the truth about the dragon clan.

"You should have told me." Christian sat back down. "I would have found a way to get to you."

"It wasn't something to bring up over the phone." Devan breathed a sigh. "Mostly, I just wanted to get back to you and DOCHAS. Rick Hunter's a part of my past. I want to keep him there. You're my future . . . I hope."

Christian leaned forward. His lips caught hers in a searing kiss that left them both breathless and promised much more than hope. When he finally released her lips, he took a deep breath.

"You know that eejit never deserved you, right?" He searched Devan's face. "You're one-of-a-kind. I'm not even sure I deserve you."

She chuckled.

"But let's get one thing straight. You'll tell me if you ever spot that rat bastard." It wasn't a question.

Devan searched Christian's deep blue eyes before she nodded.

He relaxed, then gave Devan a cocky grin, hoping to lighten the tension. "Good, cause no one messes with my Yank. I don't know what I'd do without you in my life, a ghra."

"Back at you, mo chroi." Devan winked, then got serious again. "So tell me about Finley."

Christian rubbed the back of his neck. "Logan's out of gaol and back to shaking down hard-working people. And he's trying to pin his criminal dealings on me. I'm working on something that will see Logan back in gaol for a very long time, I hope." Christian told Devan all that had happened in the past week, ending with finding Sergeant Finley at Lough Gur yesterday and his relief that the garda was aware of the Tuatha Dragon Clan.

Devan nodded. "I've always had a good feeling about him."

Christian stood and pulled Devan to her feet. "Let's go so you can spend some time with DOCHAS. Then I have plans for tonight. Just you and me." His mouth found hers, open and demanding.

# Sixteen

*Lughnasadh—Scotland*

The sun streamed through the kitchen window, bathing the snap Liam held in its golden glow. The beloved faces of his family stared back, the images faded from the constant caress of his fingers, but Liam just couldn't bring himself to stop. It was the only contact he'd had in over six weeks and, as it did every day, Liam felt the familiar frustration building in his heart. Tearing his gaze away, he looked out the window toward mainland Scotland, his real home. He knew Merida was enjoying her mum's help with the newborn twins, but he longed for his wife. And he was missing all the joys and tribulations of being a da for the first time. He'd even been looking forward to changing nappies. Something he'd never dare share with his mates.

Graeme had kept his promise of updating Liam with periodic visits, but they never lasted long enough. He never tired of hearing about his bairns. Liam was sure that his brother-in-law was disobeying The MacLean by coming out to this isolated spit of rock, yet Graeme never wavered in his duty to his sister. The latest news from two weeks ago was of how Merida was getting back to her usual perky self and how Rhys and Riordan didn't like being separated from each other when they went down for a nap or bedtime.

"I'm going completely radge here with no one but myself and KENNETH to talk to." Liam dragged a hand through his hair that had grown too long. "At least the garden's in full bloom. I'll have plenty of vegetables and such to see me through the winter. God, please don't let me be exiled for that long." He'd taken to holding a conversation aloud as he would with Merida to keep the loneliness at bay.

Liam watched as the familiar outline of a dragon grew larger on the horizon. He squinted as the sun's rays obscured the dragon's color. A dragonrider was due today or tomorrow with fresh supplies, but Liam held out hope that The MacLean would come to end his exile instead. When the dragon banked right, Liam saw the rust color of REED's wings along with Graeme's Fraser tartan across the beast's back.

"Second best visitor." Liam kissed the snaps he held, then placed them in his pocket. He rushed out of the bothy to greet Graeme.

REED landed and lowered the large wooden crate of supplies he held in his forelegs. Graeme climbed down, patted his dragon's chest, then waved to Liam.

"I thought I'd bring the supply delivery. REED wants to fly with KENNETH for a bit. Is he up to stretching his wings?"

"That'd be grand. He wretched his wing a bit yesterday. I've been experimenting with some peppers, Arnica, and Devil's Claw ground into a paste that I've used for my own muscle aches. I rubbed it into KENNETH's wing joint earlier, so I'm hoping it'll help him." Liam mentally called his dragon, rousing the yellow dragon from his late morning nap. "KENNETH will be along in a moment."

Liam picked his way through the garden to help Graeme heft the supplies and carry the crate back to the bothy. "Tell me how Merida and the bairns are doing."

"I'll do better. I've new snaps for you. The twins have grown so much since they were born." Graeme stopped talking when he stumbled on the edging of the raised herb bed. When he recovered, he continued. "Merida is talking about going back home—back to your home."

Liam halted so suddenly, he almost dropped the crate. "But who would help her with the bairns? Is she ready to be alone with them? Blast it! The MacLean must free me from this prison."

Graeme glared over his shoulder at Liam. "You didn't have to pull my arm out of its socket. Anyway, Mum and Da convinced Merida to stay a while longer. I swear I don't know who was more relieved, Mum or Merida. And I like that she and my nephews are near me in the Fraser clan compound."

"Good." Liam continued walking.

KENNETH shuffled out of his lair and he and REED launched into the warm summer sky. They flew northwest toward the Outer Hebrides and the standing stones of Callanish. KENNETH had stayed close by on his solo twice-weekly Celtic pattern flights since they'd been here, so flying to the Isle of Lewis would be a treat for him.

Liam felt his dragon's spirit soar as KENNETH caught an updraft.

"Thank REED for flying with KENNETH. He shouldn't be punished for my recklessness." Liam led the way inside the bothy and, together with Graeme, set the crate down by the front door.

He waited anxiously as his brother-in-law pulled an envelope from his inside coat pocket. Graeme handed Liam two new snaps.

In the first one, Merida sat in a rocker with a bairn in each arm. Both boys wore tiny blue caps over their mops of curly light brown hair and were wrapped in dragon-print blankets. The second snap was a close-up of the bairns lying side-by-side, but Rhys's feet were next to Riordan's head and vice versa. "Oh God. They've grown. Without me." Liam's voice caught on the last word. He tried to be strong, but tears fell down his cheeks and into his scruffy beard.

He stumbled over to the couch and sank down on it, his gaze not leaving the colorful images of his family.

"Aye. I'll make tea. Want some?" Graeme banged a mug on the counter. At Liam's shake of his head, Graeme set about his task.

Liam was vaguely aware of Graeme wandering the bothy's interior, sipping his tea.

Graeme stopped at the dilapidated bookshelf. "Have you penned another bedtime story for the bairns?"

At the sound of parchment being unrolled, Liam looked up and focused on what Graeme had said. "No. That's just some auld rubbish I found." He hoped his tone was blasé enough that Graeme would leave the scroll alone.

"It's auld all right, but I wouldn't call it rubbish. It's a prophecy. Probably came from the druids or the faerie folk. It should be in a museum." Graeme read silently, then whistled low. "There's some potentially scary stuff in here. Where'd you find it?"

"Behind that broken-down bookshelf. There's a hole at the base of the wall." Liam shrugged. "I was bored enough to dig around." He lovingly tucked the two new snaps in the pocket close to his heart, next to the older ones.

Graeme squinted, changed the angle of the parchment toward the light. "There are words missing. At least four or five on the last line, maybe even another stanza."

Liam knew that Graeme wouldn't leave the prophecy alone. No, he was like a mutt with a bone when it came to anything historical or magical. The man should have been a university professor, a kind of bookish Indiana Jones.

"I should take this, have it analyzed," Graeme said.

"No." Liam jumped up and snatched the scroll away. "It's my destiny, my way off this godforsaken spit of rock." When Graeme didn't reply, Liam continued. "Don't you get it? I'm The Exiled. We just need to figure out who these others are, then I'll be able to stop the magic from waning."

"But the magic isn't waning."

"Yes it is." Liam waved his hand to indicate everything around him. "There's no magic on this damn skerry."

Graeme gasped.

"KENNETH must go to Colonsay or one of the other islands near Mull to fly his pattern. The standing stones to the south are useless. At least that's been the case since I've been here. KENNETH and I have tried to restore the magic at the stones. Nothing has worked. Didn't you wonder why our two dragons flew north?"

"I thought they were off to have a bit of fun, maybe catch some fish for supper. I had no idea." Graeme was silent for several minutes. "But, I can still communicate with REED while I'm here. Are you saying you can't bespeak KENNETH? Have you told The MacLean?"

Liam shook his head. "Dragon-to-rider communication is the only bit that still works. I've noticed my usually close bond with KENNETH has been affected since I'm not allowed to leave this godforsaken place and fly with him. And I feel off . . . like I'm in a stupor all the time." Liam rubbed his eyes. "I've had no direct contact from my uncle."

"What about the dragonrider who brings your supplies?"

"That's usually one of my mates. I wouldn't trust any of them with something this monumental. Besides, the prophecy's no good until I can sort it out." He cocked his head toward Graeme. "This sounds a bit dafty, but I think I was meant to find the prophecy. It's my task that will see me back in the good graces of The MacLean and prove I can be an asset to the clan. You could help."

"How?" Graeme finished his tea and placed the mug in the sink.

"Well, first off, you're smart. You could research to see if there's any mention of this prophecy. Maybe you'll come across more clues. And you and REED can scout around to see if there are other spots where the magic might be lessening."

"Yeah, dropping in on rival clans, that'll go over well." Graeme rubbed the back of his neck. "REED and I'll be flamed before we could explain. Then who'll get you updates of your family?"

"I meant you have access to Fraser and MacLean lands but also MacKenzie and MacKay as well. Probably others." Liam sat back down.

Graeme joined Liam. "Okay. Say I believe you. How would you go about finding the people listed in the prophecy? Don't tell me you're planning to go against The MacLean's orders, I won't help."

"No, see you'll need to be my proxy." Liam unrolled the scroll and smoothed it flat. "Find The One Who Hears All, The Seer, and The Wronged."

"Great. I'll travel all of Alba and ask everyone I meet if they are one of these three people. Then plead with them to come here. Easy peasy." Graeme leaned over the parchment and muttered the written words. "The only part that I understand is the first two lines—they refer to midnight on Samhain, but it has to be storming at that time." He looked at Liam. "Do you have a talisman?"

"No, but I've three months to find one and for the two of us to figure out the rest of the clues." Liam felt KENNETH's joy as he and REED circled the skerry.

Graeme rose. "The dragons are back. I should get going."

"Will you help me?"

After a brief hesitation, Graeme nodded. "Let me copy the prophecy." He found a paper napkin and copied the words, then tucked the napkin into his inside coat pocket. "I'll see what I can find out. No promises."

Liam stood and walked Graeme to the door. "Thanks. Give my love to Merida and the bairns. Remember, don't tell anyone about this. Not even Merida. Don't ruin my destiny."

# Seventeen

*Autumnal Equinox—Loughcrew, Ireland and America*

Devan worked on Padrick's office computer. "I've got you now," she muttered. She was in the middle of a research project to find Christian's mother, Erin. Each time Devan thought she'd found Erin, it had been a misdirection or a dead end.

"What have you found?" Padrick glanced up from working on the flight schedule for the week.

"Erin, or Lan O'Casey as she was known back then, headed south after giving up Christian at the orphanage and leaving Dublin. Probably putting as much distance as she could between herself and your mother, Kiely." Devan reached for a map of Ireland and beckoned Padrick over. "Lan worked at a small store in Bray for a few months, then moved on to Wexford. She changed her name again sometime between the two locations. That's why I've had such a hard time. I've set up a search for any names close to yours, Erin's, Christian's, or similar combinations. That summer, there was a gardaí report at a Wexford seaside pub where a twenty-something named Nola Riley witnessed a stabbing death. I believe that witness was Erin."

Padrick ran his finger along the eastern coast of Ireland. "So close and yet so far away. I was still in Beaghmore back then. It would have been several years before DECLAN hatched and chose me as his rider. And several more years before I left Northern Ireland for Lough Gur." His voice had roughened with emotion.

Devan patted his hand. "If she's to be found, I'll find her."

*"Ring Wearer, can ye hear me? It's KIERAN, from Beaghmore."* The brown dragon partnered with Matthew, Sean's son, bespoke Devan.

*"Yes. You're FIANNA's mate."*

*"Aye. It's why I bespeak ye. The eggs have hatched. FIANNA's compeer, Maggie, thought ye might come."*

*"Oh God. I forgot the eggs were near that time. How are the hatchlings?"*

*"They are perfect."* KIERAN's voice rang strong with pride. *"We have added two new dragonets to the Tuatha Dragon Clan."*

Devan glanced up as the telephone rang. Padrick answered it. She closed her eyes to concentrate on bespeaking with KIERAN. *"I'm a terrible friend. Please have FIANNA apologize to Maggie for me. I'll be there as soon as I can."*

*"We shall await yer arrival. Matthew and Maggie will be happy to see ye."*

KIERAN withdrew from Devan's mind. Her eyes popped open when she heard Padrick's voice.

"Aye. Devan's right here," Padrick said. After a brief pause, he grabbed his flight schedule and answered, "Sure, I can work around them being in Loughcrew for a few days. And with the equinox today, it's perfect timing. I'll let them know. Expect them by midday." He hung up.

"Sean has an idea he wants you and Christian to work on with GRAYSON that might extend the communication range between dragons."

"But KIERAN just told me FIANNA's eggs have hatched. I want to go see the newborn dragonets and my friends, Maggie and Matthew. And I've just had a major breakthrough," Devan said, indicating the computer and her notebook.

"I'm sure Sean knows of the hatching and will allow time for you to visit Beaghmore soon. And you can continue your work on Sean's computer." Padrick rubbed the back of his neck. "I'm the one who has to redo the schedule. Sean said to pack enough for a week." When Devan didn't start to pack up her notes, Padrick snapped his fingers in her face. "You need to get going. It's not wise to keep the clan leader waiting."

Devan wanted to protest but knew she could continue her research at Loughcrew—and probably without the rise or fall of Padrick's hopes with each new bit of information she found on Erin. And Sean was a fair clan leader. He was sure to give her some time to visit Beaghmore, especially since it was less than an hour's flight from Loughcrew.

After jotting down the locations and timeline she'd found so far, Devan shut down the computer and went to find Christian. In less than an hour, the two of them were packed and ready to leave Lough Gur. They flew on their dragons to Loughcrew.

Sean met the pair at the grassy-topped dragon lair entrance. "I've an idea I want to try."

"Okay," Devan said, "but after that, can we go see the new dragonets?"

Sean chuckled. "I guess when you can hear all dragons, nothing is a surprise."

"KIERAN bespoke me earlier. To be honest, I was so caught up in my research that I'd forgotten the hatching time was drawing near." Devan felt the heat of the blush creep up her neck. "I should have been there for Maggie."

"The Beaghmore contingent had everything under control. You'll get to see for yourself soon. I promise," Sean said.

Devan nodded. *Sean's a man of his word, so I'll just have to believe him and hope this idea of his doesn't take too long. Maggie will understand. And I'll make sure to be at the next hatching on Samhain. No matter what.* Satisfied with her promise to herself, she gave Sean her full attention.

"Getting back to my idea . . . I'd like to test your telepathic capabilities, as well as GRAYSON's. We need to develop a central communication system that keeps track of every dragon pair. Without overburdening you." He looked at Devan, then continued. "FIONN mentioned he felt a change in GRAYSON after the poison purging the dragons performed on Beltaine. I had my idea back then but needed to wait until Timothy cleared GRAYSON medically to implement it. Since GRAYSON isn't able to oversee a county in the typical fashion, I believe he can be the clan's central communication focal point."

"So, what am I doing here?" Christian asked.

"I want you and ROARKE to try communicating with GRAYSON, see if he's receptive to others beside Devan and DOCHAS. I thought maybe it would work since your two dragons are so closely bonded as well as you and Devan."

"I'm confused," Devan said. "GRAYSON heard FIONN on Beltaine when he cauterized GRAYSON's wound after the rest of the clan dragons infused him with their magic."

"Yes, but we tried again yesterday with no luck," Sean said. "I'm wondering if the effect was only short-term, or if there's something else blocking it. There is so much we don't know about GRAYSON."

"So you envision two-way communication between GRAYSON and each Tuatha dragon. What about between him and the human riders?" Devan raked her windblown hair out of her eyes.

"One step at a time," Sean said. "I need you and DOCHAS to listen in, let me know if it's working. Provide GRAYSON with encouragement."

"But the dragons can already communicate with each other," Christian said. "ROARKE took direction from FIONN or DECLAN on each of our flights. How's this different?"

"Distance. Right now, dragon-to-dragon communication is limited to around five kilometers. I'm hoping to change that. Also, dragons don't listen in on random thoughts of other dragons. Each dragon must tune in, so to speak, with the other dragon. That works well in close range, say over the area of the clan compound, not so much when out of line-of-sight."

The three riders entered GRAYSON's lair. He perked up.

"GRAYSON, we would like to test your abilities to hear other dragons," Sean said aloud.

*"Ring Wearer,"* GRAYSON bespoke Devan. *"Please tell FIONN's rider I will do whatever the clan needs. Please, do no' send me away."*

*"Oh,* GRAYSON. *No one will send you away. You saved my life. Without you stepping into the dagger's path, I would have been killed as the other four*

*dragons and riders were before me."* Devan reached her hand to stroke GRAYSON's neck scales. His sapphire eyes whirled faster.

"He's scared that he'll be sent away," Devan said to Sean.

Sean shook his head. "Don't be silly, you're a valued member of the clan. And I believe you're quite special."

*"Special in the same way as ye?"* GRAYSON bespoke Devan. *"Then I am at the clan's service."*

"He's excited to help the clan in any way he can," Devan relayed.

"As much as I want to stay, I've other business that needs my immediate attention," Sean said. "Can I leave this first phase in your hands? I've several issues to deal with before the equinox ceíli."

"Is that what Padrick meant when he mentioned the equinox? You want us to keep our dragons engaged and away from any temptation?" Devan asked. At Sean's nod, she continued. "Is Padrick scheduling a mating flight today in Lough Gur?"

"Yes." Sean looked chagrined. "After the mishap on the summer solstice, I thought it best to keep DOCHAS and ROARKE away from any mating flights."

"Smart," Christian said. "We'll get started. When's the ceíli?"

"You've got a couple of hours. I'll check in on you before it starts. Aisling's preparing one of the guest cottages for you. I'll let you know when it's ready." Sean clasped a hand on his pendant. "Dilseacht. Fáil. Saoirse. Loyalty. Destiny. Freedom."

Devan and Christian repeated the clan motto. After Sean left, Devan and Christian began testing Sean's theory.

By mid-afternoon, GRAYSON was adept enough to handle the communication with both DOCHAS and ROARKE, but at a distance of no more than five kilometers. The drake was mentally exhausted, yet trembling with excitement.

When Sean returned, Devan explained their progress and limitations.

"That's great. I'm relieved it isn't short-term. Perhaps it's like a muscle that needs to be exercised to keep it working," Sean said. "Tomorrow I'd like to start with the distances and see if, when he's fresh, that will make a difference. Your cottage is ready. Aisling left the front door open for you. You've some time before the ceíli starts." He headed out.

Devan scratched GRAYSON's eye ridges until he swooned, then she spoke aloud. "Rest now, GRAYSON. We'll work some more tomorrow."

"Rest for you as well, *a storin*." Christian pulled Devan close to him, then kissed her temple. "You look as worn out as GRAYSON."

"Yes, but I feel like I'm contributing. GRAYSON does too." She hooked her arm in Christian's and let him guide her to their temporary home.

By the following afternoon, GRAYSON could hear up to fifteen kilometers away, but no farther. Devan sank into a chair next to the woodsy, smoky scent of the glowing peat fire burning in the fireplace at Sean's and Aisling's house. The cottage she and Christian shared needed chimney repairs before they could use it to warm the space. Christian had spent the morning flying with ROARKE and testing GRAYSON, so the repairs would have to begin this afternoon, hence Devan's pilgrimage to the clan leader's warm home.

Devan raked both hands through her hair, pulling at the ends until her hair stuck up in the Celtic warrior fashion. She wanted to help with the repairs but was too tired and mentally worn out to do more than close her eyes.

At the clomp of Christian's boots on the front stoop, Devan rousted herself. *I must have accidently infused GRAYSON with my energy while helping him increase the distance he could hear other dragons. Or could it be something else causing my weakness?*

Christian walked in, slapped his riding gloves against his thigh, and halted in mid-stride. "What the bloody ifrinn are you doing to yourself?"

Devan started to push off from the chair, but he quickly strode to her and pushed her back down. He knelt in front of her, blocking any attempt on her part to escape.

"You're white as porridge, save for the dark smudges beneath your eyes." Christian glanced around. "What have you been doing?"

"Nothing." Devan sighed when Christian narrowed his eyes.

"You were not this worn out yesterday, and you were knackered then. Tell me what you've been doing, or I'll be forced to have ROARKE keep an eye on both you and DOCHAS." Christian ran a gentle hand down her cheek and lifted her chin until she was forced to look at him. "I'm worried that you're pushing yourself too much."

Devan closed her eyes briefly, then swallowed hard at the concerned look on Christian's face. "GRAYSON was feeling bad that he wasn't progressing . . ."

"So, what did you do to help him?" Christian asked. The weariness was evident in his tone.

"I'm not sure. I just wanted to boost his spirits. Somehow I was able to boost his range." Devan shivered even though the room was warm with the blazing peat fire. "By the time I realized what was happening, I was drained." She closed her eyes against the sting of threatening tears. "Please don't say anything to Sean, or in front of GRAYSON. He wants so much to be a contributing member to the clan. I just don't know how we can get past this distance barrier."

"I don't know either, but that's something for Sean to figure out. You and DOCHAS can't undertake the extra task. You have a county to look after, and you've been pushing hard in your efforts to locate my mother." Christian leaned in and brushed a light kiss across Devan's lips. "We'll figure this out. But you can't assist GRAYSON any longer."

Devan nodded. Christian stood and pulled her to her feet.

"Let's get you back to the cottage before Sean comes home. You can rest. Then we'll figure out what to tell him." Christian tucked his arm around Devan's waist and led her out the door.

A light rain began to fall, so they hurried to their cottage.

"Looks like no fire again today," Devan said.

Christian grabbed a flashlight and stuck his head into the cold, empty fireplace. A few minutes later, he emerged with a smile on his face. "As far as I can tell, there's no damage, just something blocking the chimney, near the top. I'm going to see if I can unstick whatever is there." He shrugged into his rain slicker, pocketing the flashlight. "Can you start some tea?"

"Of course. Are you sure you want to climb on the roof in the rain? I think the heater will be sufficient."

"A little rain won't hurt me. Besides, this is more what we Irish call a typical soft day than rain anyway. I'll be back in shortly." Christian ducked out of the parlor as Devan filled the kettle for tea.

*"DOCHAS, my sweet, can you gauge how* GRAYSON *is faring? Without rousing his suspicions?"* Devan bespoke her compeer. *"I want to make sure he doesn't realize how much we helped him today."*

*"The Wingless One is content and none the wiser at our intrusion. He is resting comfortably. How are ye?"* DOCHAS's concern threaded through her tone.

*"To be honest, I'm quite tired. I'm not sure exactly what happened, but somehow when I pushed to extend* GRAYSON*'s hearing, it sucked the energy from me. Are you as tired as I am?"* Devan asked.

*"I am fine. No ill effects. The Wingless One must have pulled the magic from ye alone. Do ye need the healer?"*

*"No. I don't wish for anyone else to know of my error. Christian has brought me back to our cottage. I'll rest and no one'll be the wiser. Please don't mention this to* FIONN.*"* Devan scooped up the whistling teapot and set the tea to steep. Christian liked a strong brew.

She sat on the couch facing the fireplace, her hands wrapped around the warmth of her teacup. At a loud bang, Devan jumped. Colorful Irish swearing followed as a clump of dried clay, twigs, and feathers landed in the fireplace.

"Hello down there," Christian's voice echoed, followed by the beam of his flashlight. "Can you hear me?"

She went to the fireplace, bent down, and called back to him. "I'm here. Is this nest what was blocking the chimney?"

"Yes. Everything else looks good here. I'll be down in a moment." The light disappeared.

Devan strolled to the kitchen and prepared Christian's cup of tea.

Moments later, he entered, removed his wet slicker, and hung it on a post by the mudroom door. Christian shook the rain from his hair, then scooped up the remnants of the bird's nest from the fireplace and tossed it in the rubbish bin.

He took a sip of his tea. "You know exactly how I like my tea. Thank you." He winked at her, then went into the mudroom and returned with a stack of peat. He arranged the bricks, then lit the fire. He refilled his cup, then joined Devan on the couch.

"So, what should we tell Sean'?" Devan asked.

"Tell him the truth. That it appears the telepathic range between dragons doesn't alter. No need to tell that you boosted GRAYSON's abilities by draining your own." Christian linked his fingers with Devan's. "Somehow, we'll find a way."

Devan nodded. "You're right. DOCHAS believes GRAYSON is unaware of my interference. How do we keep him from communicating what he believes he achieved today?"

"I hadn't thought of that." Christian shrugged. "Perhaps it's best if we explained everything to Sean. He may even know how GRAYSON was able to draw your energy."

"Can we wait until I don't look like death warmed over?" Devan pressed her fingertips to her closed eyes.

Christian chuckled. Devan opened her eyes. "What's so funny?"

"You are." He sighed. "You're bound and determined to not let anyone see that you're human. He's the clan leader. He needs to understand when he's asking too much of you. Besides, I asked ROARKE to tell me when Sean and FIONN return from patrol. You've some time yet."

Christian stood, reached for her empty cup, and placed the dishes in the sink. "I'm going to see what's available for lunch in the dining hall. I'll bring back something. I want you to rest." He scooped up his raincoat and headed out the door.

*"Do you know where the clan leader is? Without speaking directly to FIONN?"* Devan asked her compeer.

DOCHAS responded immediately. *"I would need to question FIONN."*

*"Never mind. If you hear that he's on his way back, please let me know."*

Devan closed her eyes and tried not to think about Sean's reaction to her mistake. GRAYSON wasn't the only one concerned about his standing within the clan. Devan needed what she'd found here in Ireland just as much as the drake needed to belong.

At the sound of the front door opening, Devan roused herself from her light doze. Christian strolled in carrying two bags of what smelled enticingly like beef stew and freshly baked bread. He set the bags on the coffee table and carefully unpacked two large covered bowls and a foil-wrapped loaf. He retrieved cutlery and a pot of freshly made butter from the tiny refrigerator. They ate in silence, mopping up the remainder of the stew with the last of the brown bread.

*"The Clan Leader approaches."* DOCHAS bespoke Devan.

"Sean—" Christian began.

Devan held up her hand. "I heard. From both dragons."

Christian shook his head. "I don't think I'll ever get used to your ability to hear all the dragons. Thank God you can't hear what I'm thinking."

"Something you're hiding from me?" Devan joked.

"No, but some things should be sacred. And a man's thoughts are at the top of the list." Christian gathered up their empty bowls, bent to kiss Devan, then stacked the dishes in the sink. "You look better. Why don't I go ask Sean to come here?"

Devan agreed. "Take your time. I want to freshen up."

"You look fine. Besides, I'm sure Sean would like to see the effect helping GRAYSON had on you today." Christian headed for the door.

Devan rushed into the bathroom and splashed cold water on her face. There was nothing she could do about her pale complexion and the dark circles under her eyes, but she ran a brush through her hair. "Damn, you need to stop screwing up." She returned to the couch just as Christian ushered Sean in.

The clan leader took one look at Devan and rushed to her side. He reached for her trembling hands, then raised his eyebrows as concern etched his face. "Are you sick? Hurt? What happened?" His questions tumbled together before she could answer.

"Please sit," Christian said. "We have something to tell you, but I need you to stay calm."

Sean's eyes widened as he looked first at Christian then back to Devan. "Tell me. It can't have anything to do with the dragons as FIONN has said nothing to me."

Christian started to say something, but Devan pulled her hands free and held one up. "It's my mistake. I'll explain it." She took a deep breath. "While I was working with GRAYSON, I inadvertently pushed some of my energies into helping him increase the communication distance. We were able to more than double the distance, but it was not GRAYSON's doing. It was mine. In the process, I ended up completely drained."

Sean gasped. "What of your dragon?"

"DOCHAS was not affected. GRAYSON doesn't even know that he didn't accomplish this on his own. I don't know what I did. I was trying to encourage GRAYSON since he was feeling down about not being able to break the distance barrier. In my consoling him, I somehow opened myself up to boosting his reception of ROARKE's communication."

"You were trying to help." Christian reached for her hand and gave it a reassuring squeeze.

"Do we know if GRAYSON has retained the extra distance?" Sean asked.

Devan shook her head. "I never thought to check. When I realized something was wrong, I broke my connection with GRAYSON and asked DOCHAS to tell him we were finished for the day."

"And I didn't question ROARKE when he said the experiment was over for the day. I just assumed that everything was fine. I didn't know there was a problem until I returned." Christian rubbed the back of his neck.

"Okay," Sean said. "I want Padrick's opinion. You need to rest, Devan. After a good night's sleep, we'll test GRAYSON and determine the effects on him. But you can't put yourself in danger again."

Rick Hunter sauntered into his boss's office with a steaming cup of espresso in one hand and his cell phone in the other.

"What's up?" He waved the phone around. "I've got a hot lead on that police corruption story."

"I told you last week you're off that story." The paunch-bellied, balding man slammed a fist on his cluttered desk. "Dammit, you threatened the chief of police. You're lucky you're not cooling your designer Ferragamos in lockup."

"Yeah, yeah." Rick sipped his drink. "The chief wouldn't dare arrest me. Freedom of the press and all. So . . . ?"

"The higher ups want you out of here until this whole debacle of yours blows over. Your career here's in jeopardy. You've pissed off the wrong people this time. Besides, you've been a complete pain in my ass since that little lady of yours left you." The boss held up his hands as Rick started to protest. "You've got two choices. You can either take a sabbatical through the end of the year, unpaid." He shuffled papers on the desk until he found what he was looking for. "Or you can accept this special assignment with our media partner in Great Britain. Your choice, but—"

"Great Britain?" Rick snatched the paper from the boss's hand. "That includes Ireland, doesn't it?"

"Only Northern Ireland. The rest of the island is its own country."

"Perfect. I'll take it." Rick perused the page and grinned. "I'll see you next year. Or not," he muttered as he spun on his heel and headed for his desk. *That paper pusher wouldn't know a Pulitzer Prize winning story if it jumped up from his desk and kissed him. He's just another wannabe that doesn't appreciate me.* He collected his electronics, several notepads and pens, and his credentials.

*Well, well. Looks like we're going to have that reunion after all, Devan. Maybe we'll even get married in your adopted country. I'll make a name for myself over in Europe. And you'll be mine again. I told you, no one leaves Rick Hunter. No one. Ever.*

# Eighteen

Christian crept into the cottage as quietly as possible, shucked out of his wet raincoat, and tiptoed into the living room to check on Devan. She lay curled under the blanket he'd tucked around her before he'd left. Her breathing was slow and steady. The fire had died down to embers, so he stoked it and added several peat bricks.

At a gentle tapping on the front door, Christian glanced at Devan's hair and pixie-like face surrounded by a puff of blanket to see if the noise woke her. Her eyes fluttered open and met his. Christian rose to answer the door.

Padrick stood, rain dripping from the porch overhang behind him. "I wanted to check on Devan, see if there was anything I could do for her."

"She was asleep." Christian gestured Padrick in. He stamped his feet, dislodging most of the wet from his rain gear, then entered the parlor.

"Who is it?" Devan's sleepy voice drifted to the two men.

"It's Padrick, a ghra." Christian entered the living room with Padrick in tow. "He came to see how you're doing after this morning's exertions."

Devan sat up, and Padrick was instantly at her side.

"Jesus, Devan, you need to take better care of yourself. The clan needs you healthy, not so worn out that you can't fly DOCHAS." Padrick glanced from her to Christian and back. "When was the last time you and DOCHAS flew the stone circles?"

"I can't remember." Devan groaned. "Do you think that's why I'm so exhausted?"

Padrick shrugged. "It's a possibility."

Devan's eyes widened. And her mouth dropped open.

"What is it?" Padrick asked.

"GRAYSON—"

Padrick leapt to his feet. "What about him?"

"I just saw him sleeping in his lair. He was fine," Christian said.

"Yes. He's okay. I didn't mean to frighten you. I just thought of why we may not have had any luck in increasing the distance of the telepathic communication." Devan raked a hand through her hair. "GRAYSON has been recuperating from his near-death experience. He hasn't been near the stone circles. Does he require the same exposure to restore his magic? How does he do it without flying overhead?"

At Devan's question, Christian breathed a sigh of relief. He hadn't thought of how GRAYSON acquired his magic.

"Normally, the drake would walk the stone circles with the same pattern that the dragons fly overhead. With all that has gone on since the Chosen Ceremony, I guess no one thought to take GRAYSON." Padrick sat. He reached for Devan's hand and squeezed. "There you go, once again thinking of someone other than yourself. We'll take GRAYSON and fly or walk Loughcrew's stone dances tomorrow."

"What happens when a rider is unable to fly their dragon for an extended period? I don't mean the short time Devan and I were away and you took DOCHAS and ROARKE for the twice-weekly flight, but if a rider was injured or died?" Christian asked. "Will the dragon allow another rider to perform the magic rejuvenation flights long term?"

Padrick held Christian's gaze. "While it isn't optimal, it has happened a time or two. It's not ideal because the dragon and, by extension, the rider gather that magic to use as a pair. The flying of these stones circles help bond each dragon and rider pair to work as a cohesive team. When another rider flies the pattern, that special bond is weakened. Why do you ask?"

"Just wondered."

"Do you think if Timothy has a makeshift harness for GRAYSON, DECLAN would mind flying GRAYSON?" Devan asked.

"I'll check with Timothy." Padrick rose. "I'm sure DECLAN would enjoy the challenge."

The next morning dawned clear and bright. Devan supervised Timothy and his grandson, Niall, as they buckled GRAYSON into a special harness held in DECLAN's gentle claws for the ride to the stone circles.

Once Padrick, Christian, and Devan were seated on their dragons, Padrick lifted his right arm and gave the signal for DECLAN to launch into the blue sky. ROARKE and DOCHAS leapt after the black dragon. Within moments the three dragons hovered above the large stone cairn on the eastern slope of Loughcrew's most predominant hill.

DECLAN swooped down toward the outcropping of the stone circle and began his ritualistic weaving in and out of the standing stones. The great black dragon finished, then returned and hovered beside DOCHAS.

Devan directed her dragon forward, concentrating on the intricate flight pattern. DOCHAS flew with nary a pause. As the surge of power surrounded and infused her, Devan pumped a fist in the air and shouted with joy. She returned to hover beside DECLAN and ROARKE.

Christian grinned at her, then his compeer performed the same flyover.

The three dragons completed the ritual at the other two stone circles, then Padrick indicated Christian and Devan should land their dragons once more near the large stone cairn. DECLAN slowly lowered GRAYSON to the grassy ground below, then landed. The humans dismounted and gathered around GRAYSON. The drake swooshed his tail and set his neck ridges bristling.

*"I am much better now. My body and essence are filled with power. Even my battle wound tingles, and the ache is dissipating,"* GRAYSON bespoke Devan. *"Do ye feel the rejuvenation?"*

*"Yes, GRAYSON,"* Devan mentally answered in kind.

Padrick spoke aloud to GRAYSON. "Do you feel up to testing the distance once more?" He gave Devan a stern look. "This time with DECLAN and me—without your help."

GRAYSON's blue eyes whirled faster in excitement. *"I am ready."*

At Devan's nod, Padrick remounted DECLAN. The black dragon launched himself into the air and flew until he was out of sight.

Ten minutes later, GRAYSON snorted. *"DECLAN has instructed me to inform ye that he is on the borders of Counties Meath and Westmeath. That is approximately twenty kilometers from our present location. He asks for a confirmation to be provided by first ROARKE, then DOCHAS."*

Devan clearly heard ROARKE bespeak a confirmation message to the drake that signified it was indeed from ROARKE. GRAYSON transmitted the message, then DOCHAS bespoke her message. Again, Devan listened in as GRAYSON mentally sent the message to DECLAN.

A squawking bugle from GRAYSON brought a quick laugh from Devan. The flying of the stone dances had indeed lengthened the distance the drake could hear another dragon. And Devan's abilities were not being drained from her.

Christian pulled her into a fierce hug, his eyes smiling down at her as he pressed a quick kiss to her lips. "Your idea worked."

GRAYSON nudged his snout between Devan and Christian. *"I completed the task."*

Devan laughed and reached to scratch GRAYSON's snout. *"Yes, you did it. All on your own. We'll practice some more, but I don't want to overtax you. Even though the dragon magic has you feeling indestructible, you're still recovering from a life-threatening injury."*

DOCHAS and ROARKE stepped up behind Devan and Christian. DOCHAS nuzzled GRAYSON. The group turned and watched as DECLAN and Padrick flew toward them. The black dragon back-winged his massive wings and landed with a soft whoosh that flattened the grass around them.

Padrick grinned down at them before sliding out of his saddle to congratulate GRAYSON with an affectionate fist bump to the top of his head. "I think we have a winner. Let's report back to Sean. I'm sure he'd like to hear the news in person. Mount up."

At the clan compound, the dragons landed. DECLAN released his foreclaw grip on GRAYSON's riding harness. Sean emerged from his office. He tilted his head in question and looked at GRAYSON, then up at Devan.

Devan laughed aloud as her joy couldn't be contained. "After we all flew the magic rejuvenating Celtic knot pattern over the stone circles, GRAYSON's communication worked splendidly. All by himself."

"Terrific. Did you attempt any other distances? Or more than one dragon speaking at a time?" Sean asked.

Padrick slid from DECLAN. "No. I didn't want to tire the drake out. Besides, we were eager to let you know of his accomplishment."

Christian and Devan dismounted, unbuckled the riding harness, and freed GRAYSON. The drake lumbered toward the lough.

*"Did I no' tell ye that all would work out? That the fates are in our favor?"* ROARKE included Devan in his telepathic communication with Christian.

"The fates?" Devan leaned into Christian.

"Aye. ROARKE is ever the optimist," Christian said aloud, then glanced at his dragon. "But sometimes the affairs of men are complicated and don't always work in the favor of the fates."

Over the next two days, GRAYSON improved his ability to differentiate between the Loughcrew dragons. And his joy suffused Devan. In the evenings, she continued her research of Erin's whereabouts. Devan had tracked Erin from Wexford to Ardmore—the location of the first murder victims of the Irish dragon killer last year. The next time Erin surfaced was in Cobh, in County Cork. There she boarded a ship headed for Great Britain.

At supper on the second night, Devan's lips curled into a smile. "The flyover of the stone circles worked magic on GRAYSON. He has a knack for handling the various personalities of each dragon."

Padrick snorted. "That's quite an accomplishment. Now, if only he could handle humans as easily. Tomorrow we'll begin to tackle the dragons at Beaghmore."

Day three dawned without a cloud in the sky. The three dragons and their riders headed to Beaghmore with DECLAN once again carrying GRAYSON in the harness. The closer they flew to the Northern Ireland compound, the more agitated GRAYSON became.

*"Calm yourself, GRAYSON,"* Devan mentally reassured the drake. *"This time, you're with friends and on an important task at the clan leader's insistence. No one will hurt you. I promise."*

*"The dark-haired one is no longer there?"* GRAYSON asked.

*"No. And I'll be with you. There's nothing to fear."* Devan said. *"Besides, there are two new dragonets to coo over. You won't be the youngest dragon anymore."*

*"Still, I shall spend as little time there as possible."* GRAYSON's tone strengthened.

The three dragons landed in the outer courtyard. Beaghmore's leader, Michael, joined them. Padrick slid from his compeer and extended a hand. The two men talked briefly as Christian and Devan unhooked GRAYSON's harness. The gray drake trembled slightly. Devan stroked his head and whispered reassurances.

A commotion at the dragon lair mound brought everyone's attention to two emerging dragons. TULLIA waddled toward GRAYSON, her plum-colored tail swishing the cobblestones clean. Pearl-white CALHOUN followed his mate at a discreet distance. The elderly female dragon sniffed at the young drake. Her deep blue eyes whirled slowly in recognition of her offspring.

Kiely and Ronan emerged from the communal dining hall, leading a pack of curious riders. At the sight of their two dragons huddled around the drake, they halted briefly, then cautiously approached Padrick and Michael.

Devan and Christian remained at GRAYSON's side.

"What are you doing here?" Kiely's irritated tone was directed at Padrick. "And why is that damn Yank with you?"

Padrick narrowed his eyes, his mouth in a firm line of disapproval. "That damn Yank, as your prejudiced, ice-filled heart insists on calling her, has been working to implement Sean's idea of a near-instantaneous communication system. Perhaps if we had Devan and her talent before, we wouldn't have lost four dragons and their riders."

Kiely cackled out a laugh that echoed bitterly in the early morning. "Is this the best that whelp of a clan leader can do? He puts the future of the Tuatha Dragon Clan in the hands of an inexperienced, and probably mundane, Yank. Typical."

Ronan gripped his wife's shoulder hard and turned her to face him. "That's enough out of you. You, more than anyone, have been a destructive force for the clan. Your attitude has been nothing but toxic. I should've done something before now. I'm ashamed to be associated with you. GRAYSON is our dragons' offspring. You'll apologize this instant, or so help me . . ."

Kiely stared open-mouthed at her husband.

"I mean it, Kiely. Apologize. Or don't bother coming home." The look Ronan gave his wife left no room for argument.

Kiely stormed off, then stopped. With fists clenched, she spit out a perfunctory apology over her shoulder, then stomped away, muttering to herself.

"She'd try the patience of Job. And I don't have anywhere near his patience." Ronan sighed as he looked at his son. "And I am sorry. I, too, was wrong, particularly with my inactions. I should have reigned in your mother long ago. Maybe then she wouldn't have taken out her prejudice on Erin. I better go." He caught up with Kiely and guided her away from any other dragonriders.

"That was awkward," Devan said. Before Padrick could open his mouth, she lifted a hand to silence him. "Don't apologize for your mother. I've dealt with my share of obnoxious people, but she may take the cake. Her negative attitude will be her downfall. I know that what GRAYSON and I are doing will benefit the clan. It's a shame Kiely can't be happy for her dragon's offspring."

Christian brought her hand to his lips and pressed a kiss to the center of her palm. "You amaze me. She was rude to you, to all of us. Her own flesh and blood. If it wasn't for Ronan and his embarrassment, I'd have gladly smacked her. And I've never hit a woman in my life."

Padrick chuckled. "I like you, Devan. You have more class than some royalty." He glanced in the direction where his parents continued their animated discussion. "It's good to see Da not taking any more of her prejudicial shite. I just wish he'd grown a backbone earlier. Twenty-eight years ago would have suited me just fine."

"We can't change the past." Christian's soft words drew Padrick's attention. "We can only try our best to live in the present and not make the same mistakes. This wonderful Yank has taught me to revel in the here and now, not dwell on the things we can't change."

"Besides," Devan said, "I believe things happen for a reason. Perhaps fate guided Kiely's actions, for without her attempt to breed TULLIA and CALHOUN, GRAYSON wouldn't be here. And the clan needs him." She lowered her lashes a moment, before lifting sorrowful eyes to Padrick. "I don't mean to diminish your love for Erin. Perhaps she's meant for a greater fate than we can even guess. If not for my parents' deaths, I would probably never have found my great-grandmother's ring. And I wouldn't have come to Ireland in search of my heritage. If Christian hadn't been in Dublin, we wouldn't have met." She squeezed Padrick's hand and smiled. "You get my meaning. The dragons talk of fate as if it's predetermined. Without all those past happenstances, none of this would have transpired."

Michael cleared his throat. "I'd like to set up a schedule for GRAYSON to meet the other dragons and their riders. We can leave him with TULLIA and CALHOUN for now. Why don't we get comfortable in my office?"

"GRAYSON's nervous about his reception here," Devan said. "I explained that his attacker is no longer here, and that he wasn't in his right mind when he attacked the drake."

"He has nothing to be afraid of here. I will ensure it." Michael held up his hand as if swearing an oath.

Devan nodded. *"GRAYSON, I am going to the Beaghmore leader's office with the others. You should enjoy the time with TULLIA and CALHOUN. If you need me . . ."*

GRAYSON blew a warm breath over Devan's head, ruffling her hair. *"I shall be safe. TULLIA and CALHOUN will provide me a meal. I am famished."*

Devan laughed and told the others what GRAYSON said, then turned to Michael. "Once we get settled, I'll see the new dragonets. And I've been remiss in my friendship with Maggie and Matthew."

"There'll be time for visiting. I'll make sure of it," Michael told her.

"Thanks," Devan said.

As they strolled to Michael's office, he asked Padrick what his plans were for the next couple of days.

"Devan's doing some research. She's trying to track where Erin went twenty-eight years ago," Padrick said. "I hope she can continue while she's here."

"Of course."

The four riders sat in comfortable chairs around Michael's enormous desk.

Michael ran down the list of dragons and riders and their counties. Devan recommended GRAYSON work with TULLIA and CALHOUN first. The remaining dragons would be phased in tomorrow. Michael agreed.

Devan and Christian ate supper with Matthew and Maggie then were shown the two newest additions to the dragon clan: copper-colored MALACHY and oatmeal-colored ROISIN.

"So, who gets the honor of naming the dragonets?" Devan asked Maggie.

"FIANNA introduced us to her hatchlings." Maggie rubbed her visibly pregnant belly. "To be honest, I'm relieved. Matthew and I are arguing over names for our bairn. Can you imagine having to come up with dragon names too?"

Devan chuckled. "At least the dragonets were born earlier than your little one will be. There should be less for you both to do with the dragonets as they grow. More time to concentrate on yourself and your baby when he or she arrives."

After much cooing over the clumsy but adorable dragonets, Devan promised herself once again that she wouldn't miss another hatching.

The next day, during GRAYSON's rest periods, Devan continued her research. By the time they were ready to head to Lough Gur, Devan had tracked Erin all over Great Britain. She hadn't stayed in one place for more than a few months. The trail went dead in Inverness. That had been more than twenty years ago.

# Nineteen

*Samhain Eve—Scotland*

Erin Casey jerked awake as the haunting portent invaded her restless sleep. Lately, she'd been dreaming of her past in her homeland of Ireland, escaping from her mistakes. Yet, she wasn't in Ireland anymore, and this wasn't a normal dream. No, it was a vision—her curse. And they always played out with her in the center of the action. Her heart pounded and her breath came too fast. Usually the visions came too late to change the outcome, but she had to try. She closed her eyes and brought the horrible scene back into focus.

An oily fountain of black fury geysered through the pinkish-orange tinge as dawn strengthened into day over the oilrig in northern Scottish waters. Bright blue and green MacKay tartans, used as padding on her adopted clan's dragons' backs, caught Erin's gaze as four dragons and their riders hovered at the corners of the rig. Their magic fluctuated as they tried to control the flow of oil.

The sulfurous odor of crude assaulted her senses as it washed over the platform deck, over her boots, and dripped from the skeletal rigging high above her. Wind whipped sticky black splatters across her face and into her eyes, temporarily blinding her. A construction crane maneuvered the hydrant-shaped steel cap toward the wellhead. The crew slipped and slid in the sludge, manhandling the cap into position. One roughneck shouted, drawing the red hard-hatted foreman's attention as the roughneck pointed to the massive secondary crane used for safety while placing the cap. The backup crane sat stark and unmanned. The foreman pointed to his wristwatch, shook his head, then signaled the primary crane driver to continue.

Groaning from the crane's huge engine cut through the roar of gushing oil. The cap swung wildly from the end of its cable. Several roughnecks lunged for the renegade cap, only to be bowled over. Morgan's smoky gray dragon, BOYD, swooped toward the closest human—the foreman. As the enormous well cap scraped across the decking, the crane toppled, sweeping several roughnecks over the side. BOYD plucked the foreman before he would have fallen into the icy waters.

A spark from the cap ignited the oil bursting from the wellhead. Flames licked hot and quick over the steel platform. Sirens wailed. Red lights flashed, throwing a ghastly blood-red hue everywhere. Roughnecks poured from every platform, scrambling as the rig exploded in a giant mushroom cloud of red, orange, and smothering black. Men screamed and jumped into the water, frantic to escape.

At the far corners of the platform, two dragons backwinged furiously as their riders could do little more than cower at the oncoming conflagration.

Erin pulled herself out of the vision, shaking off the terrifying images. No light penetrated from the drape-covered windows; dawn had not yet broken.

*"TEAGAN, I need you. Morgan and BOYD are in trouble."* Having mentally called her dragon, Erin leapt from the warm bed. She struggled to button her shirt. A sob escaped as she yanked a jumper over her head, pulling the sleeve clear of the wing-shaped silver bracelet her da had specially commissioned for her before he'd died. The inscription inside of family, honor, and loyalty brought tears to Erin's eyes as those words symbolized her da perfectly. No, she thought, she couldn't survive another loss. In the dream, it was early morning. Perhaps there was still time.

She sprinted out her bedroom door and grabbed her boots on the way outside. Erin burst through the thick oak doors of the communal dining hall and slid in her stocking feet, stubbing her toe on the cubbies along the wall as she halted in front of the duty roster. Which oilrig was in Morgan's patrol zone? Stomping her foot into her boot, she searched for Morgan's name. The roster listed the Morey. She jammed her other foot into its boot. Several clan members stared, open-mouthed as she ran past them to the outer courtyard where her dragon waited. Erin swung up onto her dragon, sans saddle, with her boots still unlaced.

Erin commanded her dragon to fly. She leaned against TEAGAN's iridescent moss green neck scales as she launched into the pre-dawn sky. Within half an hour, Erin spotted the Morey platform in the distance. She could just make out the metallic superstructure gleaming yellow through the brightening sky. Squinting, she tried to see if the crew had tapped the oil reserves far below. Thick, black liquid rose from the center of the platform in a gusher. She thought she heard shouting but couldn't be sure. Recklessly, she urged TEAGAN forward. Moments later, a gray speck streaked down toward the oil plume. Erin screamed with all her might, "No!"

BOYD, with Morgan anchored in his riding harness, slowed, then hovered over the far side of the platform. Erin watched in horror as the fifteen-story rig ignited.

In the heartbeat that followed, the resounding concussion and volcanic blast sent waves of heated air and burning oil in all directions. The two dragons on the far side of the rig tumbled through the air as their wings caught fire.

Too close to the blast, TEAGAN somersaulted backward. Erin scrambled for a hold, but she was wrenched awkwardly against her dragon's heaving side. Erin clawed for the lead shank that was always anchored to TEAGAN's neck spikes but missed, coming away empty-handed. She cursed loudly and inventively. *Must not fall. Must not fail Morgan and the others.* She struggled to calm herself.

TEAGAN dipped to the left. Erin smacked into her dragon's

diamond-hard scales. Her chest and face stung from the collision, but she pushed the pain from her mind and finally reached the shank to pull herself upright onto TEAGAN's back.

They sped toward the burning hunk of twisted metal now collapsing into the Pentland Firth. Morgan and his dragon were lost in the flames and the black smoke that blanketed the doomed Morey. Erin and TEAGAN circled the burning platform, dodging the open flames. Searching. Burned and blackened roughneck bodies bobbed in the water before sliding below the oily surface to their watery graves. One inflatable orange raft drifted away from the platform—empty.

Black smoke billowed toward them. Tears streamed down Erin's cheeks as she forced herself to be methodical in her search for Morgan and BOYD—alive or dead. The roar of the flames and the pounding of her heart threatened to overwhelm her.

"Please, not again. I can't lose another," Erin whispered through a throat raw with emotion.

A dragon and rider emerged from the smoke. Erin glanced up and saw Noreen, on her mauve-colored dragon, RHONA, waving frantically, then pointing down. Below them, a gray bulk floated precariously on the white-capped waves.

*"There,"* Erin urged her compeer. *"Get to them before they sink!"* She flattened herself once more against her dragon's neck as TEAGAN dove toward the rough sea.

Erin pressed her knees tight and hung on as TEAGAN swooped down, backwinged, then landed in the water. Drifting up and down with the waves, TEAGAN dipped her wing underneath BOYD's torn and ragged left wing.

"Can he fly?" Erin shouted to Morgan.

Morgan shook his head and tried to yell, but his words were lost in a coughing spell. He stood in his harness and pointed at the limp form of the foreman grasped in BOYD's outstretched front claws.

Torn between saving the unconscious man or her clan mate and his dragon, Erin hesitated. If TEAGAN left BOYD's side, the injured dragon would surely sink. Just as Erin was about to command her compeer to save the foreman, RHONA came in low and hovered before them. She clasped the unconscious man in her foreclaws before lifting him away.

Erin exhaled a shuddering breath. She turned and searched for the other two dragons assigned to the Morey—the ones with their wings aflame. They had disappeared. Sadness crept into her heart.

Regaining control over her emotions, Erin shouted to Noreen. "I'm sure the alarm's gone out for rescue boats. Leave the foreman at the rescue dock. Then get back to the compound. Bring help. We'll keep BOYD afloat. Hurry!"

Noreen nodded and wheeled RHONA back toward the coast.

Erin angled her body away from her dragon to examine BOYD's injuries. Seawater peeked through burn holes in the translucent wing membrane. The wing hung at an awkward angle from the quickly tiring dragon's body.

"Are you all right?" Erin called out to Morgan.

He nodded. "BOYD tumbled arse over snout, then his left wingtip caught on something. We spun into the sea. I don't know how bad he's hurt." Morgan gently rubbed his dragon's neck ridges. "You weren't on the duty roster today. Why're you here?"

"A vision. I saw BOYD swoop down to grab the foreman just as the fire ignited." Erin narrowed her eyes. As her fear waned, her anger rose. "What the bleeding ifrinn were you thinking? Trying to get yourself killed? Did you think about your dragon or your clan?"

Morgan ducked his head. "I couldn't let them all die. We're sworn to protect, aren't we?"

"So you put yourself, your dragon, and the others in danger? All for someone who obviously didn't care enough about his men to run a safe rig? He waved off the second crane that would have prevented the explosion." Erin glared at him. When Morgan didn't respond, she continued, "And *who* do you think that bloody eejit foreman will say saved him?"

Again Morgan didn't answer.

"Besides Noreen, who flew with you?" Erin asked.

"Ian and Darlene." Morgan coughed again. He whipped his head around and searched the smoke-filled skies above the torched platform. "Are they . . . ?" His voice trailed off as he closed his eyes and shuddered.

Erin shook her head and softened her tone. "I don't know. They're missing. When Noreen returns, we'll look for them."

*I can't tell him I saw their dragons aflame.*

"Dear God," Morgan murmured. He locked gazes with Erin; his gray eyes reflected the storm clouds moving in, as well as his misery. "You should . . . should leave me and search for Ian and Darlene, and their dragons. They could be . . ." Morgan rubbed a grimy hand over his face, smearing soot.

Erin leaned toward Morgan. "Don't be a bloody fool. BOYD will drown without us. Besides, Noreen will be back soon."

She searched the lowering skies for the telltale dots that signaled approaching dragons. Nothing crossed the coastline toward them. *How much time since Noreen left? I'm not sure TEAGAN can keep BOYD afloat much longer.*

A breaking wave bounced BOYD over its crest and he slipped away from TEAGAN. BOYD blew out a stream of flame that the next wave doused into a puff of steam.

Erin commanded TEAGAN to circle and reposition herself under BOYD's injured wing.

Again Erin scanned the skies, her panic rising as BOYD groaned and flapped his front legs in the choppy water to maintain his precarious balance. From the west, Erin spotted several dragons headed straight for them. *Why would MacKay clan dragons come from that direction?*

TEAGAN flinched, causing BOYD's injured wing to dip under the water and the surprised dragon to squawk. TEAGAN recovered quickly.

*"What happened, my love?"* Erin bespoke her dragon. *"Do you recognize them? Are they from the Western Isles?"* Erin's pulse quickened at the possibility of rival clans invading MacKay territory.

*"Nae. The human rider aboard one of the dragons is communicating with me,"* TEAGAN bespoke, a deep weariness coloring her tone.

"What? How's that possible?" Erin spoke aloud as she focused on the approaching dragons. *No rider communicates with another rider's compeer. What the hell's going on? Are we under attack?*

"Is help coming?" Morgan called out.

Erin's gaze flew to Morgan. "I'm not sure, but they're not MacKay. Three dragons. One of the riders spoke directly with TEAGAN."

Morgan's mouth gaped open.

*"She is asking if they may be of assistance,"* TEAGAN bespoke Erin. *"They are of the Tuatha Dragon Clan of Ireland."*

Erin felt the blood drain from her face. *She? Has Kiely, my old nemesis, caught up with me? No matter. To save my clan mates, I'd gladly forge a deal with the bloody devil.*

# Twenty

At the thought that her past could collide with her present, Erin's heart stuttered. Her hands trembled and her eyes widened as the three newcomers flew closer. The dragons hung in the smoky orange sky for a heartbeat, then backwinged and landed in the waves directly across from her and Morgan.

The largest dragon was the black of midnight and significantly larger than her own. An imposing man with salt-and-pepper hair sat in the saddle. Beside him, atop a green dragon, sat a near replica of her long-lost love, Padrick, when he was twenty-years-old. The young man held a rigid posture, similar to a military man, but his black hair grazed his shoulders. His piercing blue eyes caught her staring, so Erin glanced at the spiky-haired woman atop the blue dragon.

*Obviously not Kiely, but could it be . . .?*

"You okay?" Morgan asked. "Take a breath before you pass out. You're deathly pale. What's wrong?"

Erin shook her head, struggled to draw a breath, and wrenched her gaze away from the strangers. Her heart pounded. *Maybe?*

The black dragon's rider addressed them. "We heard the explosion, saw the flames. Are there others? How can we help?" The man's deep voice carried a rich Irish lilt.

Erin nodded toward Morgan's dragon and pitched her voice low. "His wing is burned. Probably several broken joints. I can't get him out of the water. I've been unable to leave him to see if anyone else survived." Her curiosity gnawed at her, but she didn't want to be caught staring again. She averted her face, using her matted curls to camouflage herself. "Can you do a pass to see if there are any more survivors? There were two other dragon and rider pairs caught in the blast. Maybe you can find them."

"Of course. I'm Devan, I ride DOCHAS," the female dragonrider said. "My companions, Christian on ROARKE and Padrick on DECLAN."

Erin gasped aloud at Padrick's name as the blue and green dragons leapt from the sea. A smoky gust of wind blew her hair clear of her eyes. *Could it be? Could this rider be my Padrick?* "Padrick Nolan?"

Padrick's gaze whipped from the injured dragon and its rider to Erin. "Good Lord. Erin? Erin Casey, is it really you?"

Erin could only nod. She drank in the sight of the middle-aged man before her. Now, she could see in him the young man she'd been forced to leave behind over twenty-seven years before. "What are you doing here?" Her voice hitched as the shocking truth began to settle over her. *It's him. God, he looks good. So like his da, Ronan.*

"We've been looking for you," Padrick said.

"After all this time?" Erin couldn't tear her gaze away from Padrick, the man she'd loved all those years ago.

"For the last six months or so." Padrick waved at the injured dragon. "Let's get this one to safety, then we can talk."

Erin's cheeks heated as she recalled she wasn't alone with Padrick and had forgotten the urgency of the moment.

"Yes, of course. This is Morgan and BOYD. And TEAGAN." Erin indicated her own dragon.

Padrick inclined his head at each dragon and turned his deep blue gaze back to Erin.

"Do you have any ideas?" she asked.

"He's too big and bulky for DECLAN to carry in his foreclaws, but I think my dragon can support him on his back. Morgan will have to ride with someone else." Padrick rubbed his chin as he gauged the injured dragon's size.

The blue and green Irish dragons returned.

"I'm sorry, we didn't see anyone else," Devan called out.

"We've got to get BOYD onto DECLAN's back," Padrick said as BOYD submerged briefly. "He won't last much longer. Morgan can ride with Devan. ROARKE can lift BOYD by the saddle. Once they're clear of the waves, I'll position DECLAN underneath and we'll fly back to your clan compound."

"How will we keep BOYD from falling off?" Morgan scrambled out of his saddle. "He can't balance with his wing all torn up."

"I have netting and rope in my rucksack," Christian suggested. "Once he's atop DECLAN, we could use that to hold him secure."

Padrick nodded. "Let's give it a try."

DOCHAS paddled close to BOYD, then Morgan jumped into the churning water and scrambled onto the blue dragon to sit behind Devan.

Christian retrieved his rucksack. He tossed the rope and netting over BOYD, then directed ROARKE into position to lift the injured dragon.

The maneuver failed as ROARKE couldn't lift BOYD by the saddle. On the third attempt, the leather saddle ripped away and dangled from ROARKE's front talons. Twice BOYD sank below the surface before TEAGAN could reposition herself under his damaged wing.

Morgan, soaked through from his earlier swim, shivered as he yelled for help for his compeer.

The wind whipped smoke from the platform into a vortex. Fast approaching storm clouds mixed with the smoke, obscuring the sun.

Padrick stood in his saddle and shouted, "BOYD's strength is fading fast. DECLAN needs to dive under the waves and catch BOYD if we're to have a chance at saving him. Right now, before these waves get any larger with that approaching storm."

"You can't stay on DECLAN. You'll drown. How will you get clear?" Erin twisted in her seat to look at Padrick.

"I'll hitch a ride with Christian on ROARKE," Padrick said as he slid from his saddle onto DECLAN's foreleg. "No time to waste." He jumped and quickly swam clear as DECLAN dove under BOYD.

Erin directed TEAGAN out of the black dragon's way.

DECLAN broke from the water with a badly shaken BOYD, still wrapped under the netting, scrambling for purchase on DECLAN's back. A joyous shout erupted from Morgan.

Padrick dipped underwater as a wave knocked him away from ROARKE. Erin screamed. *No, he can't drown. We've just found each other again.* Padrick came up sputtering and floundered toward ROARKE.

Christian helped Padrick climb onto the green dragon's back. "Let's go. I don't want to get caught flying if lightning strikes," Christian shouted to Erin as DOCHAS and ROARKE flew into place on either side of the weighted down DECLAN.

"What of Darlene, Ian, and their dragons?" Morgan called to Erin.

"I'll have Noreen and whoever she brings look for them," Erin said.

"I can't hear any other dragons, just the Irish three and your two. I'm sorry," Devan said as she hunched her shoulders to ward off the pounding rain.

Lightning lit up the sky and thunder rumbled. The dragons headed toward the distant coastline. As they crossed over the rocky shore, Noreen approached with two MacKay dragons and riders. Erin urged her compeer faster to intercept the party.

TEAGAN circled the three Scottish dragons, then hovered in front of Noreen's RHONA.

"Why did you bring only two teams?" Erin demanded.

"The others were still grumbling about you taking off without saying a word. I didn't want to waste any more time, so I grabbed the ones ready to fly."

"Fine. We've done a quick look, but go ahead and search the wreckage for dragons and riders and survivors from the oil platform. Shut down the fire and plug the oil flow," Erin said, trying to derail any questions.

"What about BOYD and Morgan?" Noreen squinted into the distance, then pointed over Erin's shoulder. "Who are they?"

Erin glanced back to see the rescue party had closed the distance. "Irish dragons and riders. They've got BOYD. We need to get him back to the compound before shock sets in." Erin dismissed the MacKay riders as Padrick and the others caught up to her.

"Trouble?" Padrick shouted to her.

"No." Erin shook her head. "I sent them to do a more thorough search and to cap the oil and put out the fire. Let's keep going."

They flew for another ten minutes before Erin directed them toward a grove of trees. She circled and pointed to a clearing with buildings on the south side pasture and a small loch to the north.

DECLAN spiraled down slowly until he could dump the air from beneath his wings to land. He landed hard on all four legs, grunting and nearly toppling over from the massive weight strapped to his back.

ROARKE and DOCHAS landed on either side of the black dragon. Everyone scrambled down from the dragons' backs. The Irish dragons took up the entire landing courtyard. Erin and TEAGAN landed on a patch of overgrown grass closer to the clan houses. A growing group of MacKay riders and the clan healer ran to the black dragon.

"Any ideas on how to get BOYD off DECLAN without further injury to either one?" Morgan twisted his fingers together.

Devan's eyes took on the far away look peculiar to a dragonrider in mental communication with a dragon.

"He says he can hop off. I told him that perhaps ROARKE could lift him clear using the netting, so as not to have him stumble and fall on his injured wing." Devan focused on the noticeable claw marks on DECLAN's back. "Or cause more serious tears to DECLAN."

Christian and Morgan secured the netting under BOYD'S belly as best they could.

Before BOYD could get it in his head to move without assistance, ROARKE leapt into the air and used all four of his claws to grip the netting. He lifted BOYD slightly, then DECLAN scuttled out from under the injured dragon. ROARKE, careful to keep the damaged wing from crumpling against the cobblestones, lowered BOYD.

DECLAN folded his wings and waddled away, like a ship in heavy seas, to give the Scottish dragon healer room to work. DOCHAS and ROARKE followed.

The healer knelt by the dragon's injured wing. "What happened?"

"BOYD and I got caught when the platform blew." Morgan shuddered and soothed himself more than his compeer by rubbing BOYD'S neck ridges.

"Well, let's get him inside so I can set the broken joints and get some salve on those burns." The healer motioned for a few of the larger riders to assist him. "He won't be flying for several months, at least. We'll have to see how he heals." The healer looked around as BOYD was led away. "What of the other dragons that flew with you today?"

Morgan rubbed his arms to warm up as his teeth began to chatter. He thrust his chin toward Erin.

"I sent Noreen and the rescue crew to look for them," Erin said.

The sound of murmurs from the MacKay clan rose in volume as they eyed the Irish dragons and riders suspiciously. Someone shouted, "Who are they?"

"They saved BOYD. They are from the Tuatha Dragon Clan of Ireland." Erin narrowed her eyes at George, the clan's troublemaker.

"The young woman . . . I'm sorry I don't remember your name." Morgan began.

"Devan Fraser, rider of DOCHAS."

"You should know, Devan can hear and speak to other dragons," Morgan said, awe in his voice. "She helped calm BOYD."

A collective gasp sounded from the crowd. Devan backed up warily. Padrick and Christian put themselves between her and the restless crowd. DOCHAS growled, spreading her wings, ready to defend her rider.

Erin held up her hands. "I need a quick word with our guests. Since there was an explosion, we can expect neighboring clans to arrive soon. So, we need everyone ready."

Several of the MacKay riders held their ground.

Morgan, hands raised to placate, stepped between his clan mates and the Irish contingent. "We don't have time for this. You need to get prepared."

But the face-off continued. Morgan clenched his fists and pulled his shoulders back. "Go now. These riders saved BOYD."

Still grumbling, the crowd dispersed. Erin ushered the Irish riders toward her home.

Devan turned to Morgan. "Your dragon tells me that you shouldn't worry. He'll heal in time for the next mating flight on Beltaine."

Morgan stumbled, his blush rose high on his cheeks. "Ah, right. I'll just go see if Healer Kelvin needs my help."

Padrick caught up to Erin as Morgan followed the healer into a large barn. "Prepare for what?"

Erin stomped to her front door. "To defend ourselves."

Padrick reached for Erin's arm, but she opened the door and slipped past him into the entry. The only sound she heard was the shuffling of footsteps behind her. Erin bit her lower lip to keep it from trembling. She needed more than a quick word and a few moments with her guests but knew the Sinclairs and Sutherlands would be on MacKay land within the quarter-hour.

Her mind reeled. *Padrick had been searching for me?* The young man in the trio was a dead ringer for a younger version of Padrick. She wondered if it was their son, Riley. But no, he had been introduced as Christian. Perhaps he was Padrick's son from another woman. Erin risked a glance at the young man. Yes, he had Padrick's lean face, piercing deep blue eyes, sensual mouth, and long rangy limbs. Christian's black hair was longer than Padrick wore his, even during his rebellious university days.

Padrick cleared his throat. "I'm sorry to show up without warning. I can see you have trouble brewing. Just direct us on how we can help. And where I can change out of these soaking wet clothes. We can talk later."

Erin nodded, but before she could think what to do with three very large Irish dragons and their riders, Padrick spoke again.

"There is one thing you need to know, above all else." Padrick gripped Christian's shoulder. "Erin, meet our son, Christian Riley."

Erin brought a hand to her mouth to stifle a sob. "Riley." She whispered the name with anguish. The tears came as she reached a trembling hand toward the grown man—her baby boy. Her past stood before her, the gaping hole in her life waiting to be filled.

Christian stepped back, out of reach and from Padrick's grip, and reached for Devan's hand. His blue eyes darkened with emotions Erin didn't understand.

She wiped her cheeks. "Sorry."

Christian broke the awkward silence. His voice, so like the young Padrick Erin had been forced to leave. "The sisters at the orphanage named me Christian and kept Riley as my last name."

Erin shifted her gaze from Christian to Padrick. "How long have you known of each other's existence?"

"About seven months," Padrick said. "This wasn't the way I imagined this reunion. I promise we'll have time to figure it all out. But now we need to—"

Devan interrupted. "Dragons are approaching, not from the MacKay clan. Your own dragons' thoughts are jumbled. Perhaps we should make ourselves and our dragons' presence known."

"Have your dragons stay in the courtyard. Our dragons will be assembling and we don't want any misunderstandings in the chaos," Erin said to Padrick as she pointed to a closed door. "We have a few minutes. Go ahead and get changed. Though it's still storming outside, so not sure changing will help much."

"Rain's better than water permeated with oil." Padrick scooped up his rucksack and disappeared into the loo.

An awkward silence permeated the storm-darkened room until Padrick reemerged.

Erin led them outside. The MacKay riders mounted their dragons and arrayed themselves in a loose semicircle.

"Defend the east and south boundary," Erin yelled to the mounted pairs. She turned to Padrick. "With BOYD out of commission, can you back me up?"

"Aye."

Lightning flashed across the darkened sky and thunder followed mere seconds later.

# Twenty One

Padrick settled into his saddle aboard DECLAN in the steadily falling rain and hoped the thunder and lightning moved away. *"What can you sense from the local dragons?"* Padrick asked his compeer.

*"Trepidation and fear from some, bravado from others,"* DECLAN bespoke.

"The incoming dragons will be here soon," Devan said.

Padrick stared into the distance before addressing Erin. "Would it be better if we left and came back later? After dark?"

"No," Erin said. "If they're friends, I don't want to show disrespect. If they aren't, then your presence might give them pause if they're thinking of attacking. Though it might not do for them to know you've been searching for me, specifically."

Padrick cocked his head. "Why?"

"There's no time to explain. Trust me. I need to welcome the visitors—be they friend or foe." Erin turned to face the incoming dragons.

Padrick counted twelve MacKay dragons on the ground. He squinted into the storm-drenched sky and made out at least three times that many approaching from the south.

"Is the whole of Scotland arriving?" Padrick muttered under his breath.

At DECLAN'S snort, Padrick turned to look over his shoulder as another group appeared from the east. The stormy sky darkened further with the bodies of so many dragons flying in close formation.

"Friend or foe?" Padrick asked Erin.

"Foe." Erin's chin came up and her shoulders thrust back, readying herself for the imminent confrontation. "The ones with green tartans under their riding harnesses coming from the south are Sutherlands. The red tartan ones from the east are Sinclairs."

Erin turned as Morgan sloshed through the mud toward her. "Did you get the call off?" she asked.

Morgan nodded.

"Prepare yourselves," Erin called to the dragons and riders.

Morgan moved to stand in front of his clan mates that faced the incoming Sinclair dragons, leaving Erin and the Irish contingent to deal with the Sutherlands.

A great rustling tore through the storm caused by so many dragons in the air. The trees swayed, buffeted.

*Do the Scottish dragons not need to stay hidden from non-dragonriders. Or, perhaps this place is too remote for anyone to notice.* Then another, more dangerous thought struck Padrick. *What do these vast numbers of dragons do to the earth magic?*

Three-dozen dragons of various colors, all smaller than the Irish dragons, hovered over the muddy, plowed field to the south. Another two dozen alighted on the hill to the east. Five dragons landed: three from the south and two from the east.

Three men clad in Sutherland green dismounted and approached Erin. Two of the Sinclairs followed suit and faced Morgan.

"So far, their dragons are just curious about us," Devan whispered to Padrick and Christian. "The humans, I'm not so sure about."

A bear of a man from the Sutherland trio stepped forward. "Clan MacKay. We hear you had some trouble." His lips curled into a sneer. "We're here to offer help."

"No trouble we can't handle. A minor incident on one of the smaller oil platforms," Erin said.

"Not so minor, from what I've heard. What with all aboard dying, except one." The man raised a bushy brow.

"Your spies work fast. Too bad they couldn't be counted on to assist in the explosion," Erin said. When the man shrugged, she continued. "We have it under control. And as you can see," she indicated the Irish dragons, "we have guests."

"You dare go against Alba clan law and seek to reinforce your numbers with these?" His voice thundered. He flipped his hand dismissively at the trio of larger dragons. "You know the penalty for this type of infraction. I could claim MacKay lands right now." The man smirked. "I have witnesses."

Padrick straightened in his saddle.

Erin stood her ground, though she swept her rain-soaked curls off her face. "Your claim is without merit. I didn't seek out our brethren from Ireland. Though they were most gracious in lending their assistance." She spoke deliberately; her gaze never strayed from the Sutherland chieftain. "Furthermore, you don't have a quorum. Your clan and that of Sinclair does not constitute a majority."

Padrick realized Erin was stalling. *Awaiting reinforcements? Was that the call Morgan had made? Think, dammit. Help Erin.* Padrick slowly slid from the back of his dragon and strolled to Erin's side. He held out his hand to the Sutherland chieftain. "I'm Padrick, rider of black DECLAN." His voice rang with authority. "My clan mates and I bring greetings from the Tuatha Dragon Clan of Éire."

The brute clasped Padrick's hand in his own beefy mitt and squeezed. Padrick squeezed back.

"Clan Chieftain Sutherland." The man released his grip on Padrick's hand. "As you are not from Alba, I will tell you now that you've aligned your wings with the wrong clan. MacKay will not last the year. You'd be well advised to look to the Sutherlands and Sinclairs for any dealings."

"It was my understanding that Scotland is a civilized land where all the clans work for the betterment of the whole. Are you stating otherwise?" Silently Padrick asked DECLAN where the devil were the reinforcements? This was a dangerous game he played in a foreign land. Technically, he had no jurisdiction here. Though he could claim to be informing the Crown's other dragon clans of the dangers the Tuatha clan had just escaped.

Sutherland brooded for a moment, then burst out laughing—a sound that sent a chill down Padrick's spine. "We're not the interlopers here. You bloody Irish are. You're trespassing." He waved a hand to his clansmen. "Perhaps it's time to teach you some proper manners, eh?"

"Perhaps you overstep, sir," Padrick returned, far more calmly than he felt. "We answer to both the British and the Irish governments. We are not here to interfere. We had urgent news to relay and saw the aftermath of the unfortunate incident on the oil platform. We offered our assistance, nothing more."

"What news?" Sutherland asked. "You'll tell me now."

"The message was private." Padrick's gaze shifted slightly over the man's shoulder. "Ah, it seems we have more company." He nodded as two groups of dragons circled overhead.

DECLAN bespoke Padrick. *"The Ring Wearer has summarized the incident with the oil platform and the present standoff to the lead dragons from the new arrivals. And is telling them we are from Ireland and have come in peace, seeking a missing friend."* The dragon paused, then added, *"The newcomers are astonished at the boldness of the rival clans. And, they are taken aback that someone other than their rider can speak to them all."*

The rain eased to a steady drizzle. One dragon from each of the two new groups landed in the space between Erin and Morgan and their clan mates. The riders disembarked and joined Erin, Morgan, and Padrick.

"What have we here?" A gray-haired man wearing a dark green and black tartan asked. He focused on the surly Sutherland chieftain. "Is it a céilidh? Was our invitation lost?"

Sutherland stared holes through Padrick, then Erin. The Sinclair man fidgeted.

"We were offering assistance to our MacKay brethren," the Sutherland chief said. "Apparently, Clans MacKenzie and Fraser approve of interference from Ireland. I shall bring it up at the next council meeting. We shall see who has the power then, eh?" Sutherland mounted his dragon. "Move your stinking beasts from above my clan mates or I shall order them to flame at will."

The gray-haired gentleman flicked his hand once and the hovering dragons wheeled away to allow the Sutherland and Sinclair contingents to leave.

Morgan set about posting sentries on hills overlooking the south and east, then headed back to the barn to check on BOYD.

With the marauders gone, the remaining newly arrived dragons landed. The MacKenzie and Fraser riders glared at the Irish dragonriders, and each of their dragons held a similar snarl.

*"What's that all about?"* Padrick bespoke his dragon.

*"The newcomers are frightened because the Ring Wearer bespoke them,"* DECLAN replied.

*"Stay ready for anything. You'll have to endure the weather as I'm not sure there is room inside anywhere for you, DOCHAS, and ROARKE."*

*"Do no' fash. Tuatha dragons are hearty. We shall be fine, unless the lightning returns,"* DECLAN replied.

"Which rider had the audacity to communicate with my own dragon?" The newcomer turned to Devan and held her gaze. "A fine talent you have there, Lass." He bowed but didn't take his eyes from her face. "MacKenzie, at your service." When he straightened, he indicated the man next to him. "And this is Fraser."

Devan nodded to both men. "Sorry to startle you and your compeers, but it was the fastest way to explain the situation. The tension was escalating. I didn't want dragons fighting dragons."

"We should discuss this inside," Erin said, indicating the crowd of dragons and humans milling about in the cold drizzle. A couple of the newly arrived riders eased close enough to eavesdrop.

A ruckus broke out as the search party returned without the two missing dragon and rider pairs.

Erin inclined her head to Noreen.

"No sign of them," Noreen said. "I'm afraid they were caught in the blast."

"And the foreman?" Erin spoke in a hushed tone.

"I handed him off to my brother, Ned, on his fishing trawler. He'll say he was fishing and rescued the lone survivor. I didn't want to waste time lugging the foreman all the way to the rescue station in Durness." Noreen raised her hands in front of her. "Before you get too mad, the fool was unconscious."

Erin nodded, then ushered the chieftains and guests to the home she shared with Morgan. When everyone was settled, she made formal introductions. "The MacKenzie and The Fraser, clan chieftains." She indicated the two tartan-clad men. "This is Padrick Nolan, Christian Riley, and Devan Fraser from the Tuatha Dragon Clan of Ireland."

Fraser stared at Devan as the silence dragged on.

"I was informed of the explosion. How many did you lose?" MacKenzie asked Erin.

"Two dragons and their riders. Morgan's BOYD will be out of commission for several months." Erin spit the words out like a snake spewing venom. "No other survivors from the forty souls aboard the platform, save the foreman."

"*Mí ádh.*" MacKenzie discreetly used his thumb to hold down his middle and ring finger on his right hand in the 'horned hand' gesture warding off bad luck. "Can you hold off another challenge from Sutherland and Sinclair?"

Erin heaved a sigh and rubbed the back of her neck. "Losing two dragons puts us at a disadvantage, for sure. But, we'll have to hold them off. At least until next week's council meeting."

"I can spare some dragons and riders. Fraser can as well." MacKenzie looked to his associate, who nodded in agreement.

"Sutherland will come after the Frasers and MacKenzies now," Erin said. "This is the most overt you've been in standing up to their plans for annexing MacKay territory to Sutherland and Sinclair lands. Not that Sinclair needs any more profits from the oil platforms, but Sutherland has Sinclair under his thumb." She shook her head. "You should watch your borders." She glanced at Padrick. "Besides, my friends here might have a trick or two we can learn."

MacKenzie's eyes narrowed. "Would that entail communicating with dragons other than your own?"

"The Tuatha dragons can communicate between themselves, not just to their human partners," Erin said.

Padrick interrupted. "Devan's the only one with the unique talent of being able to communicate with all dragons. Until recently, the Tuatha dragon-to-dragon communication was limited to a five-kilometer radius."

"What changed?" Fraser asked, clearly intrigued.

"Devan and the other Tuatha dragons empowered our drake, GRAYSON. He acts as a conduit." Christian frowned. "It's a long story, but GRAYSON has a special kinship with Devan. He saved her life."

"You and I saved his first." Devan waved the comment away. "The point is, GRAYSON will never have a rider, but he works hard to be a vital part of the clan. We don't fully understand his new ability."

"A drake, you say." MacKenzie rubbed his chin. "We have no such thing here that I know of. Tell me how dragon-to-dragon communication works."

"It comes naturally with our dragons," Padrick spoke up. "Communication starts after each dragon hatches, though on a limited scale. Our dragonets can easily communicate up to one kilometer right from the hatching. The distance increases to its full potential when the dragons bond with their compeers at the Chosen Ceremony. The extended communication range is a recent development—in the last six months. The results vary depending on the bonds developed between the dragons. We've been testing the range on this trip. So far, Devan's unequaled in communicating over the hundreds of kilometers."

"I wonder why our dragons don't communicate with each other?" Erin asked.

"Perhaps the sheer number of dragons in each clan?" Padrick wondered aloud. "Or, because our riders wear clan pendants that assist with the magic? I didn't notice if any of you wear a talisman."

Erin shook her head. "It's something to look into, but the ability surely is more than a manmade, magic-infused talisman."

Morgan entered and took a seat. He stared openly at Padrick. Curiosity warred with angst.

"A survival mechanism?" Devan murmured. She glanced up when the room fell silent. "DOCHAS and I had no trouble with your dragons, but that might be because of my ability. Perhaps it has more to do with choice than ability. A trust issue." At Erin's blank look, Devan explained. "It seems the Scottish dragons and riders are constantly on guard against invasions of other clans. If I were a dragon, I'd operate from a position of strength, not let my rivals know my thoughts."

"But that wouldn't explain why the dragons don't communicate within the same clan," Erin said. "We aren't exactly rivals."

# Twenty Two

Erin fingered the bracelet on her wrist, then focused on Fraser as he cleared his throat.

"Sure and it does," Fraser said. The weathered skin around his whisky-colored eyes crinkled. "Since time began and men pledged their loyalty, there has been jealousy. Ye have experienced it yerself when TEAGAN chose ye, an Outlander."

Morgan interjected. "True. Even more so since I rely on Erin in helping lead the MacKay clan."

"I'd say you're back to the lack of communication being a trust issue," Devan said.

"How long ago did you partner with TEAGAN?" Padrick asked Erin. "What exactly is your connection here?" He shifted, and Erin felt his complete attention on her.

She rose and gazed out the window into the fierce storm. She didn't want to get into all this right now—not with the Fraser and MacKenzie chieftains here. The friendship bonds with the three clans were still tenuous. Shortly after Morgan's da's death, Morgan had, with her reluctant acceptance, pursued an alliance with the two powerful leaders. She didn't want her past mistakes to jeopardize that friendship.

"It's a long story. One that can keep until the threat from our rivals is thwarted," Erin said as she faced the others. "I'd like to hear more about how your dragons communicate with each other."

MacKenzie cleared his throat and addressed Devan. "I'm

fascinated with your talent. When did you know you could communicate with other dragons? You're American, no? Yet, you ride with the Irish."

"I'm a new dragonrider. I partnered with DOCHAS on May first, Beltaine, this year," Devan explained. "But I heard something, what I thought of as whisperings, about a month earlier." She looked to Fraser. "And I only know of my Irish heritage on my mother's side. My father never mentioned where his ancestors were from."

Fraser nodded. "'Tis possible ye are descended from the Scots as well. Ye should ask your da."

"Both my parents died in an accident last February." Devan closed her eyes and her shoulders drooped.

Christian reached for Devan's hand and twined his fingers with hers. He leaned in and murmured something Erin couldn't hear.

"'Tis sorry I am to hear of yer loss," Fraser said.

Devan gave a slight smile, accepting the condolence. "I'm getting through it day by day. Pairing with DOCHAS has helped, as has Christian."

Padrick broke the awkward silence that ensued. "About the dragon communication . . . I've asked my compeer, DECLAN, how the communication is different between dragons, and between longer distances. He says he must concentrate on envisioning the particular dragon he wishes to communicate with and that bespeaking over longer distances sounds different—kind of flat or hollow."

"Hmm." Erin returned to her seat. "Perhaps it's just a matter of practice. Or, as Devan said, a matter of trust."

"A suggestion? Have TEAGAN try communicating with BOYD." Devan shifted to face Erin. "First, BOYD is still sedated from the surgery to mend his wing and he'll be less likely to have any mental barriers up. Second, you already have a working relationship with BOYD's rider."

Erin snuck a peek at Padrick. *What must he be thinking?*

"As long as you don't think it'll traumatize him, I'm willing to try." Morgan glanced from Erin to Devan.

For a moment, Devan's eyes took on the glazed, far away look of a human communicating telepathically with a dragon. Then she refocused on Morgan. "Two of the phalanges nearest his wingtip and one near the joint are broken. The healer has realigned them and screwed a plate to the one closest to the joint. The others, he has immobilized. Also, he has slathered the burns with an ointment to numb the pain. BOYD is fighting the anesthesia. I've sent him reassuring thoughts." She faced Erin. "It may be some time until we can try communicating."

MacKenzie stood. "In the meantime, we'll return to our own lands. Keep us informed on your wee experiment."

"I can check records if ye wish, about yer da," Fraser said to Devan as he rose and extended his hand to her. "How long will ye be here?"

"I'm not sure." Devan shook his hand. "My dad was Joseph Michael Iain Fraser, if that helps. He turned fifty-five on February second, just before he died."

Fraser pulled a small notepad and pencil from his pocket and wrote down the information.

Erin walked MacKenzie and Fraser to the foyer and the front door. "Morgan and I appreciate your assistance today and, most of all, your continued friendship. Have a care with Sutherland and Sinclair."

"You as well," MacKenzie said. "Our best wishes for BOYD's quick recovery."

"I'll leave my cousin Graeme in charge of a squad and at yer disposal," Fraser said. He called Graeme to him and relayed instructions. Graeme chose several men from each clan to stay behind.

The two chieftains signaled the other riders, then mounted their dragons and directed them skyward. The flock of dragons arrowed into the stormy sky and were gone from view within moments.

Erin lingered at the door, her emotions jumbled. *Sweet Jesus, Mary, and Joseph, what do I do now? I've a grown son and the only man I've ever truly loved back in my life. But, are they really in my life?* She wiped at the sudden tears that threatened to fall. *What life? Fecked that up when I didn't go back to Ireland. And what about Morgan? I may not love him as more than a brother, but I still care.* The sound of voices intruded into her thoughts.

"BOYD will be all right," Devan said. "The plate and screws are necessary to make sure the joint heals strong enough for flight."

"Right." Morgan sighed. "I should never have tried that stunt. I should have protected my dragon. If not for Erin's foreseeing, BOYD and I wouldn't be here to tell the tale."

"What do you mean Erin foresaw? Wasn't she with you at the rig?" Christian asked.

"No. Erin needs to explain that part. It's her story to tell, or not. I'm going to check on BOYD. Let me know when you want to try the dragon communication." Morgan hurried from the house.

As Erin stepped back into the room, Christian asked, "You weren't at the rig when it blew?"

"I was still a kilometer away." Erin walked to the fireplace to warm her hands and give herself time to control her emotions. She was never comfortable discussing how she knew things were going to happen.

"Morgan said you foresaw the accident." Christian waited for her response.

"That was not an accident. That was a foreman's complete disregard for the safety of his crew." Erin whirled around. "By not using the second crane, the bloody fool killed everyone on the Morey. And he cost us two dragons and riders. I may not have gotten on well with Ian and Darlene, but they were dragonriders—part of the clan. Morgan should've let the foreman die with the rest of his workers."

Devan gasped. "You can't be that callous. Didn't you swear to protect the land and the people on it?"

"Yes, I did. But what price do we pay? One careless foreman for two dragonrider pairs? And BOYD won't be able to fly for months. You saw how quickly Sinclair and Sutherland marshaled their forces against us. I don't want to think of what would've happened if

MacKenzie and Fraser hadn't come with a show of force as quickly as they did." Erin shoved a hand through her damp curls. "Besides, drilling for oil is dangerous. The clan does what it can to mitigate the hazards, both to the people and the environment. We're lucky that the Morey was a small platform. No one will suspect we used dragon magic to staunch the spill and douse the fires. It won't be like the Piper Alpha disaster of 1988."

"What happened then?" Devan asked.

"One hundred and sixty-seven killed—"

Christian interrupted. "You haven't answered my question. What did Morgan mean when he said you foresaw the explosion?"

Erin faced the fire. She took several deep breaths. Then, at a hand on her shoulder, she turned.

"Tell us," Padrick said as he briefly squeezed her shoulder.

"I . . . had a dream, a vision." She met Christian's unflinching gaze. "I've had them before. I feel as though I'm there, even if I'm nowhere near the actual location. I can hear, see, smell, taste, feel everything." She lowered her gaze to the floor. "Usually, there's nothing I can do to stop the vision from becoming a reality. I stopped talking of this talent after some of the clan members blamed me for bringing mí ádh, bad luck. Morgan is the exception."

"Did the dreams start when you became a rider?" Christian pressed.

Erin nodded. "I think I've always been able to sense danger. Perhaps I learned this from my father. I don't know. But, that sense has kept Kiely from finding me." She raised her head to stare at Padrick, then Christian. "I assumed the visions stemmed from that. They always involve danger."

"Looks like I inherited something from you after all," Christian said. His deep blue eyes never wavered from hers.

She gasped. "You . . . have them as well?"

Christian nodded. "Bloody inconvenient, at first. Especially since, as you say, most times there's no way to prevent the disaster."

Erin memorized the look on her son's face, the same look

Padrick had when he first introduced her to his destiny. The love she felt for these two men, one her first love and the other her son, threatened to close her throat. Sweet memories of the past flooded her mind.

"But it led me to the Tuatha Dragon Clan," Christian said. "To Devan, to becoming a dragonrider, to helping stop a killer." He gripped Devan's hand.

"Erin," Padrick said, "tell us more about your visions."

"I will, if you explain how you found each other."

Padrick agreed.

Erin motioned for Padrick to sit, tossed another peat brick on the fire, then joined him. "I have had a few visions that involve the dragons. Usually I see disputes between the clans. While we aren't as organized as you in Ireland, we do have alliances and boundaries. Troubles arise around those boundaries."

"Invading clans like the Sinclairs and Sutherlands?" Devan asked.

Erin nodded. "Yes, it's an issue of each clan scrambling for the most profitable land and prestige. And a tug-of-war between the highlands and the lowlands. The alliances in the highlands are constantly in flux. One particular concern is Parliament's division of profits from oil exploration. Not just between England and Scotland, but the dispersal within Scotland itself. Many citizens believe the money should belong to the areas along the Pentland Firth, the Atlantic, and the North Sea and to those that have had to endure the ugly oil platforms. Others believe the black gold is a national treasure that should be dispersed evenly, based on population. Hence, the constant shifting of peoples and clan alliances."

"And your clan, where do they stand?" Christian asked. "Who can you count on for an alliance?"

"We're lost among the larger clans. But, we're becoming more prominent as the quest for oil expands. As you witnessed today, the MacKenzie and Fraser clans are our staunchest supporters, thanks to Morgan's persistence. The MacGregors and MacLeans next, through the bonds of marriage. The Sutherlands and Sinclairs regularly invade, with an eye on expanding their own territories."

Erin waved a hand. "As I said, the alliances shift. One thing is certain. The differences between the highland clans are nothing compared to the ill will between Scotland and England."

No one spoke for several moments.

"Your turn. Tell me how you found each other," Erin said to Padrick, trying to divert the conversation and her reawakening feelings.

Padrick took a deep breath. "Christian and Devan have recently become dragonriders. They stopped a killer who'd been trying to strip the dragon magic from Ireland to bring his dead wife and child back to life. The killer had already murdered four dragons and their riders."

Erin goggled. "I hadn't heard of this."

"The Tuatha Dragon Clan still operates in secret. The murders were never reported as such," Padrick said.

"The first murder took place last year, on the autumnal equinox," Christian said. "That was the beginning of my visions. I didn't know what to make of them at first. Each vision was so intense. I felt as though I had committed each murder."

Erin's eyes widened as she reached a hand toward Christian's cheek. He pulled away. *Too soon. He's not a bairn anymore.*

Padrick briefly told of the other three murders, over six months, always on Celtic holidays, and of the clan's realization that the murders weren't isolated incidents.

Christian described his mounting fear that somehow he was responsible for the deaths of four people he had never met, at four locations he had never been to. The last one died on the spring equinox.

"I don't understand," Erin said. "You told me you'd just met each other about seven months ago, right before Beltaine."

"When my parents died in February, I began sorting through their estate. I found a ring." Devan held out her right hand to Erin.

"That's the same—" Erin began.

"Yes, it's the Tuatha Dragon Clan symbol," Padrick said.

"I found a letter from my great-grandparents, written to my grandmother." Devan worried the ring on her finger. "It spoke of Éire. And destiny. I had to come. And I met Christian."

Christian stilled Devan's fingers. "When I saw her ring, I knew it matched my pendant. I was curious about the matching pieces, how one belonged to a Yank while I inherited the other."

"So, you received my letter and the pendant on your eighteenth birthday?" Erin asked with hope in her heart.

"No." Christian shook his head. "I was ten when Mother Superior called me into her office. She gave me the pendant then."

"But . . ." Erin's brows lowered.

"There was a couple in Mother Superior's outer office. I was to go with them as a possible adoptee," Christian spoke over Erin's protest. Then he lowered his voice. "It didn't work out."

"When did she give you the letter?" Erin asked.

"Padrick and I went back to the orphanage just before Beltaine, this year," Christian said. "Mother Superior had been gone a long time by then. We were given the letter. We read it together."

Erin's gaze widened. *My son didn't have anyone in all that time?* She opened her mouth, then closed it without speaking. *I was a fool for taking so long to go back for him, then not demanding they return my son to me, regardless of Kiely's threats.*

Devan broke the awkward silence. "Christian and I teamed up to get answers about my ring, his pendant, and most importantly, his dreams. We traveled from murder site to murder site until—"

"We drew the attention of the clan," Christian said. "That was the first time we knew the dragons of my dreams were real. We were taken adragonback to Loughcrew to meet the clan leader. The next morning, Devan heard the cries of pain from GRAYSON at the same time that I had a vision. We rode with Sean to rescue the injured drake." Christian squeezed Devan's hand.

"That's when I met our son," Padrick whispered.

"With Devan and my special abilities," Christian continued, "we set a trap for the killer. My visions led to the identity of the murderer. I foresaw that he meant to kill Devan at the Chosen Ceremony on Beltaine."

"And you as well," Devan interjected.

Erin glanced at Devan, then back to Christian.

Christian shrugged. "After the ceremony, Devan and I were separated. That's when the killer attacked. If not for GRAYSON's intervention and him taking a poisoned blade meant for Devan, she would have died."

"If you were not as quick with your blade, you would have died yourself," Padrick said. "As it was, both GRAYSON and Christian were hit with poisoned daggers."

Erin gasped. "Please, tell me the rest."

# Twenty Three

Erin sat mesmerized as Devan told the tale of first GRAYSON's then Christian's narrow escape from death.

Devan's gaze cleared as she once again focused on the present and Erin. "Later, when both Christian and GRAYSON were stronger, we realized the dragons' infusion of magic had changed GRAYSON. While he will never have wings to fly, he can hear all the other dragons. We have spent the last couple of months training him to be a communication conduit between all the clan dragons."

Erin absorbed what had happened in the past six months—both to the Tuatha Dragon Clan and to the men she loved.

Padrick rose. "And we've spent a bit of time searching for you." He waited in silence, his penetrating gaze never leaving Erin's face.

"How did you find me?" Erin asked.

Devan answered. "I'm a researcher. Or, I was before I came to Ireland. Anyway, Padrick tracked down Sully."

"I remember Sullivan. He was one of Kiely's men back in the day." Erin sighed. *Such a nice man, but he worked for Kiely.*

"Well, Sully provided Padrick with a starting point," Devan said. "It took me this long to weed out misinformation and track your movements until you ended up here in northern Scotland."

"Bloody hell, Erin. I don't know what to say," Padrick said. "I'll apologize for Mother and what she did to you twenty-eight years ago, but why did you run?" He twisted his fingers until his knuckles turned white, then he sank back down onto the couch.

Erin stole a glance at Devan and Christian before leaning forward and placing her hands on Padrick's. She caressed his hands until he settled them, holding hers. *How do I explain?*

"I never wanted to leave you. Your mother gave me no choice. The information she had on my father would have seen him die in gaol." Erin shook her head as she played with her bracelet. "I would have stayed if I thought we could have won." Erin stared into the flames licking at the peat in the fireplace.

"Kiely called me into her office the morning after you asked me to marry you. The morning after Riley was conceived," Erin's voice shook as she recounted the incidents that shaped her destiny.

Snaps of Da working with a man named Billy from the IRA lay across the oak desk. Kiely sat ramrod-straight behind the desk, in a position of utter authority.

"Sit down." Kiely indicated a low chair with a nod. Her thin lips curled in contempt.

Erin sank into the chair, her legs no longer able to support her shaky knees. She watched Kiely through lowered lashes, wondering how she might explain Da's political beliefs to this uptight, upper-class, protestant dragonrider.

Kiely rapped her knuckles in the middle of the damning snaps spread across the desk. "What have you to say?"

Erin said nothing.

"So, you do not dispute the fact your father is a . . . traitor." Kiely sneered.

"I . . . I can't say," Erin mumbled, terrified.

"Speak up, chit. Surely you know who that man is with your father? That's an IRA member. And that, my dear, is a bomb." Kiely's finely manicured index finger pointed to a small, rectangular box with a timer taped to it and wires exposed on one end.

Silence hung between them.

Kiely scooped up the snaps and shoved them into a manila envelope. "I won't turn over what I know to the gardaí, not yet. In exchange for your father's freedom, you'll remove yourself from my son's life. I want you gone. For good."

Erin opened her mouth to protest, but Kiely's next words stopped her.

"Padrick is destined to be clan leader someday. His dalliance with you would bring shame to all. He'll do what is best for the clan. That means leaving you behind."

Erin rubbed her chest where Padrick's grandfather's pendant lay warm against her galloping heart. *Did Kiely know of Padrick's proposal? Of their lovemaking?*

"If you think to get around me on this, I'll have your father, and the rest of your family, in the hands of the gardaí before you can take two breaths." Kiely leaned forward, her elbows resting on the desk, her hands steepled. "What shall it be? Gaol for all the Casey clan, or you forgetting ever meeting my son?"

Gaol with a charge of treason meant sure death.

"You leave me no choice," Erin said, her shoulders slumped at the prospect of never seeing Padrick again.

"I'll be watching. No contact, not a whisper or . . ." Kiely stood abruptly. "Even a Catholic chit understands the consequences."

With that insult, Kiely dismissed her.

Erin stole away like a common thief. She had very little money, but she made her way to Dublin. In the city, she cut her hair and blended in with the students at Trinity College. Erin cleaned classrooms during the day and scrounged a little-used utility closet to sleep at night. She made no contact with Padrick. Then one night, a little more than nine months later, she spotted Kiely's man searching for her. Erin had just returned from the market with a meager dinner for herself, so she'd have enough milk to nurse her baby. It was the night she realized her son would never be safe from Kiely. The night Erin made the fateful decision to give Riley to the orphanage. The night she had grieved for every single day since.

"What about us?" Padrick asked, pain deepened the lines around his mouth.

Erin pressed her eyelids closed before the tears that threatened to overflow could escape. Then she faced Padrick—the man he was today, not the boy of her past.

Padrick's pleading blue eyes looked into hers. "Did you ever love me? Why didn't you trust me?"

"Trust you?" The words exploded out of Erin. "What about your trust in me? You knew Kiely's attitude toward me, yet you believed whatever lies she told you. I had to look after my family. I'll not apologize for that. I'm serving a self-imposed exile. What more do you want?"

Padrick looked stricken. "I . . . I still believe we could have stopped Mother's treachery and been together if I'd known about your meeting that morning. I would have told Da. Forced him to put a halt to Mother's blackmail."

"Do you think your father could have reined in Kiely?" Erin shook her head. "Kiely would have steamrolled over anyone who stood in her way, even him."

Padrick sighed. "You may be right, but we'll never know. You didn't give me a chance."

"Perhaps we can discuss this privately." Erin tilted her head toward Devan and Christian.

"We need to check on our dragons. We'll look in on BOYD as well," Christian's voice was husky as he pulled Devan to her feet.

When the front door closed, Padrick said, "For Christ's sake Erin, why didn't you tell me you were pregnant? I might have been naïve, but I would have been there for you. Protected you and our child. I loved you. I wanted to marry you. Have a family with you."

"I didn't know," Erin mumbled. "Not when Kiely called me into her office that day."

"Bollocks! What about later?" Padrick exploded. He rose quickly and rubbed his neck. "You didn't trust me."

Erin looked into Padrick's stormy face. "Later, well . . . it was too late. I was already going against my family in seeing you. Mum told me seeking above my station in life would get me into trouble. And her words seemed to be coming true. Kiely made sure I knew she didn't make idle threats. I loved you. I couldn't hold you back. I knew your desire to become a dragonrider. I had to let you go." She wiped her eyes. She didn't want him to see how much she ached, ached with love for him.

Padrick strode to the window, his breathing ragged. He spun to face her. "You still haven't explained why you never told me about my child."

"I . . ." She closed her eyes and drew a deep breath. "I was frightened, dammit. And, I thought I would always have a piece of you, of our love for each other. I never—"

"Never what? Never thought I would want you and our child? Never thought I would have gladly given anything to be with you?" Padrick accused.

It was Erin's turn to rise. "That's just it, don't you see? You would have given up your dreams for me, for someone who could bring you nothing but trouble." She twisted her fingers into knots. "I believed it was the only way to keep everyone I loved safe. You would forget about me in time, but I would have a part of you. Always. If I stayed out of your life, Kiely would leave my family and me alone."

"Then why did you give up our son when he was born?" Padrick's anguish tore at Erin's heart.

"Twice I caught sight of Kiely's cronies. I immersed myself at Trinity College. I changed my name, my appearance." Erin waved her hand dismissively. She sank back on the couch. "I stayed well-hidden and hadn't seen any of Kiely's men for months. I thought I was safe. The second day after being released from hospital, I was returning from the market when I literally ran into one of Kiely's watchers. He recognized me. I managed to lose him, but I was scared enough that I believed he knew my secret. I still carried some of my pregnancy weight and had on my hospital ID bracelet."

Erin turned away. "All I could think of was to protect my son. I was an unmarried Catholic girl. Back then, unmarried mothers could be enslaved at a convent. And Kiely held quite a bit of power. What if she found out, what would she do? Would she take my son and have me locked away in prison? Or worse, have Riley killed to keep her precious Nolan bloodline from my lowly, traitorous one? I couldn't take the chance."

"Instead, you left him at an orphanage," Padrick accused. "Without his mum *or* his da."

"It was supposed to be temporary." Tears fell unheeded down her face. "I left a note saying that I was in trouble and would be back for Riley when it was safe. But I couldn't explain without risking my family. Not knowing what Kiely knew, I also left your pendant and a letter for our son, in case I couldn't come back right away." She wiped her tears with her hands. Padrick sat beside her and gave her his handkerchief. "It was the hardest thing I ever did. Not only had I lost you, but also our son."

Padrick ran a hand over his face. "God, Erin. I'm sorry you felt you had to protect our son from Mother."

"All I can say is that I felt Riley was safer if Kiely never found out that he was your son. At the beginning, I couldn't even risk communicating with Mother Superior at the orphanage for fear that someone had seen me the night I left him there. I wasn't yet twenty years old. I had very little money. I was barely existing." Erin closed her eyes and willed back her tears. When she had control over her emotions, she opened her eyes. The anguish etched on Padrick's face kept Erin from saying any more.

"I looked for you," Padrick said. "At your parents' house, back at Queen's University, even with your friends." He wiped a solitary tear from her cheek with his thumb. "I never suspected Mother of such prejudice and downright treachery. I believed her when she said you no longer wanted to be with me. That my life in the dragon clan wasn't for you. I should never have stopped looking."

Erin shook her head. "I tried my damnedest to make sure no one could find me. The first few years, I moved around a lot. I stayed in Ireland, in Bray, then Wexford, and finally Ardmore, for a while after I left Dublin. One day I saw dragonriders and thought Kiely had found me, so I caught a ferry out of Cobh for England. Years later, when Da died, I returned to the orphanage. I went back for our son. Mother Superior berated me. Told me Riley was placed with a good family. One that could give him a secure life. One that was well off and could provide for him better than I, a single woman, ever could."

Erin's eyes widened. "My God! That must have been when Riley, um Christian, was with the couple who planned to adopt him."

She wiped at the tears that filled her eyes. "When Da died, Mum fell apart. The family blamed me. Said I crushed his spirit when I didn't come home. I left again and made my way back to Scotland—a sort of penance. I needed distance and time to help me deal with my grief and guilt over leaving you. Both of you." Restless, now that the shock of seeing Padrick again had worn off, Erin stood and made her way to the large rock fireplace.

"I never realized there were other dragon clans," Padrick said, obviously changing the subject. "I don't know why, but I thought Ireland was unique. How did you find them?"

Erin fumbled, trying to add a peat brick to the fire. It crumbled all over the hearth. "Damn."

Padrick went to her and clasped her hands in his. He pulled her back to the couch, then turned and cleaned up the mess. "It's all right. We can talk of this later."

"Just give me a moment, please." Erin rushed from the room. More tears threatened and she willed them back. *Damn it. I gave up too easily. If I'd stayed, fought for my rights as a mother . . . fought for my son. But I didn't even try.* She took a steadying breath and hugged herself to stop the shaking. *Can't change the past. Just have to live with my mistakes and hope Padrick and my son forgive me.*

When Erin returned, more composed yet weary, she warmed her hands briefly at the fire before taking her place once again next to Padrick. Her thigh brushed his and she savored the brief contact.

"I, too, had no idea there were dragons outside of Ireland," Erin said. "I stumbled upon the MacKay clan when I was in a precarious situation. At one point, I called out for help. One moment I was being beaten. The next, a dragon had my attacker in his foreclaws. The man was shouting bloody murder. And there I was, staring up into the snout of a snarling dragon. Needless to say, the rider—Morgan's father—was quite shocked that I could see them." Erin's lips rose in a slight smile.

"So they took you in," Padrick said.

"In the beginning, I was an outsider. They watched me as though I might steal one of their beloved dragon's eggs." She chuckled. "When I bonded with a newborn hatchling, TEAGAN, I was provisionally accepted into the clan. Begrudgingly."

# Twenty Four

Padrick sighed. "Forgive me. I really should check on DECLAN. Then, if you have a landline, I need to call my clan leader. He needs to know what's happened and that there are dragons in Scotland."

"Of course. You can use the phone in the kitchen," Erin said.

He glanced in the direction Erin pointed, then walked out into the lightly falling rain to check on his compeer.

When Padrick returned, he called Ireland. He filled in Sean on the explosion that led him to find Erin and all that he'd learned in the hours since.

Morgan came in the back door and halted when he spotted Padrick.

Padrick hung up and turned. "Erin said I could use the phone."

"Of course." Morgan's glance flitted around the room. "This is a bit awkward. I, um, live here with Erin."

"I see." Heat rose in Padrick's cheeks. *Are they married? She didn't mention it.* "I—"

Morgan interrupted him. "She helps me run the clan. She has a knack for organization, and along with her dreams . . ." He trailed off. "We're there for each other. We keep the clan running smoothly." His neck and face glowed a deep fuchsia.

"None of my business," Padrick said. "We'll get out of your way." He started for the door.

"Christ, man." Morgan lowered his voice. "Can you not see it? She's still in love with you."

Padrick turned slowly. He opened his mouth but couldn't speak.

"Erin was never in love with me." Morgan's tentative voice strengthened. "This arrangement is for the benefit of the MacKay clan. I thank the fates every day that she partnered a dragon from this clan and not one of our enemies." At Padrick's stunned look, Morgan continued. "I have feelings for her, strong feelings. I even love her, but . . . her feelings aren't the same." He shrugged, then shoved his hands into his pockets. "She's found a life here, something important. I don't want her hurt. I will feck you up if you mess with her."

"What has she told you about her past?" Padrick asked.

"Not much. I know she's from Ireland. I can still hear it in her voice, though her Irish lilt has faded over time. I rode with my father the day we found her in an alley. It was my first adventure as a dragonrider, as BOYD'S compeer. Erin was broken, beaten senseless." He yanked his hands out of his pockets. "I don't want her beholden to MacKay for that. She has more than repaid any debt she thinks she owes." He paused. "Will you take her back to Ireland with you?"

Padrick gawked. "She's a dragonrider. A Scottish dragonrider. If I know anything about Erin, it's that she takes her commitments seriously. I would never ask her to give up her position. And I don't know if her dragon would let her go anyway. Irish dragons are quite obstinate when their rider tries to go against what the dragon believes is their fate. I assume Scottish dragons are the same." He ached when he realized he and Erin were bound to their own destinies—on two different lands.

Erin called from the other room. "Are you finished with your call? We need to make some plans."

Padrick motioned for Morgan to precede him. Morgan shook his head. "I need to . . ."

"You need to lead your clan. Difficult times lie ahead. You and Erin must work together if you're to get through it," Padrick said. "You should join us."

"I don't think Erin needs me just now, but my dragon does." Morgan left.

Padrick shook his head and walked back to where Erin waited. His heart lurched when Erin smiled up at him. *Could she still be in love with me after all these years? Lord, I'm confused.*

He needed time to sort through his feelings. Yes, he felt love. But was it the youthful love of a young boyo just starting out in his life? Or a more mature love? After all, what did he know about the woman Erin had become? She'd lived a life without him, without their son. By her own admission, and by what Morgan revealed, she had endured some horrific things. She seemed to be thriving here in Scotland. *I have no right to mess up her life, even if I do still love her.*

Erin looked puzzled. "What is it? Did you get some bad news?"

"No. Sean sends a hello. You remember my best friend back in the day?" Padrick sat. Erin nodded. "Well, he's the Tuatha Dragon Clan leader."

Erin grinned. "Bet that just burns Kiely's arse. She wanted the position herself, or if not her, then you."

"I never wanted it. Sean's by far the better choice," Padrick said. "I have no problem taking orders, helping out in any capacity required. I'm not dictatorial like Mother." He blushed when he realized how that made his best friend sound. "Not that Sean is in any way like Kiely. In some ways, he's her exact opposite. Where she is rash, he is thorough. I try to balance him out, add some urgency to his decisions. I could never juggle all the egos he has to deal with. I'd more likely knock a few stubborn heads together than use diplomacy. I suppose with so many clan members, that's more of a problem here?" He raised a brow.

"Yes. Morgan relies on me for that—though not through force. I don't owe anyone, other than Morgan, any allegiance. Nepotism has no influence with me." Erin shrugged. "Perhaps that attitude is a hindrance."

Padrick inclined his head. "When did you take over clan co-leader duties?"

"After Morgan's father died fighting a clan skirmish. And after Morgan's dragon mated with mine for the first time. Morgan and I, we never . . . he's like a brother to me." Erin fell silent. When she spoke again, there was sorrow in her voice. "I had to give up my wish to return to Ireland and to you and our son. I'd been partnered with TEAGAN for over four years. That dictated that I remain here."

Padrick took her hand and held it tight. "I understand about duty." He closed his eyes tight, then opened them to hold Erin's gaze. "Why didn't you somehow get word to me? I would have moved heaven and earth to protect you. And our son."

"I was scared," Erin said. "I didn't know whom to trust." Erin pressed a hand to his cheek. "Remember, it all happened during the height of the Troubles, and I was Catholic."

"Your religion never mattered to me." Padrick turned his face to her hand and pressed a kiss on her palm.

"I know. But I had no way of fighting your mother. Or the times we lived in." Erin dropped her hand into her lap. "I agonized over what to do. Then, when Mother Superior spoke of the life Riley would have with his adopted family, I . . . well, I didn't fight it."

"Why not?"

"Life. Life got in the way. I had to do some things that I'm not proud of to survive back then. I had to pay the piper, and he wasn't lenient. I knew I wouldn't stand a chance of custody, even if my case went that far." Erin lowered her gaze.

Padrick lifted her chin with his index finger. "I'm trying to not judge you. I'm angry at the circumstances that brought you to that point in your life." He held her gaze. "I loved you, Erin. By God, I think I still do." He shook his head when she started to speak. "I'm very confused. And I'm not here to screw with your life."

Erin closed her eyes and breathed deeply.

"Morgan told me about your arrangement," Padrick said.

"He was here?" Erin glanced at the kitchen door.

Padrick nodded. "He left. Listen, I don't want to compromise your position. I just wanted to find you, make sure you were okay. Introduce you to our son. We need to be there for Christian. Maybe even become friends." He paused. "I've been in a relationship with

Meara. Though I don't know where we stand now. A lot has happened recently. She's a dragonrider and helps me with my leadership duties at Lough Gur."

"Kiely can't complain, at least not about you sharing your life with another dragonrider. Though not married?"

Padrick shook his head.

"Bet she's right pissed that you never made the relationship official."

"I stopped being under Kiely's thumb a long time ago. Mother couldn't control me when I was no longer under her roof. I avoid her as much as possible. And, my sister—you remember Tess? She gave Mother more grief when she fell in love with someone from outside the clan and moved away. She's quite happy."

"And you?" Erin asked. "Are you happy?"

Padrick lifted one shoulder. "I'm content. I'm the leader of the dragons that are based in the south and west of Ireland, in Lough Gur. Though we have lost four in the last year to the killer. Our son and Devan are based there with me. We're still short-handed, but with the leaps GRAYSON has made, we're not stretched so thin that Devan and Christian and I could not take some time to search for you."

Erin nodded thoughtfully.

"How about you?" Padrick asked.

"I learned I'm responsible for my own happiness. I'm useful here. And I feel far safer than I did before I partnered with TEAGAN. I can't complain," Erin said. "And I'm happy that you found me. You and our son."

# Twenty Five

Devan sidestepped a growing mud puddle as Morgan passed her and Christian in a rush. He didn't stop when she called out to him. She tentatively probed BOYD'S mind, searching for a setback, but found him still sleeping deeply. Whatever troubled Morgan had nothing to do with his dragon.

Devan rapped the bronze Celtic knocker against Erin's door. Christian stood quiet, brooding. Devan wasn't sure how to broach the subject of finding Erin alive and ensconced as a dragonrider with a Scottish clan. Before Devan could say something, Erin opened the door.

"Come in. How's BOYD doing?" Erin asked.

"He's sleeping, but the healer talked about moving him out of the drafty barn," Devan said as she and Christian entered. "What's up with Morgan? He stormed past us without saying a word. I wanted to try dragon-to-dragon communication between the two of you and TEAGAN and BOYD while his mental defenses are down."

Erin sighed as they joined Padrick in the living area. "My guess is he's overwhelmed, what with BOYD'S injuries, losing two dragon and rider pairs, and the confrontation with Sutherland and Sinclair."

"Having us show up during a crisis didn't help," Padrick said.

Christian grunted but didn't add to the conversation.

*"Ring Wearer, can ye hear me?"* GRAYSON bespoke Devan.

*"Yes. Are you okay? Has something happened?"*

*"I am well. I have news. The two dragon eggs are hardening. They may hatch*

*soon."* A moment passed before GRAYSON continued. *"When will ye return?"*

Devan sent a soothing mental caress to the drake. *"As soon as we conclude our business here. It shouldn't be too much longer."*

*"Hurry home. Ye are missed."*

Devan broke the mental connection, then interrupted the terse silence. "GRAYSON relayed that the pair of eggs should hatch any time now."

"That is good news indeed," Padrick said.

Devan nodded. "Yes, but . . . I'd like to get back tonight."

"What's the hurry?" Erin asked.

"The mating happened out of cycle," Padrick explained.

"What does that mean?" Erin looked from Devan to Padrick.

Padrick sighed. "The mating flight took place on the summer solstice, not Samhain." He paused for a moment, then raised an eyebrow. "How often do you have your dragons mate?"

"Whenever a female comes into season. There are usually two or three females rising at a time, two or three times a year."

"No wonder you have so many dragons in each clan. How many eggs does each mating produce?" Padrick asked.

"One or two dragonets per female," Erin said. "It's been this way ever since I've been here."

Devan leaned forward, clasping her hands together with her elbows on her knees. "That could explain the Scottish dragons' smaller size. Maybe even the lack of dragon-to-dragon telepathic communication."

"Meaning, what?" Erin focused on the younger woman.

"Just thinking aloud," Devan said.

Erin narrowed her eyes.

Devan threaded her fingers through her hair. "I meant that with so many mating flights and dragons, there might not be a need or desire for closeness between individual dragons." At Erin's raised eyebrows, Devan quickly continued. "And that didn't come out right. I meant that it might be difficult to trust so many dragons . . ."

"I understand," Erin said. "I still want to attempt the dragon-to-dragon communication. TEAGAN and BOYD have only mated with each other. At least get us started before you leave."

Christian stood. "I'll get Morgan." He strode out muttering about not wanting to hear the details his mother's sex life, even obliquely.

Perfect, Devan thought. Open mouth, insert foot. And by the shock on Padrick's face, she now had both of Christian's parents pissed at her. She hung her head and called out to DOCHAS for comfort. *"Will I ever learn to keep my thoughts to myself?"*

*"Why would ye want to?"* DOCHAS bespoke. *"Tis why we are compeers. Bonded."*

*"Yes, my sweet. I meant in my discussions with other humans, not with you. Humans are not as simple to deal with. They have complex feelings and emotions that twist my words or take them out of context."*

DOCHAS snorted. *"Humans fash too much over what is no' in their control."*

*"You're correct. But worrying is part of human nature. It helps us plan for whatever trouble might be ahead."*

*"Planning for an unknown problem does no' make sense,"* DOCHAS replied. *"But, I will leave human fashing to ye."*

*"Thanks,"* Devan bespoke, dryly.

Several minutes later, Christian reappeared with a subdued Morgan. They sat in a loose circle around the room.

"What do you need me to do?" Morgan asked. "Remember, I've agreed as long as BOYD'S in no danger."

Devan turned to Erin. "Let's have TEAGAN mentally call out to BOYD. His defenses are already lowered because of the anesthesia." Her face took on the blank stare of a dragonrider communicating telepathically. "He's waking, but he's a tad groggy."

Erin concentrated on her dragon. *"Focus on BOYD. Ask him how he's feeling."* She sent the request to her puzzled compeer.

Several silent moments passed.

*"I do no' hear BOYD. I have called to him, yet he does no' reply,"* TEAGAN bespoke.

*"Keep trying. Ask him for just his name. Perhaps he can't think clearly."*

*"BOYD, 'tis TEAGAN. If ye can hear me, bespeak yer name."*

Erin concentrated on Morgan, silently pushing her compeer's telepathic words to him. If only he would look at her, show some sign that BOYD might be responding.

Morgan continued to stare at the floor.

Devan's gentle whisper broke the strained silence. "Morgan, ask BOYD to open himself to TEAGAN. She's calling to him."

"I have been. I can barely get through myself. He's in so much pain," Morgan's voice broke. He scrubbed his hands over his face. "He needs more medication."

"If he has any more, he'll be too far under for anyone to get through, even you," Erin said.

Morgan jumped to his feet. "Feck the bloody communication. I'm going to be with my dragon. You can do whatever you like. Stay or leave. I don't care." He strode to the door and out.

The door slammed, its crash ricocheted in the silence.

Padrick cleared his throat. "I'm sorry."

Erin snapped her gaze from the door to Padrick. "What for?"

"For arriving unannounced. I think we—or more specifically, I—have intruded on your relationship with Morgan."

"Your coming here shouldn't affect any of that." Erin sighed. "Morgan's the clan chieftain. I'm the co-leader because BOYD and TEAGAN mated, not because Morgan's in love with me."

"Are you sure?" Padrick said.

Erin hesitated. *I've been clear with Morgan, with any man that had shown a hint of feelings, that I didn't want a relationship. How could I after what happened to me before being rescued by Morgan's father?*

"What about trying with another dragon and rider pair?" Devan interrupted Erin's thoughts. "Perhaps, the rider that reported there were no other survivors. She seemed close to Morgan."

"Noreen?" Erin shrugged. "I've always suspected she was in love with Morgan. I could ask, but Noreen tolerates me because of him. I'm still an outsider to her and most others here." Erin raised her hands, palms up when she noticed Devan's sympathetic look. "I hear grumblings, especially after incidents happen that I've dreamed about. Some suspect our hard times are because Morgan's da, The MacKay, found me and saved me—that I'm some sort of seer-witch."

"Good to know prejudice is alive and flourishing even in a society that includes the use of earth magic and dragons," Christian said, dryly. "No wonder they eyeballed Devan so closely when Morgan announced she could communicate with all dragons."

"I still want to give this dragon-to-dragon communication a go," Erin said.

"If your relationship with the others is tenuous, perhaps your dragon should try communicating with ROARKE or DECLAN," Devan said. "Maybe I can convince Morgan and BOYD to try with another dragon pair. Besides, someone should check on Morgan." Devan held up her hand to forestall Erin's protest. "I'm the logical choice—I'm not related."

"I don't want you wandering around alone," Christian said. "We don't know these people, and they turned hostile when they found out you were different."

Devan squeezed Christian's hand. "I'll be fine. I'm going to check on BOYD. Morgan won't be far away. Right now, Morgan knows BOYD's recovery is of foremost importance to me." Devan rose and headed for the door. She turned back before opening it. "Morgan needs to trust someone. Without trust, this whole endeavor will fail."

Outside, in the steady rain, Devan opened her mind to seek out BOYD. She headed right and passed several houses before turning toward a craggy rock formation. The Fraser and MacKenzie riders were leading their dragons through an opening. When she started to follow, Morgan intercepted her.

"What now?" He shoved wet hair out of his eyes.

Devan displayed her open hands. "I came to check on BOYD. DOCHAS and I have had success in keeping injured dragons calm." At Morgan's shrug, Devan continued. "How is he?"

"Resting, and out of the cold barn. His wing's bandaged and strapped to his body so he can't use it."

"How's his pain?"

"The medication seems to have numbed the worst of it. His speech is a bit muddled."

"And how are you doing?" Devan lightly touched his forearm.

"I feel like a fool. First, putting BOYD in harm's way with that stunt. Losing two dragon and rider pairs. Then, telling Padrick Erin's still in love with him."

Devan sputtered. "What?"

Morgan shrugged. "Erin paired up with me after my da was killed, mostly because I needed someone strong to help me lead the clan. She's not been in a relationship since she's been here."

"You mean—"

"Our dragons have mated for several years, but we haven't . . ."

Devan's embarrassment heated her cheeks. "Sorry. I assumed."

"Don't fash. It's the impression we give everyone." Morgan toed a pebble. "Da smoothed the clan's concerns about Erin, but after he died, there was a faction that blamed her for our tempestuous relationship with the Sutherlands and Sinclairs." Morgan led Devan farther into the cave structure to the alcove where BOYD lay sedated.

*"Can you get through to BOYD?"* Devan bespoke DOCHAS.

*"The burns and broken bits of the wing pain him. He is no' listening."*

*"I'd like to attempt communication between BOYD and another MacKay dragon. Can you penetrate the pain medication?"*

Devan listened to DOCHAS's soothing words to BOYD, then spoke to Morgan. "Will you work with Noreen and RHONA to test the communication?"

Morgan glared at her. "Can't you wait? BOYD's been through enough today."

"His mental defenses will be down with the pain meds. Now may be the best chance to get any of the dragons communicating with each other," Devan gently explained. "I'll monitor him the whole time. I promise it won't hurt him."

"If it didn't work with TEAGAN and BOYD earlier, what makes you believe it will work with RHONA?"

Devan inclined her head toward the injured dragon. "Do you think he doesn't feel your confusion, your turmoil? The strain between you and Erin affects his mood, just as much as yours."

Morgan grumbled under his breath.

"Can I ask you something—quite personal?" Devan once again brushed his arm. She didn't wait for his answer. "When BOYD and TEAGAN mate, what are you doing, if not . . . you know?"

Morgan's blush spread to the tips of his ears, but he wouldn't look at her.

"What I mean is . . . are you and Erin both mentally engaged with your dragons? In the same room? Connected in an intimate way, though not physically?"

Morgan continued to stare at his dragon and nodded.

"Even though you and Erin aren't . . ." Devan's last words hung unspoken.

"It's not that I don't want to. She's beautiful. And until recently, I'd never told her how deep my feelings run." Morgan clenched his hands into fists. "We're friends. Erin trusts me. Believe me, it took a while for that to develop. She confides in me about her visions. I don't want to feck that up."

"That's my point," Devan said to his blank stare. "Through everything, during the most intimate of times, you and Erin are in sync with each other. Our visit today changed that. Not intentionally, but you noticed Erin's shock at having Padrick find her. You said she's still in love with him. Seeing them together has struck you hard. Your feelings are clouding BOYD's thoughts, keeping him from wanting to communicate with Erin's TEAGAN."

Morgan shuffled his feet and gazed at BOYD. "So he's picking up on my confusion, my fear."

"Yes. That's why I want to try with another dragon and rider pair." Devan shoved her hands into her coat pockets. "Erin said she thinks Noreen is in love with you."

"What?" His glance was sharp. "That's not true. Noreen and I grew up together, like brother and sister."

"You are friends though, right? You trust her? Have a good working relationship with her?"

"I suppose. I've never really given it much thought."

"Would you have BOYD at least try with Noreen's RHONA?"

Morgan nodded, then pointed the way out to find Noreen.

Erin pressed her palms to her knees and addressed her son. "Would you and your dragon like to try the dragon-to-dragon communication?"

Christian shook his head as he rose. "Padrick and DECLAN would be better suited." Christian wandered to the window and stared out.

"Right," Erin said before shifting her gaze to Padrick.

"Give him some time." Padrick lowered his voice. "He's been on his own for so long, surviving as best he could on the rough streets of Dublin. Tied up with the wrong boyos when he was younger."

Erin drooped.

"I'm sorry." Padrick rushed to continue. "I don't mean to be critical. After hearing your side of what happened, I don't blame you."

"I do," Erin said. "I should never have given him up—regardless of your mother's threats, or Mother Superior's promises."

"What's done is done." Padrick rubbed Erin's shoulder. "We can't change the past."

# Twenty Six

Morgan sat in a corner of the communal dining hall with his eyes screwed shut. "Blast it all. I know BOYD is trying his best, how can RHONA not hear him?" Morgan opened his eyes and glared across the table at both Devan and Noreen.

"Keep your frustration in check," Devan warned him. "Your dragon can pick up on your feelings."

"I bloody well am! Besides, he can't hear me from here."

Devan sighed, then leaned forward and tapped Morgan's temple. "He can hear you perfectly well—telepathically. You're shouting louder than a thunderclap."

Morgan slumped in his chair. "Sorry."

"Don't apologize to me." Devan turned to Noreen and spoke in a whisper. leaving Morgan to apologize to his compeer.

*"BOYD, mo chroí. I'm not upset with you. I'm frustrated that my actions got you injured. And I'm . . ."*

*"Do no' fash. We have been through much this day,"* Boyd bespoke him.

*"That's no excuse. I've been out-of-sorts ever since the Irish dragons showed up."* Morgan rubbed the back of his neck. *"That's not quite true. It's more since I realized how tenuous my relationship with Erin really is. I have eyes, don't I? She's still in love with Padrick and, for sure, he's in love with her."*

*"But she 'tis yer mate."*

*"I'm not so sure that's enough. But let's get back to trying this dragon-to-dragon communication. Are you up for it?"*

*"Aye, but I grow weary."*

Morgan tapped the table, drawing the two women's attention. "Let's try once more. BOYD is getting tired."

"Right," Devan said as her eyes glazed over as she spoke telepathically to a dragon. "Remember, have BOYD and RHONA let down their mental barriers. They must trust one another."

Devan rubbed her temples, trying to relieve the pounding headache that had formed after the futile hour of no communication between BOYD and RHONA. "Okay, let's stop now."

Noreen snorted. "Mary, Mother, and Joseph! If dragon-to-dragon communication is this draining, you Irish can have it. My brain hurts."

"It isn't this difficult for you, is it?" Morgan narrowed his gaze at Devan.

She shook her head. "Not for me, but then I can hear all the dragons. And when I joined the Tuatha Dragon Clan, their dragons could already communicate amongst themselves."

"Cripes," Noreen said. "What's it like to have that many voices crowding your mind?"

"Disconcerting." Devan shrugged. "After a fashion, I learned to tune out the dragon speak that didn't pertain to me. Now I know which dragon is bespeaking me right away."

"How?" Morgan clasped his hands and leaned forward.

"Each one has a different timbre, a different tone, even unique word choices. I picture each dragon in my mind when I hear him or her. That helps me focus. It also helps that the clan is divided into three areas, with about a dozen dragons in each. I usually don't have to keep more than four or five dragons clear in my mind at one time."

"But you can hear our dragons. How do you know who is bespeaking?" Noreen asked. "I couldn't handle more than my own."

"BOYD was easy because he was in so much pain. TEAGAN and RHONA are quite different in their thought patterns, so within just a few minutes, I could tell them apart. The Sinclair and Sutherland dragons—I just got a sense of their anger, their emotions, more than honing in on specific voices." Devan stood. "Let's go check on the others. It might be time to try using some type of talisman."

The three headed back to the house where Devan had left Christian with his parents. The rain had increased, and Devan inquired after her dragon.

*"DOCHAS, my sweet, are you warm enough?"*

*"I am well. The weather is no' so different than home, yet I do no' relish flying in this."*

*"Hopefully the storm will abate. Or we can hold off until morning,"* Devan bespoke. She splashed through a puddle before following Morgan and Noreen through the front door.

"Any luck?" Devan asked as she entered the living room.

"No." Erin pounded one fist into the other palm. She shoved her jumper sleeves above her elbows. "TEAGAN can't seem to hear anyone but me."

"It's the same with BOYD and RHONA," Morgan said, then skirted around the couch. "Can I get anyone a drink?"

"Some tea would be lovely, thanks," Erin said.

Morgan nodded, then asked Noreen to help him in the kitchen.

Christian stood gazing out the large picture window, lost in thought. Devan went to him. "Are you okay?"

A negative jerk of his chin and he whispered, "I don't know what I expected—finding my mum. But I never thought that they would still have feelings for each other." He shifted his gaze to the couch where his parents sat next to each other, knees nearly touching.

"Have you had a chance to talk with Erin, alone?"

"Not yet. I thought if the dragon-to-dragon communication worked, it would be between the two of them and their dragons."

Devan clasped Christian's hand in hers, then they joined the others. "I have an idea I'd like to try. If you'll trust me."

"What?" Erin asked.

"Sean told us the clan pendant helped with the bond between rider and dragon and the telepathic link. I noticed the MacKay dragonriders don't seem to have a talisman of any kind."

"Of course," Padrick said. "Why didn't I think of that?"

"You were a bit preoccupied with finding Erin, saving BOYD, and dealing with hostile neighbors," Devan said. She squeezed Christian's hand. "Padrick gave your pendant to Erin first, who left it for you. Would you be willing to let Erin wear your pendant? Just as an experiment."

Christian reached for the pendant, holding it protectively before he finally removed it from around his neck and held it out to his mum.

Tears filled Erin's eyes, but none spilled over as she reverently accepted the silver dragon pendant and put it on. She reached for Christian's hand and held it. "Thank you."

"Perfect," Devan said. "Now let's have DECLAN bespeak—"

*"Ring Wearer!"* GRAYSON's frantic mental shout broke into Devan's mind. *"Can ye hear me? There is a problem with the dragonet hatching. Ye must come. Hurry."*

Devan bolted to her feet.

"What?" Christian grabbed her before she could run for the door. "What's happened?"

Devan blinked to shove the image of dead dragonets from her mind. "GRAYSON. The two hatchlings are in trouble. I need to go."

"Slow down," Christian said. "Tell us what's happening."

Devan took a deep breath and sent DOCHAS a quick mental command to be ready to leave. "GRAYSON is frantic. He said there is a problem with the hatching. That's all I know. Have you had any visions?"

Christian shook his head.

"Doesn't matter. I just need to go. Now."

"I'll go with you," Christian said.

Padrick rose. "Let me call Sean. See what's going on. GRAYSON may be exaggerating, in all the excitement." He headed for the kitchen and almost collided with Morgan carrying a tray filled with a large teapot, cups, saucers, and an assortment of biscuits.

"Bloody hell. What's the rush?" Morgan stumbled but managed to keep the tray and its contents from smashing to the floor.

Erin rescued the tray before answering. "There might be a problem with a hatching in Ireland."

Devan tried communicating with GRAYSON, to no avail. She willed her speeding heart to slow down. There could be any number of reasons why she couldn't reach GRAYSON. *Don't worry. Probably just distance limitations.*

Padrick came back. "Sean said they lost communication with the two as-yet-to-be-hatched dragonets and haven't been able to re-establish it. GRAYSON is beside himself and believes the pair are dying."

"How long has it been? Is it typical to lose contact like that?" Devan paced. "Oh, I should be there. I promised myself I wouldn't miss another hatching."

"Can't Sean just break the eggs and get the dragonets out?" Christian wrapped his arm around Devan's shoulders, halting her.

Padrick held up his hands. "It's been over an hour. And no, it isn't typical, so there is a definite concern. But breaking the eggs could injure the dragonets. The eggs have hardened to the point we would need a sledgehammer to crack them."

Devan shuddered. "I don't want to risk their lives. Not when I can be there in a couple of hours."

"Then we'll all go." Padrick turned to Erin. "We can come back once the situation is resolved."

"No," Devan said. "You two should stay. Continue working on the communication. Spend time with Erin, get to know each other. I'll be back before you can even miss me."

Christian shook his head. "It's near gloaming. You'll be flying into the teeth of the storm. You shouldn't fly alone."

"If it was you they needed?" Devan stepped away from him. "What would you say if I demanded to go? And don't you dare say something idiotic about the situation being different because you're a man." Heat suffused her cheeks. "I'm a dragonrider and can take care of myself."

Christian mumbled something she couldn't hear.

Erin interrupted. "I can have one of the Fraser riders guide you safely through to the coast. Then you'll just need to steer around some of the uninhabited islands, cross a bit of ocean into Northern Ireland, and you'll be there."

"That works," Devan said. Erin hurried out. "I'll stay in contact with ROARKE for as long as I can, then I'll contact FIONN." Devan hugged Christian and gave him a quick kiss. "I need to be there. This is what I'm meant to do—help the clan. I'll be careful, I promise."

Erin led a Fraser dragonrider past them and said, "Use the phone in the kitchen, Graeme, but hurry. Ms. Fraser needs to get going."

"Just need to check in with my family," the dragonrider said, then quickened his pace.

Christian walked Devan outside to her waiting dragon. "You watch yourself. I mean it. Be careful. We've stepped into more than just a little spat between neighbors. Keep in contact. I'll have Padrick call Sean and let him know you're on your way."

Devan nodded, then climbed up DOCHAS's foreleg and into the saddle. "I'll be back as soon as I can. *Is breá liom tú, mo chroí.*"

"Not bad, my stubborn Yank. You've been practicing. I love you too." Christian smiled. "Now go, alleviate GRAYSON'S fears. And hurry back."

The Fraser dragonrider returned and readied for flight.

Devan directed her compeer to follow the Fraser dragon and rider pair that leapt into the sky from the nearby courtyard cobblestones. She placed her hand over her heart, blew a kiss to Christian, and flew into the stinging rain.

# Twenty Seven

The Faerie Glen on Scotland's Isle of Skye was reputed to hold secrets—and more. Rick Hunter needed answers. When his fiancée, Devan Fraser, ran from him in San Francisco, he'd found her dual citizenship application for Ireland. Then using his investigative journalist credentials and his special assignment to Great Britain as cover, he'd traveled from city to town to village, scouring Irish police reports and talking to the locals. He heard fantastic tales of dragons and of an American woman, fitting Devan's description, at the center of it all. A news report that mentioned a possible dragon sighting in Scotland led him to this godforsaken place, even though he didn't believe in anything magical.

"Damn her," Rick muttered as he slammed the rental car door and made his way along a partially obscured path. "That mousy bookworm thinks I'm controlling? Thinks she's better than me? Wait 'til I catch up to her. I'll show her. Who does she think she is? Without me, she's nothing. She won't get away with leaving me. She's mine, only mine."

He trudged over tall grasses, gnarly tree roots, and broken bits of stone. He stumbled and caught hold of a tree branch.

Thunder rumbled overhead and the steady drizzle of the late autumn afternoon increased as he shoved the branch away from his face. It broke with a loud crack.

"Aye, have a care!"

*What the . . .?* Rick whirled around in search of the owner of the deep brogue. The wind increased and the rain slashed sideways, causing the broken branch to slap his cheek.

"Who's there? Show yourself."

When no one answered, he wiped the water from his face and surveyed the area. The glen stood quiet. Only the steady plop-plop of rain on his Macintosh broke the eerie silence. He continued his ascent over the bracken-covered ridge toward a flattopped rocky prominence.

"Castle Ewen?" he said when he spotted the peak above the tree line. "That can't be right. It's just a rock-strewn mound—not even ruins. The Scottish people have a few screws loose if they call that pile of rocks a castle."

"Watch yerself, boyo."

The hairs on the back of Rick's neck bristled. He ducked his head and glanced from side to side as surreptitiously as he could but still couldn't locate the speaker.

"Now I'm hearing things. What's next, a damn faerie? Ha!"

He hurried to follow the dirt trail around the ridge that descended into a boggy hollow. He skirted to the left, staying on solid ground, passed several cone-shaped hillocks, then halted.

In the distance, water cascaded over rocks with a deep-throated roar. The spray from the waterfall mixed with the falling rain, casting an ethereal image of a flying silver horse. He heard the voice again.

"Magic resides here, but only for the believer. Ye are no'."

Rick approached the waterfall. "Enough with the games. Stop hiding. Show yourself like a man."

"Think ye a man? A true man does no' gain pleasure from a woman's tears . . . or her fears."

Rick clenched his fists and shook them at the space between him and the waterfall. *Has that bitch been telling lies about me?* "I don't know who you think you are, but I won't stand here listening to some crazy asshole who refuses to show himself."

He retreated to the trail and escaped around the next hill. Ominous clouds so obscured the meager sun, he couldn't tell if it was near dusk. Rain fell harder.

"Where the hell is the path that leads to the rocky formation?" Rick grumbled aloud. "I just want answers, then I'm outta here."

"'Tis answers ye want, but nae answers ye'll receive." The voice came from behind.

Rick glanced over his shoulder, but he was alone. A few moments later, the path split. To the left were several hand-sized stone spirals laid out in the grass. In the center of the spirals, he could make out old coins and other bits of detritus that were the foolish offerings made by equally foolish and superstitious people. He took the path to the right, scrambling up the muddy, rocky trail. He hoisted himself through a tight opening between two boulders, slipped twice, and banged his elbow and scraped his palms.

"Fuck." His frustration grew as he neared the top. "Probably another wild goose chase. When I find that lying wench, she'll answer for this too."

He took a moment in the growing twilight to catch his breath, shake the rain from his sodden hair, and scrutinize the unique landscape. Scattered patches of ferns and rocks punctuated the grassy carpet. It wasn't like anywhere he'd ever seen. "What *is* this place?"

"'Tis the tip-top of the Faerie Glen. Me home."

Rick spun toward the voice and nearly slipped. An old man, dressed in black, sat on a boulder on the edge of the prominence, fresh and dry in the downpour.

"Who are you? Where'd you come from?" Rick stepped back, tripped, then fell on his ass.

The man leaned forward, pulled one knee toward his chest, and rested his foot on the rock. A wicked grin spread over his face, revealing razor-sharp pointed teeth. "I'm the one ye have insulted at every turn. I'm Cuillin, the Faerie Prince."

Rick guffawed. "A Faerie—"

Cuillin ground his boot heel on the rock.

Rick struggled to draw in a ragged breath. A crushing pressure seized his lungs. He couldn't move, couldn't feel his arms or legs. *What the hell is he doing to me? Am I dying?*

"I command the magic here and I come and go as I please." The man snapped his fingers and disappeared.

Rick blinked, clutched his chest, and felt his heart race as the pain eased. Pins and needles tingled in his extremities. He scrambled to his feet and brushed the mud from the seat of his trousers. "This is crazy. Someone's messing with me." He took a tentative step toward the unoccupied rock, but the pungent odor of ozone stopped him. "What the hell? Did I just imagine all this?"

He turned to start back down, but Cuillin blocked the path.

"Ye've trespassed. Why should I permit ye tae leave?"

Rick focused on the narrow path, then straightened his shoulders. "You can't force me to stay. Besides, I don't believe in magic . . . and certainly not faeries."

Though he saw no lightning, thunder boomed across the glen.

"Why are ye here if no' for answers tae questions that concern magic?"

"I'm an investigative journalist. I've heard about dragons in Scotland. I've come seeking the truth. Know anything about that?"

Cuillin raised one brow but said nothing.

"I demand you tell me where I can find the person who claims to be the leader of dragons." Rick pulled a crumpled piece of paper from his coat pocket and squinted at the barely discernable words. "I found this passage written in old Gaelic and had it translated. It says, 'Voyage to the Isle of Skye, Traverse the Faerie Glen afore dusk settles, Humble yerself atop Castle Ewen on Samhain, to find that which ye most desire.'" He stuffed the soggy paper away. "I've done what the cryptic passage instructed. I want—"

"Ye claimed tae no' believe in magic. What evidence do ye have there be dragons?"

A shiver skated down Rick's spine. He tugged his coat collar closed. "I have my sources, folks in Ireland and here in Scotland. They've said they've encountered the beasts. Now, answer my question."

"'Tis no' like I'm a genie granting ye wishes," Cuillin growled.

"I'm the Faerie Prince. And ye have nae manners."

"Then point me in the right direction and I'll leave you in peace."

"And what of the lassie? Will ye leave her in peace?" Cuillin leaned against one of the boulders at the path's exit and crossed his arms.

"She's not your concern."

Lightning slashed across the sky as Cuillin pointed a gnarled finger at Rick. "Ye lie!" Thunder punctuated Cuillin's words. "She's yer reason for coming here."

Rick stiffened. *He can't possibly know anything about Devan. He must have heard me, that's all.*

"Ye do ken what today is, aye?"

"Of course. I'm not an idiot," Rick said. *Though I might be losing my mind.* "It's what you call Samhain. That's why I'm standing on the top of this blasted mound of rocks, drenched, seeking what I most desire—answers."

"I ken the passage ye speak of. 'Tis no' correct in its translation." Cuillin pushed off from the boulder, yet moved no closer. "Ye mayhap should have come on Beltaine, no' Samhain. For tonight is when the veil between yer world and the otherworld is thinnest. Ye'll no' be finding yer heart's desire. Only yer own fears." Cuillin's moss green eyes gleamed as his wicked laughter rang clear.

Rick retreated, glancing around wildly for another way down. He spied flattened grass behind him and scrambled over the backside of the prominence. He slid until his foot caught a rock, then he tumbled head over feet. A thicket of ferns at the bottom stopped his out-of-control descent.

# Twenty Eight

Devan and DOCHAS followed the Fraser dragon and its rider southwest toward the base of the ever-increasing wall of cumulus clouds. Diffused gray light backlit the farthest clouds and thunder clapped. Devan shivered. While the magic kept her and DOCHAS invisible to all but other dragonriders, it didn't stop the rain from penetrating her Mackintosh and riding cap. *Perhaps I shouldn't have rushed off to Ireland. GRAYSON was probably exaggerating the trouble with the dragonet hatching. Or I could have accepted Christian's offer to come back with me. Too late now.* She huddled deeper into her coat and leaned against DOCHAS's neck to block some of the wind and rain.

*"Hope the weather stays to the north. I don't fancy flying in the midst of all that lightning,"* Devan bespoke her dragon.

*"Clan leaders FIONN and Sean will no' appreciate it if we are singed,"* DOCHAS replied.

As if to drive home the danger, three jagged lightning bolts exploded in rapid succession just off DOCHAS's right wingtip. The shock wave sent the dragon tumbling. Devan struggled to hold on and stay in her riding harness. Just as DOCHAS righted herself, thunder crashed. Devan dipped her head as pain pierced her ears. Everything went silent. Fear, jagged and debilitating, clawed at her stomach as she clung to her dragon. *Where the hell are we?*

Another lightning strike lit up the sky. Menacing dark clouds stormed and crashed into each other, pressing down on Devan's head. She ducked as the eeriness of a full-blown storm raged oddly silent all around her. *I've never heard of a storm growing this vicious so fast. Taranis, the storm god, must be truly pissed.*

*"ROARKE, tell Christian the storm is brutal here. DOCHAS and I might need to find shelter for a bit."* Devan telepathically called out, then waited for a response but heard nothing. She hoped her message was at least received.

She strained to see the Fraser dragon and rider they had been following—to no avail. All she could make out in the brief flashes that lit the sky were the gray clouds that seemed to be one with the storm-tossed sea.

*When did we leave land? Where's our guide? Christ, where are we?*

*"FRASER's dragon? Damn I don't know your name. Where are you?"* Devan mentally called to the other dragon. *"I've lost sight of you."*

The Scottish dragon didn't reply.

*They couldn't have flown too far ahead.*

And still, Devan could hear nothing—not the wind howling, not the crash of the waves, nor the storm raging all around her. No sounds in her head but her thoughts.

She searched ahead for a place to land where she could calm down and make sure her compeer wasn't injured. *"We need to find shelter until the storm passes. I can't see anything out here and I don't relish crashing."*

As another bolt streaked across the sky, Devan's attention lingered on a swirling whirlpool—a maelstrom creating a spiral effect on the surface of the boiling sea. *"Pull up! Pull up! We'll be sucked into that cauldron,"* Devan frantically bespoke her dragon.

DOCHAS beat her wings, seemingly endlessly, then finally surged forward and higher into the storm.

Devan heaved a sigh of relief. When she regained her composure, she resumed the search for a safe place to land.

"Over there," she yelled and pointed at a small, boulder-strewn island jutting from the roiling sea. Even though she couldn't hear, she spoke aloud to lessen her anxiety about flying with her dragon in a fierce storm over unfamiliar territory.

DOCHAS circled the island, buffeted by hurricane-strength gusts. She twisted her wings at the last instant to dump the air underneath. A wild gust wretched her right wing, and she hissed in pain. DOCHAS crash-landed, stumbling onto a grassy slope near a group of standing stones. She barely remained upright and managed to fold her left wing tight to her body to avoid tumbling with another shove of the wind, but her right wing hung awkwardly.

*"GRAYSON,"* Devan called to the Tuatha clan drake. *"ROARKE, can you hear me? DECLAN?"* After a few panic-filled moments, when none of the dragons answered, Devan whispered, "Hope it's just the storm."

She guided DOCHAS to the leeward side of a massive standing stone to wait out the nasty storm. Devan climbed down from her riding harness, fumbled with stiff fingers to un-cinch the buckle, and managed to pull the harness off her compeer. *Metal and lightning, not good together.*

DOCHAS stretched her injured silvery-blue right wing and rested it on the top of one of the standing stones. She used her triangular head to nudge a soaked and shivering Devan underneath, then used her body to block the rest of the wind and rain from her rider. *"Ye are safe."*

Devan slumped against the warm, scaly body of her dragon and gave in to her tears. Tears of relief that she could still bespeak DOCHAS blended with tears of fear because no one would know she was lost and in trouble. *Oh Christian, I shouldn't have been so stubborn. Wish you were here with me. I'm scared.*

After a time, the tears stopped. Devan dragged her riding harness closer and pulled her first aid kit from the built-in saddlebag. She found sterile gauze and placed a square in each ear then pulled them out one at a time. Fresh blood spotted both squares. Devan sighed as she tucked the makeshift bandages back into her ears. *Not much I can do about it right now.* She popped a couple of ibuprofen in her mouth, leaned past DOCHAS, cupped her hands to capture some rain, and drank until she swallowed the medicine.

*"You saved us. Are you injured, my sweet?"* Devan bespoke.

*"The lightning grazed my wing, but the rain extinguished the burns. The wind twisted it a bit, but do no' fash,"* DOCHAS replied. *"Yet I can no' bespeak the others."* Concern tinged the dragon's tone.

While lightning and thunder continued to crash overhead, Devan attempted to communicate with ROARKE, DECLAN, and GRAYSON. None of her dragon companions bespoke her. *Where is the Fraser dragon and rider pair? Are they hurt? Have they abandoned us?*

Time seemed to drag under the merciless pounding of the storm.

Christian watched his mother and father try for god-only-knew-how-many times to break their dragon compeers' telepathic communication block. He leapt from the couch. "Quiet. ROARKE has heard from Devan." His parents immediately stopped talking.

*"ROARKE, tell me again what Devan bespoke to you."*

*"The Ring Wearer spoke of a fierce storm. They needed to land,"* ROARKE bespoke. *"Then, I could no' hear her."*

Christian repeated aloud what his dragon said, so Erin could hear. He was sure DECLAN and, by extension, Padrick had heard ROARKE.

*"I continue to bespeak The Ring Wearer and DOCHAS, but there is nigh response,"* ROARKE's anxious tone rang clear to Christian.

"DECLAN can't reach Devan either." Padrick rose. "I'll call Sean and see if she's been able to bespeak either FIONN or GRAYSON." He awaited Erin's quick nod then rushed out of the room.

"It could just be the storm," Erin said, still clutching Christian's pendant. "Or Devan's too far away from us."

Christian shook his head. "If ROARKE heard her, then she's still in range. No, there's something wrong. I can feel it."

"Have you had a vision?" Erin asked as Padrick came back into the room.

"No," Christian said. "Has Sean, or any Tuatha dragon, heard from her?"

Padrick grabbed his coat. "No. And now he's concerned." He turned to Erin and clasped her hands. "We need to go."

"Absolutely." Erin handed Christian his pendant. "The Fraser pair would have stayed along the north coast for ten kilometers, then zigzagged to just south of the Isle of Skye to avoid clans aligned with Sutherland. And the clans along the southern coastal lands aren't allies either. Do you want a guide?"

"No need," Padrick said. "We should be able to pick up Devan's and DOCHAS's magical signatures unless the storm plays havoc with us."

"When you find her, please call to let me know."

"I will. I have your number," Padrick said. "And after the dragonets hatch, we'll come back. Definitely before your clan council meeting next week."

Christian rushed out the door, jumped aboard ROARKE, then gave the signal to fly.

ROARKE leapt into the stormy sky with DECLAN and Padrick close behind.

Rain pelted down, but Christian urged his compeer onward. *"Faster. Christ, I have a terrible feeling."*

# Twenty Nine

Graeme Fraser, temporarily blinded by the ferocious lightning storm, blinked the rain from his eyes and scanned the coastline below. Nothing.

REED darted away from a lightning bolt, nearly unseating Graeme.

*"Cuillen is in a fierce temper today. Wonder who the fool is that could have riled up the Faerie Prince?"* Graeme bespoke his dragon.

*"The Faerie Prince should no' waste his talents on intensifying this storm. It harms the citizenry and the dragons who fly,"* REED's tone showed his frustration with having to fly in such weather.

*"Doesn't matter. We'll be far enough south soon."* Graeme patted REED's neck scales. *"Nice bit of flying."*

Then Graeme blocked his thoughts from his dragon. *Where the bloody ifrinn is she? Could she have heard my thoughts, discovered my plan, and ditched me?* He shook his head, sending raindrops scattering from his long hair. *Not possible . . . unless the auld prophecy is true. If so, I must find her. She's our only hope to restore the magic.*

He decided to rendezvous with Liam. Graeme hoped his cryptic phone call message to Liam's friend had reached him. That way, Liam could help search for the Yank. He'd just have to break his exile. In this storm, no one would know.

Graeme directed his dragon around the whirlpool in the center of the Gulf of Corryvecken and onward to the cloud-shrouded, minuscule rocky island halfway between the isles of Jura and

Colonsay. The skerry that was too small to show on any map—that mysteriously thwarted the magic.

"At least the storm helped me steer the Yank and her dragon toward the skerry. We'll have some time before anyone starts the search for her. But will it be enough time to convince her to use her powers to help us figure out why the magic is dwindling from Scotland?" Graeme muttered before he guided his dragon to land.

Liam stood, hands on hips, at the entrance to his tiny bothy. "So, where is this 'thing' that I've been searching for? Why all the secrecy?"

"I figured you hadn't said anything about the prophecy or the loss of magic to anyone other than me."

"Right. My friend passed on your message when he brought me supplies." Liam inclined his head. "So, where is it?"

"It's not a thing, but an American dragonrider." When Liam didn't seem to understand, Graeme continued. "She's the Keltoi who comes from across the ocean, the one who can hear and speak to all dragons."

"Well, where is she?"

"I lost her in the bloody storm just as we left the mainland," Graeme said as he dismounted and removed his gloves to rub the feeling back into his icy fingers. "But she couldn't have gone far. I was able to change her heading before we were separated. Nasty storm. They're getting worse. Do you think it's the loss of the magic?" He started for the bothy to change into dry clothes.

"Where are you going?" Liam blocked the way. His upper lip curled in a snarl and spittle gathered at the corners of his mouth. "We need to find her. Fast. Before she's able to call for help."

Christian and ROARKE followed DOCHAS's flight path over Scotland, but it took a while to maneuver around the worst of the storm. They lost the magical signature once they left the mainland.

With the Isle of Skye off Christian's right side, he flew over several modest-sized islands scattered amongst the dozens of others that were nothing more than hillocks and jutting rocks harboring colonies of birds. He couldn't find a trace of DOCHAS's blue hide or silver wings. The torrential downpour continued, but the lightning had moved eastward.

*"They could be anywhere,"* Christian bespoke ROARKE. *"Let's land so we can plan our search."* Christian signaled Padrick his intentions and chose the island to his left.

ROARKE circled the tiny island then landed on a flat beach, away from the squawking clusters of white birds with black-tipped wings. Christian thought they were Gannets, but he'd never seen any this large. DECLAN touched down at the edge of the beach. The large birds swooped at the humans and dragons until ROARKE roared, then they dived into the churning ocean.

Christian waited for Padrick to dismount then pulled a map from his saddle pack. ROARKE spread one wing and Christian and Padrick huddled underneath.

"According to the map, that large island to our north is Skye," Christian said. "DOCHAS should have flown directly southwest from here to reach Northern Ireland, then on to Loughcrew." He sighed. "If they were forced to land because of the storm, they could be on any of the hundreds of islands that run along the coastline."

"So why isn't Devan or DOCHAS answering?" Padrick asked. "Were they knocked unconscious? Or worse?"

Christian raked his gloved fingers through his soaked hair. "I don't like this. We never should've trusted any of the Scottish riders."

Padrick cleared his throat but said nothing.

"Let's split up," Christian said. "We'll cover more territory and find them faster. We'll meet up before nightfall." He used his index finger on the map and tapped a fairly large-sized island directly west of Glasgow. "Here. The north side of Islay." He refolded the map and tucked it inside his coat.

They left the sanctuary beneath ROARKE's wing.

"We'll find them," Padrick said as he mounted his dragon.

Christian nodded, then climbed into his wet saddle and urged ROARKE to take flight. "I'll tear this place apart if I must."

# Thirty

Darkness surrounded Rick. He wasn't sure if he was blind or if he'd blacked out and night had fallen. Rain continued to pelt his upturned face. Pain and nausea washed over him in waves. He rolled over and retched.

"Ye'll no' terrorize the lassie again," Cuillin's voice echoed across the glen. "She's beyond ye. Devan's fulfilling her destiny."

Rick lurched to his feet and waited a moment to make sure his stomach wouldn't revolt. *How does he know Devan's name?* He could make out the darker shape of the rocky prominence with the help of the rising moon as he staggered toward his rental car. Several times he fell and cried out in pain but didn't slow his pace until he saw his vehicle. He sagged against the driver's door while he fished the keys from his torn trousers.

Jamming a key into the lock, he wrenched the door open and slid into the car's warm, dry interior. He slammed the door shut, rested his battered body for a moment, then looked in the rearview mirror. His blond hair stood on end, caked with mud, grass, and blood. Dilated pupils darkened his brown irises to black. A jagged cut oozed a thin trail of blood over the bridge of his nose.

He started the engine. His skinned hands shook as he gripped the steering wheel. "I took a tumble, it was dark. There's no magic in the world, no Faerie Prince threatening me. A good night's sleep, then I'll get back to searching for Devan."

"Go ye back tae America, for ye'll find nae help here." Moonlight outlined Cuillin, sitting astride a gleaming silver horse. He guided the beast across the road in front of Rick's car. "It'll be me pleasure tae ensure the lassie's safety from the likes of ye. Go now, afore I change me mind and drag ye under Castle Ewen—forever." Cuillin leaned against the horse's neck and whispered something. Shimmering wings unfurled from the horse's back. In two long strides, the beast took flight.

Rick shuddered and lowered his head to the steering wheel. "There's no such thing as flying horses. Or faeries. I'm hallucinating. Probably have a concussion. I'll be okay once I get away from this crazy place."

Rain pounded the windshield to the same staccato rhythm beating incessantly in his head. Lightning lit up the sky. Thunder followed.

He drove away as fast as he dared, but not before the crushing pressure returned to his chest, like a vise squeezing his lungs and stealing his breath.

Then he heard Cuillin's deep brogue one last time. "Ye will never find Devan Fraser. The lassie has found her family. Her true calling. We protect our own. Always."

I don't need this much trouble, Rick decided. "You can keep her. I won't be saddled with wacko faeries—or magic."

Graeme squared off with his brother-in-law. "For God's sake, there's a hellacious storm over the whole of Western Scotland. And the magic out here on these islands is sketchy at best. There's no way she can communicate with anyone. My dragon hasn't heard her since we left the mainland. For all I know, she's dead."

Liam shoved Graeme. "I need both the dragon and the Celtic foreigner who hears all dragons safe and unhurt. They must be found—before midnight."

"Why? What happens at midnight?" Graeme shook the wet from his hair.

"The prophecy says 'He who joins with The One Who Hears All before Samhain will command the power to control all dragons.' I must be that person. I must have the power. It's the only way to be released from this exile. With the Celtic foreigner's powers, I will control the Alba dragon council. I'll be a god!" Madness etched Liam's features.

Graeme stumbled back. "But . . . that's not what the prophecy says. It speaks of The One uniting three entities. One being The Exiled, which we assume is you. And there is something about power and restoring magic, which is why I redirected the lass here—where the magic is leaching away. Not for you to steal—"

"I don't need your holier-than-thou attitude. Find her. Now!" Liam spit out the venomous words, his eyes blazed with fury.

Graeme had never seen his brother-in-law this crazed, not even when Liam had been banished for killing Auld Alain and his dragon on Beltaine. *Was this what Merida had feared? Had Liam shown signs of madness before that incident six months ago?* Graeme turned away from the warm and dry bothy. *Think of clan loyalty. How far should I go for my family?* No answers came to him. He trudged back to his dragon, climbed onto the sodden riding saddle, and directed REED aloft.

"We'll find the Yank lass, deliver her to Liam, then be done with that daft bastard. I've done my duty to Merida. I found the person that might restore the magic and get Liam back home. Now it's up to him," Graeme spoke aloud, hoping his words would loosen the tightness he felt in his chest.

Graeme and his dragon circled above the unnamed spit of land that he had come to think of as Exile Skerry. He was about to direct his dragon toward the larger island of Colonsay when he spotted a movement near the standing stones.

*"Hover here,"* Graeme bespoke REED. A moment later, Graeme was positive he'd found the missing rider and dragon. *"Land on the flat just south of the stone circle."*

On the ground, Graeme cautiously approached the pair. He called out, but neither responded. The blue and silver dragon had her back toward him, her right wing stretched awkwardly, resting atop the shortest standing stone. He assumed the lass was staying dry under the dragon's wing. Not wanting to startle the large beast, Graeme raised his voice to a near scream to be heard over the storm.

The dragon's triangular head rose quickly and her neck twisted so her body and wing never moved. Her deep blue eyes whirled furiously, showing her alarm. She bared her gleaming, razor-sharp teeth in a snarl.

Graeme backed up several steps and raised his hands in front of him to show he was unarmed. *Christ, up close, she's so much larger than REED.*

"Ms. Fraser," Graeme yelled. "'Tis I, Graeme Fraser, your escort. I'm glad to have found you. Thought I lost you in that storm. Ms. Fraser?" His accent was more pronounced with his nervousness.

Several moments went by before a drenched lass with bandages stuffed in her ears emerged.

Relief swept through Graeme, followed swiftly by concern. "Are you hurt? And your dragon too?"

The lass didn't respond right away, so he pointed to his ears.

"Damn storm has damaged my hearing. Too close to a thunder-clap. And DOCHAS's wing was hit by lightning," the lass spoke loudly. "Why didn't your dragon respond to my calls for help? Where have you been?"

"I've been searching for you," Graeme shouted. No way would he mention the waning magic. That was for Liam. "Ms. Fraser, can your dragon fly?"

She shook her head. "DOCHAS wretched her wing, and she has several burn holes from the lightning strike. And please call me Devan."

Graeme approached slowly. "Will she let me look at her injuries? We need to get someplace dry before you catch your death."

Devan's expression softened and her eyes lost focus as she communicated with her dragon. "She says her phalange nearest the joint is too painful to fold properly. And the burns sting."

The disheveled and drenched lass rubbed her dragon's eye ridges until the faceted blue eyes slowed—the same way Graeme soothed his own dragon.

"I need to find the salve I have to soothe the burns, but I'm not sure it will help the wing joint. First, we need to get out of all this rain," Devan said.

Graeme jerked his thumb over his shoulder. "There's a small cave on the far side of the rocky outcropping that might work. Larger caves are impossible to get to without dragon flight, and my REED can't lift DOCHAS. Come on, let's go."

Devan ducked under her dragon's wing and emerged moments later with a leather riding harness. Graeme rushed to help her mount it on her dragon's back, in front of the wings. She quickly buckled the harness in place, then patted the dragon's neck.

The dragon listed like a drunk, one wing folded to her body, her injured wing outstretched.

Graeme led them to the small cave—a nook created from several massive granite stones crashing together during the Ice Age. He hoped the indentation would shield the Irish dragon. She was nearly twice the size of REED. *It's the best place. I can't leave them in Liam's care now that they're hurt. The gods only know what he'd do to them.*

He helped Devan cross the rocks made slippery from the storm. At the cave entrance, the dragon halted and ducked her head into the darkness. Devan scooted past her into the cave.

Devan emerged a moment later. "It'll be tight, but I think it'll work. DOCHAS will have to squeeze in sideways."

DOCHAS's eyes whirled faster, and she blew smoke from her nostrils.

"Come now, my sweet," Devan soothed her dragon. "You can fit. Then I will tend you, and we can rest without fear of the lightning."

The dragon scrunched into the cave sideways. Devan gingerly guided the injured iridescent wing clear of the rock walls.

Graeme scanned the horizon for any sign of Liam. With no one in sight, Graeme directed REED to remain outside, but close by. He didn't want Liam or KENNETH to find them. Graeme followed the Irish dragon and her partner. He found an old rag-wrapped peat torch within the cave and lit it. At least they'd have light for a while.

Devan had removed the riding harness from her dragon. She staggered and lifted a hand to her head.

"Are you okay?" Graeme asked.

"Just a bit dizzy. Probably from whatever's wrong with my ears. I'll be fine." Devan reached into one of the saddlebags and produced a small, brown jar. She opened it, scooped a glob, and gently rubbed the brownish, pungent salve into the wing joint. She repeated the process over six silver dollar-sized holes on the wing itself.

Graeme plugged his nose. "That's god-awful. What is it?"

"A special salve our healer makes. It works miracles on dragon-fire burns." Devan resealed the jar and wiped her fingers clean. She glanced at Graeme and his dragon. "Are either of you injured?"

Graeme shook his head.

"Okay. Can you help me with DOCHAS's wing?" Devan ran her hands over the wing joint. "I think we can manipulate it so she can fold it."

Together, Graeme and Devan gingerly rotated and massaged the joint until DOCHAS let out a soft huff as the wing folded.

"Do you think she'll be able to fly soon?" Graeme asked.

Devan shook her head.

*Damn. How do I protect them from Liam? The Irish riders are probably looking for her by now. Maybe I can intercept them and they can help. That still won't fix the waning magic. Christ, what a mess.* Graeme rolled his shoulders to ease the tension. *One step at a time. Tell Liam I can't find—*

"Good. I see you've found her." Liam's ragged voice echoed in the small cave.

# Thirty One

Christian and ROARKE had been searching for what seemed like an eternity but found no sign of Devan and DOCHAS.

"Where the bloody ifrinn could they be?" Christian blew into one gloved hand then the other in an attempt to warm them. His gloves were soaked and his fingers rubbed raw from holding the lead shank tightly. *I shouldn't have let her go by herself. It's not like I was bonding with my mother anyway.* Christian roared with frustration, and ROARKE followed suit.

Icy pellets battered Christian's face as the temperature dropped with the setting sun.

*"We have overflown this island twice,"* ROARKE bespoke. *"Are ye seeing something I am no'?"*

*"No. Just a feeling."* Christian tried to clear his mind, willing a vision to come. *Come on, Devan. Help me.* He struggled to slow his pounding heart. *Give me a hint on your whereabouts, a ghra. You're the first person I've trusted with my heart, my feelings. I can't lose you.*

*"Night is closing in. DECLAN is commanding us to meet as planned."*

Christian opened his eyes. *What fecking good are my visions if I don't have one when Devan needs me?*

ROARKE banked hard to the left. Christian had to press his thighs tight against his dragon's flanks to keep his balance.

Lights begin to pop on all over the larger inhabited islands. Clusters indicated small towns, while one or two lights showed a number of scattered homesteads.

Christian saw Padrick and DECLAN on a deserted, rocky outcrop on the north side of Islay. When ROARKE touched down, Christian slid from his dragon, his knees buckling.

"Whoa." Patrick lunged forward and caught Christian. "You're dead on your feet. Didn't you land once in a while to rest and get the circulation back in your legs?"

"No time. Devan's in danger. I can feel it."

"A vision?"

Christian shook his head.

Padrick glared at Christian. "You need to take care of yourself. And your dragon." When Christian didn't respond, Padrick rubbed the back of his neck, then continued. "I picked up a faint magical signature that I think was DOCHAS's—"

"Where? Why didn't you contact me as soon as you felt it?" Christian stormed over to a cluster of rocks. Using his teeth as pinchers, he worked his hands free of his sodden gloves. He pulled his map out and laid it over a waist-high boulder. "Show me."

ROARKE spread one wing over Christian and Padrick as they huddled together to inspect the map.

"Calm down. I just picked it up on our last pass before heading here. I can't even be sure it's them. And I asked DECLAN to bespeak ROARKE, but he couldn't get through." Patrick trailed his finger along the coastline on the map. He stopped and tapped a section of the mainland near the island of Mull. "I can't figure out why they would be this far south and still be on the mainland. It doesn't make sense."

"Maybe the storm made it safer to stay over land than out to sea." Christian scanned the map. "Christ, they could have been forced down anywhere along this bloody coastline. And we've wasted hours searching these islands." He pounded a nearly frozen fist on the boulder, unaware that the jagged stone tore his skin. "Let's start from where you picked up the magical signature—" He trailed the path to the end of the mainland. "To here. This point is also the closest to Ireland."

"But Erin said the Scottish clans that far south aren't MacKay allies. Why would the Fraser dragonrider lead Devan and DOCHAS into hostile territory?" Padrick leaned to get a closer look at the map.

"The storm may have driven them off course." Christian scrubbed his hands over his face, smearing blood along his nose. "We can't even be sure Devan and DOCHAS were still with the Fraser dragon and rider at this point. When Devan bespoke ROARKE, she didn't mention the other pair."

"DECLAN can't reach any of the Tuatha dragons. Either we're too far away or this storm's wreaking havoc with our communications," Padrick said. "Let's fly one quick pass along the coast, then get ourselves to Beaghmore. We can get in touch with Sean and set up a search party. I'll also call Erin to see if the Fraser dragon pair have returned. Maybe she's heard something."

Christian nodded as he folded his map and stowed it away.

Darkness enveloped them and the rain continued its onslaught as the two men mounted their dragons and took flight. When they reached the southernmost peninsula of Scotland with still no sighting of Devan or DOCHAS, Padrick directed DECLAN and ROARKE to cross the channel toward Northern Ireland.

"I can't," Christian shouted to Padrick. "You fly on. Bring help. We're going to keep searching."

DECLAN turned a tight half-circle and hovered in front of ROARKE.

"We've been searching for hours," Padrick said. "The darkness and the weather aren't helping. My eyes are burning. Yours must be too. We need to rest."

"I don't care how tired I am." Christian straightened in his riding harness. "I've got to find them. I won't give up on Devan. Not ever."

"I'm not asking you to, but you need to rest. Eat something to keep up your strength. Get warm for God's sake."

"Not until I find her. Don't you understand? I should never have let her fly off by herself. And if you weren't so caught up in finding and reconnecting with Erin, you'd have insisted on one of us going with Devan. You know it's true." Christian started to guide ROARKE back to the north. Once again, DECLAN intercepted them.

Padrick's usually robust face appeared pale and drawn. "That may be true, but I can't change what's done. I can only make the best decisions I can going forward. Not just for Devan's sake, but for you and the clan. Right now, you need to think about your compeer. ROARKE must rest, or he'll hurt himself. Then we'll be down a dragon in the search. Would Devan want you to fly your dragon into the ground?" Padrick pleaded. "You're so knackered, you could fly right over them and not even know it."

As if to validate Padrick's words, ROARKE suddenly plunged several meters. The green dragon struggled to rise. *"I am weary."*

*"Christ, I'm so sorry. I wasn't thinking. You should have told me . . . No, I should know better. It won't happen again. I promise."* Guilt seared through Christian. *"I just want to find them."*

*"We shall. But* DECLAN *and his rider are correct, we both must rest and gather our strength."*

*"You're right, mo chroi. There is still so much to learn about being a dragonrider."* Christian's shoulders slumped.

*"We shall learn together. As compeers."* ROARKE followed DECLAN across the black, storm-tossed water.

*"I'm afraid you'll need to be patient with me. I've only been responsible for myself. I'm bound to bollocks things up, either with you or with Devan."* Christian wrapped his numb hands in the lead shank, trusting ROARKE with his life, then closed his eyes and prayed to every deity he'd ever heard of to keep Devan safe.

*I'll find you, a storin. I can't live without you.*

# Thirty Two

Just inside the entrance to the cave stood a madman. His features were twisted and terrifying in the peat torch's dim red glow.

"Who . . . who are you?" Devan stumbled backward until she came up against DOCHAS. A deep growl started in her compeer's chest and vibrated against Devan's back. *Oh Christian, I'm so sorry. I shouldn't have been so stubborn, so self-righteous. I wish you were here with me.*

The man before her easily towered over six feet. His rough clothes did little to disguise his muscled breadth. Unkempt, his scraggly facial hair matched his grizzled face. But it was the air of madness that surrounded him that horrified Devan.

She glanced at Graeme and that seemed to shake his stupor.

"Devan Fraser, this is my brother-in-law, Liam MacLean," Graeme said. "Though he's clearly not at his best just now."

"So, you're the foreigner who can speak to all dragons." It wasn't a question. Liam's dark, beady eyes scrutinized Devan from head to toe. "Just a wisp of a thing, aren't you? But the Ancient Ones weren't much larger, I suppose. It'll make what is required easier."

"And what is that, exactly?" Though every fiber of her being urged her to shrink away from this man, Devan straightened and kept one hand on DOCHAS. *Be brave. Be strong.*

"What I must. Though it is distasteful for me to go against my marriage vows, it needs to be done if I am to control what is to be gifted to me from the prophecy." Liam stepped closer to Devan.

"Yes, that certainly clears it all up for me," Devan muttered.

Graeme started to step between Devan and his brother-in-law just as Liam backhanded Devan. DOCHAS used her talons to pull Devan clear and shot a mouthful of flame toward the two men.

Screams echoed in the cave.

"Stop! Enough!" Devan shouted. "You'll kill them." She raised a hand to her stinging face and tasted blood from her split lip.

*"No one hurts my compeer. No' ever. He is lucky I held back."*

Devan stared in horror as Graeme sank to the dirt floor. Liam stumbled backward through the cave's entrance and into the rain, his face and hair on fire. She scrambled to Graeme's smoking form and, disregarding her safety, patted the remaining flames that burned through the back of his riding jacket and shirt.

Graeme moaned and tried to sit up. His exposed skin was already blistering. A large patch of hair on his head was scorched and brittle. Devan gagged at the stench. She swallowed hard and murmured to Graeme to lie still.

A triangular head poked its way into the cave—Graeme's dragon. His eyes whirled fast, either in anger or fear.

Devan attempted to calm the smaller, yet no less dangerous, dragon, but found she still couldn't communicate telepathically with any dragon except her own.

DOCHAS snorted puffs of smoke at the rust-colored dragon.

"Hold yerself, REED," Graeme managed to croak. "I've no wish to be caught between two flaming beasts. She didn't mean to harm me."

Devan found the burn salve jar among her things and carefully applied a thin layer over Graeme's back and neck. She dusted the burnt hair away from the back of his head and dabbed at the new bald patches.

REED sniffed his rider. Either satisfied or repulsed by the salve's odor, he pulled his head from the entrance.

Relief swept through Devan. *That was close. No way do I ever want dragons fighting dragons.*

Without REED's body filling the cave entrance, the wind howled and the rain blew into the cave.

Devan shivered, but she wasn't sure if it was from the cold or the horror of the situation.

A moment later, Liam staggered in, beet red and blistered. Much of his mud-brown hair was now singed off. The skin under his eyes and around his mouth sagged.

"Fecking bitch," Liam slurred. "I'll kill you."

DOCHAS growled.

Liam backed up; blackened hands held out.

Graeme managed to roll onto his hands and knees, then push himself up until he knelt facing Liam. "Shut the feck up, ye bloody gobshite. Ye attacked her. Did ye not think her dragon wouldn't retaliate?"

Liam dropped his gaze to Graeme but didn't say another word.

"Your impulsiveness almost killed me." Graeme took a shuddering breath. "Remember why I brought the lass here in the first place. Get your head on straight before you start a bloody dragon war—"

"Wait." Devan interrupted. "What do you mean you brought me here? We had to land because the winds battered DOCHAS and she was hit by lightning. I don't even know where we are."

Graeme shifted so he could see both Liam and Devan. He grimaced but waved Devan away as she started toward him. "I'll explain. But first, can you put some of that medicine on Liam's burns? I don't want him to die. Merida, my sister, loves him. God knows why."

"I won't have that foreign witch touching me," Liam snarled.

"Don't be an eejit," Graeme said. He waved a hand to encompass Liam's head and face. "You're near burnt to a crisp. At least second degree from what I can tell. You could die. Is that what you want? Think of Merida and the bairns."

"I don't need this Yank for anything other than what the prophecy dictates. Once we mate—"

Devan snorted. "That's rich. You need physical contact to mate."

*Don't antagonize him.* She waved her hands in front of her. "But that doesn't matter because I'd die before having sex with you." She glanced at Graeme. "Can you believe this crackpot?" *What is it with wacko men? First Kelly in Ireland, then Rick in America, and now this creep.*

She shifted her gaze back to Liam. "The salve will help heal the dragonfire wounds, but it needs to be applied as soon as possible."

"But your dragon . . .?"

"DOCHAS won't interfere . . . unless you try to hurt me again." Devan started forward, then changed her mind. "You know what? Graeme can do it. He's your family." She handed over the jar, then bespoke her dragon. *"Keep on guard, but don't do anything rash."*

Graeme eyed DOCHAS, then slowly nodded. "Aye, perhaps we should go to the bothy. You can recover there, and I can borrow a shirt." Liam hesitated, his gaze on Devan before he grunted and exited the cave. Graeme nodded to her. "I'll get him fixed up, then come back and explain."

"You best get his head on straight. I don't know what's in some prophecy, but if he thinks I'm going to let him rape me, he's got more than a screw loose. And you, too, if you're in it with him." Devan fisted her hands on her hips. "What DOCHAS did earlier will be nothing compared to the fury the two of us will unleash on you. And remember, my friends must be searching for me by now."

"The prophecy doesn't say anything about mating. Liam's confused. I'll get him straightened out. There's no need for more violence. I promise." Graeme glanced once more at DOCHAS before heading out to catch up with Liam.

Devan felt dizzy and nauseous, so she sat with her back against her compeer. Her knees pulled to her chest; she rested her aching head on her crossed arms. Her ears were ringing. She fingered her cheek and flinched at the soreness that indicated she'd have a bruise.

*"DOCHAS, my sweet. How are you feeling?"*

*"My wing is stiff. I can no' open it. The salve has stopped much of the burning. I am quite weary."*

*"Rest. I will keep watch. Besides, I think the storm is letting up, so I'm going*

*to keep trying to reach* ROARKE *or* GRAYSON.*"*

*I wonder if my hearing loss is contributing to not being able to communicate with any other dragons? Or if it's this storm?*

DOCHAS lowered her head onto her outstretched foreclaws and curled her tail, effectively cocooning Devan. *"I did no' intend to flame the Fraser rider."*

*"I know."* Devan was careful to hide the guilt she felt at her dragon inadvertently injuring Graeme, someone who claimed to have her best interests at heart, though that remained to be seen. With no one to witness her weakness, she let her tears fall.

*I'm trapped on an island with two men I know nothing about, at least one other dragon, and* DOCHAS *can't fly. Be strong. I can't let them know how scared I am. Christian and Padrick are searching for me. I just have to hang on.*

*"I am with ye. Together, there is nothing we can no' endure,"* DOCHAS's sleepy voice whispered to Devan.

*"Rest, my sweet. As soon as you can fly, we'll escape."*

When Graeme returned an hour later, Devan pounced. "Where am I? Why did you bring me here?"

Graeme pointed to the cave entrance. "We should go to Liam's bothy. It may be small, but there's a fireplace and places to sit that aren't on a dirt floor. And we can have a proper supper."

"You can go after you answer my questions." Devan glared. "I won't be going anywhere without DOCHAS. Stop delaying, or I'll unleash my Irish temper. I bet there's nothing in your damn prophecy about how to handle an angry half-Irish, half-Scottish Yank, now is there?"

"No." Graeme, now dressed in a baggy shirt and cloaked in a tartan blanket, handed Devan the salve jar. "Thank you for sharing. I figured you wouldn't leave your dragon." He handed her an apple and two protein bars, then gingerly sat to her right. "That should take the edge off any hunger, at least until tomorrow." He glanced at the entrance several times. "I apologize for my brother-in-law. He's . . ."

"Bat shit crazy?" Devan tore the wrapper from one of the bars and took a bite.

Graeme shrugged. "He's lost it. Being exiled on this skerry—"

"What's a skerry?" Devan rubbed at her tender ears.

"A small, rocky island," Graeme said. "Anyway, Liam's been here for six months, away from his wife and bairns."

"Why?" She polished off the first protein bar and bit into the apple.

Graeme relayed the incident from the Beltaine festival at Lochbuie, The MacLean's subsequent proclamation, Merida's risky pregnancy and delivery of the twins, and his own sparse visits with his brother-in-law. "About two months ago, Liam showed me an old parchment scroll he'd found hidden in the stone walls of his bothy. The Keltoi Prophecy. I copied it." He pulled out a worn, folded piece of paper and handed it to Devan. "Liam asked me to help him. He thinks this is his chance to end his exile."

Devan read the scrawled words. "I don't understand."

"The dragon magic is waning. This skerry is now devoid of all magic. Even the standing stones where I found you aren't regenerating their magic," Graeme explained. "Liam believes, and I do too, that the prophecy was meant to be discovered in our time of need. And that you are at least one piece of the solution the prophecy alludes to."

Devan reread the prophecy. *Damn, it certainly could pertain to me. And to Christian. Is Liam the Exiled? But who is the Wronged? There's no way I'm telling this man about Christian's gift.*

"As you can see, there are words missing." Graeme pointed to the paper. "But it seemed likely that you—as the one gifted with hearing—could restore the magic. It's possible, and I haven't told Liam this, that Erin Casey is also involved."

"Erin? Why?"

"Rumors within the Fraser clan say that Erin has visions. She might be the Seer. The Fraser won't confirm this, but . . ."

Relief swept through Devan. *At least no one suspects Christian.* "So, now what?"

"I don't know. I guided you here in the hopes that between the three of us, we could figure this out. Maybe restore the magic before anyone else finds out there is a problem."

"Why not tell others? Perhaps get everyone working together to fix this?"

"You saw the confrontation between the MacKay clan and the Sutherlands and Sinclairs. This whole country is being torn apart because of clan feuds. Can you imagine what would happen if more areas lose the magic?" Graeme shuddered. "It would be all-out war. Dragons fighting dragons. Complete dragon extinction, just like in the prophecy."

Devan slowly nodded as she envisioned the massacre. "I'll help. But you've got to keep that madman away from me."

She yawned and her ears popped. Pain stabbed both ears, and she groaned.

"You should get some sleep. REED is guarding the entrance. He'll alert me if Liam comes round. I'm sorry I wasn't truthful from the beginning, but I didn't know Liam had completely lost his mind until I got here." Graeme laid with his burnt back to the cave wall and covered himself as best he could with the tartan. "I'll protect you. I promise."

"We'll talk more about this in the morning." Devan grabbed her saddlebags to use as a pillow and tried to get comfortable. Thoughts swirled in her mind, but she was so tired, they eluded her.

# Thirty Three

*Beaghmore, Northern Ireland*

The standing stones of Beaghmore came into view. Padrick breathed a sigh of relief. The storm had lessened the farther away they'd flown from Scotland, and he'd fretted over compelling Christian and ROARKE back to Ireland. It was the right decision, but Padrick couldn't help wondering if they shouldn't have done a more thorough search in the area he'd felt the magical trace.

*The boyo was right. I've lost my head since finding Erin. I've got to set my feelings for her aside, at least until we find Devan and DOCHAS.* Padrick shook his head, hoping to clear his mind and focus on what he needed to do next. *No more mistakes. Start acting like the leader you are. Analyze the facts and make choices based on those facts, not on emotions.*

As they circled the Northern Ireland clan compound, Padrick indicated ROARKE should land in the outer courtyard first. After the dragon folded his wings and lurched to the edge, Padrick gave DECLAN the go-ahead. For a weary dragon, DECLAN landed perfectly. Padrick dismounted as the Beaghmore leader's office door opened and Michael stepped outside.

"I'll call Sean and Erin," Padrick said to Christian.

Christian nodded as he leaned heavily against ROARKE's glistening body, then bowed his head.

*Right. Start by taking care of your son.* Padrick chastised himself. *Remember, he's only been a dragonrider for six months. He and ROARKE have never been pushed to their physical limits before. Guide them as you would any other dragon and rider pair.*

Padrick rested a hand on Christian's shoulder. "Take a few minutes with ROARKE to make sure he hasn't hurt himself, then meet me in Michael's office." When Christian didn't respond, Padrick continued. "We'll find them, but you must take care of your compeer. Understand?" When Christian nodded, Padrick headed for Michael.

"Damn. What happened to you?" Michael wrapped an arm around Padrick as he staggered toward the office door. "Are you injured?" He guided Padrick to a chair and eased him down.

"I'm not injured, just exhausted. I need to call Sean. Can you get someone to tend to DECLAN and ROARKE? They both need food and a warm, dry place to rest."

"Sean called, filled me in. Did you find—?"

"Not yet. We need fresh eyes. More eyes. And some luck. It's a bloody mess out there." Padrick reached for the telephone.

"I'll be back." Michael strode from the office and shouted to someone to prepare lairs for DECLAN and ROARKE.

Christian stumbled into the office just as the call to Sean went through. Padrick engaged the speaker function on the phone as he indicated Christian should take a seat.

"Sean. Christian and I just landed at Beaghmore. Any word from Devan?"

"No." Sean's voice floated out of the base of the phone. "GRAYSON's in a panic. He can't reach her either."

Christian cursed as he collapsed into the remaining chair.

"So no sign of her?" Sean asked.

"We caught their magical signature near Skye, then lost it. We thought it was because they were over water, so we split up and searched as best we could. There are hundreds of islands on the west coast of Scotland," Padrick said. "Just before full dark, I thought I picked up a faint flicker of Devan's telepathic plea for help, but it was farther south on the mainland. We flew another pass, but either we were too tired, or the magic had faded."

Padrick heard rustling and voices in the background, then Sean came back on.

"I'm sending Aisling, Meara, Aiden, and their dragons to you. Together with Matthew and KIERAN, you'll have your search party. BRIANNA will transport GRAYSON. Maybe he'll be of use since Beaghmore is closer to where Devan was last known to be."

"Hold off on sending Meara." Padrick rubbed his forehead.

"Why? This doesn't have to do with you finding Erin does it?"

"No. Meara's more valuable leading the Lough Gur dragons. Especially since that area's going to be shorthanded again." Padrick glanced at Christian. "There's no way Christian and I will return until we find Devan."

Christian nodded but didn't say anything.

"Besides," Padrick continued, "Meara's been flying with Braeden since his wife's murder and he's finally adapting to his new life without Mary. I don't want to interrupt his progress or the way he's bonded with Meara." *It's not about my tentative relationship with Erin. It isn't. We're both committed to our dragons and the clans we've each sworn to protect. Regardless of our personal feelings.*

Sean broke into Padrick's self-recriminations. "Okay, I'll keep Meara in charge at Lough Gur. But have Michael send another team with you. I want no one flying alone."

"Right. I'm going to call Erin to see if she's heard anything from Devan's escort," Padrick said. "DECLAN and ROARKE need rest, as do Christian and I. We'll be ready to go at first light."

"I'm ready now," Christian said. "I can ride with Matthew."

"I want to use a search grid. With six rested dragons, we can move faster and cover more ground," Padrick said. "You'd be no good to the search team if you can't keep your eyes open. You might be our best hope of finding Devan, but you must be alert. Also, I need you to sleep."

"Why?" Christian pushed his hands through his wet hair.

"Have you ever had visions while awake?" Padrick asked his son. Christian shook his head. "That's why you need to sleep. I'm hoping you'll have a vision that will give us some clue as to where Devan and DOCHAS might be."

"I hadn't thought of that," Christian said.

"You're too knackered. It fogs the brain," Padrick told Christian, then slapped his own forehead and spoke to Sean. "Speaking of a fogged brain, what's the word on the hatchlings?"

"GRAYSON was so insistent they were in danger, I had the healer break their shells."

"Are they all right?" Padrick asked.

"Yes, but . . ."

Padrick leaned forward. "But what?"

"Both dragonets are smaller than we've ever had before. And both are pure white with red irises. Timothy called them albinos."

"Wow. I've never heard of such a thing. Is that why they stopped communicating?"

"I don't know," Sean said. "Once their shells were broken, GRAYSON was able to communicate with them again. Our best guess was they were too tired trying to break free, so they ignored GRAYSON. Timothy examined them and found no other anomalies. REGAN named them ANNE and STRUAN."

"That's good." Padrick sat back in his chair. "I'll be in touch if there's any news from Erin. We'll be awaiting your contingent of dragons and riders."

"Expect them at dawn. Safe flight. *Eitilt sábháilte,*" Sean said before Padrick ended the call.

Padrick gazed at Christian. "Why don't you check with Michael for some dry clothes and some supper for us?"

Christian nodded and pulled himself from the chair.

After the office door closed, Padrick rubbed his face hoping to revive himself. He pulled a scrap of paper out of his coat and punched in the numbers that would connect him to Erin. *Please let her have some good news.* She answered on the fourth ring.

"It's me. Christian and I are at Beaghmore. Has the Fraser dragon and rider pair returned yet? Any word on Devan and her dragon?"

"No," Erin said. "And I'm starting to worry. Graeme Fraser should have returned by now."

Padrick told Erin of his failure in finding Devan and the confusion of the second faint dragon signature. "You said the clans to the far south are not allies. So who are they?"

"That would be clans Donald and Campbell. They are enemies of each other." Erin's tone indicated disgust. "The Campbell's territory is between where you think you felt DOCHAS's signature and Donald territory. Graeme would not steer Devan and DOCHAS that far south. He wouldn't even have dared to cross into Campbell territory by himself."

"Bloody hell. And I thought the Tuatha Dragon Clan politics were complicated." Padrick rubbed the back of his neck. "We need to rest for a bit. ROARKE isn't even two years old yet and we pushed him too far today. My fault. I keep forgetting Christian didn't grow up around dragons, so he doesn't know his dragon's limitations. Anyway, Sean is sending a few dragons and riders up from Loughcrew. I'll work out a search grid. We'll get a fresh start at dawn. Is there someone in the area that you trust who can work with me?"

"I'll get in touch with MacKenzie and Fraser, see if they can help."

"Is it possible the Fraser rider would have just gone back to his own clan after leaving Devan, without sending word to you?"

"No. Graeme is very conscientious. He wouldn't consider his task complete without reporting back here. Besides, the rest of his flight wing is still serving as protection against the Sutherlands and the Sinclairs," Erin said. "The storm's been a nasty bitch. Maybe Graeme and Devan had to land for safety. I'm sure he'll do everything in his power to keep Devan and DOCHAS safe."

Of course, Padrick thought, that's only if Graeme Fraser was still with them when they went missing.

"I'll give you a call back as soon as I talk to the two chieftains."

"Thanks. We'd appreciate any help we can get."

There was silence on the other end of the phone line before Erin spoke. "How's our son handling this?" Her voice trembled.

"He's blaming himself. And me. Rightfully so."

"Why?"

Padrick leaned back in the chair and rubbed his eyes. "One of us should have gone with Devan."

"If anyone's to blame, it should be me for monopolizing your time and dragging you into our stupid clan feud. Besides, if I recall correctly, Devan was adamant about going by herself and allowing the two of you to stay here with me."

"Yes, and she's no pushover. But their relationship is still new, so Christian is very protective of her. He has been since I've known him." Padrick straightened. "I got caught up in seeing you again. To be honest, I let my feelings overrule my leadership."

"How?"

*Was that hope in Erin's voice? Don't go there. Concentrate on finding Devan and her dragon.* Padrick pulled his thoughts back to the conversation. "When we were searching for the killer last spring, Sean and I laid down the law, no dragon and rider pair flies alone. I broke that policy. And the worst part is I did it for selfish reasons. I wanted the time with you. If something's happened to Devan and DOCHAS, I'll never forgive myself."

"We'll find them. I'm sure there's a reasonable explanation for what's happened," Erin said. "Get some rest. I'll get back in touch as soon as I have more information." She paused and her voice softened. "Tell our son—"

"I'm sure he knows. I'll await your call. Thanks, Erin." Padrick hung up as Michael and Christian entered. Both men carried trays filled with steaming bowls of Shepherd's Pie and buttered slices of fresh baked brown bread.

Michael set a tray on the desk. "Your dragons have been fed and settled. Eat up. I'll find you both some dry clothes." He spared Padrick and Christian a meaningful glance, then hustled out the door.

Christian waited until the door closed before inclining his head toward the telephone. "I take it there's no word yet."

"Erin hasn't heard from the Fraser dragonrider, Graeme. She gave me a bit more background on the clans in the area and believes Graeme wouldn't have stayed over the mainland that far south because of who inhabits that territory. She's going to contact the two chieftains that we met earlier to find out if they've heard anything. And to see if they would be willing to provide us a contact person for our search tomorrow."

"I don't trust them."

"Who?"

Christian shoved a hand through his disheveled hair. "Any of them. Devan's got a talent that any nefarious eejit would love to exploit. The tension at the MacKay compound was palpable. I wouldn't put it past any of them to use Devan to seize control. If you ask me, the Fraser chieftain was a little too interested in Devan. For all we know, this Graeme Fraser kidnapped her."

Padrick nearly choked. He held up a hand until he swallowed the spoonful of food in his mouth. "But no one could have predicted we'd show up. Or that GRAYSON would bespeak Devan and she would insist on returning to Ireland alone. No. It's more likely the storm forced them to land. Besides, we don't know if Graeme was even still with Devan. Or why she can't communicate with anyone?"

Christian brooded. His food sat untouched.

"You should eat. You'll need energy for tomorrow." Padrick picked up his spoon and made a point of eating, even though he'd lost his own appetite now that he'd thought about all the possibilities. *Damn. I hope Devan's not caught in some fecking clan conflict.*

"I'm going to check on ROARKE. Probably catch some sleep on the bed in his lair. Wake me if there's any news." Christian grabbed his tray and stormed from the office.

*"DECLAN, please keep an eye on Christian and ROARKE. Make sure they don't sneak off. Maybe ask Matthew and KIERAN to keep watch as well."*

*"Aye,"* DECLAN bespoke Padrick. *"ROARKE will no' be ready to fly until the sun rises again. I will bespeak KIERAN. We will watch over the young ones. Do no' fash."*

*"We've got to find Devan and DOCHAS safe. If we don't, I'm not sure I can keep Christian from causing an international incident. Or worse, exposing the secret of the dragon clan in his search for them."*

*"DOCHAS and The Ring Wearer are still here. We would know if either was gone."*

*"How do you know that for certain?"* Padrick asked, intrigued.

*"I do no' understand the mechanics of how we dragons know, yet the certainty of that knowledge has been in my mind since The Ring Wearer and DOCHAS paired on Beltaine. It is as though we can sense their mingled spirits in this plane of existence, though I can no' determine their exact location."*

*"So it's not something the dragons can do with anyone?"*

*"Nigh. Only with The Ring Wearer and DOCHAS. It is the reason I know they will be rescued."*

Padrick was disappointed that his compeer couldn't pinpoint even a place to start the search, but he hid his dismay. *"Maybe you should reinforce that notion to ROARKE and have him comfort Christian."*

*"Aye. Sometimes I forget the yearling is so inexperienced. I will reassure him. Now I must rest. Ye should as well."*

*"I'll try."* Padrick shoved the remainder of his food across the desk and waited impatiently for Erin to call back. "You're not such a great father so far," he chided himself. "But that stops now."

The phone rang and Padrick rushed to answer it.

"It's Sean. Are you alone?"

"Yes. What's up?"

"Sergeant Finley just called. Apparently Logan Walsh and his man, Kelly, have been spouting off to anyone who'll listen about a government cover-up having to do with a wild, talon-clawed creature."

Padrick rubbed the back of his neck. "Bollocks!"

"The superintendent and I are handling it. I wanted you to know without Christian hearing. He's got too much to worry about without this added stress," Sean said. "The good news is Logan's managed to continue his crime spree while in gaol. He got caught and is now in solitary confinement."

"Maybe that'll stop the rumors, but you'd better have another explanation ready. You know the media will be all over a story like this. Nothing better than administrative or political corruption to boost ratings." Padrick sighed. "God, I'm so cynical."

"Check in tomorrow," Sean said before he hung up.

When Michael returned with a stack of dry clothes, Padrick asked him to find a detailed map of Scotland's western coast and the numerous islands from Skye to the southern tip that lies just across the channel from Northern Ireland.

After changing into the borrowed clothes, Padrick studied the map, working out a search grid. Just about done, and the phone rang.

"Yes?"

"It's Erin. No word from Graeme, but I have a contact that's familiar with the area. A MacLean dragonrider. The MacLean's are loosely linked with the Frasers via several marriages. He'll meet you on the westernmost tip of the Isle of Mull about eight o'clock."

Padrick found the island of Mull on his map and marked the location for tomorrow's rendezvous. "Listen. I hate to ask, but how trustworthy is the Fraser clan chieftain?"

"I'd trust him with my life. Why?"

"Christian thought he was a bit too interested in Devan," Padrick said. "I didn't notice. I just figured he took an interest because they shared the same last name."

"That's all I picked up on. I've known Fraser for a long time now. He was mates with Morgan's father."

"I'm sure Christian's just overthinking it because he's so worried. I'll call before we head out for the search. If you find out anything while we're out, call Michael at this number. He'll try to get in contact with me."

"Be safe, Padrick. You and our son." He heard the wistfulness now, and a bit more of the Irish lilt in her voice.

"Will do," Padrick said, then he hung up and returned to his search grids. He focused on the area where he'd thought he felt something. "Hang in there, Devan. We're coming for you."

# Thirty Four

Christian wanted nothing better than to chuck the tray of food against a wall, but he restrained himself. The act might relieve his frustration, but it wouldn't bring Devan back to him. He stormed into the grassy mound that housed the dragon lairs and found ROARKE curled on the dry hay, snuffling softly in his sleep.

"Sure, leave me raging and nowhere to vent," Christian muttered as he set his tray on the cot next to a pile of dry clothes. He sighed. *It's not ROARKE's fault. I'm the one who should have insisted on accompanying Devan. To hell with hanging around my parents. And wasn't that awkward? I don't know what I expected anyway. Some loving reunion?* He peeled off his wet clothing, tossed them in a heap by the entrance, then put on the borrowed pants.

Christian sat on the cot and picked at the Shepherd's Pie. When he couldn't eat any more, he placed the tray outside the lair, moved the rest of the clothes to the end of the cot, and climbed under the covers.

He tried to clear his mind but was still too stirred up. He punched the pillow and flopped back down.

ROARKE interrupted Christian's pity party. *"Do no' fash. DECLAN says he knows DOCHAS and The Ring Wearer are out there somewhere."*

*"How can he possibly know that?"*

*"It is more a sense we dragons have, ever since the Chosen Ceremony on Beltaine. We are connected to The Ring Wearer. Though we can no' determine her location."*

*"She could still be hurt,"* Christian bespoke. *"And that doesn't explain why we've lost communication with her."*

*"That is a question for when we find her. For now, ye need sleep. And so do I."*

Christian rolled onto his side and snuggled deeper into the warm bedding. Sleep finally came and a vision enveloped him.

*Rage flooded his bloodstream as he spied* REED *through the binoculars. "That fecking waste of air. I send him to find the lass, and where is he? Holed up in a bloody spit of a cave." He tossed the glasses on the makeshift kitchen counter and slammed out of the bothy. "Looks like I have to do everything around here."*

*He slipped and fell several times on his way to the south side of the skerry, but his fury fueled him.*

*When he stepped into the dimly lit cave, he saw an enormous blue dragon with silver wings folded against her back. The beast had to hunch down due to the low ceiling. A wisp of a lass stood in front of it, which made the dragon appear even larger.*

*In the dimness, he spotted movement off to his right, knew it was his traitorous brother-in-law, but he couldn't take his eyes off the behemoth.*

*"Good. I see you've found her." His voice echoed off the cave walls.*

*"Who are you?" The lass stuttered and fell back against the beast. It growled—a deep, menacing sound that reverberated through his body and soul.*

*He heard the deep rumble of words, but he was still fending off his shock at the size of the dragon to pay any attention.*

*Words came and went from his mind. He wasn't sure if he spoke them aloud, but when the lass snarked at him, he backhanded her. The sting reverberated up his arm.*

*Flames spewed forth from the dragon's enormous maw.*

*Pain! Screams. Searing agony.*

*He stumbled backward and flailed to put out the flames. When he felt the rain, he lifted his seared face skyward. Needles of rain stung his tortured skin. Agony spread white-hot over his face and head. He was too scared to pat his cheeks to see if the fire was out, so he let the rain pummel him until numbness set in. Finally, he lowered his head and tried to open his eyes. His eyelids felt gummy and stuck. He forced them open and found his vision clouded.*

*The wind blew strong, billowing his sodden shirt. He shuddered. His heartbeat drummed in his ears. He forced an unsteady hand to his head but pulled it away when his fingers found hot, bumpy skin. Disregarding the pain, he staggered back into the cave.*

*"Fecking bitch," he screamed. "I'll kill you."*

*The fiery dragon snarled.*

*Can't think straight, he thought. Concentrate. I need her. But how am I to fulfill my destiny, fulfill the prophecy, if the foreign bitch is protected by such a beast? I'll find a way. I have to.*

*More nonsense spewed from the traitor's mouth as he knelt, his back scorched from dragonfire. The man wanted the bitch to put medicine on my face.*

*No way in hell am I trusting her to touch me. At least not until I'm ready to fulfill my duties of the prophecy.*

*The numbness began to fade and the searing pain returned. He didn't know if he responded aloud or in his mind.*

*I've got to get out of here.*

*The dragon shifted and drew his attention. Fear surpassed his anger.*

*Retreat, he decided. I'll find a way to end this exile.*

Christian gasped and yanked himself from the vision. He sat up and scrubbed the sleep from his face. He squinted at the muted glow of his wristwatch, just past four o'clock.

ROARKE was still sleeping, though his tail twitched and his neck ridges bristled.

Christian pulled back the covers and noticed the pile of his clothes, dry and folded, next to where he'd kicked off his boots last night. He dressed and reminded himself to thank Michael for taking care of his compeer and himself.

While he laced up his damp boots, he ran through the dream in his mind. He didn't want to forget any clue to where Devan was. He went in search of Padrick.

Christian found his father in Michael's office, chatting with the clan leader. Sean's son, Matthew, poured mugs of steaming coffee and passed one to Christian.

"Thanks." He sipped the delicious brew then turned to Michael.

"And thank you for taking such good care of ROARKE and me."

"It was the least we could do," Michael said as he stood. "I'll tell the cook to start breakfast. The Loughcrew dragons and riders will be here soon. Matthew can help ready your dragons."

The two Beaghmore riders headed out the door.

Padrick inclined his head at the empty chair as he sipped his coffee.

"I had a dream, a vision. Devan and DOCHAS were in a small cave. It's a bit myopic."

"What do you mean?"

"As with my dreams of the Irish dragon killer, I see things from someone else's point of view." Christian rubbed his chest where his pendant lay against his skin and thought back to when Erin was describing how she dreamed of the oilrig explosion. "My visions are different than Erin's in that respect. That's not important." He waved the wayward thought away. "I envisioned Devan and DOCHAS through the eyes of someone else. And I believe they're both hurt."

"Why?"

"Devan had cotton or something stuffed in her ears and DOCHAS's right wing was tight to her body at an awkward tilt. Burn holes ravaged her wings." Christian relayed the rest of the dream to Padrick.

Michael entered with Aisling.

"Oh," Aisling said when Christian suddenly fell silent. "You've had a vision, then?"

Christian started in his chair. He took a deep breath. "Yes, for all the good it did. They're in a cave somewhere. A rocky landscape. It was dark and raining." He rubbed the back of his neck. "Hell, that could be hundreds of places. Maybe thousands."

"Any lights?" Padrick asked.

"A dim glow inside the cave. I think it was from a torch of some kind, it flickered like a flame in the fireplace."

"And you saw only Devan?" Padrick asked. "Besides the angry person whose point of view you were seeing through?"

Christian shook his head. "Someone else was there. Someone the angry person thought was a traitor. But I couldn't get a clear visual or hear a voice. It was like a distorted film."

"Breakfast is ready," Michael said. "Perhaps you can relate your vision to us all over a hot meal. Maybe it will help in the search."

"You aren't going with us?" Padrick asked as he stood.

"No," Michael said. "Sean wants me here with GRAYSON to communicate with you. Matthew, Ryan, and their dragons will round out your team."

Padrick nodded then led the way to the communal dining hall where Christian relayed his vision once everyone was settled.

As the sun peaked over the horizon to collide with the lingering storm clouds, Padrick spread the map over the table. He pointed to three overlapping grids that covered the coastline of the mainland and all of the islands west of Scotland. He assigned responsibilities to each two-person, two-dragon team.

"We'll fly together to this location." He tapped the spot on the Isle of Mull where the MacLean rider was to meet them. "We'll adjust as necessary. Your dragons are to check in with DECLAN at least every hour. Understood? No lone dragonrider." He made extended eye contact with Christian, then folded his map. "Gear up. The weather is rain. Pack extra energy bars. When we find Devan, she may need food. I've got a phone call to make, so we leave in ten minutes."

Christian grabbed extra food from the kitchen's walk-in pantry. He found GRAYSON nuzzling up to ROARKE.

"I'll find her and bring her home," Christian said aloud as he rubbed the drake's snout. GRAYSON leaned into Christian's hand.

*"The Wingless One says to fly safe and hurry back with The Ring Wearer and DOCHAS,"* ROARKE bespoke Christian.

He climbed aboard his compeer as Padrick exited Michael's office.

"No word from Graeme Fraser, I'm afraid," Padrick said. He swung onto his dragon, fisted his hand into the air, then gave the signal to take flight.

After DECLAN launched into the air, it was ROARKE's turn. Christian gave a silent command. ROARKE spread his sea-green wings to their full extension, bent his powerful legs, and leapt into the air with one swift downstroke. His next wingbeat increased their altitude by several meters, allowing him to catch an updraft before veering toward the east.

The other dragons quickly followed. Though they flew toward the rising sun, the late autumn skies were cluttered with menacing clouds that obscured the light.

Christian felt the urgency to find Devan weighing him down as much as the stormy conditions. *I hope this clears. Otherwise it'll be impossible to see below.* He straightened in his riding harness. *Doesn't matter. I won't stop until I find you, Devan.*

# Thirty Five

*Scotland*

Graeme woke, cramped and cold, on the dirt floor of the cave. The rain and wind had stopped. Now, though more clouds were stacked on the horizon, the cave was blessedly quiet. If he concentrated, he could hear the waves crashing against the jagged rocks on this side of the skerry.

The peat torch sat guttered in its sconce. The scant light of dawn barely lit the dirt floor where Devan slept curled against her dragon.

Graeme shifted to sit and pain ripped over his back. He cried out.

"Graeme? Is that you?" Devan whispered.

"Yes. Sorry to wake you." He grimaced as he managed to sit upright.

A beam of light flashed toward him as Devan pointed a torch his way. He tried pulling the borrowed shirt away from his blistered back and hissed as this action seared his skin all over again. Nausea rolled in his gut.

"Wait. You'll tear the scabs." Devan approached him. "I'll put more salve on. What you really need is proper care in a hospital. Timothy's salve works wonders, but I have nothing to stave off infection."

"The salve and whatever Liam has in his first aid kit will have to suffice."

"Why not let me patch you up, then you can fly off to the local hospital?" Devan carefully worked the shirt over the red and blistered skin. "You've got some serious burns here. The remaining salve won't go far, especially since you'll need to put another coating on Liam's burns."

Graeme squirmed as Devan's cool fingers pressed against his hot skin. "I can't leave you here alone with Liam. God knows where his mind is, especially now that he's injured. You've heard of the auld adage, an animal is most dangerous when injured. That fits Liam perfectly."

Devan pulled the remaining fabric away from his back. "Hold your shirt for a minute. I'll dab some salve on the worst burns and cover them with gauze."

When she opened the jar, Graeme plugged his nose with his free hand. He wondered how his brother-in-law could stand the stench, especially since Graeme had applied it liberally to Liam's face and head. *Perhaps you get used to it. Or, maybe you'd deal with just about anything if it meant saving your life.* He shuddered at the thought that Liam might die.

*What would happen to Devan and DOCHAS if the MacLean clan found out about the attack? Even though Liam started it, the flaming wasn't exactly an even response.*

*I can't take the chance of anyone finding out. Not until we solve the problem of the magic waning. Perhaps by then, Liam and I will be healed. I'll just have to convince Liam it's in his best interests not to mention the incident.*

"Done." Devan lowered his shirt.

Graeme shifted to check his mobility. He nodded, then stood. "Thanks." He reached for the jar Devan held out. "I'll see to Liam. You'll not be wanting to go with me, aye?"

She shook her head. "I'll stay with DOCHAS."

"Right." Graeme stopped at the cave entrance and turned back. "I know KENNETH, Liam's dragon, fishes for his food, will DOCHAS mind? The skerry doesn't run to sheep. Any red meat comes when one of the MacLean's pops by with the monthly delivery. I don't think Liam would be too keen on me taking it all for the dragons."

Devan's expression softened as she bespoke her dragon. After a moment, she said, "DOCHAS will be pleased to share in the bounty from the sea. Her phrasing."

Graeme nodded. "I'll be back soon with peat for a fire and the torch and some food and water. Is there anything else you need?"

"Get Liam to take any antibiotics he might have. It wouldn't hurt for you to have a dose or two as well." At Graeme's nod, she continued. "Perhaps some soap and socks and a shirt or two?"

"I'll get what I can." Graeme glanced at the dragon. "If you and DOCHAS decide to stretch your legs, don't stray too far. The terrain can be treacherous."

He left them and made his way to Liam's bothy, watchful of his steps. *Who would look out for Devan if not me?* He knocked on the front door, then let himself in when he heard a crash inside.

Liam stood shirtless next to the rickety wooden counter. The large pot he used to heat water was on its side against the fireplace.

"Come to gloat, have ya?" Liam slurred as he waved his fingers near his face. "I'm nothing but an ugly bastard now. What has that bitch to say for her dragon attacking me?"

"You provoked the attack. You should be grateful Devan was generous with her special burn salve." Graeme held up the jar. "I've come to treat your burns. And to see if you've any antibiotics."

"You should save that crap for yourself."

"Don't be a bloody eejit." Graeme motioned for Liam to sit. "I've had my second treatment. Now it's your turn."

"It reeks something awful. Ripe dragon dung smells better."

"You ain't lying, but it's powerful stuff. The skin around your eyes looks better already. And that's from just one treatment. Some of the blisters look smaller too." Graeme opened the jar and quickly, yet gently, smeared the salve over Liam's face and the exposed skin on his head. "Done." He closed the jar and set it by the door. He returned to stoke the peat fire, then retrieved the dented pot. After washing his hands, he filled the pot with water and set it on the grate to heat.

While Liam sat and stared into the fire, Graeme rummaged in the first aid kit. He found antibiotic cream and a dozen antibiotic capsules. He placed two in his shirt pocket and set the remainder on the counter. He also took several gauze squares, medical tape, small scissors, two packets of aspirin, and alcohol wipes.

When he finished, he dipped a mug into the hot pot, spooned in fresh tea, stirred it, then gave the beverage to Liam, along with one of the antibiotics. "Take this. It'll help keep the blistered and exposed skin from possible infection. Have another one tonight with your supper."

Liam swallowed the capsule and sipped the tea, but continued to stare at the flames.

"Have you eaten?"

No answer.

Frustrated, Graeme shook Liam's shoulder. "What about KENNETH? Have you neglected him?"

"KENNETH can take care of himself. He caught enough Gurmard and Plaice earlier to last us a week. He ate his fill. Now he's asleep."

"With such an abundance, you won't mind sharing then." Graeme grabbed a box and tarp left by the MacLean dragonrider who'd last brought provisions. He stacked a half dozen fish along with other foodstuffs in the box. He grabbed some toiletries from the loo and a couple of Liam's T-shirts, socks, and pulled on a jumper. The non-food items he stuffed into a sack, along with six peat bricks, a small, battered pot, and two mugs. The tarp covered everything. He carried it all outside, then went back inside for one final check.

"Liam, I'm off. I'll be back later today to check on you. Make sure you eat something."

"What for?" Liam grumbled.

"For Merida and the bairns, ya bloody eejit. You need to stay strong for them. They need you."

Liam nodded but didn't look at Graeme.

"I mean it. Don't make me kick your arse. Merida would be devastated to see you like this."

This time Liam looked at Graeme. "Aye, but I'll not be getting to see my beautiful wife anytime soon. That bastard The MacLean still hasn't set a timetable for my return. And now I've missed the deadline to mate with that witch and fulfill the prophecy." His tone was flat and defeated.

"The prophecy never said anything about mating," Graeme replied. "We'll figure out what the prophecy means. Then you'll be reunited with Merida and the bairns. I'm sure of it."

Liam snorted. "Be careful of that Yank witch. Don't let her put a spell on you."

Unwilling to argue with Liam over what was clearly lunacy, Graeme shrugged. "Don't fash. I'll take care." He scooped up the salve and headed outside. *Is Liam drunk? Either that or he's gone over the edge.*

The rain held off until Graeme reached the cave, but once it started, it came down in sheets.

Devan had made a small fire pit on the left side of the cave with stones laid in a circle. She was taking inventory of whatever was in her saddlebags. She broke he second protein bar from last night in half, ate her piece, and left the other half resting on one of the fire pit stones. "Breakfast." She inclined her head toward the half bar.

"Thanks. I brought some food for us and fish for DOCHAS and REED." Graeme unloaded the fish from the box and offered the blue and silver dragon three of the plump Gray Gurmards. DOCHAS daintily took the fish from him with her foreclaws, then proceeded to swallow each whole.

Graeme grinned, then took the remaining fish outside to REED. *"How are you doing?"*

*"This rain is a nuisance. If we are no' flying home, perhaps I could share KENNETH's lair?"*

*"Aye. That would be fine. But don't let Liam talk you into flying him anywhere."*

*"I wish to sleep in a warm lair with no rain pelting down on me. Will ye be all right within?"*

*"Yes. I'll check on you later. Remember, only the quick flight to KENNETH's lair. No other flying."*

REED butted his triangular head into Graeme's shoulder with affection. *"I remember."*

After his dragon had flown north, Graeme went inside. He knew Devan would be expecting him to expand on his story from last night.

Devan found the extra clothing and exchanged her damp socks for a pair of Liam's. They came to her knees and looked like the highland socks Scotsmen wore with their kilts. The sight brought a smile to Graeme.

The wind drove rain into the cave. Graeme shivered. "I sent REED to share KENNETH's lair to get out of this weather. I've got some rope and a tarp to tie across the opening to block that wind."

Together, they managed to double the rope and string it through the tarp eyelets, then anchor it between outcropped rocks high on either side of the entrance. It made for a cozy space with enough clearance to let the smoke from the peat fire escape.

Graeme replaced the ash from the wall torch with a fresh peat half-brick and lit it. Shadows danced along the cave walls. He dashed outside with the pot and filled it with rainwater, then lit a small fire and heated the water for tea.

When there was nothing else to do, he sat by the fire with Devan. He swallowed one of the antibiotic capsules as they sipped their tea.

Graeme cleared his throat. *Might as well get it all out in the open. Show Devan that I trust her.*

"As I said last night, the dragon magic is waning. So far, I know of a few places where it is obvious. This skerry—because Liam told me. A small area south of Inverness where Fraser territory butts up against Grant land and the western end of MacGregor territory that meets Campbell land. There could be more, but I'm not in a position to find out. And I wouldn't have even known about the Fraser and MacGregor areas if I hadn't surveyed those lands after Liam told me of the loss of magic here and filled me in on the prophecy.

"The way the clans have been feuding lately, no one from an outside clan escapes notice. I've done as much as I dare."

"So, there could be other areas where the magic is waning or completely lost?" Devan asked.

"Aye."

"Then we need to perform a thorough search."

"Have ye not been listening? The clans are feuding like mad. I've not seen it this bad in my lifetime. And historically not since the auld clans chose sides on who was to be king in the 1700s. Where'd that get us? Between the battle at Culloden and the subsequent Clearances, nearly wiped out, that's where." Graeme pounded a fist on his knee. "I'm not sure who to trust."

"What are these latest feuds about?"

"Auld grudges. I don't think anyone really knows what started them." Graeme lifted his hands in wonder.

"I'll never understand why people go on holding grudges, inherited at that. Why not treat each new acquaintance as a clean slate?" Devan sipped her tea.

"I guess folks want a ready-made enemy to blame their problems on. You said you're half-Irish and half-Scottish, so you should be well versed with long-term grudges."

"I was born in America, so I didn't grow up hearing all the history of how the Irish or the Scottish were oppressed by various peoples. Anyway, can you trust your clan chieftain?"

"I was to confide in The Fraser, but then Morgan called and we were away north. When I heard that you could hear and speak to all dragons, I decided to enlist your help. I tried to intercept you outside the dragon lairs, but Morgan caught up with you. I bided my time. It was fortuitous that you decided to fly back to Ireland. When Erin asked for an escort for you, I volunteered."

"Why didn't you just speak to me instead of essentially kidnapping me?"

Graeme shrugged. "I started to several times but thought it best to show you. Then Cuillen threw a tantrum and the storm blew massive. It was all I could do to guide you in the general direction of this skerry and not smash REED and me in the process."

"Who the hell is Cuillen?"

"He's the Faerie Prince that rules the Isle of Skye. The storm took on magical properties the closer we flew to Skye. I believe it's due to Cuillen. He can affect the weather when he's in a snit."

Devan stared at him. "So faeries are real? Have you actually seen one?"

"I haven't, no. But Cuillen's a legend in Scotland."

"Never mind Cuillen." Devan downed the last of her tea. "How did Liam know I was here if he's been exiled for so long? Wait. You called someone before we left the MacKay compound. Who?"

Graeme ducked his head. "I wanted to let Liam know I might have part of the answer to the prophecy, so I gave one of Liam's mates a message. He passed it on when he brought supplies out here yesterday."

Graeme rose to pour them more tea. When he sat again, he continued. "I lost you in the storm, so I landed near Liam's bothy, hoping to warm up a bit before I continued my search. It was the first time in a while since I'd seen and spoken to Liam. He was crazed. Demanded I find you and bring you to him."

Devan sucked in a breath.

"When I found you and realized you and DOCHAS were hurt, I decided there was no way I'd take you to Liam. I brought you to this cave to hide you. That didn't work out so well."

At the mention of her name, DOCHAS opened her eyes and curled her top lip at Graeme, showing her sharp, powerful teeth.

"I have so many more questions, my head is spinning. But I'm exhausted." Devan settled back against DOCHAS.

Graeme retrieved his tartan and laid it over Devan. "I'm not going anywhere, except to check on Liam later," he said as he sat by the fire. But Devan had fallen asleep.

# Thirty Six

The rain hit just as Christian and the other searchers left Ireland and flew over the choppy waters where the North Channel merged with the Atlantic Ocean.

*"I'd hoped the rain would bypass us, but it looks like we're in for a miserable day,"* Christian bespoke ROARKE.

*"It will be worth all the discomfort when we find The Ring Wearer and DOCHAS,"* ROARKE replied.

*"Yes, it will, mo chroí."*

Padrick gave Christian the signal for him to take the lead. Christian nodded and glanced over his shoulder to make sure his fellow dragonriders were still in close formation behind him. Padrick guided DECLAN to fall in beside Aisling and her dragon, BRIANNA.

*Was it Padrick's choice to pair me with Aisling, believing she'll act like a mother? Or Sean's? No matter. I'll do whatever it takes to find Devan. The gods above won't be able to save any who try to thwart me.*

Black clouds that matched Christian's mood bunched and stacked atop one another the closer they flew toward the western islands of Scotland.

*"ROARKE, have you had any luck hearing Devan or DOCHAS?"* Christian asked.

*"Nigh. However, I am able to bespeak The Wingless One as well as the others flying with us. Do no' fash. I will inform ye if I catch a whispering from either one."*

*"Do you remember the Fraser dragon?"*

It took several moments before ROARKE answered. *"Aye."*

*"Maybe call out to him as well. He could be with Devan."*

*"I do no' believe that will work without The Ring Wearer."*

Frustration rolled through Christian. *"Right. I forgot. It's a bloody nuisance that the Scottish dragons don't have the same communications skills as the Tuatha dragons."*

The Isle of Mull grew more distinct through the sheeting rain. DECLAN flew to the lead position for Padrick to assume command of the search team. ROARKE followed the black dragon in a wide, sweeping right turn. Christian saw a rider atop a dragon waiting on the westernmost point of the island. With a small area between the Scottish dragon and the sea, DECLAN and ROARKE landed while the remaining search team dragons hovered just off the coast.

All three riders dismounted.

Padrick made the first move. "Padrick Nolan, friend of Erin Casey and Morgan. This is Christian Riley. Thank you for agreeing to help us."

"Trace MacLean." The man extended his hand in greeting.

*Let's get on with it.* Christian bristled at the pleasantries.

"So what's this I hear of a missing dragon and rider? Possibly two?"

Christian started to speak, but Padrick cut him off. "Yesterday, one of our companions that was visiting the MacKay compound needed to return to Ireland. Graeme Fraser was to guide our friend near here."

"Bloody rotten day to be traveling yesterday, what with the fierce storm and all." Trace rubbed his whiskered chin. "Would the missing dragon and rider pair be the one who can hear and speak to all dragons?"

Padrick nodded. "Seems word travels fast."

"Aye. Especially when an anomaly is amongst us."

"Devan is not an anomaly," Christian swore and clenched his fists. "She's a human being. The best person I know."

"No offense meant. Just that Scottish dragonriders, regardless of clan affiliation, are only able to communicate with our own dragons."

Padrick signaled for DECLAN to spread his wing. "Let's get out of the wet."

The trio ducked under the dragon's outstretched wing. Padrick pulled the map out of his coat pocket and opened it.

"We've worked up a three-pronged search grid to include some overlap. Our plan is to fly in pairs, each pair assigned a grid." Padrick inclined his head toward the colorcoded boxes that broke up the western coast and islands of Scotland.

Trace leaned in. "From what you've indicated, I don't ken that there's any reason to believe Graeme Fraser and your missing dragon and rider pair would have gone anywhere near the Outer Hebrides." He pointed to the farthest western group of islands. "They're too far north and west from Ireland. I wouldn't waste resources searching there. No, I'd adjust your grids to maybe include a bit more of the mainland instead." He drew an extended box to the east and south of the Isle of Skye with his finger. "If I was flying adragonback and came up against that beast of a storm, which reports said emanated from Skye, I would have vectored back over the mainland."

"Even if those lands belong to clans not friendly to Fraser, MacKenzie, or MacKay?" Padrick asked.

"I understand your concern, but if the reports are true, then most dragons and their riders would not have been flying. And those that were would have found safe shelter. I don't believe any clan lookout would have endangered themselves on the offchance a non-friendly dragon flew over their territory."

"What about today? What can we expect?" Christian asked.

"You'll have trouble with nearly each clan territory you fly over. At the very least, you'll be looked at as outsiders, and that's with the more friendly clans such as MacLean and Stewart. You'll face overt hostility with the Campbell and Donald clan. The smaller Scottish clans may feel threatened by the size of your dragons, but that might work in your favor."

"Great." Christian raked his hand through his hair. "How will we know if we're searching friendly or hostile areas?"

"You'll just have to be ready for trouble. Mull, Coll, and Tiree are MacLean lands, along with this area to the east." Trace pointed on the map. "If you run into anything you can't handle, get back here as quick as you can."

Padrick nodded, then folded the map and stowed it in his coat pocket. "Thank you. We appreciate your help."

"I'll be in this general vicinity all day. If you find them, let me ken."

"Will do." Padrick shook Trace's hand.

Christian nodded to the Scotsman.

All three left the shelter of DECLAN's wing and climbed upon their respective dragons. Each dragon took flight.

Once reunited with the other Tuatha dragonriders, Padrick shouted to be heard. "We're not going to search the far outer islands. It's too far out of the way. Instead, stretch your search area to cover more of the mainland. We'll be in hostile territory. Stay together. We've larger dragons, but two against ten smaller, more agile dragons won't be good. If necessary, this island and the two to the northwest are safe. Understood?"

The five other dragonriders confirmed.

"Have your dragons keep in contact with DECLAN every hour." Padrick closed his hand over his pendant, then said, "Safe flight. Let's find them."

Christian clutched his own pendant and closed his eyes. *Call out to us, Devan. Help us find you, a ghra.*

Padrick watched Christian, Aisling, and their dragons head toward the Isle of Skye. *I sure hope that boyo reigns in his guilt about letting Devan go off on her own. It's more of a hindrance than a help.* He shook his head. Pot calling the kettle, as you've to do the same, old chap, he chastised himself. *No one's to blame, just bad luck. Plain old mí ádh.*

Aiden, on his pale blue dragon, SEBASTIAN, gave Padrick a two-fingered salute, then steered Matthew and brown KIERAN toward the islands to the immediate northwest. They would search the area around the Isle of Mull and a large stretch of the mainland. Padrick, joined by Ryan on teal QUINN, would take the most southern territory. And as the team leader, Padrick reasoned he was best equipped to handle the search area that was the most likely to cause conflict.

Padrick led Ryan to the southernmost tip of the mainland—the dreaded Clans Donald and Campbell territories.

The first hour passed without incident, mostly because Padrick didn't see any Scottish dragons and riders through the sodden rain.

*"DECLAN, please check in with each search team,"* Padrick bespoke his compeer.

Each team responded that no one had found even a hint of DOCHAS's magical signature. Communication from ROARKE was spotty and Padrick attributed it to the weather.

Padrick had DECLAN, through GRAYSON, update Michael.

As the morning edged toward noon, Padrick and Ryan crossed over into Campbell lands. They were met with a chevron of fifteen fierce-looking riders atop their dragons.

"Bloody hell," Padrick muttered. *"Be prepared for anything."* He indicated Ryan and QUINN should stay behind and to his left as DECLAN flew toward the dragonriders.

Ten meters from the Scottish dragons, DECLAN hovered.

"Greetings. I'm Padrick Nolan of the Tuatha Dragon Clan of Éire."

"Ye are trespassing," the grizzled man in the lead position said. "Ye've not leave to fly over Campbell lands."

"Yes, I'm sorry about that. We're searching for one of our own that was caught in the storm yesterday."

"Storm or not, no one's allowed to cross our lands without permission."

"And how does one request permission? Especially a neighbor from another country who doesn't know the boundaries? We believe the whole of Scotland to be one nation within Great Britain." Padrick eyed the other fourteen dragons and riders, but no one so much as glanced away. *Definitely not a friendly group.*

"Hah! Ye lie. We ken ye visited with the MacKay clan yesterday. Surely, ye were informed of the lay of the land, so to speak."

Padrick nodded. "Yet we are not here to interfere in Scottish clan politics. We are simply searching for our missing dragon and rider. With your permission, may we proceed?"

The Campbell rider seemed to ponder Padrick's request. After a thorough survey of the size of DECLAN and QUINN, the leader spoke. "Ye will have one hour to search. My son will accompany ye. After that, with or without yer dragon and rider, ye must be off our lands." He waved his hand at the rider on his right side. "See to it."

*Better to be diplomatic and have the hour to search than get into a pissing contest with the arrogant eejit.* Padrick bowed his head briefly. "Thank you."

"One hour. Do not test my good humor."

The designated rider nodded to Padrick, then urged his sleek, pale red dragon up and away from the other Campbell dragons. Padrick and Ryan, on their dragons, followed.

The rain and the wind made for a miserable hour of flying, but Padrick wanted to cover as much of the wooded glens, coastal dunes, and especially the craggy peaks as possible. If Devan was holed up in a cave, the rocky areas near the coastline seemed the best bet.

When the hour ended, the Campbell rider led them to the coast where the northern tip of Jura lay across the narrow body of water.

"Thank you. Please express my gratitude to your father," Padrick said.

"I'm sorry we didn't find your missing dragon and rider." The man looked Padrick in the eye. "I shall return to our southern border where my father awaits. You understand?" Padrick nodded. "The auld grudges of the past shouldn't impede the possibility of newfound friends. I will keep a watchful eye as I patrol. I wish you well in your search." He gave a quick salute, then wheeled his dragon around and flew directly south.

"Did he just hint that we could continue searching for a bit longer?" Ryan asked.

"Yes he did. So, let's not waste a moment." Padrick directed his dragon eastward toward the area they hadn't had time to search.

Not wanting to be found out, Padrick limited their search to half an hour. With still no sign of Devan and her dragon, Padrick headed toward the Isle of Jura. Once there, he called for a rest. They had been flying for hours and he and Ryan needed to get the circulation back in their legs and food in their bellies.

Four hours later, Christian directed Aisling and their dragons to land on a craggy hilltop that, according to the map, was called Castle Ewan. There wasn't a castle, but from a distance, the top of one of the hills looked like a ruin. Once they landed, Christian and Aisling shook out their stiff and cold legs, sipped lukewarm tea from thermoses, and nibbled on energy bars. There was not even a hint of DOCHAS's magical signature nor a whisper of Devan's mental communication.

The weather had changed several times, shifting from a wisp of sunlight to a downpour and everything in between. Right now, a fine mist fell through broken rays of sunlight, giving an ethereal glow to the grass and rock-strewn valley that was aptly named, Faerie Glen.

"Feck." Christian kicked a boulder, then turned to take in the 360-degree view. "I was hoping since yesterday's storm originated here, maybe they'd be holed up in one of those caves we searched."

A deep brogue sounded from atop the boulder. "What about me storm from yesterday? Who's gone missing?"

Christian spun back around, positioning himself between Aisling and the voice. A man, small in stature and with a wry grin, sat cross-legged on the boulder. His eyes twinkled.

"Who are you? Where'd you come from?" Christian asked.

"I've tae ask ye the same, but 'tis obvious ye be dragonriders. Though no' from Caledonia."

"Are you from one of the local dragon clans?" Aisling asked.

"Nae. I am Cuillen, the Faerie Prince. 'Tis me home." He spread his hands to encompass the top of the hill. "And who might ye be?"

Christian's frustration and anger bubbled over. "Don't be

slagging me. I'm in no mood for games. Not with—"

"Whist. Ye be a dragonrider, yet ye question the existence of other magical beings? Perhaps ye need to see for yerself." Cuillen threw his left arm skyward. Lightning flashed. His right arm followed and thunder rumbled.

Christian ducked.

"'Tis a sad day when I am obliged tae deal with eejits. Though ye are no' as wretched as the boyo yesterday."

"A man was here yesterday? Was he a dragonrider? What about a woman and her dragon? Did you see where they went?" Christian fired off his questions, not waiting for the answers.

"'Twas no' a dragonrider. Nor a lassie. Only the black-hearted Yank searching for Devan Fraser. And I sent—"

"You've seen Devan Fraser?" Christian closed the distance between Cuillen and himself. "Where is she?" He reached for the man's shirtfront, but his hand hit an invisible barrier. Christian gawked as Cuillen folded his arms across his chest and raised an eyebrow.

"Where is she?" Christian repeated. "Tell me, or I'll—"

"Ye'll what?"

ROARKE rumbled a growl.

"Oh, aye. Ye dragon fancies a skirmish, does he?"

"Enough!" Aisling stepped forward and closed her hand over Christian's shoulder. "Devan and her dragon are members of the Tuatha Dragon Clan of Éire. I'm Aisling, rider of BRIANNA. This is ROARKE's rider, Christian. He is Devan's mate. She went missing yesterday after flying into a nasty storm."

Cuillen stood without seeming to move. "'Tis untrue. The lassie was safe with the MacKay clan. She did no' come here."

"No. There was an incident in Ireland. Devan headed back early." Christian parsed his words. "She was being guided by a Fraser dragonrider, but no one has heard or seen either of them since they left. Devan last bespoke my dragon, saying there was a hellacious storm and she might have to land. Then nothing after that."

"Why cannae yer dragon communicate with the lassie? She hears and speaks tae all dragons." Cuillen tilted his head to view the two dragons perched behind Christian and Aisling.

"That's one of the mysteries," Christian said. *I'm not trusting this wee chancer. How does he know of Devan's talent?* "Devan hasn't contacted anyone. She's disappeared. We fear she's hurt."

"Nae. Devan must be a'right. She cannae be lost because of me temper." Shock etched worry lines on Cuillen's face. "I shall imprison that evil Rick Hunter beneath Castle Ewan, I swear."

"Rick Hunter? He was the man searching for Devan?" Christian narrowed his eyes.

"Aye."

"Who's Rick Hunter?" Aisling asked.

"Devan's ex-fiancé. He was stalking her in America." Christian snarled. "I'll kill him myself if he's harmed Devan."

# Thirty Seven

Devan woke snuggled under Graeme's tartan. She thought she'd heard Padrick's dragon calling out to her telepathically. She sat up and concentrated. The small fire to her left had been carefully banked. Graeme was nowhere in sight.

*"DECLAN, is that you? Can you hear me? I'm in a cave on a tiny island that I've been told has lost its magic,"* Devan bespoke. She waited, but no reply came. *Why am I not able to communicate with any dragon, except my own? It can't just be the island losing its magic. Otherwise, I wouldn't be able to bespeak DOCHAS either. And Graeme wouldn't be able to communicate with his dragon.* She raked her hand through her hair in frustration.

*"DOCHAS, my sweet, can you bespeak ROARKE or GRAYSON?"*

*"Neither one answers."* DOCHAS sounded weary.

*"Have you rested any?"*

*"Nigh. I am no' comfortable cramped in this place. I watched the Fraser rider who shares our cave. He has gone."*

*"What? Graeme left the island? Are you sure?"* Devan scrambled up. Before DOCHAS could respond, Devan heard footsteps splashing near the entrance. *Oh God. That maniac's come back.* She grabbed the banged-up pot Graeme had used for tea earlier, turned to face her attacker, and froze.

Graeme stood just inside the makeshift door covering, his arms full of peat bricks and other necessities.

"You're still here," Devan whispered. Even though he was partially responsible for her and DOCHAS being trapped on this island

and she'd told him he should get to a hospital, Devan was grateful he hadn't left her alone.

"Aye. I'm not going anywhere." He shook the rain from his head and lowered the box he carried. "I needed to check on REED. I also wanted to see how Liam was faring." He inclined his head toward the fire. "Knew we'd need more peat if we were going to stay here. You were sleeping soundly, so . . ."

Devan stood, still holding the pot as a weapon. *Why's he acting so casual?* She narrowed her eyes. "Why haven't you gone for help? At least gotten Liam to a hospital?"

"I can't suddenly show up at a hospital with Liam and myself covered with burns, especially since it's probably been reported that I've gone missing with an Irish dragonrider." Graeme raised an eyebrow at Devan and the pot she clenched in her fist.

She set it down. "You can tell the truth—we got separated. You landed here, then had an accident. Yes, that's it, an accident with the peat stove."

"No one would believe our burns were from a peat fire. Besides, Liam's unpredictable. He's still talking of the prophecy and how the foreign witch's dragon nearly killed him."

"DOCHAS was protecting me," Devan said.

Graeme held up his hands. "I know. But even you have to admit; the flaming wasn't necessary."

Devan ducked her head but didn't reply.

"The MacLean chieftain would not hesitate to retaliate. He doesn't suffer fools gladly. He exiled his own nephew."

Devan gasped.

"Yes, Liam is The MacLean's own kin, and he showed very little mercy for what was essentially an accident. I'd hate to think of what would happen if The MacLean learned an Irish dragon attacked his clansman. And he would find out, make no mistake." Graeme shook his head. "No. It's better to treat Liam here where I still have some control over him and his actions while you and I try to figure out the meaning of the prophecy."

Devan could find no fault in Graeme's logic, but she wanted off this island. She wanted nothing more than Christian's strong arms around her. Him whispering Gaelic in her ear as he made love to her. She pushed those thoughts to the back of her mind and concentrated on what she could control.

"How are Liam's burns?"

"I swear that salve is magic. I've seen some horrible burn scars on oil workers. Thought for sure Liam would lose his vision with the way his skin around his eyes was sagging and blistered, but it looks better today. He says he can see fine, but . . ." Graeme shrugged. "I'd like him to see a doctor, but I won't take the chance of The MacLean finding out. He's a valuable ally for the Fraser clan. He'd be a merciless foe. And if we're to stop the magic from extinction, it may come down to which clans are friends versus enemies."

"Then we better figure out this prophecy," Devan said. "But first, I need to stretch out DOCHAS's wing. Will you help?" Graeme nodded.

The dragon lifted her head from her foreclaw.

"Come, my sweet," Devan said aloud. "We need to get your wing working again. Step into the center here. Give yourself room."

DOCHAS uncurled herself and lumbered from the back wall, head lowered to avoid the low rock ceiling. She tried to unfurl her wing but whimpered.

Devan rushed to her dragon's side. "Let us help. We'll go slow, I promise."

Together, Graeme and Devan attempted to rotate the dragon's shoulder joint, but to no avail. In the end, Devan massaged the wing joint, then dabbed a small amount of the dwindling supply of salve over the burn holes she could see. *Dammit. I hope her wing isn't as damaged as BOYD's was. That could strand us here for weeks.*

# Thirty Eight

*Scotland and Ireland*

Padrick had DECLAN check in with each of the teams, none of which had heard even a whisper from Devan or DOCHAS. *Oh, God! What will my son do if Devan is lost?*

As dusk crept closer, Padrick was forced to call a halt to the day's search. The teams regrouped on a deserted beach where all six dragons could safely land on the leeward side of the Isle of Mull. The rain had finally slackened to a drizzle, and a heavy fog rolled in.

"We've done all we can for today," Padrick said. "Based on Christian's vision, we can surmise that Devan and DOCHAS are tucked away in some cave."

"They may be drier than us, but I could see they were both injured. And scared." Christian rubbed a hand over his face. "I'm positive there's at least one person near them that's deranged. I can feel it."

"We'll fly back to Beaghmore for food and rest, then get a fresh start tomorrow. Hopefully, the weather will be better. And maybe Erin will have heard something from Graeme Fraser." Padrick clasped a hand on Christian's shoulder. Before he could shrug it off, Padrick continued. "This will give us time to get someone searching for Rick Hunter. Find out all we can about him. If he's anywhere near the Isle of Skye, we need to find him."

"Devan's had to deal with that bloody gobshite," Christian said.

The anguish in his tone broke Padrick's heart.

"Don't give up on her. Devan is strong. She'll find a way to reach us," Padrick said. "In the meantime, we need more people searching—those who know the land. Maybe Erin will have suggestions."

Padrick surveyed the Irish dragonriders. They were cold and exhausted, but no one looked defeated. He closed his hand over his pendant. "Dilseacht. Fáil. Saoirse. We swore an oath to protect Éire and that includes our clan mates. We will prevail in our search, I promise."

The search members repeated the Tuatha clan oath, then mounted their dragons and flew back to Beaghmore.

*"I have failed Devan and DOCHAS,"* Padrick bespoke his dragon.

*"Nigh. Believe in yerself as The Ring Wearer believes in ye. Each step must be taken. Every possibility considered. The Ring Wearer and her compeer are destined for greatness within the Tuatha Dragon Clan. She is The One. This all dragons know to be truth."* DECLAN's tone was firm, yet kind. *"I know yer heart to be steadfast. No one has failed yet."*

Once at Beaghmore, Padrick dispersed the team. He, Aisling, and Christian met with Michael in his office. They called Sean and updated him on the day's fruitless search.

"Michael, Matthew tells me you're handy at finding out things," Christian said.

"That depends on what you need to know."

"There's an American, Rick Hunter. We need to know if he's in Scotland." Christian tapped his chin. "I believe he's some kind of journalist. Lives in San Francisco. He was engaged to Devan, but she broke it off well before she came to Ireland in March."

Michael whistled low. "You think he might have abducted her?"

"We've heard this Rick was searching for Devan on the Isle of Skye, and he was a right bastard about it. Also, he might have talked to people here—I don't yet know who—about dragon sightings." Christian raked a hand through his damp hair. "Devan said he harassed her when she was in America over the summer. There was an incident in a bistro and a breaking-and-entering at Devan's parents' home."

"Did Devan give you his age? Or better yet, his birthdate?" Michael shooed Padrick out of the desk chair and booted up the computer.

Christian shook his head. "That's all I can remember. She put on a brave face, but Devan came back to Ireland abruptly, even skipping her favorite American holiday. She wouldn't have done that unless she felt threatened."

"Okay," Michael said. "This will take time. Why don't you grab some supper while I get started."

While Michael worked the keyboard, Aisling slipped her arm in Christian's. "Take me to dinner, young man. I'm near to famished."

Christian barked a laugh, which was probably Aisling's intention.

Padrick telephoned Erin.

"Did you find them?" Erin asked.

"No. And by your question, I take it Graeme hasn't surfaced either."

"No one has seen or heard from him. The Fraser is restless and hinting that either one of his enemies or MacKay is to blame. We nearly came to fisticuffs this afternoon. Morgan had to step in and point out there was no logical reason we would kidnap a dragon and rider from our most loyal ally. In the end, reason prevailed."

"What can you tell me of Cuillen, the Faerie Prince?" Padrick asked in hushed tones.

Michael glanced up from the computer screen and raised an eyebrow. Padrick waved him back to his work.

"How did Cuillen's name come up?" Erin asked.

"Christian and Aisling ran into him atop Castle Ewan. It seems he was in a Faerie Prince-sized snit yesterday and intensified the storm. He was quite taken aback when he learned Devan and DOCHAS were caught in his temper tantrum."

"I've heard the legends, never knew he was real. It's told that he has the power to affect the weather, so his tantrum could very well have caused the storm to turn dangerous. Do you know what caused his fury?"

"Aye. Seems an eejit from Devan's past was stalking her."

"Could that person—"

"We're looking into it now," Padrick interrupted. He didn't want to get into more detail with Erin until he knew more. *No sense anyone believing Devan had been kidnapped by an ex-lover then deciding to not help search for her. Besides, it didn't explain why Graeme was also missing.* "In addition, Cuillen said he knew we were coming to visit you."

"Seems Cuillen's legendary talents include some sort of second sight, or precognition," Erin said. "I don't think it's anything similar to our son's or my dreams. From what Christian described of his visions, he's sort of in the body and mind of a person, looking through their eyes, feeling what they feel. And in mine, I'm separate, like an out-of-body observer." Erin paused. "Why didn't Cuillen know Devan was heading back to Ireland?"

"Good question. We can ask him if we see him again tomorrow. Will you be able to help us? We need searchers who know the area, the places where a couple of dragons can get out of the elements. Maybe a cave."

Erin sighed. "Fraser's asked for and been granted an emergency council meeting. There'll be representatives from all the clans. Morgan and I are required to be there. You and Christian should come with us."

"Can't. There's no way Christian will stop searching as long as there's a chance Devan and DOCHAS are still alive. And neither will I. It's the one thing I can do for our son."

"But this might be the best chance to get the searchers you need," Erin said. "Don't you see? Tensions are escalating in Scotland."

"That's not our priority. I know that sounds cavalier, but—"

"Fraser wants to find his cousin, but most of the Scottish clans don't care about Graeme. They certainly don't have a stake in Devan and her dragon. One of those might have had a hand in her disappearance. Morgan and I can only plead your case up to a point before our rivals would view the MacKay clan as traitorous."

Padrick rubbed his temples to ease the vicious headache brewing there. "I don't see how Christian or I could help. Our presence would surely intensify that perception and cause more strife."

"You and our son would appeal as one dragonrider to another, without all the rival clan politics. Perhaps even invoking our countries' close ties."

"I know Christian won't want to stop searching. It's a battle to get him to rest his dragon, let alone himself."

"His devotion is what makes him the perfect one to ask the council for help. His love and willingness to sacrifice for Devan might spur these auld cynics to act for someone other than themselves, or for their own interests." When Padrick didn't say no, Erin rushed on. "It'll be for a few hours, then we can search on our way. Let's meet at Castle Ewan on Skye at nine o'clock. Maybe we'll get lucky and Cuillen will grace us with his presence."

"No promises on the council meeting, but we'll be meet you on Skye. I'm sorry for the trouble this is causing with the Fraser chieftain."

"Don't fash. Once Morgan pointed out the absurdly insane odds that Devan would head back to Ireland, that you and Christian would stay here, and Graeme would volunteer to guide her, Fraser calmed down." Erin sighed. "We'll find them. Scotland has more places to get lost in than people realize. And the weather hasn't cooperated. I'm sure with more searchers, we'll find them sooner."

"I hope you're right. We'll see you in the morning." Padrick ended the call. *Now I just need to convince Christian he needs to be the one to ask the Alba dragonrider council for help. Should be easy—not! That boyo doesn't trust anyone. God willing, we'll catch a break and find Devan and DOCHAS without stirring up trouble or causing an international incident.*

# Thirty Nine

*Scotland*

Dusk gave way to night as Devan settled DOCHAS in her spot along the back of the cave. Devan was surprised at the speed in which the darkness permeated the cave. She'd never been anywhere that didn't have some form of lighting. Even on the rare occasions that the electricity had failed, there was always some building or neighbor who had a generator, or the flashing red of signal lights. Besides the utter blackness, the cave dampened and distorted sound. *Or is it damage to my eardrum?* The eeriness here gave her the shivers. She wrapped her arms around her body and thought, not for the first time, how she could protect herself and her dragon if Graeme decided to team up with that wacko, Liam. *I just have to get to know Graeme better, build trust, without divulging too much and making myself vulnerable.* Not for the first time since she and DOCHAS had crashed, Devan wished Christian was here with her.

She turned around to find the wiry, ginger-haired Graeme kneeling to add a peat brick to the fire. He had lit the torch that was mounted in a sconce in the rock wall. Devan grabbed the pot she had discarded earlier and rummaged about in the supplies for something to heat up for dinner. She found several cans of soup and decided to mix two different kinds.

"Great idea." Graeme pulled a tool from his pocket and opened the cans. "I'm starving. You must be too."

Devan nodded. "Though I haven't done much today to work up an appetite." She emptied the soups into the pot and set it on the fire. She retrieved the two mugs they'd used for their tea and found them clean and dry. *Someone taught Graeme well. His mother, or perhaps he has a wife.*

"It's a bit unnerving to be sharing a cave with you when I know next to nothing about you," Devan said. "Are you married?"

Graeme raised an eyebrow.

"I . . . I mean—" She felt heat rise to her cheeks. "It's just you tidy up after yourself." She indicated the mugs and the organized supplies.

"Right. No, I'm not married. My mum raised us, my sister and me, to keep a clean house. Besides, I think better when I'm not surrounded by clutter. What about you?"

"I'm not married either, but I'm in love with Christian, one of the dragonriders I flew with. Oh, and I'm a researcher. I'd be in deep trouble if I wasn't organized." Devan stirred the soup. "So, your family . . .?"

"My parents and my sister, Merida. She's married to Liam. They have the twins, Rhys and Riordan. Merida and the bairns are my whole world. That and being REED's rider. My da and The Fraser are distant cousins. What about you?"

Devan poured soup into the two mugs and handed Graeme one. She blew on the hot soup, then took a tentative sip. It was surprisingly good. When she glanced up, Graeme was looking at her expectantly. She steeled herself for the sadness that enveloped her whenever she spoke of her family.

"My parents died this past February." Her voice trembled and she firmed her resolve. "I'm an only child. And I just know my mother's brother and parents from photos, as they all died before I was born."

"I'm sorry. That must be hard. I'd be devastated if something happened to anyone in my family. I guess that's why I've stuck by Liam through all his troubles. Merida loves him. She sees the best in everyone, especially her husband. I'm not quite as compassionate, but

Merida knows I'll do anything for her."

Devan sipped more soup while she processed this information. "Tell me more about the history of the clans, especially the feuds."

Graeme nodded, seemingly thankful to talk about something less personal. "So, what do you know about Scotland?"

"Erin explained a bit about the various attitudes between highlanders and the lowlanders and those between the Scots and the English, especially as it pertains to the oil production and where the profits should reside." Devan shrugged. "I don't have a good grasp of Scotland's history, just the basics. And since I don't have access to a computer, you're the next best thing."

Graeme finished his soup and made himself comfortable. "Scotland has a checkered past. We've been independent, pulled back under British rule, then back to partial independence over the centuries. Wars were fought, enemies and allegiances formed, changed, then changed again. Although there were clans in the lowlands, the clans were stronger in the highlands, perhaps because the landscape here was well-suited to the clan system. All the mountains, glens, rivers, and islands meant that it was fairly easy for groups to stay away from each other.

"Each clan was tightly bound together, by blood and by loyalties. They tended to develop their own customs, traditions, and laws. Devotion to their own clan was strong. There were often feuds with rival clans, where the auld grievances were passed down through the generations. The ill will never diminishing over time. Many vicious battles were fought over clan territories.

"The power of the clans never sat well with the crown. The efforts of some kings to control the clans' power bordered on the fanatical. King William of Orange demanded powerful Highland families swear allegiance to the crown, which led to the tragic and avoidable Glencoe massacre. Feuds intensified during the 1700s. Two rebellions were fought and squashed by the English. The aftermath of the Battle of Culloden in 1746 was shocking. Reprisals were swift and bloody. The clans were almost destroyed." Graeme shuddered.

Devan nodded. "I've heard of Culloden and the Clearances that took place after. But what of the dragons? When did they appear?"

Graeme rubbed his chin. "I don't know exactly. Seems like they either weren't around during the Clearances, or they weren't interested in human conflicts." He shrugged. "I've never thought about it overmuch. I do know that being a dragonrider has been in my family for at least three generations. My parents are also riders." He inclined his head. "Why? Do you think it might be important?"

"Maybe, or not. Either way, I like to collect as much information as I can." Devan yawned, then grimaced as her ears popped.

Graeme rose and collected the pot and mugs. "I'll clean up. You should get some sleep. You're still recovering from your injures. How are your ears? You seem to have your hearing back."

"For the most part, but it's like I'm underwater. And my balance is still wonky. The stabbing pain has subsided to a dull ache. How about your burns?"

"They're healing, thanks to your salve." He pulled open the makeshift barrier.

"Do you think my injuries are what's keeping me from communicating with the other dragons? I can't hear another dragon, except DOCHAS."

"Maybe. Or it could be because of the lost magic."

Devan nodded and hoped it was the former and that she would recover quickly. "Graeme, thanks for catching me up on Scottish history. One never knows when something from the past might resurface to cause trouble."

# Forty

Erin sat at the kitchen table and brooded over a steaming cuppa. The rich aroma of her favorite Irish tea scented the fire-warmed air, yet did little to distract her. She turned Padrick's words over in her mind. The idea of a stalker taking out two dragonriders was ludicrous. And she firmly believed Graeme was still with Devan. *No, the weather caused the dragons to land. Probably they are holed up somewhere to wait out the storm. But why isn't Graeme getting word to anyone? The Frasers have allies in the area. Unless the Campbells . . .*

A cool waft of moisture spilled into the room as Morgan entered and the winter wind slammed the door shut.

"How's BOYD?"

"Restless. I don't ken how I'm to keep him grounded for another day, let alone the weeks the healer said it would take for his wing to heal." Morgan shrugged out of his raincoat and toed off his wellies. "Any word from Graeme or your friends?"

"I just got off the phone with Padrick. They searched until the last light bled from the sky. Not a single sighting of Graeme or Devan, nor their dragons." Erin rubbed her temples.

Morgan filled a mug with hot tea, plated a half-dozen biscuits, and sat opposite her. "Did you tell him of the council meeting tomorrow?" He pointed to a biscuit. "You need to eat something as I can see a monster headache brewing."

Erin frowned but broke a biscuit in half and popped a piece into her mouth. "I convinced Padrick to meet us at Castle Ewan on Skye before the meeting. I thought it best for them to accompany us to the meeting. That way, we won't be breaking any sacred rules. We certainly don't need to give Sutherland any ammunition to use against the MacKay clan. And maybe we'll get a bit of insight from Cuillen on how to sway the MacLeod council leader to our side. After all, the Faerie Prince's rath is under MacLeod land."

"Good plan." Morgan sipped his tea. "How do we want to handle the meeting tomorrow?"

"I think it would be best if I deferred to you as much as possible. Otherwise, it might appear as though I'm siding with the Irish dragonriders over our own," Erin said.

Morgan nodded. "And if it came down to it, with whom do your loyalties lie?"

Erin opened her mouth to speak, but no words came out. She was that shocked. Finally, she spoke. "I am a MacKay dragonrider. I can't believe you'd question that."

"But you're also a mother."

"I was a mother when your da found me in that alley." Erin jutted out her chin. "Maybe I wasn't a good one, but I made the best choice possible based on my circumstances at the time. I just didn't tell anyone here."

"You know what I mean," Morgan said. "Now you've come face-to-face with your grown son and his father. And both are dragonriders for the Tuatha Dragon Clan."

"That doesn't change my allegiance." Erin rubbed the back of her neck. Her headache had grown.

"What if I told you Padrick was still in love with you?" Morgan pressed.

"How can he be? Twenty-eight years have passed. I'm not the same girl I was back then. He's moved on."

"But you never have."

Again Erin was stunned. *I haven't, have I? But is it because Kiely sabotaged my relationship with Padrick, or because of what I suffered at the hands of Sutherland?*

"I think you should marry me," Morgan said.

"What?" Erin gaped at the man she thought of as her clan mate, her rescuer, her only true friend in her adopted land of Scotland. "Where's this coming from?"

"First, I love you. And not as a sister—"

"But—"

"I ken you don't have the same feelings toward me. I'd hoped, with time and mutual respect, our relationship would progress from friendship to love. I still believe we can build on what we do have." Morgan uncoiled his lanky frame and paced. His hopeful tone contradicted the waves of frustration emanating from him.

Erin sat gobsmacked. She was still reeling from seeing Padrick after all this time. And meeting her son, Christian Riley. She'd wished for, even dreamed of—though not in a vision—the day she'd get to see her boy. Though she'd never expected him to be a grown man when she finally saw him again. In her mind's eye, she saw the wee babe swaddled in a warm blanket as she'd placed the letter and Padrick's dragon clan pendant under her Riley in the basket she left at the orphanage. Absently, she rubbed her hand over her pounding heart.

"And second, it's the only way to protect you," Morgan said, interrupting her thoughts.

"Protect me from whom?" Erin raised one eyebrow.

His thin lips pressed together in a gesture that Erin recognized as him trying to figure out the best way to tell bad news.

"Morgan, just say it."

"How long have we had our arrangement?"

Erin shrugged, her shoulder-length auburn curls bounced. "Since shortly after your father died, when you became MacKay chieftain. So about ten years."

"Right. And in all that time I've kept several of the more hotheaded clan members from drumming you out."

"Well, pardon me." Erin's Irish temper rose. "And here I thought me partnering with TEAGAN, a Scottish dragon—no, a MacKay dragon—ensured my safety. Are some in the clan demanding you toss a dragon and her rider out into this desolate patch of bogland? Why now? Why not before TEAGAN and I bonded?"

"Da protected you until he died. And I'm doing the best I can." Morgan rubbed his face as if to erase what he would say next. "It's your visions."

"My visions?" Erin sputtered. "But, I haven't relayed a vision to anyone except you in ages. We agreed that keeping them secret was for the best."

"That's still my belief, but . . ." He glanced out the window into the darkness. "The most vocal naysayers suggest you've envisioned something horrendous and you don't have the guts to tell anyone. Some are threatening a revolt, saying I'm keeping secrets. They're demanding we marry to seal the bond between us legally."

"But we've agreed. Our relationship isn't based on that type of love. I think of you as my younger brother. We're family. Not by blood, but through honor and loyalty. Our relationship is based on mutual respect and what's best for the leadership of the MacKay clan." Erin surged to her feet. "You know what I've been through. I told you I'd never put myself in a position of vulnerability again. You said you understood."

She wrapped her arms around herself, holding in her fear. *When will I ever learn? Having feelings for anyone makes me vulnerable. I'm better off not in a relationship, even as friends. Just me and TEAGAN.*

Morgan started toward her, but forced himself to step away.

"I do understand. But I'd be lying if I said I haven't had strong feeling for you ever since Da and I found you, broken and bleeding in that alley all those years ago. Those feelings have blossomed into love. And as I said earlier, I'd hoped your feelings for me would grow, and the memories from your past would fade. I can see now that isn't going to happen."

Erin clutched herself tighter. "I'm sorry if I've given you mixed signals, or if I've kept you from falling in love with someone else." She turned toward the door. "Perhaps TEAGAN and I should—"

"Don't you dare run away. Not from me." Morgan blocked the exit, though he was careful to keep from touching her. "The naysayers can blow smoke for all I care. But I worry about rumors of your special talent spreading to other clans." He blew out a ragged breath. "I've not missed out on love. I can find someone if that's what I want. Besides, you and I, together with our dragons, are a great team. We've kept the Sutherlands and Sinclairs from taking over MacKay territory. We'll figure this out. I promise."

"Is The Fraser questioning our relationship?"

"Not that I've heard. He's just upset with Graeme and REED going missing."

Erin nodded and relaxed her arms. "I need you to understand, I'd never betray my sworn loyalty to you or my dragon." *No matter what my heart might be wishing for.*

"Funny, that's what Padrick said. Seems he knows you after all." Morgan sighed as he gazed at her. His shoulders slumped, but he held his head high. "I'm going to check on BOYD and TEAGAN one more time. Get some rest. Tomorrow's going to be hellacious."

The door clicked closed behind Morgan.

She sagged back down into her chair, defeated. *Why can't one thing be simple? I should have known better. No matter what I do, I lose.*

# Forty One

Cuillen tucked his booted feet underneath him as he sat cross-legged on his favorite boulder atop the rocky hill known as Castle Ewan on the Isle of Skye. The boulder was worn smooth from centuries of the Faerie Prince sitting in the same spot—watching and contemplating. He'd speculated about everything from the ever-changing seasons in Scotland to the mysteries of humans constantly changing their minds over trivial matters. His thoughts shifted to Devan, the Yank lass who, according to the Irish dragonriders, had gone missing on Samhain. *Why are humans always on the move? Why cannae they enjoy the here and now?*

Oblivious to time and the elements, Cuillen pondered the lass's role in a centuries-old prophecy. Afternoon slipped into dusk and the soft mist turned to dense fog.

Guilt gnawed on Cuillen's conscience. "Devan cannae be lost because of me temper." His gnarled fingers twisted, then smoothed the hem of his royal blue tunic. "I 'twill help find the lass, I swear."

Ghilli Dhu popped into view in the grassy center of the hilltop. "Cuillen, you spend too much time with the humans. You are turning into one—brooding and all." He shuddered, sending the leaves that covered his naked body aflutter. The tree-like faerie was Cuillen's closest friend, but also his harshest critic.

"What brings ye tae me home? Ye rarely leave yer blessed forests, except when trouble 'tis afoot." Cuillen jumped down to properly welcome the faerie.

Ghilli Dhu scratched his whiskered chin with bony fingers. "Have you not heard the summons? Dagda is on the warpath. He has convened a conclave. All are to gather at midnight at his rath."

Cuillen despised Dagda's faerie fort, not so much for its location on the Scottish mainland just east of the Isle of Jura, but for his proclivity toward extravagant décor. Ornate Victorian-era furniture adorned each great hall. Gold and diamonds dripped from every magical chandelier. And there were a dozen sleeping chambers. Who needed all those beds when one lived alone?

The otherworld leader was a pretentious poser, at least in Cuillen's opinion, Faerie King or no'.

Ghilli Dhu's birch leaves rustled as he sighed. "Did you hear me? Or is your jaunty-capped head still in the clouds?"

"I heard ye just fine. 'Tis nothing wrong with me ears. Do ye ken what has the Faerie King so riled that he'd call for a conclave of all the faeries?"

"No, but there is conflict brewing amongst the humans you are so fond of. I hear Dagda is displeased with you and your continual interference with their inferior race. And whispers on the wind speak of a diminishing of the earth magic."

Cuillen gasped upon hearing another faerie speak of the potential loss of magic. *So, the Keltoí prophecy 'tis in motion. I believed 'twas so. Me eolas draíochta, me magical knowledge, has nae been wrong. And Devan Fraser 'tis at the center of it all.*

He startled out of his thoughts when Ghilli Dhu's hand gripped his shoulder.

"What is wrong, my friend? You look as though you've seen the end of the world." Ghilli Dhu withdrew his touch. Most faeries didn't enjoy the physical contact of another, even when offered in comfort.

"Mayhap I have," Cuillen whispered, then spoke louder. "I shall see ye later. 'Tis something I must find afore the conclave." He vanished without waiting to hear his friend's rejoinder. "Quite rude," he chastised himself, but Cuillen knew his friend wouldn't hold it against him.

Once inside his own rath under Castle Ewan, Cuillen lit each wall sconce he passed with a flick of his fingers. He scowled at the parchments overflowing the large oak table in the alcove of his sleeping chamber. More rolled and banded scrolls lay atop one another in the dozens of shelves cut into the walls.

"Och, 'tis thousands of scrolls, mayhap more, tae be gone through. 'Twill take forever tae find the proper one. I need tae organize me scribblings." Cuillen sighed. He closed his eyes, waved his hands over each shelf, and murmured, "*Iarr ar an tuar Keltoí.* Seek the Keltoí prophecy."

Hours later, Cuillen's bony shoulders sagged in defeat as he slumped in a chair. "Gone. The Keltoí prophecy scroll 'tis truly gone. Could someone have stolen it?"

The clock in the hall chimed, interrupting Cuillen's musings. On the twelfth bell, Cuillen snapped out of his funk. "Ye daft eejit, ye'll be late." He waved his fingers in an intricate pattern, muttered the teleportation spell, and transported himself to the solitary, rocky hill above Dagda's rath.

Cuillen placed his right boot in the deeply carved footprint embedded in the Inaugural Stone and waited for the Faerie King to acknowledge his arrival. In the time between one breath and another, Cuillen stood before Dagda's gold and purple throne that sat upon the gilded dais of the Great Hall.

"As ye summoned, O' Great One." Cuillen, as a faerie prince, knelt before his king, even though he detested the auld custom Dagda had reinstated.

"Rise," Dagda's voice echoed through the chamber. "You are late, as usual. What have you to say for yourself?"

Cuillen stood. Though his heart beat a quick tattoo, he held his gaze steady on the Faerie King's impassive face. Someone coughed, and Cuillen dashed the cap from his head. "'Tis sorry I am, I 'twas lost in searching through me scrolls." He knew the chamber was filled with faeries from every region of the Celtic nations, but the eerie silence grated against his nerves.

Dagda inclined his crowned head. "Your scrolls are more important than attending to your king?"

Cuillen's ears burned red at the rebuke, but he wouldn't forget he was a powerful prince in his own right. "I wished tae be prepared for the conclave."

"Prepared?" Dagda raised one black brow. "How?"

"Ghilli Dhu mentioned the earth magic was waning and I suspected . . ." Cuillen trailed off as the murmurs from the other faeries grew louder.

"Silence!" Dagda roared. He rose from his throne and stalked toward Cuillen. "What do you know of such matters? And speak the whole truth. Have you done something to affect the magic?"

"Nae. I have born witness tae the possibility. 'Twas centuries ago, when I 'twas just a wee laddie. Back then, 'twas me first experience with me eolas draíochta. I scribed a prophecy as the images and words came tae me. 'Twas that scroll I sought which caused me lateness."

"Where is it?" Dagda curled his fingers in a gesture that demanded Cuillen turn over the scroll.

Cuillen offered empty hands. "'Twas no' in me rath. I searched every place."

"So you have nothing—"

"But I remember the whole of it." Cuillen snapped his fingers. Fresh parchment, a quill, and inkpot appeared in his hands. *Why did I no' think of this afore? Me brain's gone soft.*

"By all means, enlighten me." Dagda returned to his throne.

Cuillen closed his eyes and murmured an incantation. The prophecy sprang clear in his mind. In quick strokes, he recreated the stanzas. When he had finished, he read the spidery words to himself to make sure he hadn't left anything out.

The hall fell silent once more as Cuillen vanished his writing implements. He scanned the faces of the assembled and noted Ghilli Dhu nodding his support.

Cuillen read the prophecy, his voice strong and clear.

"On the eve when the veil between the worlds 'tis thinnest,
When the darkness 'tis deepest, and the tempest 'tis most fierce,
Seek The One who comes from the land across the sea.

For in the age when The One Who Hears All
Unites The Seer, The Wronged, and The Exiled,
Long sacrificed bonds shall be forged anew.

Loyal tae one another, their destinies interwoven.
Each bares a talisman tae harness gifts of the soul.
Through these gifts, truths shall be unveiled.

With faith, grace, insight, and respect,
The One must heal a fractured nation
Afore securing the magic from extinction."

"Again," Dagda said. "Slowly."

Cuillen enunciated clearly and paused at the end of each stanza. When he finished, he saw the stricken looks on the faces of many of his brethren.

"Who are these entities that are mentioned? And what talisman?" Dagda asked. "You should know as you proclaim your magical knowledge brought the words and images forth."

""'Twas centuries ago and the images rushed and blurred. I 'twould no' have remembered it, but for another envisagement on Samhain Eve. Many hours I have contemplated the images and have puzzled out some of the prophecy." Cuillen waited for the sarcastic chuckles to subside. Many of his brethren scoffed at his magical gift. "I saw a trio of dragonriders come from Éire tae seek a kinswoman. One rider, a lass named Devan Fraser, wears a dragon signet ring. I believe The One mentioned in the prophecy 'tis Devan. She 'tis a Yank, and I ken she has the ability tae hear and speak tae all dragons. The other two riders 'twere nae so clear in me visions." Cuillen paused a moment. "But now there 'tis a problem. The lass, she—"

"She what?" Exasperation colored Dagda's tone.

"She 'tis missing. And 'tis me own fault. I 'twas angry with another Yank who stalked the lass. I fear 'twas me own temper that increased the storm on Samhain. And the first stanza of the prophecy bears out the timeline. Devan has no' been seen nor heard from since. Her mate and others from the Tuatha Dragon Clan of Éire search for her."

"Arrgh. You and your damn curiosity for the humans. This is why faeries should not interfere in the goings-on above the otherworld. I forbid you from having contact with humans forevermore."

"But, I'm the sole one amongst us 'tis spoken with the humans. I need tae help find the lass. She is the key tae restoring the waning magic."

Dagda pounded a fist on his throne. "And what of your own race? Will you see our magic diminished or faeries killed because of the humans' constant petty clashes?"

"'Tis precisely why I must find Devan." Cuillen straightened his shoulders and his voice grew stronger in conviction. "The Keltoí Prophecy applies tae us as well. Faeries and humans only survive if in harmony with each other. If 'tis no' fulfilled, our world, our magic, nae our very lives, 'twill cease tae exist."

Several faeries gasped aloud. Others shook their heads in denial. At least Ghilli Dhu nodded in support.

"Search yer heart. Ye ken it tae be truth," Cuillen said to Dagda.

The Faerie King studied Cuillen. Time hung still. "Aye. Go then, but remember who you are, Prince Cuillen. Find the lass, but do not meddle further in human affairs. And do not mention your prophecy. Humans are notorious for killing the harbinger of an ill wind. We have our own troubles, and I would be very angry if I had to lead without my son."

# Forty Two

*Beaghmore, Ireland*

Christian paced the length of his dragon, from ROARKE's triangular head to his spiked tail thumping the dirt floor. Christian's frustration mounting, he flopped on the unmade cot. *Where the bloody ifrinn is Devan? Oh God, what if she's seriously hurt?* Thoughts of one disaster after another invaded his mind until he couldn't take it anymore. He sprang off the cot and started out of the lair.

*"Where are ye going? Ye need rest. Mayhap ye will dream of the Ring Wearer again, and we shall find her and my mate on the morn."*

*"Nothing would make me happier than finding Devan and DOCHAS tomorrow. They've been missing for too long."* Christian returned to stroke ROARKE's eye ridges. *"I just need to walk off some of my excess energy, or I'll never get to sleep. I'll be back soon, mo chroí."*

*"Do no' fash yerself into exhaustion. We must be sharp on the morrow."* ROARKE blew a puff of warm air over his compeer's head, ruffling his hair.

Christian strode outside into the moisture-laden autumn night. Most of the houses in the compound were dark. He spotted a light in Michael's office and headed there. Christian tapped on the door, then entered.

Michael sat hunched over his computer, fingers working the keyboard in a steady rhythm.

"Have you found anything yet?" Christian asked.

"Don't crowd me." Michael blew out a breath. "Come on, ya little wench. Spill your secrets," he cajoled his computer. "That's right." He straightened in the chair and stretched his arms over his head. "The Yank reporter used his credit card to buy a ticket on a flight from London into Dublin two weeks ago. I'm still checking on when he arrived in London from the states. But, he caught a shuttle to Glasgow two days ago, hired a car, and rode the ferry onto Skye yesterday. He left a clear trail—credit card purchases for everything. But I've had no luck in tracking him further. The bastard could still be on Skye, or he could have left over the Skye Bridge heading toward Eilean Donan Castle. He's not booked a room anywhere."

Christian rubbed his neck. "Do you have a snap of him?"

Michael jerked a thumb toward the printer in the corner. "Easy peasy. He's some big-time investigative reporter. His headshot is on many news websites."

Christian snatched the paper from the printer and stared into the smarmy face of Devan's ex-fiancé. Hunter's expensive haircut showed not a blond hair out of place. The headshot didn't show much of the man's physique, but his sports coat hung too big for his shoulders. The phony smile highlighted bleach-white perfect teeth—too perfect. A narrow, patrician nose was centered over thin lips.

"Don't know what Devan ever saw in this eejit. He's a complete fraud. You can see it in his fake smile and the way his gaze isn't quite straight on. Not trustworthy." Christian threw the snap on the desk and strode back toward the door. "I'll leave you to it. Can you make sure the rest of the search team gets copies of this? I want everyone on the lookout for the gobshite."

"Will do." Michael waved him away.

Christian made his way toward the small lough and stood staring out at the storm-ravaged night sky. *Please be okay, Devan. I'll give up anything the gods demand as long as you're safe.* He pulled his pendant from underneath his shirt and fisted it. His gaze shifted to the northeast where Scotland lay. *Come back to me, my sweet. Coinníonn tú mo chroí. You hold my heart.*

From the corner of his eye, Christian caught a shooting star. "I'll take that as a good omen. Be safe, a ghra. Visit me in my dreams. Help me find you." He tucked his pendant away, rubbed his chest over his heart, and whispered a quick prayer. Then headed toward the lair.

A swooshing sound brought Christian to a halt. A lone figure was approaching. Christian tensed until he realized the intruder was Padrick.

"It's late. What are you doing out here?" Christian asked.

"I could ask the same of you." Padrick dragged his hands over his face. "I talked with Erin earlier. I've something to tell you." He spoke of the need for the two of them to attend the Scottish council meeting.

"You go play the politician. I don't have time for that shite." Christian pushed past Padrick. "I'm finding Devan. I'll not stop until I do." He stomped back to the lair mound, his temper near boiling. *Calm down. I won't have any visions if I'm wound up again.* He breathed deeply until he felt his pulse slow, then he entered his dragon's lair.

He crept past the sleeping ROARKE, undressed, and slid under the covers. He consciously relaxed his mind, thought of snuggling with Devan after a satisfying round of lovemaking, and drifted into sleep. The vision soon began.

*Rage had him gripping the steering wheel, driving the winding tracks the Scots considered roads far too fast. "Who the hell does that little man think I am? Some third-rate journalist? Cuillen, Faerie Prince or not, he won't sidetrack me from why I came to this Godforsaken place—to get my Devan back. That stupid bitch thinks she can dump me and get away with it. Looks like she needs another lesson in who rules this relationship. And I'm just the man to give it to her. Faerie Princes be damned."*

*He laid on the car's horn, urging a slow-moving truck to speed up. When the truck driver wouldn't cooperate, he veered wildly and scraped the driver's side of his car against the overgrown verge. The old man in the truck slid his vehicle into a rut, trying to avoid a collision.*

*"Where the hell do these people learn to drive? They should get off the road." He slammed his right hand against the door trying to downshift before he*

*remembered the shifter was on his other side. "And why don't they drive on the correct side of the road?"*

*The windshield wipers beat a steady tattoo. Find Devan. Control Devan. Possess Devan. I'll teach her who's boss. Rick Hunter, that's who.*

Christian gasped and yanked himself from the vision. "Bloody gobshite. You'll never get your hands on Devan again. I'll make damn sure of that, even if it takes my last dying breath to do it."

*"Do no' waste yer energy on that sack-o'-dung,"* ROARKE's sleepy tone soothed Christian.

He tucked the covers up to his chin and fell back asleep. And a new vision bloomed.

*The sky above was a soft blue after the last two days of storms. They were flying over the forest, circling in the pattern, waiting for their turn to land. He saw several of the clan chieftains from the high council milling about the three stones that made up the Cothiemuir Wood Stone Circle, better known as the Devil's Hoofmarks.*

*"Damn Fraser for calling this meeting. If he's lost one of his own, then perhaps he shouldn't be chieftain. What's it to do with me and mine anyway? And if the rumors are true, then he and the MacKay leaders have their arses where their heids should be. Aye, glad I've kept my clan clear of that lot."*

*Off in the distant west, he spied an enormous black dragon accompanying one normal-sized moss green one. Is that one of the Irish dragons I've been hearing about? He shuddered at the thought but couldn't tear his gaze away. Wouldn't want to have to battle that great beast.*

*He bashed his chin on his own dragon's neck ridges when his dragon swooped down to land. Once on the ground, he heaved his bulk out of the riding harness and slid to the grass and boulder-strewn ground. His knees buckled, and he would have fallen if he hadn't leaned against his dragon.*

*"I'm getting too auld for all this gamboling around."*

*"Ah, MacDougall," he heard the gravelly voice of the Campbell clan chieftain call out to him. "If ye've a minute, I've something of import to discuss with ye."*

*He wanted to pretend he hadn't heard the bloody dolt, but that'd just bring out the nastiness of the auld man.*

*"Aye, what is it?" He turned around with what he hoped was a neutral expression on his face.*

*"Did ye allow those Irish dragons to cross yer lands day afore yesterday?"*

*"The day of the massive storm?" He shook his head. "Didn't see anyone flying in that mess." He turned to leave, but Campbell grabbed his coat sleeve.*

*"I told ye afore, ye'd be wishing yer son was chieftain if I caught ye or any others crossing into Campbell territory from yer lands."*

*He pulled his coat free and stared past the auld coot. "Well, you didn't catch me or any others crossing into your lands, did you? No, you didn't. Now if you'll excuse me, I've to meet with the high council before this nonsense begins." He strode away without daring to look back. The breath hitched in his chest at the thought of the threat Campbell had proclaimed last summer when one of the young lads had accidentally poached from Campbell lands. The auld man dared suggest the next time someone crossed into Campbell territory, he'd castrate the MacDougall chieftain.*

*And he believed the loon. After all, there were rumors the auld coot was turfing out his own son because the young man didn't share the same views as his auld da.*

*No way would the smaller MacDougall clan stand a chance against the Campbells and their allies.*

*The high council was smart to hold this impromptu meeting in neutral territory—couldn't get more neutral than on Leslie lands as they weren't rightly seen as a highland clan.*

*He was here today in part to form some alliances of his own. But would the missing Fraser dragon and rider interfere in his plans?*

Christian rolled over, breaking the dream sequence. And the scene shifted once again.

*More than forty highland clan chieftains gathered in the cleared circle of Devil's Hoofmarks. Sunlight filtered through the scattered high clouds, allowing the meeting to be outside. The high council had taken their seats with their backs to the recumbent stone and its two guardian stones. Chairs were scattered in loose groupings based on alliances.*

*To his right sat his sworn enemies, the MacKay clan leaders. They had the gall to invite one of the Irish dragons and its rider to accompany them. Another reason the MacKay clan should be disbanded and their lands given to the Sutherlands and Sinclairs. And next to Erin sat the reason the highland clans were convened at this meeting—the Fraser chieftain. Word was his cousin was missing. Good riddance. Maybe the high council would finally consider the reorganization plan he as the Sutherland chieftain had proposed last year.*

*He turned away from Fraser and stared daggers at Erin. The damn bitch never learned to keep out of the business of her betters. As far as I'm concerned, the Irishwoman's not to be trusted just like the lowlanders and the bloody English.*

*Auld Morgan and his dimwitted son were too soft on the woman. Or perhaps she was keeping it all in the family. One thing he knew for certain, if Auld Morgan hadn't interfered that long-ago night in that alleyway in Inverness, the fiery, red-haired Irishwoman would have been his, and he'd have taught her some proper respect. She damn sure wouldn't be a co-leader of a highland clan.*

*He laughed at the thought of Erin scrubbing the floors of his castle by day and warming his bed at night. Maybe he should just take what should have been his anyway. What would that wimp Morgan do? He shifted his gaze to the dragonrider. The lad can't even keep his beast from serious injury supervising a small oilrig. No, he'd be of no consequence.*

*Or I could force her out of Scotland altogether. Then I could lay claim to MacKay territory due to the negligence shown at the oilrig explosion and in the Fraser lad and his dragon going missing. Yes, I could stir up some trouble. Might even liven up this joke of a council meeting.*

*So, what interest does the Irishman have in Erin? He might be a problem. I'll have to neutralize him. And get Sinclair to deal with Morgan. Do it quick, before anyone can react.*

*McLeod, as council leader, banged his fist on the portable table in front of him. "Come to order." The murmurs of the gathered chieftains quieted. "Fraser has the floor."*

*Fraser stood and faced the other clan chieftains. "Two days ago my cousin Graeme disappeared while escorting a fellow rider and her dragon from MacKay land to the southwestern coast on her way back to Ireland. The storm—"*

*"Maybe your cousin was convinced by Erin to fly off with the Yank."*

*"Why? What could be gained from that?" Fraser asked.*

*"The MacKay leaders could be playing you. Weakening the Frasers. The missing Yank and this Irishman suddenly appear in Scotland, specifically visiting the MacKay clan. There's something nefarious going on. I've never trusted that outlander." He rose from his seat, playing to the crowd. "The Yank spoke to my dragon. How could she do that? The logical explanation is she's a witch. You've all heard the rumors that Erin has visions." He used air quotes around the last word. "I say she's a witch as well. And you ken what our ancestors did to witches. Let's see if she can envision that." He lunged for Erin, knocking her out of her chair and to the ground.*

*The Irishman leapt to her defense a split second before Morgan. Sinclair pulled Morgan away while Sutherland freed his sgian dubh from his belt and bashed the Irishman in the side of the head with its hilt. The Irishman crumpled next to Erin. The black dragon roared.*

Christian jerked awake. "Christ." He dragged a hand through his sweat-dampened hair. "Is there anyone not wanting to kill us?"

ROARKE opened one eye. The sapphire blue facets swirled faster. *"What has ye so fashed?"*

*"Seems most of Scotland is gearing up for battle. And we're caught in the middle. I don't care what these rival highland clans do to each other, all I want is Devan and DOCHAS back."*

*"Ye had a vision?"*

*"Aye. Several. But I didn't see Devan in any of them. And I'm beginning to lose hope."*

*"The Ring Wearer is meant to be wherever she is at present. Ye can no' give up. I will no' let ye. Remember, I am with ye always, as is the Ring Wearer. All shall be as the fates dictate."*

*"That may be, but how am I supposed to keep my parents and Morgan from being ambushed while I search for Devan? I can't do both. And sending just one Tuatha dragonrider into that fractious meeting could be suicidal."*

*"Ye know what ye must do."*

Christian rolled off the cot and dressed. He scratched under ROARKE's chin before heading out to talk with his father. *"Aye, but I don't have to like it."*

# Forty Three

*Ireland and Scotland*

The morning dawned bright and crisp. Icy tendrils hung from the bare branches of trees and a coating of frost covered the rooftops. Weather forecasts expected snow flurries by late afternoon all across the Scottish Highlands. Padrick stood just inside the office doorway, sipping his coffee. He wasn't sure how best to convince his son to attend the Scottish council meeting. As if the boyo sensed Padrick's dilemma, Christian emerged from the dragon lair mound and headed straight for the office. His black hair was sleep tousled, and there were dark circles under his deep blue eyes.

*"DECLAN, how is ROARKE this morning? Did he rest, or did he and Christian disobey orders and go back to Scotland last night?"* Padrick bespoke his compeer.

*"Nigh. The young one slept deeply after his rider returned from his restless wandering,"* DECLAN answered.

Padrick cocked his head toward the coffee pot inside the office as Christian entered. "There's fresh coffee. Looks like you could use some." Christian grunted. "What did your visions show?"

"Why do you think I had a vision?" Christian poured himself a large mugful of black coffee.

"The bags under your eyes tell me you've not slept well. And you're about to inhale my coffee without complaining that it's thick as mud. So why don't you tell me about it?" Padrick sat in one of the chairs in front of the desk and waved his son to the other. He didn't want to be the leader right now, he wanted to be a father.

Christian spoke bitterly of his first vision through Rick Hunter's perspective. Then he gave brief accounts of the Scottish council meeting from two different chieftains' points of view, one being from the Sutherland leader Padrick had verbally sparred with two days ago.

"So no vision of Devan specifically?" Padrick finished his coffee.

"No." Christian rose and paced the office.

"Is that what has you so worked up, or is it something else?"

"Isn't Devan and DOCHAS missing enough? We've been unable to communicate with either of them. Devan wouldn't be incommunicado unless something was wrong. Even hurt, she'd try to get our attention somehow. Yet we've not seen any signs of her or this Graeme boyo." Christian drank some coffee, then spit it back into his mug. "This is god-awful. How can you stand it?" He started for the door. "I've gotta have a decent cup of coffee. Today's going to be brutal between us going to Skye, then to this bloody meeting. And to top it off, it's supposed to snow later." He raked a hand through his hair. "I'm not the diplomat in the family, but I'll do whatever it takes to find Devan, even plead for help from people I don't trust. Devan's my priority."

Padrick wasn't sure what had changed his son's mind about attending the meeting, but he wasn't going to complain. "I'm sure there's better coffee than mine in the communal dining hall, and we can eat a hearty breakfast as well. Might be a while before we get another chance. Let's go."

The two men strode out of the office. Christian dumped the sludge from his mug into the tall grass at the side of the building.

"Oh sure, kill the foliage," Padrick joked.

"Better the grass than my stomach lining," Christian retorted.

After breakfast, Padrick released Matthew, Ryan, and their dragons so each could perform their original duties. He then asked Aisling and Aiden to fly GRAYSON through the standing stone pattern to enhance his magic.

Each dragon and rider pair needed to restore the magic, or all the searching would be for naught. If the magic waned, they could fly right over Devan and DOCHAS and not even know it—especially if they were injured or sheltering from the weather.

Padrick made plans to rendezvous with the Tuatha dragonriders in the early afternoon on the beach on Mull. He hoped to have several Scottish dragons and riders who knew the terrain to help in the search. He knew the longer Devan and DOCHAS were missing, the worse the odds were of finding them.

Michael caught up with Padrick and Christian as they were readying their dragons for the flight across the ocean to Scotland.

"Can't find hide nor hair of your bloke, Rick Hunter. And it's not like him. He's one for the spotlight, he is." Michael pulled his knit cap low over his ears. "I'll keep searching. Just wanted to keep you in the know."

"Thanks," Christian said.

Michael turned to Padrick. "If you've a minute?"

Padrick nodded and guided Michael away. "What's up?"

"Sean just called. He said the government cover-up story is gaining traction. The Gardaí Superintendent and the *Taoiseach* have been called before Parliament. Both are hopping mad. They demand Sean answer for the sighting of a dragon."

"What's Sean going to say?" Padrick stole a glance at Christian. *Christ. He can't handle another thing until we find Devan.*

"Sean's telling the officials to remain calm and stick with the story that Logan's man, Kelly, is crazy. That he's wanting out of gaol and he'll work any angle, including saying crazy things. That there's no proof." Michael tilted his head in Christian's direction. "Are you going to tell him?"

"No. We'll deal with one problem at a time. Finding Devan's our priority." Padrick clasped Michael's forearm. "Thanks for telling me. But Sean's got the right of it as far as how to handle the media and Irish bureaucracy."

"Eitilt shábháilte," Michael said. "Bring Devan and DOCHAS home."

The flight to Castle Ewan on Skye was uneventful. As DECLAN and ROARKE approached the hilltop at the northern end of the island, Padrick spotted Erin flying atop TEAGAN. Morgan was seated behind Erin. Padrick sketched a quick salute, then indicated DECLAN and ROARKE would land first.

When they had gathered near the boulder where Christian had seen the faerie, he called out. "Cuillen, are you here? I've more questions for you." When there wasn't a response, Christian kicked the boulder. "Come out, you bloody Faerie Prince. It's your fault Devan's missing, so you can damn well answer some questions."

Erin gasped at Christian's brash tone.

"Quit yer havering," Cuillen's voice came from behind the four dragonriders. "The Faerie Prince does no' answer tae a summons from the likes of ye." Thunder rumbled.

The humans turned around. Morgan stumbled back as Christian stepped past him toward Cuillen.

"Listen, you wee bugger, enough of your games. Devan's still missing, possibly injured. If you hadn't thrown a temper tantrum the other day, she'd be fine now." Christian stood with his hands fisted, ready to strike.

The thunder died down and no lightning followed. "'Tis sorry I am me storm caused the lass trouble. She has no' contacted ye?"

"No," Christian said. "And we've some questions to ask you."

Erin stepped forward. "How is it you knew Devan and these two," she indicated Padrick and Christian, "were coming to MacKay territory?"

"And ye are?" Cuillen glided between the riders and sat cross-legged on his boulder.

"I'm Erin and this is Morgan." She indicated her clan mate. "We're from—"

"The MacKay clan." Cuillen nodded his head toward Padrick. "Ye be the brash boyo's da?"

"Yes. Padrick Nolan of the Tuatha Dragon Clan of Éire."

"So, the lass succeeded in reuniting yer family." Cuillen seemed lost in thought, no longer aware of the riders standing before him. "I shall ponder this development."

"Answer the question," Christian demanded.

Cuillen blinked. "I ken because I've a talent me brethren call eolas draíochta or magical knowledge. Though, apparently 'tis fallible as I didnae foresee the lass going off on her own, nor her loss of communication." He stared at Padrick. "Ye have been ill-treated. Can ye move past it? Time shall tell." With that cryptic remark, Cuillen vanished.

"Dammit. What was that all about?" Erin said to no one in particular. "I didn't get to ask how his magic works. Or his thoughts on how to handle the McLeod council leader."

"Cuillen! Come back here." Christian shouted. His hands balled into fists. "Do you know where Devan is? Or that bloody gobshite, Rick Hunter?"

"Nae. And me magic 'tis no' a vision per se, but a prescience of acts with lasting consequences." Cuillen's deep brogue echoed all around the riders. "Beware, magic always exacts a price."

"That was a colossal waste of time," Christian said.

Padrick turned to Erin and Morgan. "We'll follow you to the council meeting, but we're staying just long enough to recruit some riders to help in our search."

Christian wondered if he'd done the right thing by not telling his parents or Morgan of the ambush that Sutherland was planning. *I'll be there to stop it. The vision clearly showed only Padrick with Erin and Morgan. By me attending, I'll change the outcome. If nothing else, I can keep an eye on everyone, especially that Sutherland eejit.*

The plan settled in his mind, Christian guided his dragon to follow the others. ROARKE lost communication with GRAYSON shortly after leaving the Isle of Skye, so Christian spent the flight deep into Scottish lands encouraging ROARKE to call out to Devan and DOCHAS. Though to no avail. They didn't see any dragons until they neared the forest where the meeting would take place, where

Christian felt a number of eyes focused on him. He sat taller atop his dragon. *Don't be intimidated. They'll respect me more if I'm confident.*

Erin caught Christian's attention, indicating they were to land in the clearing to the north.

Once on the ground, Christian reminded himself to stay alert. His attendance might have thwarted Sutherland's attack, but the man could just as easily try another avenue to disrupt the meeting and take down the MacKay leaders, Padrick, and himself.

Several clan chieftains openly gawked as Morgan and Erin led Padrick and Christian through the crowd toward the Fraser leader. Whispers penetrated the hushed reverence of the ancient site.

Sutherland shifted so his heated gaze focused on Erin. Christian crossed the chieftain's line of sight and made sure the large man knew he was watching him.

*"Be ready to cause a distraction,"* Christian bespoke ROARKE.

*"Are ye giving yer permission to flame the obnoxious eejit that ogles yer mum?"*

*"What? No. Maybe. Just watch for any sudden movement from the Sutherland or Sinclair leaders you met the day Devan went missing."*

*"If one of them hurt The Ring Wearer, I shall do more than flame them."* ROARKE's stubbornness broke through.

*"A distraction. Don't cause a war. We're here requesting help in finding Devan and DOCHAS, not gathering enemies."*

ROARKE huffed but didn't comment further.

Once seated, Christian surveyed the large group. There had to be over fifty men and women—though only a handful of women—and each chieftain wore the plaid of their clan allegiance. He noted the Sinclair chieftain leaning forward to whisper something to Sutherland. The chieftain nodded, then crossed his beefy arms and stared at the council leader who banged his fist on the portable table in front of him. He called the meeting to order, then announced Fraser.

Fraser rose, nodded to the council, then turned to face the gathering. He spoke of his cousin, Graeme, going missing while assisting Devan.

Sutherland questioned Fraser, then Sutherland's subsequent grandstanding unfolded exactly as in Christian's vision.

However, this time when he heard Sutherland spout off that Devan and Erin were both witches because of their special talents, Christian couldn't reign in his temper.

"No one denigrates Devan," Christian said, his voice low and dangerous, as he slowly stood and faced Sutherland. "It's no wonder none of the Scottish dragons will communicate with anyone other than their own rider. You're some of the most stuck-in-the-past, intolerant eejits I've ever met." Christian moved his chair and placed himself between the red-faced Sutherland chieftain and Padrick and Erin. "Your dragons are magic, yet you refuse to believe there is other magic or special talent in the world? Or are you jealous?"

Sutherland brandished a knife, but Christian didn't back down.

"You come here and toss insults at us? Who do you think you are?" Sutherland advanced, flashing the blade.

Christian held his hands out in front of his body. "I'm a Tuatha dragonrider, a seer like my mum, and a Dublin street rat. I'm your worst nightmare." He reached into his right boot and withdrew his own knife, a KA-BAR. "Let's see who'll win in a fair fight, and not the ambush you planned against my mum and da."

Sutherland retreated several steps. "Erin's your mother?"

"Yes. She's why we were here in your bloody country. Not to plot against other Scottish clans. Unlike you and Sinclair." Christian paused at the blank looks on several people's faces. "I wonder if the rest of the Scottish chieftains approve of your plans to take over MacKay territory?" Christian spared a glance at the council leader.

Murmurs rose through the crowd as people leapt to their feet and gathered around their allies.

"That's right," Christian continued. "Last night I envisioned this cowardly surprise attack. I also know you despise Erin for some long-ago slight, and you have no respect for Morgan, nor his father before him."

Erin gasped but didn't say a word.

"You let this upstart foreigner speak to me this way? Threaten one of the oldest clans?" Sutherland turned away to beseech the council members.

MacLeod, the council leader, rose. He stuck his thumb and middle finger in his mouth, blew a shrill whistle. "Order!" When the clearing was quiet, he spoke. "Weapons, even a ceremonial sgian dubh, are forbidden at council meetings. Sutherland, you ken this. Morgan, you should have ensured your guests knew and obeyed the rules before allowing them to attend. Now you'll give them to me. And I'll see arses in seats, or there'll be hell to pay."

Christian stepped back in a protective stance and indicated Sutherland should proceed him.

After both had relinquished their weapons, MacLeod sat and continued. "Mister . . .?"

"Riley. Christian Riley."

"What is your involvement in this meeting? Other than to cause trouble?"

"As Fraser was trying to explain, his cousin went missing while helping my mate, Devan, pass through Scotland safely. Apparently, they flew into the storm that was exacerbated by Cuillen's temper tantrum."

Scoffs and snickers could be heard from the Sutherland and Sinclair side of the clearing. A popping noise broke through the ridicule.

"Ye do no' believe in faeries, yet ye partner with dragons? How can this be? Why must I deal with eejits?" Cuillen stood upon the recumbent stone behind the council leaders.

Most of the council members and several Sutherland supporters scrambled out of their chairs and away from the standing stones.

Cuillen's jaunty cap sat rakishly at an angle, and his silver doublet shimmered in the weak sunlight. Sea blue trousers were tucked into black leather boots with silver Celtic knot buckles adorning the outer ankle flaps. "'Tis sad I am tae call ye Scots."

"Ah, Faerie Prince Cuillen." MacLeod rose and bowed. "So nice of you to grace us with your presence."

"Ye are a cheeky one, MacLeod." Cuillen mock-tipped his cap.

"Is what the Irish dragonrider saying true?" MacLeod asked. "Did you enhance the storm a couple days ago?"

Cuillen dipped his head. "Aye. Tae me great regret, as I now ken the lass, Devan Fraser, 'tis missing."

"As is my cousin," Fraser said, giving Cuillen the evil eye.

Christian stepped forward. "Finding Devan and Graeme is my sole concern. It's why I'm here wasting valuable search time."

"Why don't you just envision where they are?" Sutherland used air quotes as he mocked Christian's talent.

ROARKE roared and spewed a burst of flame skyward.

*"Easy, my great warrior. I've got this, but thanks for the timely show of strength,"* Christian bespoke his dragon.

Several of the smaller Scottish dragons took flight as their riders shouted war cries.

"Enough!" Cuillen and MacLeod bellowed in unison.

When order was restored, Christian squared off with Sutherland once more. "In my visions, Devan and her dragon are in a cave-like structure. I'm not sure if Graeme is with them." *No way am I mentioning that Devan and DOCHAS were hurt, or that DOCHAS flamed a madman.*

"Since the Yank lass can speak to all dragons, why hasn't she?" Sinclair squeaked out.

"In our last contact, Devan said they'd been caught in a severe storm and might need to land. With no sightings and no communication, I'm convinced something disastrous has happened." Christian raked a hand through his hair. "We came here to request searchers with knowledge of the islands and mainland coastline from Skye southward. Dragonriders, whether Irish or Scottish should be working together. I don't understand why anyone would not move heaven and earth to find missing dragons and riders."

When no one spoke, Christian gazed at Padrick. "We're wasting our time with a bunch of dragonriders that can't see past their own thirst for power." Christian stepped toward the council and inclined his head toward his blade. At MacLeod's nod, Christian retrieved his knife. He thrust it back in his boot. "If I have to, I'll search alone."

A heartbeat of silence ensued before Cuillen cleared his throat. "The lad 'tis correct. All must work together tae find the lass. Otherwise, the world as ye ken it, 'twill be lost forever."

"What do you mean?" MacLeod asked.

"The magic 'tis already waning. 'Tis pockets of land where the magic can nae longer be felt or rejuvenated." Cuillen paused while murmurs spread through the crowd, then he stared at Christian. "With the lass no' being able tae use her magical talent, I fear she 'tis in one such place."

"Christ. When did you know about this?" Christian glared at the Faerie Prince.

"Centuries ago. Last night."

"Which is it?" Christian advanced toward Cuillen.

Cuillen took his cap off and scratched his head but did not give ground even when Christian halted a mere hair's breadth away. "I ken the possibility centuries ago, yet learned the truth of it last evening."

"And you didn't think it was important enough to tell us this morning?" Christian's voice rose. "Still playing games? Or were you hoping to lay the blame of Devan's disappearance on someone else?"

"Nae. Ye gave me other things tae ponder, tae clarify the truth. 'Tis why I've come tae this meeting, shown meself tae so many humans."

"What truth?" MacLeod asked.

"The lass, Devan Fraser, 'tis the one tae bring the magic back. 'Tis her destiny. As 'tis declared in the Keltoí Prophecy."

"What prophecy? How will this woman restore the magic?" MacLeod raised his voice to be heard above the bickering that had started between several clan chieftains.

"That, I do no' ken. Only that she 'tis The One." Cuillen hesitated, then reached into his doublet pocket and flourished a parchment. He snapped it open and read the words. "The prophecy came tae me centuries ago, then 'twas forgotten and lost over time. I recreated it yesterday."

"Right now I don't care how Devan is associated with this bloody prophecy, or if she might be able to restore the magic." Christian glowered at the Faerie Prince. "She just needs to be found."

"Right," Cuillen said. "I 'twill do all in me power tae find the lass."

"Wait. How did you know where to find us?" Christian asked Cuillen.

"We have our ways."

"So, you spy on humans?" Sutherland sneered.

Cuillen guffawed. "Nae. 'Tis no need. Ye are no' much of interest tae us. The land and the magic, however, 'tis." He pinned Christian with his direct gaze. "And Devan, as the lass holds the future of all races in her grasp."

"There'll be MacLeods on Skye within the hour to assist you," the council leader said to break the tension.

"And MacKinnons," someone from the crowd chimed in.

"You can count on the MacLeans," a burly man who stood behind Fraser said.

"I 'twill see ye on Skye. Hurry. A storm approaches and 'tis too much for me tae influence," Cuillen said, then he disappeared.

*"ROARKE, let's get out of here,"* Christian bespoke as he strode past where his parents and Morgan were in deep discussion. He vaulted atop his waiting dragon. *"I'm not wasting another minute here."*

# Forty Four

Morning sunlight warmed Devan's face as she drifted between sleep and wakefulness. She mumbled to Christian to shut the blinds and let her rest just a bit longer before she remembered she wasn't in their cozy cottage in Ireland. She breathed in the scent of a peat fire, the salty tang of the nearby ocean, and coffee. Her eyes popped open.

DOCHAS rumbled and shifted behind Devan. *"I am cramped. I need to leave this dwelling. The sun shall feel good upon me."*

*"Yes, my sweet."* Devan bespoke as she rose. She turned to find Graeme pouring coffee into two mugs. As he handed her one, she rubbed the sleep from her eyes. She sipped the hot brew. "You are a godsend, truly."

Graeme nodded. "You're welcome. The sun's out, at least for a bit. I thought we might get out of here for some fresh air."

"DOCHAS mentioned the same thing. I'd like to check her wounds and get her wing joint moving." Devan stretched her aching muscles, especially the shoulder that had been dislocated several months ago. She grimaced as the ground was uncomfortable.

"Right." Graeme pulled the worn tarp that partially blocked the opening aside so Devan could lead her dragon outside.

DOCHAS squeezed her two tons of bulk past the slate boulders that made up the cave's entrance and emerged into the sunlight. Devan let out a low groan as she caught sight of the burn holes in her dragon's iridescent wings. The salve had started the healing process on the smaller holes, but there were several larger ones that she hadn't noticed in the poor lighting of their shelter.

*"Oh, DOCHAS, my sweet. Why didn't you tell me there were more burns?"*

*"I did no' feel all of the burns. Now that I am moving about, I am able to distinguish each one."*

Careful to not bump into DOCHAS's damaged wing, Devan headed back toward the cave's entrance. She ran into Graeme coming out.

He handed her the jar of salve.

She saw the puckered skin of his burned hands and frowned. "I had hoped your burns would have healed more than they have by now."

"They have. It's not even been forty-eight hours. That might be a miracle salve, but miracles still take some time." Graeme looked past her toward her dragon. "Let's see about getting that wing joint moving, then you can tend to DOCHAS's burns while I check on REED and Liam."

Devan and Graeme spent an hour slowly manipulating DOCHAS's wing joint until the dragon was able to fully unfurl the wing and tuck it back against her scaled body without whimpering in pain.

"That's enough for now. Let me take care of these burns," Devan said aloud as she wiped the sweat from her brow.

Graeme pointed to a nasty line of black clouds rapidly approaching from the west. "I'll be back in short order. Looks like we're in for a major snowstorm. Don't stay out here too long."

Devan nodded. "Since there's no way DOCHAS's capable of flying, I want to have another look at that prophecy, see if I can figure it out."

Graeme set off at a quick pace.

Devan smeared the last of the salve over her dragon's burns. "Damn. Next time I'm loading up on Timothy's special salve. I just wish it worked as well on muscles and other soft tissue injuries." She scanned the horizon but couldn't see any other landmass. "Then we'd be able to fly off this isolated rock and back to Ireland."

She tried calling out to ROARKE or GRAYSON. She even attempted to communicate with Graeme's REED, with the same negative result. *Hope I haven't lost my magical gift permanently.*

"GRAYSON's probably frantic with worry. I hope the hatching went okay. Not much I can do if it didn't." Devan spoke aloud. She shoved her fingers through her hair, positive she looked like a scarecrow after a Cat 5 hurricane. "And Christian is surely a raving mess by now."

*"Aye. 'Tis sure I am the Tuatha dragons are searching for us. The storm may have forced me to land, but it can no' keep me down for long."* DOCHAS folded her injured wing against her body. *"I shall regale ROARKE and the Wingless One with my prowess at landing safely during such a storm."*

*"Yes, well let's get back under shelter before all my careful tending of your wounds goes for naught,"* Devan said to her boastful compeer as a gust of wind blew icy water into her face.

By the time Devan had settled DOCHAS and stoked the peat fire, Graeme returned.

He shook off the sleet and removed his coat, then pulled a rolled parchment from its sleeve. "I nicked the original prophecy when Liam was scrambling to cover his fragile flowers and herbs in the garden." He handed it to Devan.

"But won't he realize it's missing? I don't want him storming in here, threatening me again."

DOCHAS snarled her agreement.

Graeme shrugged. "It was behind a stack of books, so he probably won't notice it's missing for a while. Besides, I'll return it when this latest storm passes."

Devan unrolled the yellowed paper and compared it to the one Graeme had hastily scrawled on a scrap of paper months ago. "They're the same. Still can't make out most of the last line." She rolled up the original and handed it back to Graeme. "I'd feel better if you returned this now before Liam has a chance to notice it's gone." At the weary expression on Graeme's face, Devan bristled. "Look, you might think your brother-in-law isn't a threat, but I do. The two of you conspired to bring me here. Your reasoning, though noble, isn't the same as Liam's—even you've got to admit that."

"You're right." Graeme lowered his gaze. "But I won't let Liam hurt you. If you believe nothing else, believe that."

Devan thought over everything she'd learned about Graeme through his words and his actions, and realized she could trust him.

"Still, I don't want to tempt fate. I'm stuck here until DOCHAS can fly, and you can't predict what Liam might do next. I'd feel safer if we didn't do anything that your brother-in-law might misconstrue. You said yourself he's gone wacko since you last saw him. I think his exile has snapped something in him. His rantings tell me he believes he has nothing to lose. That means he's a loose cannon."

Graeme inclined his head in thought. "So, don't do anything to light his fuse?"

"Exactly." Devan pointed to the prophecy in Graeme's hand. "Liam's fixated on what he sees as his role in that prophecy. There's no way he'll not notice it's gone."

"Okay, I see your point." Graeme pulled on his coat, tucking the rolled parchment back in his sleeve. "I won't be gone long." He secured his hood and headed out into the swirling snow.

Devan stood just inside the entrance watching the bruised sky swirl and darken as the intensity of the storm increased.

*"Come inside,"* DOCHAS bespoke, her tone sleepy. *"Ye need to take care with yer ears."*

*"Yes, my sweet. You're right. I'm just frustrated that we can't be away from this place. Though that's not your fault or mine."* Devan spoke the last words quickly so as to not have her compeer reflecting on their earlier predicament. She turned away from the entrance and settled against DOCHAS's curled body.

*"I shall attempt to fly on the morrow."*

*"We'll see whether your injured wing can handle the strain of flight. I wish I knew more about your physiology so I could treat your injury. Of course, I'd have to have the proper medicines on hand, which I don't. What we really need is more time for you to rest, but I'm afraid of staying here too long. I don't trust Liam.*

*And I miss Christian and the others so much."* Devan wrapped her arms around herself. *"I can't be losing my new family, not when I've just found them."*

*"Ye shall never lose me. We are bonded forever."* DOCHAS rested her snout on Devan's shoulder and blew warm air that lifted her hair.

*"Yes, we are. And I'll not leave you either."* Devan reached up to stroke DOCHAS's muzzle. *"Rest now, my sweet."*

Devan tilted the paper with the prophecy written by Graeme toward the flickering light of the fire. "The first stanza seems to indicate Samhain, especially during the brutal storm that Graeme blames Cuillen for." She spoke her thoughts aloud. "But I don't think Liam's The Exiled. Or at least I've not done anything yet to unite him with The Seer, whether that's Christian or Erin, or whoever is The Wronged." Devan pondered the prophecy while DOCHAS's soft snores blended with the sigh of the wind as it found its way into the shelter.

"Perhaps that's my task—bringing Liam to Erin. But then what? And the only talismans I know of are the Tuatha Dragon Clan pendants and my ring." Devan closed her eyes, trying to remember what had been said when she'd asked Erin and Morgan about talismans to help with the dragon communication. "Erin said they didn't have anything like that. But did she mean just the MacKay clan or *any* of the Scottish clans? I'll ask Graeme when he gets back."

She looked at her wrist for the time but remembered once again that she'd left her watch back on her nightstand in the cottage in Ireland. She had barely worn her watch since returning to Ireland after wrapping up her parents' estate. Without the confines of working a regular job, she'd relaxed into the natural rhythm of waking, eating, and going about her day when her body dictated, not by a ticking clock.

Devan glanced once more at her wrist, and that's when she remembered. She caught her breath at the image of a silver bracelet etched to look like two dragon wings with the tips touching, wrapped around Erin's pale wrist. "Damn. I bet that's another talisman."

# Forty Five

Erin shooed Padrick toward his dragon. "I'll meet up with you after I drop Morgan home. I won't leave the MacKay clan vulnerable to attack. And Sutherland is more than angry."

"You think he's going to try something?" Padrick used DECLAN's foreleg to climb into the riding saddle.

"I can guarantee it," Morgan said as he stared at the man in question. "But we'll have the backing of more clan chieftains now that his plans have been exposed. I'll need to get organized."

"Then Erin should stay with you to help protect MacKay territory." Padrick inclined his head in the direction of the Fraser and MacKenzie leaders who were getting settled onto their dragons. "Will they continue to assist you?"

"Aye." Morgan nodded. "And we've still the squad they lent us."

"Then I'll call you when we find Devan and Graeme," Padrick said.

"You best hurry if you're to catch Christian before the next storm hits," Erin said. "We'll be right behind you until we cross into Fraser and MacKenzie lands, then we'll head north, skirting Sutherland territory."

"Take care," Padrick said, then he and DECLAN were airborne and headed westward in the blink of an eye.

As Erin and Morgan edged past the Campbell chieftain mounting his dragon, they heard him exclaim, "No rival clan or foreigner better cross into my lands, not without expecting a battle."

Once seated on TEAGAN, Morgan leaned forward and whispered in Erin's ear, "He's as dangerous as Sutherland."

Erin nodded. "Somehow, I can't see anything getting in the way of Christian finding Devan. Not even a bloody clan war."

"Agreed," Morgan said. "But our priority is to keep the MacKay clan safe. We'll need to shore up our existing alliances. If it comes to war, our allies will be more important than ever."

TEAGAN launched into the air. She followed DECLAN and the Fraser and MacKenzie dragons into the ever-darkening, cloud-filled sky.

Erin quickly lost sight of DECLAN and ROARKE as the larger Irish dragons outpaced even the Fraser and MacKenzie dragons.

Sleet fell, hard and biting, as TEAGAN turned north, heading for home. The wind howled, forcing Erin and Morgan to huddle into their riding coats.

Suddenly TEAGAN plunged and jerked to the left as Sutherland's dragon arrowed right for Erin and Morgan. The fact that they were already hunched close to TEAGAN saved their lives.

"Bloody ifrinn!" Erin whipped around to see the dragon whirl in midair, its mouth opening. *"Dive, TEAGAN. Get us down. You'll never outrun him. Them,"* Erin corrected as she noticed Sinclair's dragon circling above them.

The moss green dragon dove. White-hot flames licked at her tail. She zigzagged, trying to shake her pursuers. Pain on her right flank poured adrenaline into her. *"Attack! I am under attack. Help. Flamed,"* TEAGAN bespoke as she folded her wings and plunged heedlessly toward the rocky landscape.

Morgan slammed into Erin's back, and she had to wrap her arms around TEAGAN's neck in an all-out effort to keep from pitching arse over head off her dragon. Morgan shouted something that was ripped away before she could understand his words.

The ground was fast approaching. Erin mentally screamed to TEAGAN. *"Pull up, pull up. You'll kill us all."*

TEAGAN rolled to the right, spread her wings, and leveled off just before she would have crashed into a rocky outcropping. Another burst of flame licked the area where TEAGAN had been. She flew onward, darting from side to side. Several more flames shot past, though none managed to find their target.

Erin squinted through the sleet and realized TEAGAN had doubled back toward MacKenzie lands. She hoped they'd reach help before Sutherland's dragon killed them.

*"They are coming. Help is coming."* TEAGAN continued her race southward, dodging rocky protrusions and winging through a Scots pine forest. She kept as low to the terrain as possible.

Morgan shouted in Erin's ear. "Have TEAGAN slow down. I'll jump clear."

"Are you crazy? That drop'll kill you. Just hang on. TEAGAN says help's coming."

"She can't know that. I'm extra weight, slowing her down. Without me, you'll have a chance."

Erin clenched Morgan's soaking wet coat sleeves and held on with all her might. "No!"

*"They are here."* TEAGAN pulled upward and flew between two dragons suspended in midair. She arced up and over until she, too, faced the now startled and backwinging Sutherland dragon.

Flames from DECLAN and ROARKE engulfed the air surrounding the Sutherland chieftain and his dragon, though neither was singed. Sutherland ranted and shouted as he was forced to land. The dragonfire ceased once Sutherland dismounted.

Fraser's and MacKenzie's dragons appeared a few moments later and herded the Sinclair dragon from the sky.

"What in hot, holy blazes are ye doing? Starting a war?" Fraser shouted down from his perch atop his dragon. "I'll have yer answer right now, or I'll have my dragon flame ye myself. And it won't be a warning."

TEAGAN trembled. Erin patted her dragon on the neck and spoke aloud, "It's all right now. We're safe. Can you land, my love? I need to see if you're hurt." TEAGAN lowered herself to the ground, and

Erin and Morgan climbed down. Erin's legs gave out from under her, and she landed hard on her knees.

Sinclair snickered but quickly subsided when a burst of flame exploded above his head.

"What right do you have interfering in my rightful dealings with trespassers? They crossed over into my land. I've warned them before, yet they continue to flaunt my sovereignty." Sutherland shoved his wet hair away and glared up at Fraser. "And you allow foreign dragons to flame me?"

"Yer dragon flamed TEAGAN and the MacKay leaders first. Unprovoked, I might add," Fraser said.

"I was protecting my territory." Sutherland folded his beefy arms over his chest, disregarding the falling sleet.

"We were never over your territory, and you know it," Morgan fumed.

"I say you were," Sutherland snarled. "And Sinclair will back me up."

"Well, you're on my land now," MacKenzie said as he directed his dragon to land.

Erin regained her footing and checked on her dragon. Several areas of scales on her right side and tail were blackened and still smoking. Erin clenched her fists and stormed toward Sutherland. "You'll pay for this, ya bloody gobshite. You nearly killed us."

"I wasn't trying to kill you, just force you down and out of Sutherland territory."

Morgan restrained Erin before she could get close enough to take a swing at the belligerent fool. "I should let her have at you. Ambushing us from behind. Waiting until we were alone. Two dragons against one. You're a fecking coward." He looked past Sutherland and spoke to Sinclair. "And you should be ashamed of yourself for going along with this."

"How . . . how did you even know we were in trouble?" Erin asked Fraser when he jumped to the ground after his dragon landed.

Fraser pointed to Padrick and Christian, still atop their hovering dragons. "The two of them almost collided with us, they were in such a hurry. Padrick yelled that ye both were in trouble. We followed."

"TEAGAN called out to DECLAN and ROARKE," Padrick said.

"Telepathically?" Erin shivered from the cold.

"Aye. I guess her fear overrode her distrust. Hell of a way to break through that barrier." Padrick inclined his head toward Sutherland and Sinclair. "What should we do with these feckless eejits?"

"Who the hell are you to call us names and interfere in our business?" Sutherland bristled.

"I'm the bloke who can have his dragon flame you faster than you can blink." Padrick stood up in his riding harness. "Want to test me, ya gutless bully?"

MacKenzie raised his arms. "Let's all calm down." He glared at Sutherland. "If you weren't trying to kill Erin and Morgan, and I'm not completely sure I believe you, then you can go. But remember, we'll be watching you both. And I'll be in contact with MacLeod and the rest of the council members. Any other harassment of the MacKay clan, and the Frasers and the MacKenzies will be on you like scales on dragons."

Sutherland and Sinclair climbed aboard their dragons, muttering the whole time.

After they left, Padrick and Christian guided DECLAN and ROARKE to land.

"Are either of you hurt? How's TEAGAN?" Padrick asked.

Erin gingerly rubbed her chest. "Shaken up. Maybe a bit bruised. TEAGAN had to do some acrobatics to keep from being singed more than she already is."

Christian pulled a jar out of his rucksack, opening it as he approached TEAGAN. "I'll just dab some of this on the burn holes in her right wing."

Erin rushed to TEAGAN's side. "Christ. I swear, if I see that Neanderthal again, I'll—"

"You'll stay the hell away from him. Let MacLeod and the council reign in Sutherland. No vigilante justice, no matter how much he deserves it," Morgan said, then he plugged his nose. "Phew. That stinks."

Christian grinned. "You're right, mate. But it's the best for dragonfire burns. Works instantly, but TEAGAN shouldn't carry a rider, let alone two, for the rest of the day."

"One of you can ride with me and one with Christian," Padrick said. "We should get going before we get stuck here. That storm's coming this way."

"What about your search for Devan and Graeme?" Erin rested her hand on Christian's shoulder as she inspected his first aid handiwork. Her heart ached at the waves of frustration rolling off her son. *He loves Devan deeply.*

"It's near blizzard conditions the closer west you fly," Padrick said. "We wouldn't do much good searching in that mess. But I'd like to check in with Michael in Beaghmore, see if any of the Irish search teams went out before the storm blew in."

Christian finished applying the salve and faced Erin. "You can ride with me. We need to go before the wet washes all the medicine off." He stowed the jar, climbed ROARKE's foreleg, and into the riding harness, then leaned down and helped Erin up.

"Right," Morgan said as he shook hands with Fraser and MacKenzie. "Thanks for the rescue."

"Call when you get home," MacKenzie said as he and Fraser climbed atop their own dragons.

"Will do." Morgan followed Padrick onto DECLAN. "Stay vigilant. I don't trust Sutherland or Sinclair. No matter what they claim, they were out to kill us."

# Forty Six

Padrick directed Christian, with Erin aboard ROARKE, to lead the way to the MacKay compound. TEAGAN flew in the middle, and DECLAN brought up the rear. *That'll be the safest formation, both to ward off another assault and in case TEAGAN falters.*

The sleet turned to snow the farther north the party traveled.

Padrick kept a close vigil for suspicious activities but didn't see any other dragons in the sky around them.

"What was that all about?" Padrick looked over his shoulder to ask Morgan. "I might understand Sutherland wanting to expand his territory, but that attack and the incident at the council meeting doesn't add up. No, that was personal."

"It's Erin's story to tell. I'm sure she'll share it with you when she's ready. We're sorry to involve you. I had thought Sutherland's animosity had waned. Apparently not."

"So this is more than clan rivalry?" Padrick asked.

"Aye."

"Erin's the one in danger. Sutherland wanted to kill her. Though your death would have been a nice bonus, right?"

"Aye. Without Erin or me to lead the MacKay clan, Sutherland could petition the council for our lands to be annexed. He is a ruthless, power-hungry gobshite who'd toss MacKay clan members off the land they've owned and protected for generations."

"If this has been going on for a while, why haven't you and Erin brought it to your council?"

"Sutherland is a canny bastard. He's got Sinclair and other, older chieftains indebted to him. And even if Erin's ready to tell her story, we have no proof that Sutherland . . ." Morgan trailed off in his explanation.

Padrick scowled at Morgan but knew the man wouldn't break Erin's trust. *I'll hold my tongue, for now. But if Erin's in danger, I'll do everything in my power to protect her. I owe her that, and more.*

The rest of the flight was spent in uneasy silence.

Once on the ground, Morgan said, "Let's give Erin some time to get TEAGAN settled. I'll have your dragons looked after. I need to set a watch on the borders. You and Christian can come with me. I'll get you dry clothes to change into." He ushered them toward his house, stopping briefly to speak with Noreen.

"How did Erin seem?" Padrick whispered to Christian.

"Shaken. Quiet. Like she was wrestling with something. Why?"

"There's more to the attacks by Sutherland, but Morgan wouldn't say much except that it's Erin's story to tell." Padrick sighed. He started to say more, but Morgan approached.

"I need to call Ireland, check on the other search team," Padrick said.

"You ken where the phone is," Morgan said. "I'll set the clothes out for you."

Padrick called Michael in Beaghmore. "Did Aisling and the rest of the search team go out?"

"No. It's a whiteout from here eastward. Storm tracker says all of Scotland should hunker down for the next forty-eight hours. GRAYSON tried to bespeak DECLAN and ROARKE. No luck. Don't know if it's the distance, the weather conditions, or something else."

"We couldn't get close to the western islands. Had to turn inland. We're back at the MacKay clan compound. Looks like we'll be stuck here until the blizzard lets up," Padrick said. "Maybe send Aisling and Aiden back to Loughcrew, if it's safe to fly. Send GRAYSON so he can dote over the new hatchlings, and that will keep him well away from Kiely."

"Great minds . . . I've already done all that, my friend. How's Christian? Frantic?"

"Aye," Padrick said. "Especially after the debacle at the council meeting, but that story'll have to wait until I fill in Sean. I'll be in touch."

"Stay safe," Michael said.

Next, Padrick called Sean to relay the incidents at the council meeting and the encounter with the Sutherland and Sinclair chieftains.

"Thanks for keeping me in the know," Sean said. "Not to add to your troubles, but I just found out that Logan and Kelly had a visitor before they were sent into solitary—an American journalist named Hunter. Aisling says he's Devan's ex."

"Aye. The last we heard, he's somewhere here in Scotland." Padrick scrubbed a hand over his face. "Damn. What's Rick Hunter up to?"

"We must keep the dragons secret. At all costs. And you and Christian should to be careful in dealing with the Scottish clans, especially if they have no scruples about going after their own brethren."

"Will do." Padrick rang off and contemplated the unwelcome news.

# Forty Seven

Devan flinched when the tarp covering the entrance was ripped aside. She hadn't heard Graeme's footsteps over the sound of the storm.

"What's this about another talisman?" Liam snarled as he pushed Graeme in front of him and entered the cave. "Answer me."

Devan stared at the wet, snow-covered men. The flash of a blade at Graeme's neck, along with his wide, fear-filled eyes, brought Devan out of her shock.

"What the hell are you doing?" She jumped to her feet, startling her sleeping dragon.

DOCHAS growled, and Devan rested a hand on her dragon's blue snout. *"Easy, my sweet. Don't be rash. I need Graeme unhurt."*

"I caught this traitor stealing my prophecy. No doubt he meant it for you." Liam's crazed expression was magnified by the patches of blistered and sagging skin near his right eye and lower lip. "Give me the talisman. Or . . ." He pressed the blade tight against Graeme's throat. Blood welled, a crimson bead shimmering against pale skin.

"I don't have another talisman," Devan said, her gaze riveted on the knife that threatened to end Graeme's life. *Think. How can I buy time? Keep Graeme alive.* "But someone I know might have one."

"Who?" Liam demanded.

*If I tell him, what then? Will he slash Graeme's throat? How can I get him away from this madman unharmed?* Devan brought her hands in front of her in a placating manner. "Erin, the MacKay clan leader, has a bracelet. It's just a possibility, mind you. Might not even be one. But if you let Graeme go, I'm sure I could convince her to give it to you."

Liam seemed to ponder this. "What talisman do you possess?"

Devan whipped her hands behind her back. "I don't have anything."

"Don't lie. The prophecy says each has a talisman." Liam pulled Graeme closer, the blade dug deeper, and blood trailed down, staining his collar. "Give me yours."

"I'll think about it, but only if you release Graeme." Devan tried to work her dragon ring off her finger and into her back pocket, without dropping it or drawing Liam's attention.

Liam cackled. "You'll give it to me, or I'll slit this traitor's throat."

Graeme grimaced.

"What will Merida think if you kill her brother?" Devan had her ring free, but her hands shook so much she dropped it. She didn't hear anything and hoped it wouldn't roll into Liam's line of sight.

"She'll never know." Spittle flew from Liam's mouth as he eyed DOCHAS. "Now give me your talisman or I'll kill him slowly. I'll leave this skerry, and you'll die as well."

"Then what? Your damn prophecy isn't any good without me." She brought her hands to the back of her neck.

"What are you doing? Stop." Liam's eyes were wild.

Devan sighed, then lifted her chin. "You wanted my talisman. I'm giving it to you." A sudden thought crossed her mind. "By now you've realized Graeme's a part of the prophecy too."

"How do you know that?"

"Graeme showed it to me. I've been working on solving it." Devan frantically searched her memory for the entities listed in the prophecy. "You're The Exiled. That makes Graeme The Wronged."

"How is he The Wronged?" Liam lowered the blade a fraction of an inch.

*Damn. Think, think.* To give herself more time, Devan unclasped her necklace—the one with the dragon head as the top of a Celtic cross. Christian had purchased it for her in Clifden, the town near the

Cliffs of Moher. I'll get it back, she promised herself.

"You know Graeme should've been the Fraser chieftain." She stepped forward, her hand outstretched. The pendant dangled from her fingers, glimmering in the firelight.

Liam nudged Graeme forward. "Take it." Graeme did as ordered. Liam snatched it from his grip, and the movement pulled the blade farther away.

Graeme shifted, lightning quick, and knocked the blade from Liam's grasp. It clattered against the rock wall.

DOCHAS filled her chest, but Devan shouted, "No. No flame. He's not in his right mind."

Graeme took Liam down with a sweep of his leg.

Liam's head banged against the ground. He cried out as he struggled to gain his feet. His face took on the expression of a young boy, lost and alone. "What'd you do that for?"

"You held a knife to my throat and threatened to kill me." Graeme wiped his throat with his thumb and held it out for Liam to see. "You cut me, ya bloody eejit." He forced Liam to his knees.

Devan scooped up her ring, and stuffed it into her pocket, then rummaged in their supplies for something to restrain the madman.

"I wouldn't have really killed you. I just needed the witch's talisman." Liam put on the necklace. "The power it wields."

She found rope and handed it to Graeme. He tied Liam's hands together, pushed him into a sitting position, and tied his hands to his ankles. There wasn't any slack for Liam to stretch out his legs, and he complained bitterly.

Devan considered taking back her necklace but decided against it. If Liam believed he'd gained what he sought, perhaps he'd be more apt to listen to reason.

Graeme picked up the knife and shoved it into his waistband at the small of his back. Then he repositioned Liam against one wall, away from all the supplies or anything that could be used as a weapon. He pulled the tarp at the entrance closed, then went to Devan.

"I'm sorry. He jumped me on my way to the bothy." Graeme pressed his thumb to the gash on his neck. "He's more deranged than ever."

"I've got a theory about that. Let me tend to your wound and I'll explain." Devan grabbed the first aid kit.

Graeme settled on the dirt floor and lowered his voice. "I'm not really a part of the prophecy am I?"

Devan shook her head and whispered, "I'm not even sure Liam's The Exiled. Based on the prophecy, the timing's wrong. I'm still working on the clues. But that was the first thing I could think of to keep Liam from harming you, more than he'd done already. Any more pressure, and he might have nicked your jugular." She cleaned and bandaged the wound.

Graeme shivered and carefully removed his soaked coat. Next came his boots and socks.

Devan retrieved his tartan and tossed it to him. She built up the peat fire while he peeled off his jeans and wrapped the tartan around himself. Then she tucked a blanket around Liam as best she could, given his current bindings. No way was she untying him, but she didn't want him to catch his death either.

Devan and Graeme sat close to the fire where they both had a clear view of Liam. He sat, transfixed on the dragon cross necklace, seemingly oblivious to his wet clothes.

"Thank you for not ordering DOCHAS to kill him. I don't know if Merida could have ever forgiven me. I promised to look after him, but—"

"I've been working on the prophecy. Based on what you told me about there being no magic on this island and the territory borders where the magic is waning, I've come up with several theories."

Devan held up one finger. "First, Liam's magic-starved. He's been on this skerry since Beltaine, right?" Graeme nodded. "That's six months. And he's not ridden KENNETH on any of his magic restoring flights?" Another nod. "Irish dragons and riders need to perform the magic rejuvenating flights every three days, I'm assuming Scottish dragons do as well. And Padrick says the flights gather the magic and help bond the rider and dragon as a pair. Liam hasn't been doing that. I believe his magic-starved condition has warped his mind. I'm hoping it's only temporary."

Devan watched as relief swam in Graeme's whiskey-colored eyes, so similar to her own. "DOCHAS and I flew our magic rejuvenating flight the morning we headed out from Ireland. So . . . three days ago. We should be flying no later than tomorrow."

Graeme nodded. "As should REED and I."

She continued with her theories. "Second, in regard to the magic waning, I believe the magic is a living, breathing entity. When it's in contact with tension, anger, conflict, it protects itself by withdrawing." She demonstrated by spreading her fingers wide, jabbing a twig toward her palm, then closing her fingers to make a fist. "The MacLean clan has probably used this skerry as punishment for a long time. So, according to my theory, it makes sense that the magic has diminished from the standing stones. I'm surprised a clan chieftain would put a dragon and rider in this type of danger."

"The MacLean never would've exiled anyone, let alone his nephew, if he'd known about the magic waning," Graeme insisted. "He'd use this skerry as a harsh punishment, but not to cause an offender to suffer madness. He wouldn't sentence an innocent dragon to certain death. No, I can't believe The MacLean knows of the magic waning." He grimaced. "Damn. I've inadvertently added to Liam's problem."

"How so?" Devan raised her eyebrows.

"In June, when Merida gave birth. I convinced The MacLean to let Liam see Merida and the bairns in hospital. I didn't allow him to fly KENNETH to the mainland. I insisted Liam ride with me." Graeme stole a glance at Liam who had turned on his side, curled up, and fallen asleep. "Yet your theory doesn't explain the other areas that I've found on the mainland."

"My guess is those places have been the sites of conflict between rival clans." Devan's mind strayed to Ireland. "Hmm."

"What?"

"Nothing. It's not important." Devan waved off Graeme's question.

He gave her a skeptical look but didn't press her. "So what do we do to fix it?"

"I believe Liam has a part to play, beyond his madness." *Could he be The Wronged and The Exiled? But that doesn't make sense either. The prophecy says I was uniting three people, but which three?*

Graeme cleared his throat.

Devan shook herself out of her distraction. "We need to get off this skerry. All of us. As soon as possible." Devan threaded her fingers through her dirty hair. "DOCHAS can't fly yet, so I need you and REED to go for help."

"I won't leave you alone with Liam. Besides, it doesn't look like this storm's going to let up anytime soon. It's a blizzard out there. Perhaps DOCHAS will be healed enough to fly in a day or two."

"I have something that will help," Liam said, sounding more coherent and less like a madman. "But you need to get your dragon out of this cave. The cold and damp are prolonging her injuries. She could probably fit in with KENNETH and REED. Their body heat will help." He sat up. "Will you take me with you when you leave?"

"Only if you're not playing us for eejits," Graeme said.

Liam looked down at the ropes binding his hands and ankles. "You can keep me tied up if you need to."

"What do you have that'll help DOCHAS?" Devan asked.

"It's a paste I made from ground-up flowers and herbs. I used it on KENNETH a few months ago when he pulled a muscle in his wing joint," Liam said. "The poultice needs to be massaged into the affected area several times a day, then kept warm. Your dragon should have enough muscle strength to fly in short bursts by the day after tomorrow, if we start treatment tonight."

"What's the catch?" At Liam's questioning stare, Devan explained. "What do you want in return?"

"I just want to see my family. My wife and the bairns." Liam closed his eyes for a moment. "Do you really believe I'm magic-starved? 'Cause I haven't felt right for some time now." He looked at Graeme. "Didn't I tell you that a while ago?"

Graeme slowly nodded. "Yes. I think it was summertime. I also remember when you told me KENNETH hurt himself, and you'd been testing your mixture on him. He flew just fine with REED that day."

"Maybe when you explain this to The MacLean, he'll end my punishment. I'm really not a bad guy." Liam's tone was wistful. "I am sorry for all the trouble I've caused. Let me help. Please."

Devan bespoke DOCHAS. *"I know you've been listening, my sweet. What do you think?"*

*"I am willing to try his medicine. And I am quite cold in this place. I do no' like the snow. A warm pallet would be appreciated."*

*"Then I'll accept. But—"*

*"I will keep up my guard. He is still a puny human. And I can still flame him, or his compeer."*

*"Keep that option as a last resort,"* Devan bespoke her dragon. Then she held Liam's gaze and said, "I'll trust you, but don't make me regret it."

# Forty Eight

After Erin saw to TEAGAN's care with the healer, she trudged home. She knew it was time to explain the origins of the feud between the MacKay clan and Sutherland—between Sutherland and herself—but how much should she tell? *How much can I bring myself to share?*

Morgan met her at the kitchen door. "BOYD told me he heard TEAGAN's call for help. I think if his wing joint could have supported him, he would have taken flight to rescue her."

"I've no doubt," Erin said, then she rested her hand on his forearm. "Can you see to our guests for a few minutes? I want to get out of these wet clothes."

Morgan nodded. "You need to consider the elephant in the room—Sutherland's obsession with you. And what you're going to tell Padrick and Christian. They saved both our lives today. They deserve to understand the extent of Sutherland's depravity. It needs to come from you, before Sutherland tries to spin the story."

"I know. I came to the same conclusion on the flight back here." Erin sighed. "It's one thing for Sutherland to go after me, but quite another when that rat bastard attempts to kill you and TEAGAN too. I'm just not sure how I can explain it in front of my son—grown or not."

"The amount of detail is up to you." Morgan caressed her cheek.

Erin squeezed his hand, then eased away.

"Take a moment for yourself, maybe a long shower. I'll fix everyone lunch."

Erin headed to her room. While hot water pounded her aching and bruised body, her mind wandered back to what had become the start of the Sutherland/MacKay feud. No matter how she tried, she couldn't have predicted the degree to which Sutherland would seek some sort of twisted revenge.

*Maybe if I finally talk about it, get it all said aloud, I'll finally find some peace. But what if Padrick and my son run for their lives after they hear about my failings? Can I handle losing them both again?*

When the water ran cold, she still hadn't decided how much of her past nightmare she'd be able to share. After so long, it felt like a confession. She dressed in her favorite Queen's University jumper, her emotional comfort blanket, and headed toward the sound of three male voices in the living area.

All three men were seated, wolfing down sandwiches and crisps. At some point, they had changed into dry clothes, though Erin wasn't sure where Padrick and Christian had gotten what they wore.

Padrick noticed her first. "Here, have some food." He pointed to the spread laid out on the coffee table. "We were just talking about TEAGAN and how, now that she's started bespeaking with our dragons, she's regaling BOYD with her harrowing escape. She's a right drama queen, knows just when to pause for effect. To build the suspense." He smiled, but it didn't reach his eyes.

Erin acknowledged Padrick's attempt to lighten the mood caused by their narrow escape from serious injury. She grabbed a sandwich, then poured herself a pint of Scottish ale. Subdued, trivial conversation resumed around her as she nibbled on her lunch.

When she could put it off no longer, she set her dishes on the coffee table and cleared her suddenly dry throat.

"I want to explain about Sutherland," Erin said.

Padrick wiped his mouth and fingers, then shifted to face her. "Okay." He set his empty plate next to hers.

Christian glanced at Morgan but didn't say a word.

"There were two incidents long ago," Erin began. Direct and to the point, she decided. She took a deep breath. *Just the facts. Nothing more.* "The first, almost seventeen years ago, shortly after my da died. I had been working at a midlevel hotel as a housekeeper. I went in to clean what I was told was a vacant room. I started to strip the bed, when this man came out of the bath in nothing but a towel. He thought I was a 'working girl' dressed in a maid's outfit. Bought by his mates for his stag party." She shuddered. "I'll spare you the details and just say he didn't believe me when I repeatedly explained I was an employee of the hotel. Not a hooker. He wouldn't let me leave."

"He raped you?" Padrick asked. His voice hoarse, his gaze steely.

Erin nodded, then stole a quick peek at Christian. His stony expression made her shudder.

"And when you reported it?" Padrick gentled his tone.

"The manager didn't believe me. Said the room wasn't booked, and that I was just trying to claim harassment to get money from the hotel. That I was a lazy arse, and he'd had complaints about my work from customers and other staff." Erin looked away. "I was fired."

"That bloody gobshite." Christian exploded to his feet. The rage contorting his normally angelic face promised pain and suffering. "I'll kill him, and the eejit who raped you. Where—?"

Erin raised her hands, halting her son's outburst. "Please. That was long ago. Besides, the manager was sent to gaol for pimping. And I wasn't able to identify my rapist."

She took a sip of her ale, then continued. "I left Glasgow. I found myself at an odd place in my life—a crossroads. Da always said, 'people are most vulnerable when they come to the end of something and have to decide which beginning they're going to take.' I was missing my da something fierce, but my family shunned me, still blamed me for his death. So I headed into the highlands."

Christian sank down in the chair. Hot fury rolled off him in waves.

"I wanted a fresh start." Erin faced Padrick, pleading for understanding. "Have you ever wanted to just lose yourself? Forget who you are, forget your past, forget your mistakes? Start over as someone else?"

Padrick closed the distance between them, held her hands, and pressed his forehead to hers. "I'm sorry. I should've been there for you. You wouldn't have even been in that god-awful situation if Kiely hadn't threatened you. Christ, no wonder you didn't tell me about our son." He seemed to realize they had an audience and let go of her hands.

The tears came out of nowhere. Erin tried to get control of herself. When she did, she brushed the wet from her checks and leaned away to give herself space. *It would be so easy to let him comfort me.*

"There was nothing anyone could have done for me. It was something I had to do for myself. I toughened up. Over time, I found work in a pub in Inverness. By then I was through with the aliases. It was my lone act of defiance. Kiely couldn't hurt me, or my family, anymore."

Padrick shifted, regret swimming in his eyes before his gaze dropped to the floor.

Erin continued. "I needed to be my da's best girl again. Foolish, I know, since he was dead." Erin fingered her bracelet. "Da had this made for me. I figured the jeweler shipped it directly to me because I received it at my flat the day I was fired. I took it as a sign. It's inscribed. 'Honor. Family. Loyalty.' I've tried to live up to those ideals ever since." She pulled her sleeve over the silver bracelet and paused reflectively.

"Anyway, one night I was tending bar and several blokes came in." Erin closed her eyes and drew in a ragged breath. Gone was the warm, quiet of the home she shared with Morgan, the comfort of having Padrick by her side. In its place was the noisy, crowded pub of her memory. The details still so vivid. The fear so real.

The jukebox blasted out a U2 rebel song, the drumbeat pounding the same rhythm as her heart. She poured old man MacQuarry a dram of his favorite whiskey and set it in front of him. The pub door opened and several burly men hustled in.

MacQuarry reached out with eighty-year-old arthritic hands to clasp one of Erin's and brought it to his thin lips for a quick kiss. "When will ye be a marrying me?" he teased. His faded blue eyes twinkled.

It was their nightly ritual, and Erin played along. "As soon as the boss gives me a Saturday off, don't you know."

"Aww, but yer breaking me heart, ye are." MacQuarry pretended to clutch his frail chest. "Saturdays are the busiest of the week. I guess I'll have to settle for a kiss."

The regulars sitting on either side of MacQuarry laughed, as they did every night.

Erin caught sight of one of the newcomers signaling her. "Time to earn my keep," she said and headed toward the strangers.

"What can I get for you gentlemen?" She wiped the scarred oak bar top with a towel.

"I'll have what he's going to get." The older of the men pointed toward MacQuarry and winked at her. His heated, lascivious gaze left no doubt as to what he was referring to.

Heat rose and suffused her cheeks. "Whiskey it is then." She quickly looked to the others. "And for the rest of you?" They each ordered a pint of beer.

She quickly filled the orders, then made her way to the other end of the bar. *Don't like the looks of that bunch.*

Twice more in the next half hour she was called to the far end for refills. And twice more she had to fend off advances from the older man while his companions ribbed him about not making headway with her. Finally, the younger men wandered off to play darts.

Sitting alone, the man pounded down the whiskey. And grew louder and more belligerent with each refill. She tried to limit him, but he wouldn't listen. Alcohol fumes assaulted her every time he leaned toward her. Now, her heart pounded for a different reason—fear.

"Come out with me, after your shift. I can guarantee you'll have a good time." The man leered and grabbed her hand.

"Sorry, no. You're blootered already. And, I'm married." Erin tried to withdraw her hand, but he held on tight.

"You've no ring and you've been flirting with everyone in this place. Besides, no one turns me down. Do you know who I am?" He didn't wait for an answer. "I'm The Sutherland. The most powerful clan chieftain in the north highlands."

Erin yanked her hand away. "I don't care who you are. You could be a faerie prince, and I'd still not go out with you."

"Bitch. You're nothing but a tease. You need to be taught some manners." He went on to call her more despicable names, then toddled off toward his mates.

Erin breathed a sigh of relief. She pasted a smile on her face and continued her shift.

About an hour later, one of Sutherland's young mates stormed up to her. He leaned over, his nose almost touching hers. "What the hell did you promise my da? Flirting's one thing, but he's almost twice your age, Tramp." The last word was spoken in a hiss of contempt.

"I wasn't flirting, and I didn't promise your old man anything." Erin twisted the bar towel in her hands. "You heard him when you first ordered drinks. You and your mates cheered him on. He took that as an invitation. He was persistent, so I shut him down. End of story. Now, if you'll excuse me, I've customers waiting." She didn't wait for the young man's response before she hustled to the other end of the bar.

By closing time, it was a madhouse. Folks wanting their last drinks, closing out the till, wiping down the bottles and tabletops. She shooed the stragglers out, then locked the doors.

She waved to the boss and began the trek home. As she passed an alley, she heard glass breaking, and the streetlight went out. Panic filled her and she ran.

Someone grabbed her arm, pulled her into the now pitch dark alley, and swung her face-first into the wall. Fists pummeled her. When she collapsed to the filthy ground, steel-toe work boots kicked and stomped on her.

She screamed for help, or thought she did. Her face ached and she couldn't move her jaw. Maybe her screams were only in her head.

"No one makes my da look the fool, Tramp." Another kick to her exposed head.

Consciousness slipped away, and with it, the excruciating pain.

Gentle hands touched her face, lifted her matted hair away. A dim light swayed as she opened her swollen and gritty eyes. She groaned, but even that hurt. Pain punched white-hot all over her body.

"Hush now. You're safe. I've got you." A distinguished-looking gentleman with round spectacles peered at her.

She tried to sit up, but darkness edged her vision.

"No. Don't move yet," the man said as he dabbed at her split lip with a green, blue, and purple tartan.

Erin's gaze shifted to the triangular, scaled head of the dragon behind the man. "D . . . dragon." She tried to draw in a breath to continue, but pain wracked her.

The gentleman looked over his shoulder, then back at her. "You can see my dragon?" She nodded. "You cried for help. My dragon heard you."

Erin took a deep breath and she was back in the present—in the warm, quiet house. "As you now know, my rescuer was The MacKay, Morgan's father." She unclenched her fists and relaxed her tense muscles.

Padrick and Christian sat, stunned.

*Christ.* She rushed to soothe them. "That was fifteen years ago. I was near death's door. The MacKay and Morgan brought me here, to the MacKay clan compound. They were shocked I could see their dragons. The MacKay sat at my bedside for a month, demanding I fight for my life at a time when I wanted naught more than to die."

"What happened to your attacker?" Padrick ground out.

Erin shrugged. "I never found out . . . no that's not true, I never wanted to know."

"My father . . ." Morgan spoke in a hushed tone, belaying the fury etched on his face. "He ordered his dragon to mete out justice, the type he knew the system wouldn't give to a barmaid, an outlander."

Erin gasped. "You never told me that."

"That still doesn't explain old man Sutherland's obsession with Erin," Padrick said. "Was he the one who raped you back in Glasgow?"

Erin shook her head. "No, he was too old. At least twenty years older than me. My rapist was younger."

Christian chimed in. "Old man Sutherland wanted Erin that night in the pub, but he didn't get her." When everyone turned to stare at Christian, he said, "One of my visions yesterday was from Sutherland's point of view. He's obsessed with you. Whether for sex, or to own you, or both, isn't clear. For sure he wants to teach you proper respect, wants to break you. If he can't have you, he'd rather see you dead."

"Right," Morgan said. "Especially since the lad who nearly killed Erin was Sutherland's heir."

"Christ Jesus." Padrick shoved his hands through his salt-and-pepper hair.

"So all this time, Sutherland suspected what, that I had his son killed?" Erin asked Morgan. "And you never thought to tell me?"

"I'd say, based on my vision, Sutherland believed you were in cahoots with Morgan and his father," Christian said. "That you were a lover to one, or both." Erin gasped, and Christian continued. "That's what the sick fecker thinks. His dead son isn't at the forefront of his mind. At least not in my vision."

"Has the body ever turned up?" Padrick asked.

Morgan nodded. "The next day. The lad's death was attributed to a murderer who had been killing blokes in and around Inverness's quays that summer."

"But Sutherland never believed that," Christian said. He leaned forward. "Could his son have been your rapist? Maybe he recognized you in the pub? Thought it was funny his old man was hitting on you?"

Erin closed her eyes and thought back to the two worst nights in her life—apart from being forced to leave her son in an orphanage. "Possibly. Though when I saw him in the pub, his hair was longer and he wore a beard and mustache. And he had on rough clothes, like an oilrig worker." She shook her head. "I just don't know for certain."

"Well, we can't change the past," Padrick said. "We must hope for the best, but plan for the worst."

A knock sounded on the front door. Morgan answered it. He brought Noreen into the living area.

"You need to turn on the telly," Noreen said.

Morgan grabbed the remote and switched on the flat screen.

The foreman that BOYD rescued three days ago stood with a blond man at the entrance to a hospital. "Tell the viewers what happened to you? How did you come to be the lone survivor from the explosion on the oilrig known as the Morey?" The interviewer asked in his clipped, American accent. He smiled, showing perfect white teeth.

"I was plucked from the inferno by a beast. A flying beast with wings, scales, and claws," the foreman said, his eyes wild. "And the government's covering it up."

Christian jumped to his feet. "Bloody ifrinn. The reporter's Devan's ex—Rick Hunter."

The segment continued with the image of the burning hulk of the oilrig. "There's been no official statement from the Prime Minister." Once again the image changed to the reporter and a grizzled fisherman decked out in foul-weather gear in front of his boat. "However," the reporter said, "I caught up with Captain Ned from the trawler that rescued Mr. Killian. Tell us, Captain Ned, what do you make of Mr. Killian's claims?"

"What do ya expect the bloody eejit to say? He's covering his arse. 'Cause his incompetence got the rest of his crew killed. Though this story is a bit far-fetched. Flying beasts!"

The reporter gazed into the camera, not one hair of his expensive cut moving in the stiff breeze that swirled snowflakes all around. "You heard it here first. This is Rick Hunter, investigative reporter, on special assignment from America. Tune in all this week as I investigate this and other mysterious happenings throughout Ireland and Great Britain."

"Sounds like the foreman's already a laughingstock," Noreen said.

"Oh, but someone will believe him. The conspiracy theorists will be gearing up, and at a time when Scotland is least prepared to handle a PR nightmare," Erin said.

Padrick scowled, then brightened. "At least we can surmise that Rick Hunter hasn't found Devan. Or she'd have found a way to contact us by now."

"True, but that doesn't make her situation any better. And now that chancer's out to reveal the dragon clans." Christian stormed over to Morgan, grabbed the remote, and punched the off button.

Morgan slammed one fist into the palm of his other hand. "Feck. I should've left that eejit foreman to die the same way he did his men."

# Forty Nine

Devan and Graeme packed their supplies, then bundled up against the blizzard that raged outside. Once they were ready, she doused the fire while Graeme untied the ropes from Liam's feet and helped him to stand. Graeme made Liam carry the boxed supplies. She followed the two men out.

DOCHAS, right behind Devan, scrunched her way through the narrow passageway and emerged from the cave.

The snow whipped at Devan's exposed skin. "Let's hurry before we freeze to death."

Graeme guided the party slowly over the slippery rocks, past the standing stones, and on to the bothy. Once there, he took Liam inside.

Devan carefully climbed the front steps and peeked in through the open door. Graeme had relieved Liam of the supplies, settled him on a chair, and restrained his brother-in-law once again.

Liam started to protest, but shut up when he caught sight of Devan's stony countenance.

Graeme led Devan and DOCHAS to KENNETH's lair. Inside the spacious cave, REED and KENNETH lay curled on top of scattered hay. Both dragons lifted their heads and stared at the intruders.

"This is DOCHAS. She's going to stay here with you until the blizzard passes," Graeme spoke aloud. He pulled three stacked hay bales apart and spread them out over the unoccupied side of the lair.

DOCHAS gingerly made her way to her new bed. Once settled, she blew warm air over Graeme's head. *"Tell him I am grateful,"* she bespoke Devan. *"The bedding and the lair are much warmer than the last."*

Devan relayed her compeer's sentiments before sitting on an extra hay bale. "I'm going to stay here with DOCHAS, make sure she is comfortable. Can you bring Liam's poultice? I want to see if it will work." She was bone-tired and wanted nothing more than to be back in Lough Gur, enfolded in Christian's strong arms.

"Don't you want to warm up by the fire first? Maybe eat something?"

"After I've seen to DOCHAS's injuries." Devan tried to bespeak each of the other two dragons, but yet again to no avail.

Graeme stared at her for a moment, then nodded and left.

Her eyes burned and she blinked furiously. Fear was catching up to her. She needed to pull herself together before Graeme came back. Glancing around to distract herself, she noticed REED and KENNETH had gone back to sleep. *Blizzards seem to be a common occurrence here.* She shuddered and wrapped her arms around herself. *Something else I'll have to get used to, living away from San Francisco's moderate climate.*

*"DOCHAS, my sweet, were you able to bespeak either of your two lair mates?"*

*"Nigh. Though I did make the attempt."*

Graeme called out to her as he entered the cave. He handed her a jar and two large, warm towels. "Liam said to spread this poultice on thick, then wrap the towels around the wing joint as best you can. I've heated them by the fire with a bit of water to keep them moist. They should adhere to the joint."

"Thanks." Devan got to work slathering the mixture where DOCHAS said she hurt the most. When DOCHAS sighed, breathing out a puff of air that ruffled Devan's hair, she cleaned her hands then wrapped the towels as snuggly as she could. She scratched her dragon's eye ridges and leaned her forehead against DOCHAS's neck. *"Rest now, my sweet. I'm going to go warm up, then I'll be back to check on you. If REED or KENNETH bother you, let me know immediately."*

*"Aye. Rest will be beneficial. Ye need to as well."*

*"I'll feel safer if I rest with you. I'm still a bit wary of Liam's abrupt change in behavior."* Devan lifted her head, then blushed when she realized Graeme had witnessed her tender moment with her compeer.

"They're like family, aren't they?" Graeme said as he checked on REED.

"Yes. Closer though." Devan looked in the direction of the bothy. "Speaking of family, how's Liam? Is it just me, or does he seem almost docile since I gave him the pendant?"

"It's not just you. It's as if a switch was flipped when he placed the pendant over his head. Or maybe when he hit his head. He's back to the way he was before the incident on Beltaine—except quieter, more reflective. Like he's finally at peace."

"Right. That makes me suspicious."

Graeme ushered Devan out of the cave. The snow was piling up all around. "You can bet I'll keep a close watch over him." He fingered the bandage on his throat. "He won't get the jump on me again, I promise."

They stomped the wet from their boots and entered the bothy. Liam was still sitting upright in the chair, asleep. His face was relaxed and made him look more like a young man in his prime than the grizzled madman Devan had first encountered. The sagging skin—like melted wax—around his eye and lip would probably scar as it healed and retain the look. The other burns had healed well, leaving several blisters and red welts that would continue to improve over the next few days.

"Here," Graeme said as he helped Devan remove her coat. "Go warm up by the fire. I've got some stew in the pot and some water heating for tea." He hung her coat on a peg near the door, then prepared a mug of tea for her.

Devan drifted to the fire. She surveyed the small room with its bed along one wall and its kitchen nook on the opposite side. The fireplace warmed her as she sipped her tea. The scent of cooking meat and vegetables made her mouth water and her stomach rumble.

"The vegetables are from Liam's garden. The last of the season."

Graeme stirred the pot that hung on a hook to the side of the fireplace. "It may be simple food, but it'll keep us warm."

Devan nodded. She wished she was sharing a meal with Christian right now, but at least she had food and both she and her compeer were dry and warm. *I'll get back to you, a ghra. When this storm blows over, and when DOCHAS can fly again. I promise.*

The telephone rang. Morgan debated about answering it but knew it would be The MacLeod. especially right on the heels of that broadcast.

"Morgan," he said into the receiver, then had to yank it away from his ear or risk a ruptured eardrum.

"What in God's name is going on up there? Have you seen the news? What did you do to that foreman? How could he have seen one of the dragons? I thought you said in your report that he was unconscious? What else is that bloody Yank reporter going to talk about?" The MacLeod shouted rapid-fire questions at Morgan without a breath in between. "Well?"

"I saved that bloody eejit's life. Should have left him to die like he did his crew," Morgan replied. "Noreen involved her brother, the fisherman. Ned did a great job with the reporter."

"I've been inundated with calls from the Prime Minister and his staff. I've even heard from the royal family." MacLeod blew out a sigh. "Incidents like this make officials want to bring us back under Britain's thumb. Rumors swirl. Politicos and pundits are havering shite."

"There's always incidents that stir people up. You just need to keep spouting the 'he's crazy' line. No civilian's actually seen one of the dragons." Morgan rubbed the back of his neck. "I've something else to speak to you about."

"If it's Sutherland's attack on you and Erin this afternoon, Fraser and MacKenzie have already briefed me. Once this latest storm blows over, I'll be paying Sutherland a visit. I'll expect a formal complaint from you by email before tomorrow morning. And Morgan . . .?"

"Yes?"

"Let me handle Sutherland. Stay well clear of him. Understood?"

"I won't go borrowing trouble, but I can't say the same for Sutherland. He's beyond deranged. Fraser and MacKenzie were a bit late coming to our rescue and didn't see the encounter. The Irish dragonriders saved our lives. Sutherland was going to kill us. I won't give him another chance, so don't dally."

"Please keep in mind the larger picture. I'm not talking about skirmishes between rival clans—no matter how vicious," MacLeod said. "That stupid broadcast might just be the final nail in the coffin for Scottish independence."

# Fifty

Devan woke as DOCHAS lifted her head and sniffed. It took Devan a moment to realize she was nestled between her dragon's forelegs, and under several layers of blankets. She listened intently, but most noises sounded as if they were underwater. *Blasted eardrums. Wait. There. Was that a footstep?*

*"Did you hear that?"* Devan bespoke her compeer.

*"Aye,"* the dragon replied in a sleepy voice. *"It is no' coming from neither KENNETH nor REED."*

Devan kicked off the blankets and rose. She rested her palm against her dragon's warm chest. *"Be ready. Just in case."*

Before DOCHAS could answer, Liam stepped into the lair and halted. He carried several steaming towels and a fresh jar of poultice. His coat had a light dusting of snow on it.

"Sorry. I didn't mean to disturb you," Liam said. "Just wanted to get another treatment started on your dragon, if she'll let me." He eyed DOCHAS. "I'm afraid the damp of KENNETH's lair isn't good for injuries. It slows the healing process. Wrapping her wing joint in the heated towels will help drive in the poultice."

Devan stole a glance at her dragon. DOCHAS's multifaceted, sapphire blue eyes whirled lazily, indicating she didn't feel threatened.

"Where's Graeme?" Devan asked, still not quite willing to leave the protection of her dragon.

"He's in the loo. He'll be here in a few minutes." Liam inclined his head toward the two male dragons. "I figured KENNETH would be awake by now. He likes to fish early in the morning. 'Course, with the storm yesterday and the snow still falling, I don't want him flying. Too much of a risk."

At the mention of his name, KENNETH opened his eyes and dipped his pale yellow snout in acknowledgment of his intentions to not fly today. He snuffled then repositioned himself, which caused REED to grumble and wrap his rust-colored spiked tail closer to his body.

Liam chuckled. "KENNETH says that no dragon in his right mind will be flying in these conditions."

Devan gaped at Liam. *Wow. He's like a normal human being again. Not the raving lunatic I met just a few days ago. Could my necklace be having some kind of placebo effect on him?* She closed her mouth. *Or is there magic in my necklace after all?*

"Shall we get started?" Liam held out his encumbered arms. "We need to get the blood flowing to her injured joint. Massage, movement, and the warm compresses will chase the night's coldness away."

Devan started forward when Graeme rushed in. He slid to a stop with his coat half on and his boots untied.

"I told you to wait for me," Graeme huffed, struggling to find the other sleeve opening.

Liam shrugged. "Did you bring the pail of water?"

"No. I—"

"You thought I came out here to accost the lass, right?" When Graeme didn't answer, Liam continued. "I might be the impulsive eejit you've always claimed, but my horrendous actions these last few days isn't who I am. You ken me better than most. I swear, it's like I was possessed before." He hung his head. "I'm so ashamed."

Devan touched Liam's forearm, startling him. "I believe you. And your previous behavior supports my theory that you've been magic-starved. But you have to understand our wariness."

Liam nodded. "Aye. I just want to help so we can get off this blasted skerry. I want to see my wife and bairns."

Devan took the armload of towels and medicine from Liam. "Why don't you get that bucket of water, then we'll get started. With three of us, we'll finish quicker. And I could use a cup of coffee."

Liam stopped next to Graeme on his way outside. "I need Merida to be proud of me. I want to be her hero, hers and the bairns. I'm counting on you to keep me from going radgy again."

When Liam was gone, Devan inclined her head to have Graeme follow her away from the two male dragons.

"Did you untie him after I left last night? Or did he get out on his own?" She whispered.

"I untied him. I'm a light sleeper, so I figured I'd hear him if he woke before me. He didn't move all night. I don't think he's slept much, at least not since I was here last." Graeme rubbed his neck and groaned. "That sofa's not comfortable. I miss my bed. I'll be glad when we can leave this place."

"Any chance of that happening today?" Devan glanced at her dragon. "If DOCHAS is able to fly, I mean."

"Probably not. While it's no longer whiteout conditions, it's still snowing steadily. And even if DOCHAS could fly, she'd be better off with a full day's treatment and staying relatively warm." Graeme had the unfocused look in his eyes, and Devan knew he bespoke REED.

DOCHAS chuffed. *"I am stronger than those two Caledonian dragons. If ye desire, we can fly away now."*

*"I've no doubt, my sweet. But we need to check your range of motion. See how you're faring. And I don't fancy flying in bone-numbing snowfall. Let's hope tomorrow is clearer."*

*"As ye wish."*

Liam came in carrying two buckets of water. He set one down near the male dragons, and the other he kept near the door, out of the way.

Devan, Graeme, and Liam spent an hour massaging, rotating, and working the poultice into the dragon's wing joint before wrapping it in the warm towels. Afterward, Liam fetched the water and DOCHAS drank her fill.

*"I feel better already. The warmth is a blessing."* Her eyes closed and she sighed.

They treated DOCHAS four more times as the snow continued to fall throughout the day and into the night.

The longer Devan was around Liam, the more she was convinced the loss of magic on the skerry was to blame for his madness. *But why has his craziness gone away? It's not like I gave him my ring.* She continued to ponder this, but couldn't come up with a satisfactory answer.

Padrick gazed out Erin's kitchen window as snow flurries swirled past. *I wonder if this'll let up by tomorrow.* He'd been restless all day, but nothing compared to Christian. He'd paced the downstairs rooms like a caged lion.

When gloaming darkened the already gray skies, Padrick went back into the living area.

Morgan turned on the telly. No one sat as the evening news broadcast began.

Rick Hunter, his hair perfect, smiled at the viewing audience. "Before I came to Scotland a few days ago, I traveled to Dublin, Ireland, where I interviewed two men down on their luck and locked away for crimes they claim they didn't commit."

Padrick watched Christian. *Oh, God. I should've told him. At least he wouldn't have been blindsided.*

Rick continued reporting. "Kelly Dunkirk and his boss, Logan Walsh, told me an incredible story. Last spring, Mr. Dunkirk, running an errand for his boss, was attacked by a beast. He said, and I quote, 'the beast had claws the size of a rubbish can. It clutched my shoulders. I couldn't see it, only its scaly claws, but I felt something solid against my back.' Mr. Dunkirk mentioned he was trying to help a young woman, an American, when he was attacked. He was genuinely frightened. And I, for one, believe him. Yet the gardaí officers wouldn't listen. Claimed he was lying. Mr. Dunkirk was incarcerated on a trumped-up charge of assault," Rick said.

Padrick scoffed. "He believes the words of criminals? Probably didn't even read the gardaí report. This boyo calls himself an investigative reporter? He's a buffoon."

"Since my interview with Mr. Dunkirk and Mr. Logan, I've learned the young American woman, Miss Devan Fraser, my fiancée, has gone missing." Rick held up a photo of Devan with the Golden Gate Bridge in the background. "I've reason to believe Miss Fraser is now in Scotland, in the company of one Christian Riley, alleged mob boss. If you've seen Devan, please contact the phone number on the screen. There's a reward for information leading to her whereabouts."

"That bloody gobshite." Christian scowled. "He's trying to get Devan back. And he'll use whatever means he can to do it, regardless of Devan's desires. He's nothing but a fecking chancer doing Logan's bidding."

Rick had lowered the photo and was still speaking. "My research suggests this beast in Ireland might be similar to the beast that rescued Mr. Killian, the oilrig survivor from my report yesterday. And once again, officials have no comment. I'm smelling a government cover-up." He smiled, showing straight, white teeth. "This is Rick Hunter, investigative reporter. Tune in tomorrow as I uncover more mysterious sightings. And if you'd like to report any flying beasts, please call the number on the bottom of the screen."

Christian stormed toward the telly as though he was going to smash it to smithereens, but spun on his heels just before he reached it. He raked a hand through his hair and swore inventively. "And he'll destroy anyone or anything that stands in his way. Including dragons."

The telephone rang, and Morgan went to the kitchen to answer it.

"It's for you," Morgan said to Padrick as he returned to turn off the telly.

Padrick stepped into the kitchen and drew a deep breath before lifting the receiver. "Hello."

"Did you see that rubbish?" Sean asked. "How'd Christian take it?"

"He's ready to tear that bastard apart, limb by limb," Padrick said.

"How's the Taoiseach holding up? What've you told him to say to the media?"

"He's ready to unleash FIONN on that sorry excuse for a reporter. I had to talk the Taoiseach off the ledge. Told him to stick with the truth as written in the gardaí report of Kelly stalking and assaulting Devan. And that Kelly's using this farce of a story to get himself and his boss out of gaol."

"Glad I'm not in your shoes," Padrick said. "I better get back to calm Christian down before he goes out into this snowstorm to hunt down Mr. Hunter."

"The weather's supposed to break by morning. So I'll send Aisling, Aiden, and Matthew to meet up with you. Take care of Christian. And find Devan before anyone else does. She's now a target for profit."

"Aye." Padrick hung up. *Bloody ifrinn. Hadn't thought of that.*

Padrick returned to the living area. At the quizzical looks on Morgan's and Erin's faces, he said, "Seems the Irish Taoiseach caught the latest BBC broadcast. He's just as furious as your Prime Minister. And our search for Devan just got harder, now that Rick Hunter's made her a target."

Christian whirled to face Padrick. "I'll kill him."

# Fifty One

Warm, winter sunlight glistened on the massive snowdrifts piled outside the lair entrance. *At least it's not snowing anymore.* Devan shaded her eyes and surveyed her surroundings for the first time since she'd spotted the tiny spit of land during the brunt of the storm that forced her and DOCHAS to land. Besides the dragon lair and the bothy Liam had been exiled to, the landscape not covered by snow was a jumble of shale rock. To the south, Devan spied the standing stones she and DOCHAS had huddled against four days ago before Graeme led them to the tiny cave.

*Has it only been four days? Feels like I've been separated from Christian for weeks. This whole island is about the same size as Alcatraz. It's a wonder anyone can find this place. I'll be glad to leave.*

*"DOCHAS, my sweet. Come outside and stretch your wings,"* Devan bespoke her compeer as she pushed her dragon ring back onto her right middle finger. *I don't think Liam will notice my ring now.*

The blue and silver dragon trundled out. Devan unwrapped the towels from her dragon's injured joint, then waited. DOCHAS gingerly stretched both wings. The smaller burn holes had healed clean and the larger ones were much improved.

*"It does no' hurt or stick as before."* DOCHAS preened. *"I shall fly now."*

*"Not yet,"* Devan bespoke. *"Wait for REED and KENNETH."*

*"Why?"* DOCHAS's tone indicated her disgust at being hampered by the two male dragons.

*"Prudence. If something goes wrong, they can help."*

DOCHAS snorted and a wisp of smoke curled from her nostrils.

*"I'll feel better."* Devan raked a hand through her hair. *"Do it for me."*

The blue dragon nodded her triangular head as Devan peered into the lair and called the two male dragons outside.

The door of the bothy opened and Graeme and Liam stepped out.

"DOCHAS wants to test her wing joint," Devan said. "Can you ask your dragons to accompany her on a short flight around the skerry? If she can fly, then we can leave today."

Excitement shimmered off Liam. "Of course."

Graeme agreed, and the two gazed at their dragons as they spoke telepathically.

In short order, the two male dragons leapt skyward and circled the bothy to hover at a safe distance away.

Above, the sky held soft and blue after the last few days of storms.

DOCHAS flapped her wings twice, sending snow swirling, then leapt into the air. She rose gracefully, banked toward the south, and bugled a triumphant cry. *"Oh, I have missed this. The freedom to take flight."*

*"No problems?"*

*"Nigh."*

*"Excellent. Come back now. We'll be ready to leave soon. I want to find Christian."*

*"Aye. And ROARKE."*

Devan grinned as DOCHAS led the two male dragons back to the bothy. She landed with no difficulty.

Liam rushed inside the bothy, packed his rucksack, and extinguished the peat fire in the hearth. He handed over the prophecy to Devan for safekeeping.

"We'll need to get the clans together to explain about the prophecy," Devan said, "but first we'd best perform the magic rejuvenating flights. Especially Liam and KENNETH. Where's the closest stone circle?"

"Lochbuie Standing Stones on Mull," Graeme said.

Liam shuddered. "I'd rather not return to the scene of my shameful actions. Let's head to one of the smaller dances on the mainland. I know just the place. It's close to The MacLean's home. We can tell him about the magic waning. And my part in finding the problem."

"All right," Graeme said. "But what if he doesn't release you from your punishment? Are you prepared for that?"

Liam shrugged. "After we explain, I believe he'll be reasonable and end my exile. Especially if I'm a part of the prophecy, as Devan says."

"And what of your burns? How will you explain those?" Devan asked the two men.

Liam and Graeme studied each other, then Liam spoke, "Tell the truth. A gross misunderstanding. I was radgy from my magic-starved condition. The MacLean and all the clan chieftains must understand what can happen if we don't stop the magic from waning."

Twenty minutes later, the three dragons were harnessed and their riders mounted and ready for flight.

Devan indicated Graeme should lead the trio, at least until they approached The MacLean's compound.

When all three dragons left the coastline of the skerry, she called out to ROARKE, DECLAN, and GRAYSON, *"Can any of you hear me?"* She received no reply.

As they flew over the coastline toward Ardtornish Castle, DOCHAS faltered and spiraled toward the ruins. *"I can no' fly much farther. I must rest."*

Devan caught herself before she banged against her dragon. She tried to bespeak REED, but still couldn't get a reply. She whistled and was relieved when Liam glanced over his shoulder. He got Graeme's attention and the two of them returned to hover in front of DOCHAS.

"DOCHAS needs to rest," Devan shouted, pointing downward.

"We are a few minutes away," Liam said. "Can she . . .?"

DOCHAS glided down. She landed heavily just north of the ruins, on a grassy knoll. Sheep bleated in a rock walled pasture to her left.

Devan slid from her riding harness as the two male dragons landed nearby. She ran her hands over DOCHAS's injured wing joint and breathed a sigh of relief that it wasn't unduly warm or swollen.

"I think she just got tired," Devan said when Graeme and Liam joined her. "Do you want to fly on ahead?"

"No. We should stay together," Graeme said. "A few more minutes won't matter."

Devan nodded as she stroked DOCHAS's dull-looking snout. *Is DOCHAS suffering from the waning magic already? Is this how it starts? Or is this dullness from her injuries?*

A half an hour later, DOCHAS bespoke, *"I am able to fly now."*

The male dragons waited until DOCHAS had taken flight before they leapt skyward.

They arrived at the standing stones within minutes. KENNETH flew the magic rejuvenating pattern first, followed by DOCHAS.

After Devan and her compeer completed the Celtic knot pattern and hovered to watch REED, she ran her fingers over the now luminescent blue on her dragon's triangular head and marveled at the noticeable improvement. *The ritual is bound to help Liam. Will one circuit be enough? He should fly the pattern twice. Or maybe another one close by.*

Her thoughts were interrupted as unknown dragon voices assaulted her. *"I shall flame Auld Donald if he dares cross into my territory." "He has been warned. Blast him from the sky." "He is no' over our lands. Stop!"*

The she heard a heartrending cry. *"Help! It burns, it burns. Help me."*

Devan gasped. *"REED, KENNETH, can you hear me?"* She concentrated on her two flying companions.

*"Aye,"* they bespoke together.

*"There are dragons fighting dragons."* Devan twisted in her riding harness, trying to pinpoint the direction of the injured dragon. *There.* Her desire to find Christian warred with what she considered her duty—to help those in need. She steered DOCHAS to the southeast, away from MacKay territory and her beloved. *"Follow me."*

The two dragons caught up to her.

"We're heading toward Campbell territory," Graeme called out. "You don't want to trespass onto his lands. Not without several clans to back you up."

"But there's at least one dragon that's been flamed." Devan leaned closer to her compeer's body. As she urged DOCHAS faster, they were overtaken by a dozen dragons.

KENNETH bugled, and Liam shouted, "It's The MacLean."

The MacLean dragons wheeled in the air and hovered in front of Devan and DOCHAS, forcing them to stop in mid-air. REED and KENNETH flanked DOCHAS.

"What are ye doing here?" The MacLean bellowed.

Liam started to speak, but Devan interrupted. "There's no time to explain. The Campbells are fighting with the Donalds. At least one dragon's hurt. We've got to stop it."

"We ken. Donald's son phoned me. How—?"

"Later." Devan pointed to a flurry of dragons in the distance. "Let's go."

The MacLean dragons spun around, and they all headed toward the skirmish.

# Fifty Two

Roused from a deep sleep, Erin willed her conscious to go back to the vision she was having in which dragons fought dragons. *Which clans and where*? The incessant pounding on her door finally pulled her from her semi-aware state. "Coming." Shivering at the brisk morning air, she threw on her robe, then opened the door. A disheveled Morgan balanced against the doorframe, shoving his feet into his riding boots.

"One of the lookouts phoned. Sutherland and Sinclair dragons are gathering at our southern border." Morgan finger-combed his hair.

"Bloody ifrinn. What's that madman thinking?" Erin turned and headed for her closet. "I'll be ready in five. Have you sounded the alarm?" She grabbed the first warm clothes she found and began dressing. "What about Padrick and Christian?"

"Every dragon and rider that can fly are getting ready, Padrick and Christian included. I've phoned Fraser and MacKenzie. They'll be in the sky and headed this way within minutes. I've also talked to MacLeod. He's coming."

Erin, still buttoning her shirt, darted into the loo. She splashed cold water on her face, brushed her teeth, then ran a brush through her curls. She waved Morgan ahead of her, and they thundered down the stairs.

Padrick and Christian were donning their riding jackets when Erin came into the foyer. She quickly pulled her coat on and found her riding gloves in the pockets.

The riders stepped outside, snow crunching under their feet. Slush dripped from the rooftops.

In less than the five minutes she had promised, Erin climbed aboard her dragon and Morgan settled in behind her. *Too bad BOYD isn't ready for this flight. We could use another dragon.*

Ten MacKay dragons had lined up in a wedge position behind TEAGAN, DECLAN, and ROARKE. When all were ready, Erin gave the signal and the dragons leapt skyward.

By the time they arrived at the southern border, Sutherland and Sinclair had amassed triple the number of dragons pledged to the MacKay clan. So far, the two sides only faced off against each other, but tensions ran high. No one had crossed the boundary line and attacked the other. Yet.

*How can I neutralize this standoff when we're on the brink of war?*

Sutherland focused on Erin. His hatred palpable.

As she took in the volatile scene, her anxiety soared. *How many will die today? All because of me.*

Erin, her gaze not leaving Sutherland, tilted her head toward Morgan and whispered, "How the hell is Sutherland keeping all these dragons and riders under his control?"

"I don't ken, but anything's possible with Sutherland. Especially after that bastard tried to kill us." Morgan glared at the man over Erin's shoulder.

"Do we land and attempt to diffuse this?"

"No. I won't put our clan mates at the disadvantage. He's instigating this confrontation."

"I agree. Just wanted to make sure we're of the same mind." Erin maneuvered TEAGAN so the dragon's left flank faced Sutherland, and he could see both Morgan and herself. "How long before we have backup?"

Morgan shrugged, then pitched his voice to carry over the distance. "What do you want, Sutherland?"

"I want the woman responsible for my oldest son, Archie's death. Hand over Erin and I'll think about letting the rest of the MacKay clan live." Sutherland spit out the words.

"Are the rest of you prepared to go to battle over an incident that happened over fifteen years ago? One in which Erin was a victim?" Morgan asked.

"Wait." A younger version of Sutherland spoke up. "You claimed the MacKay leaders trespassed on our lands. That their intentions were malicious. What is this really all about, some personal vendetta? If you truly believed this woman was responsible for my brother's death, why is this the first I'm hearing of it?"

Sutherland seethed but kept his mouth shut.

"If you're going to start a feud with our brethren, where dragons and riders are likely to die, it best be about something more than bad blood between you and one woman." The young man lifted his chin at half a dozen younger riders who nodded in agreement. Several of the more seasoned riders shifted in their riding harnesses, but no one spoke out against their chieftain.

"Hold yer whist, you ungrateful whelp." Sutherland glowered at the young man. "You dare question me, your chieftain? I demand your obedience, your respect, your loyalty." Spittle flew from his mouth and his hands shook. "You're a waste. You'll never be a leader, not like my Archie. If you won't stand by your chieftain, then get the hell outta my sight. I'm sorry you were ever born."

The young man recoiled at his father's venomous words.

Morgan interrupted the awkward confrontation. "Do any of you even ken what happened that night in Inverness?" He paused. Several riders from both Sutherland and Sinclair clans looked bewildered. "No? Then let me—"

"They ken the truth. I told them," Sutherland yelled. "That witch lured my son into an alley and killed him. I've a right to avenge his death."

"You caused your son's death," Morgan accused. "It was your behavior. I was there in that alley with my father, The MacKay. I remember as though it happened yesterday. It was the Saturday evening of my first council meeting. Da and I were visiting friends in

Inverness on our way home. Da's dragon heard a tortuous scream. Your son beat, kicked, and stomped Erin until she was unconscious. If it wasn't for my father's interference, she'd have died that night. All because your drunken flirting with Erin—a woman half your age—and her rejection of your advances, enraged your son."

"You're a damn liar. Always ken that witch could wrap weak-minded men 'round her finger. Your father wasn't fit to be clan chieftain. And neither are you. Choosing that witch-whore as your co-leader. She takes over men's minds with her witchcraft. Uses her so-called visions to spread her evil. She'll drive the Alba dragonriders into extinction. Mark my words." Sutherland swept his hand around and below him. "I swore to protect my lands. I'll not have her trespassing and using her wiles on my men. The witch must burn. She's an abomination."

Heat bloomed on Erin's cheeks, and she clenched her jaw to keep from unleashing her Irish temper. *Don't rise to the bait. It'll only fuel his crazed, sexist ideology.* She scanned the Sutherland and Sinclair riders and realized there wasn't a single woman among them. *Christ. Are there no women riders in either territory? That can't be, else how would their dragons breed?* Morgan's words broke into her musing.

"She's no more a witch than your wife or your mother were, God rest their souls." Morgan made the sign of the cross on his chest. "You're deflecting from your real reason for wanting Erin killed. And I have proof of your son's actions."

"What proof?"

"His boots." At Sutherland's gasp, Morgan continued. "Da gave them to a constable—the friend we were visiting that night. The constable bagged them as evidence. They were covered in Erin's blood."

"Not true. And if you've brought in a dirty Copper to hide the witch's murderous ways, I'll have this man's badge, I will." Sutherland's face turned scarlet. The vein in his forehead pulsed rapidly. "The police claimed—"

"The police attributed his death to the Quay Murderer to keep the dragons a secret. My father went along with the authorities ruse for the safety and future of all Alba," Morgan said. "You've already avenged your son's death when you killed my father and his compeer during that border skirmish ten years ago. And you ken it. You gloated about your revenge. Or are you going to deny that too?"

Sutherland screamed in rage, kicked his dragon, and charged.

As she flew south with the MacLean dragons, Devan once more tried bespeaking ROARKE.

*"Ring Wearer, where are ye?"* ROARKE replied. *"Christian has been frantic with worry. As have I."*

*"It's a long story. Are you and DECLAN still in Scotland?"*

*"Aye. We are with Christian's mum."* ROARKE sounded distracted.

*"Tell them the Campbells are attacking the Donalds. I'm with the MacLean chieftain. We're trying to stop it. Can you come help?"*

*"We are also engaged in a skirmish. Sutherland and Sinclair . . ."*

DOCHAS halted so fast, REED nearly collided with her.

"What the hell?" Graeme shouted as he righted himself on his dragon's back.

"I've got to go. Sutherland and Sinclair are attacking the MacKay clan. My friends are in danger," Devan said. "Tell MacLean about Liam and the magic. I'll bespeak REED later."

"But they're half the length of Scotland away. It'll take you hours to get there, especially with DOCHAS not at full strength."

"I must try." Devan fisted her hand against her heart. "We'll meet again. Eitilt shábháilte, *mo chara.*"

Graeme returned the farewell and spurred his dragon to catch up to the others.

Every nerve in Devan's body screamed for her to hurry. As she turned her dragon northward, she heard a melodious female voice bespeaking her. *"Ring Wearer, ye are alive. Thank the fates. Where have ye been?"*

After a moment's hesitation, Devan recognized the voice. *"BRIANNA, where are you? Has something happened?"* Devan kept her dragon hovering in place.

*"Nigh. I fly with KIERAN and SEBASTIAN to search for ye, as we have since ye went missing. We have left the north coast of Éire, hoping to meet with DECLAN and ROARKE on the Isle of Skye. Where—?"*

*"Perfect. I'm on my way to MacKay territory to help Padrick and Christian with an attack from a rival clan. But a second skirmish has broken out here on the West Coast."* Devan closed her eyes and recalled the map she'd studied for months while searching for Erin. She opened her eyes and gazed westward. The Irish dragons would be almost even with the Campbell/Donald border, she thought. *"I need you to head east to help stop this second attack. Look for REED, a rust-colored dragon, and his rider, Graeme Fraser. He's a good guy. I'll let him know to keep an eye out for you. We must put a stop to all this clan rivalry and dragons fighting dragons. I'll be in touch."*

*"Aye. Keep safe."* BRIANNA's soft voice withdrew from Devan's mind.

She relayed to REED to be on the lookout for the three Irish dragons and riders.

Before DOCHAS downstroked to resume her flight, Devan heard a popping sound. In the blink of an eye, an old man wearing a silver doublet and black boots sat perched on DOCHAS's neck, facing Devan.

"Whoa! Who in the world are you?" Devan jerked her head back. *Breathe. Just breathe.*

"I am Cuillen, the Faerie Prince. And ye must be Devan."

"You." Anger rushed through Devan. "You're the cause of DOCHAS and me crashing. How'd you get here?"

Cuillen quirked his right eyebrow but didn't speak.

"Never mind. Get off. I'm in a hurry." Devan tried to shoo him away, but he wouldn't budge.

"I think no'. Ye are The One in me prophecy. Ye must bring the magic back."

"I won't be doing anything if my friends die at the hands of the Sutherlands and Sinclairs," Devan lashed out.

"What do ye mean?"

Devan scowled. "Sutherland and Sinclair are attacking the MacKay dragons. My friends are—"

"Hold tight." Cuillen snapped his gnarled fingers and the landscape below them disappeared.

The MacKay dragons scattered as the Sutherland and Sinclair dragons surged across the border. Flames burst forth from dragons on both sides.

*"Fly high, TEAGAN. Don't let Sutherland get above you,"* Erin bespoke.

The moss green dragon pumped her wings furiously in a race to outpace the Sutherland dragon.

"Look out! Sinclair's about to cut us off." Morgan pointed to his right.

*"Left, left."* Erin gripped the riding harness and squeezed her legs tight to TEAGAN's side as the dragon banked at a precarious angle. *Christ, Sutherland's lost his mind. He doesn't care if dragons and riders die. Even his own clan mates.*

Dragons whizzed past, their foreclaws extended. Fire streamed from open maws.

"Sutherland's son is leaving," Morgan shouted in Erin's ear, pointing at the man. "Stop him before he brings reinforcements."

Erin glanced in the direction Morgan was pointing. "No, look. He's not heading home. He and his mates are staying out of the fray. They're not engaging MacKay dragons, so we won't attack them. But keep an eye out." She quickly guided TEAGAN away as another Sinclair dragon dove to attack.

Smoke clouded the sky. Dragon roars and rider howls permeated the air.

Erin, too busy focusing on keeping away from Sutherland and Sinclair, lost sight of the MacKay and Irish contingent. *Please, stay safe, my love. You and our son.*

Two Sutherland dragons crossed too close to each other and their wingtips tangled up. They shrieked as their scaled bodies collided and they struggled to extricate themselves. Neither was able to break free, and Erin shuddered as the two dragons and their riders, wrapped together in a sickening parody of lovers, tumbled to their deaths.

TEAGAN dodged and weaved and spewed fire at any rival dragons that flew close enough.

Erin watched, horrified, as time seemed to slow when ROARKE spiraled up and over, nearly unseating Christian, to change from being the pursued to being the pursuer. Her heart thumped wildly in her chest at the thought of her son falling to his death because of Sutherland's deranged sense of entitlement and revenge. Fear knotted her stomach and threatened to consume her thoughts, leaving her vulnerable. She wanted nothing more than to protect her son but knew he could take care of himself. And if she, Morgan, and TEAGAN were to survive this, she needed to get her mind back on the battle.

*"RHONA, bank left. Now!"* TEAGAN bespoke Noreen's compeer, interrupting Erin's moment of inattention.

She noticed the mauve dragon respond exactly as TEAGAN commanded.

Dragons bugled when caught by another's fire. And dragons plummeted toward the patchy snow-covered ground. Shrieks and wails abruptly extinguished on impact.

DECLAN flapped his massive black wings as he hovered, sending a Sutherland dragon tumbling away.

Twice, Sutherland got close enough to singe TEAGAN's tail. And Sinclair's dragon swiped at her exposed belly. TEAGAN yelped, but twisted and turned, dove and rose, and managed to flame Sinclair's dragon's hindquarters. He screeched and flew recklessly beneath one of his clan mates to get away.

Out of the corner of her eye, Erin saw the sudden, violent maneuver that unseated a dragon's rider. She watched in horror as the man twisted in mid-air, his mouth open in a scream she couldn't hear but felt to the depths of her soul.

TEAGAN bespoke other MacKay dragons, giving warnings or directions on evasive maneuvers.

*"Are the other MacKay dragons bespeaking each other?"* Erin asked.

*"Aye."* TEAGAN sounded pleased with herself.

Two dragons, one Sutherland and one Sinclair, dove toward RHONA from different directions. RHONA gained altitude at the last moment and the two enemy dragons, unable to avoid a collision, smashed into each other.

Erin quaked at the sound of the impact: bones crunching, wings tearing, and frantic cries of pain.

*"See? 'Tis already changing the fight in our favor."*

*"But . . . the cost, the useless sacrifice of precious lives."* Anguish painted Erin's every word.

As the battle waged, smoke stung Erin's eyes. *Damn. Where are our reinforcements?* She shifted in the riding harness to check on the MacKay dragons. Most were still in the sky, but several were being driven toward the ground—overwhelmed by enemy dragons. Movement in her periphery caught her attention. Dozens of MacKenzie and Fraser dragons had joined the fray. *Thank God.*

The new arrivals dove, scattering the combatants, but Erin noticed that one of the MacKay dragons was too close to the ground. One wingtip clipped a boulder, and the dragon cartwheeled wing over wing, coming to a stop in a crumpled heap. The rider, who had either fallen or jumped clear of the harness, staggered over to his mortally injured dragon and wrapped his arms around its broken neck.

Two other dragons smashed into one another, their wings ripped and torn as they collapsed toward the ground. *Christ. They're attacking without thought.*

Suddenly Sutherland was above her and swooping in.

*Feck!* "Dive, dive, TEAGAN," Erin screamed aloud. A weird popping noise sounded from somewhere behind her. *No! Not Morgan. He can't die.* She whipped her head around in time to see Devan's blue and silver dragon appear out of nowhere, a mere dragon length away. *What the bloody ifrinn?* But Erin had no more time to think.

In an instant, DECLAN flew between TEAGAN and the flaming Sutherland dragon.

# Fifty Three

Devan's vision blurred as the air shifted around her. Breathe, she reminded herself. Snowcapped mountains and rolling hills had replaced the dunes and grassy, low-lying plains of the west coast. The vast winter-blue sky was now filled with dragons flaming dragons. Sutherland and Sinclair tartan-clad dragons battled MacKay, Fraser, and MacKenzie dragons. "What the hell? How'd we get here?"

"I teleported ye. 'Twas the quickest way," Cuillen said, his tone smug.

A dragon screeched, and Devan shifted her gaze to the fighting going on all around her.

*"Where's* R*OARKE and* D*ECLAN?"* She asked her compeer.

*"There. Just ahead of us,"* DOCHAS bespoke, then surged upward, nearly unseating both Devan and Cuillen. *"Nigh!* D*ECLAN, nigh!"*

A cacophony of discordant dragon voices shouted warnings within Devan's mind, and she had only an instant to wonder which dragons were bespeaking.

Padrick screamed as dragonfire caught him.

Cuillen muttered an incantation and splayed his hands toward DECLAN and the flaming Sutherland dragon.

The flames from Sutherland's dragon stopped in mid-air and rebounded onto him. Dragon and rider were engulfed in the inferno. High-pitched shrieks broke over the roar of the dragonfire as Sutherland and his dragon hurtled in a burning mass to the ground.

Terror roiled in the pit of Devan's stomach as she fell. She couldn't think, couldn't breathe, could only be tossed around like a kite in the wind. White-hot flames consumed her. She tried to scream, but couldn't, and then . . . it all stopped. In that instant, she knew her life was over. She surrendered, longing to see her parents again. Yet, in a blink of an eye she mourned the life she would have had with Christian and DOCHAS and the family she had found with the Tuatha Dragon Clan.

*"Come back to me, Ring Wearer,"* DOCHAS's worried voice filled Devan's conscious.

She opened her eyes and found Cuillen snapping his fingers an inch from her face. Her whole body shook and she was covered in a cold sweat.

"Come out of it. Ye're all right."

"I was . . . dead." Devan's voice quavered.

"Aye. Close tae it. Ye linked with Sutherland's dragon. But ye are back tae yerself now."

*"Do no' do that again!"* DOCHAS chastised her. *"Ye near stopped my heart."*

*"Sorry, my sweet."* Devan shuddered and wrapped her arms around herself. *"I'm not sure what happened, but you can bet I'll do my best to avoid it in the future."*

Cuillen uttered another incantation, this time moving his hands as if erasing a chalkboard.

Silence ensued as dozens of dragons hung suspended in the air, their talons extended in attack mode. Their flames snuffed out.

The dragonfire enveloping Padrick ceased, and he slumped in his riding harness. Smoke billowed around him. His shoulder and upper arm glowed red where his coat and shirt had burned away. DECLAN roared.

Terror bled up Devan's spine, seizing her breath. She blinked hard as tears coursed over her cheeks. *No. I can't lose another family member.* She lifted her gaze to the heavens. *Be strong. Take control.* She scanned the skies for ROARKE and Christian but couldn't find them. *God, no! They were just there.*

*"DECLAN, land. Padrick's hurt,"* Devan bespoke the black dragon, and just then, ROARKE crossed her line of sight as he followed DECLAN down to the ground. *"ROARKE, did Christian pack any of Timothy's dragonfire salve?"*

*"Aye. Christian wants to know how ye got here so quick."*

*"I'll join you soon and explain."* Devan took a moment to calm herself, then focused her thoughts on the remaining dragons. She bespoke them as a group. *"Stop this madness. Would you kill each other to the detriment of all Scotland?"*

She heard protests from several dragons but glared at the offenders. *"What of your oath? Each of you and your riders took an oath to protect the human race, nurture the land, and guard the coveted secret of the dragons. Ask your riders if they are willing to sacrifice you and the magic over petty clan skirmishes?"* She spread her arms to encompass the dead and dying dragons and riders on the ground below her. *"How many more will die today?"*

When she heard nothing more, Devan continued. *"Do you accept whatever your rider commands, without question? Even if the command goes against your oath? What's done is done, but you've an equal say in what happens going forward. What's between you and your chosen compeer must be shared goals, or you're nothing but slaves. Is that what you desire? Or a full partnership?"*

Devan heard a couple rumblings, but most of the dragons responded positively. She pointed to several hilltops below her and called to all the riders, "Sutherland and Sinclair on that hill to the south. The rest of you on the one to the north." She issued her terse command with authority.

Not one rider complained, and every dragon complied with her orders. Whether they were exhausted from the battle or ashamed of their actions, Devan didn't care.

"'Tis a neat trick ye possess, communicating with all the dragons. Ye are surely The One. Though ye must no' link with another dragon again," Cuillen said as DOCHAS spiraled down to land next to the smoking Sutherland dragon and rider carcasses. "No' if ye want tae live."

"So, is that what happened?" Devan dismounted, not waiting for an answer. "Couldn't you have stopped him without turning his own dragonfire against him? Did he have to die?" Her stomach revolted at the stench, and she had to turn aside.

"Aye. The link 'twas strong. I almost could no' break it. If I hadnae been here . . ." Cuillen pursed his lips. "As tae the flaming, 'twas the only spell tae come tae me mind. Besides, he 'twas beyond stopping." Cuillen remained perched on DOCHAS's neck.

"You're probably right. But it's another dragon and rider dead. Their lives destroyed because of hatred or stupidity. What I believe is at the core of the waning magic." Devan sighed. *Such lovely, noble creatures—dragons. It's too bad the hearts and minds of some humans are not as noble. Thank God there are selfless riders in the world.*

*"Do no' despair. For there are more honorable humans than no'."* DOCHAS crooned soothingly.

*"Thanks, my sweet."*

Movement caught her eye, and she spied a contingent of dragons flying in from the southwest. *Lord Almighty, now what?* She shaded her eyes but didn't recognize the yellow and black tartan harness cloths on the dragons. *First things first. See to Padrick.*

Devan's soul wept as she skirted around the broken and charred dragon bodies that littered the ground and made her way over to Padrick and Christian. *I'll never understand the depravity required to intentionally kill anyone I consider my brethren, my family.*

On that thought, she bespoke another she considered family. *"REED, can you hear me?"*

*"Aye. We have contained the Campbell chieftain and his rebellious dragons and riders with minimal injuries. Where are ye?"*

*"At the south end of MacKay territory. More dragons are approaching. I hoped it was you."*

An unfamiliar female dragon interrupted Devan's conversation with REED. *"That is The MacLeod. The Alba council leader. Morgan contacted him before we left."*

*"TEAGAN, is that you?"* Devan spotted the moss green dragon in a

small area between DECLAN and ROARKE.

*"Aye. Please come see black DECLAN's rider. He suffers."*

Devan ran to where Christian and Morgan were helping Padrick from his riding harness.

*"REED, I'll bespeak you later. Seems the council leader, MacLeod, has arrived."* Devan slid to a stop, her attention divided between the newcomers and the injured Padrick.

The MacLeod dragons landed in the space between the rival clans amongst several smoldering dragon husks. The leader clamored down from his dragon, and bellowed, "What in blazes has been going on here?"

Many of the Sutherland and Sinclair riders shifted uneasily in their seats.

"Where's Sutherland?" MacLeod snapped. He balled his fists and set his jaw.

Morgan strode toward the MacLeod leader and pointed to charred remains. His eyes flashed with antipathy. "That's what's left of him. And if it wasn't for Padrick and his dragon—at significant risk of death, I might add—putting themselves between that unhinged sod and TEAGAN, Sutherland would have finished the job he started days ago. Erin and I would both be dead." Morgan's voice rose, shouting the last words.

Christian gently lowered Padrick to the ground as Erin rushed to Padrick's side. She gingerly brushed his hair away from his sweaty face.

Kneeling beside DECLAN's heaving flank, Christian glanced around until he spied Devan. He rose, scooped her up, and held on tight. "Oh God. You're here. You're finally here. We've been searching for you ever since ROARKE lost contact." He rained kisses everywhere.

She closed her eyes and breathed in the scent that was uniquely her Christian. "I've missed you so much. And an awful lot has happened."

"Where've you been? Are you all right?" His hands trembled as he stroked her back. His lips brushed the top of her head, then rested his cheek there. "I saw . . ."

Padrick groaned, and the sound of his agony made Devan aware of their surroundings. She inched away, reluctant to leave Christian's side.

"Let's take care of Padrick, then we can talk." She grabbed the jar of salve from the bag attached to ROARKE. "Help me, Christian. Cut his coat off." She opened the jar and scooped out a handful of the pungent salve.

Christian pulled his blade from his boot and deftly cut away Padrick's coat. Devan gently smeared the medicine over his whole arm and shoulder and to where the burn extended halfway across his back.

Padrick closed his eyes and moaned. Erin retrieved her MacKay tartan and gingerly draped the cloth over him. She poured a steaming hot drink from a thermos and encouraged Padrick to sip it. Color was starting to return to his pasty complexion.

Devan noticed a jagged, bloodstained tear in Christian's jeans along his right thigh. Pulling him to his feet, she bent to examine it. "You're hurt."

Christian shook his head. "Not really. Just a scratch."

She fingered the tear in his jeans and found the wound had already stopped bleeding. The coiled anxiety inside her chest loosened. *He's okay. And Padrick's going to be all right too.*

"What about you? I saw—"

"I'm okay, now. The thunder affected my eardrums and the lightning caught DOCHAS. We were stranded and had to wait until DOCHAS was able to fly again. Long story. The most important thing is the magic's waning." She glanced over Christian's shoulder at Morgan in a heated conversation with the MacLeod leader. Fraser, MacKenzie, and one of the Sutherland riders had joined them.

Morgan pointed toward Cuillen, and Devan heard the Faerie Prince snap his fingers. He disappeared from DOCHAS's neck and reappeared in the cluster of clan chieftains.

"Uh oh. Cuillen's joined Morgan and the rest of the clan leaders. We better see what's going on." Devan ran her fingertips over Christian's stubbled jaw, kissed his soft, full lips, then stepped back.

"Did I see the Faerie Prince riding on DOCHAS with you?"

"Yes. He teleported me here. That's another story. But first, let's see what kind of mischief he's gotten himself into now. Besides, the sooner I talk with the clan leaders, the sooner we can get Padrick tended to properly, the sooner we can be alone. A part of me was lost without you by my side. I don't want to spend another night alone." She clasped Christian's hand, linking fingers and headed toward the cluster of men. *Not another night, for the rest of my life.*

"Don't fash, I'm not letting you out of my sight," Christian said.

When Devan and Christian approached, Morgan introduced her to MacLeod.

MacLeod scrutinized Devan then reached to shake her hand. "Ah, Devan Fraser. I've heard quite a bit about you. Cuillen said—"

"I'm sure the Faerie Prince was exaggerating." She caught Cuillen's raised eyebrow, then tilted her head and spoke to the Fraser chieftain. "Graeme's safe. He's with his brother-in-law and the MacLean clan."

"Thank ye. I've been quite worried. As have yer family here." Fraser indicated Christian, Padrick, and Erin. "I've found information about what we discussed days ago, about yer da."

"I'm anxious to hear what you've found out, so we'll make a bit of time later, cousin." Devan smiled. At Fraser's surprised look, she continued. "You've the same color eyes as I inherited from my dad. As does Graeme. I suspect it's a family trait."

"Aye." Fraser grinned.

Devan then addressed all the leaders. "I don't want to interfere in Alba dragon clan business, but it seems whether I want it or not, I'm already involved. I've got a lot to tell you."

"You mean about Cuillen's prophecy?" MacLeod asked.

Startled, Devan stammered. "Y-you know of the prophecy? How? Wait. Cuillen's prophecy?"

"'Tis the Keltoí Prophecy, no' mine," Cuillen protested. "I 'twas only the conduit."

"Regardless," Devan glared Cuillen into silence, "the magic's waning from the land. I've seen it, experienced the ramifications firsthand. It's why Graeme stayed in the west. We had just left the skerry DOCHAS and I landed on and completed a magic rejuvenating flight when I heard a dragon call for help near the Donald/Campbell border. At the same time, I was finally able to bespeak ROARKE and found out about the fighting that was going on over here. I left Graeme, Liam, and the MacLeans to deal with that border skirmish."

"How do ye ken of the prophecy?" Cuillen asked.

Devan pulled the scroll from her coat sleeve. "Liam MacLean found it on the skerry. He . . . In the end, he gave it to me. I've been trying to decipher it, but there are words missing from the last line."

Cuillen held out his hand. "Let me see, please." She handed it over. "Ah, aye. 'Tis the original one." He snapped his fingers, produced a quill, and filled in the smudged words. Then he gave the parchment back to Devan.

She read the words, nodded, then returned the scroll to her sleeve. She addressed MacLeod. "Can you call a gathering of all dragonriders for tomorrow? It's crucial."

"Why not just the chieftains? That I could arrange for today."

"Because we have the dead to attend to, and the injured must be cared for immediately." Devan pushed her hands through her short, messy crop of hair. "And I need time to consult with Cuillen on his prophecy. The magic isn't just waning, it's disappearing from the land. That skerry I crashed on was devoid of magic, even though there was a stone dance on it. And while I was there, I couldn't bespeak or hear other dragons."

MacLeod gasped and brought a hand to his chest. "I don't believe it."

"It's the truth. Graeme's brother-in-law, Liam, was severely afflicted because he was exiled on that skerry. And based on the madness that seems to have infested Sutherland, I believe he was so magic-starved, he became irrational."

The Sutherland representative spoke up. "My father's been lax in his magic rejuvenating flights. I'm not sure when it started, maybe years ago after my brother died." He wrung his hands, then continued. "Father wouldn't listen to anyone who disputed his ideas, especially me."

Devan touched the young man's forearm in support. "Those two can't be the only ones magic-starved. I'm betting Campbell and some of his riders are too. We must know who else is affected and help them. Liam noticed a huge difference right after we flew the pattern over the stones near Ardtornish Castle. Even Graeme felt restored. And I was able, once again, to communicate with the other dragons." She twisted her ring around her finger. "And if I am The One, as the prophecy says, I must bespeak all the dragons and their riders together."

*"Ye are The One,"* DOCHAS bespoke Devan. *"Ye know the prophecy to be the truth. Trust in yerself."*

Devan's voice lowered, as if she spoke only to herself. "Yes, it has to be me."

*"'Tis yer destiny."* DOCHAS's tone held pride. *"For ye are the Ring Wearer. The Hearer of Dragons. The One. Ye ride me—Hope."*

*"The One,"* a symphony of melodious dragon voices echoed in Devan's head.

She straightened her shoulders and gazed over the groups of dragons and riders, then back to the Scottish council leader. "I am The One."

"All right. I'll have to pick a location that can accommodate the whole Scottish dragon and rider population and keep us hidden. This weather might actually help us." MacLeod stroked his chin in thought. "Somewhere with stone circles nearby. Maybe Kilmartin Glen, near Dunadd."

"I can assist ye with keeping the dragons and riders hidden," Cuillen said. "Dunadd holds ancient magic. 'Twas once the royal seat of the Scoti tribe. 'Tis the best place tae hold yer clan gathering. And 'tis fitting for The One tae stand in the footfall of past kings as she leads all in healing Alba."

"Then it's decided. Tomorrow at noon." MacLeod's watery eyes glinted in the sunlight as he surveyed the dead riders and dragons. "We'll burn them here where they died. A reminder of the enormous cost of what's happened here today."

Devan's heart grieved and tears blurred her vision, but her voice was clear. "All should understand that today's actions weren't simply rival clans disputing boundaries. No. This might be the beginning of the end of dragons and riders. For if the magic vanishes completely, it won't just be the ones we've lost today." She waved her hand to encompass the carnage before them. "All dragons will die."

# Fifty Four

Christian glanced to where his mother was caring for his father. *He must still love her if he was willing to sacrifice himself and his dragon for her and Morgan. There's no question, I would do the same for Devan.*

*"Ye know I would for DOCHAS,"* ROARKE bespoke.

*"Aye, mo chroí. That's what family means—sacrificing for those you love. I just never thought of Padrick and Erin in love with each other, especially after so much time apart. I guess most people don't see their parents as in love."*

*"Time and distance apart does no' always lessen feelings. Ye do no' love the Ring Wearer less, even though ye two were separated for days and the whole of Scotland."*

*"You're right."* Christian grinned. *"But days apart is different than twenty-eight years. Some would say, a lifetime."*

As the gathered leaders were finishing their discussion, Christian pulled Devan and Morgan aside. "We've got to get my father and the injured to shelter as soon as possible. What do you need done here?"

Morgan surveyed the dead dragons and riders. "We've only lost two dragons and one rider. That's a miracle." His gaze stopped on one battered rider with his arms around his dead dragon's neck. "Can you help me with an injured rider? I'm not sure he can bring himself to leave his compeer, not without our insistence. The MacLeod has offered . . ." Morgan wiped his eyes, unable to hold back his emotions.

Christian squeezed Devan's hand. "A ghra, can you get Padrick ready? He'll ride with me. And ask DECLAN if he would carry Morgan and the injured rider. We'll be there in a minute."

Devan nodded and headed away while he and Morgan went to the injured man.

"Look." Christian discretely pointed to the grieving man's twisted and broken leg. "We'll need to stabilize that and keep your man from going into shock. I'm surprised he hasn't passed out yet. The pain must be incredible."

Morgan nodded. "I'll see what I can find." He headed toward the tree line.

A few minutes later, Morgan, carrying a dozen meter-long branches, returned with Noreen and a couple other riders Christian couldn't name.

Noreen laid a tartan on the ground, placed five of the branches in the center, spaced apart, then layered on another tartan. The other riders removed their belts.

She handed Morgan a first aid kit and a bottle of water. "Get as much of the pain relief into him as you can. Then set him down here and we'll complete the splint around his leg."

Morgan coaxed the man into taking the medication. Sweat beaded on his forehead and upper lip. His body began to shake and his eyes rolled back. He sagged. Together, Christian and Morgan laid him down.

Noreen and the others quickly moved the makeshift splint under the rider's broken leg, added more branches and tartan to build up the sides and the top, and used the belts to hold it all in place.

"Thank God he's no longer conscious," Christian said.

Christian, Morgan, and two of the male riders carried the injured man to DECLAN.

The rest of the MacKay dragons and riders assembled nearby, and Christian observed the singed and soot-covered riders as they checked over their dragons.

Christian helped Padrick climb aboard ROARKE, then assisted in securing the injured MacKay rider on DECLAN. Christian decided the best way was to place the man back-to-back with Morgan, keeping the man's two legs tied together along DECLAN's back.

"We need to get to the compound as quickly as possible. The MacKay rider's in bad shape. He's secure, but DOCHAS and ROARKE should fly right behind DECLAN. Devan can bespeak TEAGAN if he shifts too much," Christian said to Erin.

"Would it nae be easier for me tae teleport ye all tae the MacKay compound?" Cuillen asked Devan.

"Have you ever teleported more than just yourself, and DOCHAS and me?"

"Nae, but . . ."

"Then let's save the multiple teleportations for another time."

Christian carefully wrapped his arms around his father within the MacKay tartan to shelter him from the wind. *Thank God, the salve's working. Just got to keep him warm. Keep shock from setting in.*

When everyone was ready, Erin gave the command to take flight, and the MacKay and Irish dragons leapt skyward. ROARKE flew beside DOCHAS.

Christian managed to sneak glances at Devan while he kept an eye on the injured MacKay rider and ensured Padrick was safe.

*Christ, I don't know what I'd've done if Devan or Padrick had died.* He wondered at the speed of his changed attitude toward his father. *Maybe Devan was right. I didn't understand what I had with Padrick until I almost lost him.* He shuddered at the thought, and Padrick groaned. "I've got you, Da. You're safe now."

Once at the clan compound, Erin directed DECLAN and ROARKE to land close to the buildings. The other dragons circled once and settled in the grassy area where most of the snow had melted.

"Stay here," Christian said to Padrick. "I'll help you once we get the injured rider down." Christian slid to the ground.

They were met by the healer and several other clan members who were anxious to help. The healer called for a stretcher.

Christian untied the rope used to keep the rider from shifting or falling off. Then he, Morgan, and two burly men carefully lowered the still unconscious man onto the stretcher. The healer whisked him away.

Christian returned to ease Padrick from ROARKE.

"I'm not an invalid," Padrick said as the tartan slid off his shoulder.

"No, but the burns are more extensive than when you burned yourself knocking down Sean's door after ROARKE set it aflame last spring." Christian lifted the tartan back into place. "You should have the healer look at those burns. Some of them look like second or third degree. There might be permanent scarring."

"Timothy's salve will be sufficient. Besides, the healer will be busy with that injured rider."

Devan and Erin joined them. They guided Padrick into the house and settled him on the couch. Within minutes, Devan had coated Padrick's burns with another thick layer of salve. Erin went to the kitchen to put on the kettle for tea, then came back with rolls of sterile gauze. The women laid the fresh dressings over the scorched and blistered skin.

Padrick sighed and slumped against the back of the couch, angled carefully to keep his injured arm, shoulder, and back from touching anything.

For the first time in what seemed like hours, Christian could breathe again. The tight bands of fear loosened from around his heart. He pulled Devan into his embrace and buried his face in her neck. A deep growl reverberated in his chest. *I might never let her out of my sight again.*

Devan pulled back, gently cupped his cheeks, and kissed him. "I'm here now. I'm not going to disappear on you."

"I know, but . . ." He shrugged and enfolded her in another hug.

The whistle of the kettle startled Christian. He twined his fingers with Devan's. Despite what she'd said, he wasn't ready to lose physical contact with her completely.

As Erin went to make tea, he peeked at Padrick and debated with himself about moving him to one of the upstairs bedrooms.

Morgan came in from the kitchen carrying a tray with freshly poured tea and a plate of biscuits. Erin followed. He set it all down before going to a cabinet and retrieving a bottle of twelve-year-old Macallan. He poured a dram in each cup, then handed them out.

"How's your injured rider?" Christian asked.

"Noreen and our healer have taken him to hospital. I don't know if the doctors there can save his leg." Morgan took a healthy swallow of his tea, then pointed to Padrick. "Should we get him upstairs? That can't be comfortable."

"I'll be fine here," Padrick mumbled. "Maybe a shot of whiskey?"

"Tea," Erin said as she brought a cup to him. "With a wee bit of the good stuff."

Padrick pushed himself upright, winced, then took a sip. "Bless you." He closed his eyes for a moment, then opened them and sought Devan. "I thought that was you. What happened to you after you left us?"

Letting go of Christian's hand, Devan slipped into the seat beside Padrick, careful to avoid jarring him. "It's a long story, and I'll tell you over dinner. But for now, it was Cuillen who helped me get back to you. We arrived just as Sutherland's dragon started spewing fire." She searched for the Faerie Prince and finally spied him near the hearth. He indicated she could tell the story. "Cuillen cast his magic to stop the attack, but a second too late. You caught the leading edge."

"The flaming I know." Padrick took another sip of his tea.

Christian poured three fingers of the Macallan in a tumbler and tossed it back in one swallow. "You nearly died." The words came out in a whisper.

"I saw Sutherland positioned to attack. I didn't think. I reacted." Padrick sucked in a breath, then wearily shook his head. "What happened to him?"

"Cuillen's magic caused Sutherland's dragon's flames to rebound." Devan squeezed Padrick's leg. "They died instantly. After that, the fighting ended."

Padrick nodded, then lifted his bloodshot eyes to Christian. "Have you told Devan about . . .?" At Christian's shake of his head, Padrick sighed. "She needs to be told about that bloody eejit ex of hers, and what he's planning to expose. The safety of the dragons is paramount."

"Christ." Christian scowled. "We've barely managed to get back to the MacKay compound and get another dose of Timothy's salve on you."

"What about Rick?" Devan looked from Padrick to Christian.

Christian glared at his father, then sighed. "The bloody gobshite's been on the evening news. Spouting lies and half-truths about the dragons."

"What? Wait. On the news here in Scotland?" Devan's eyes widened. "How does he know—?"

"He knows nothing. He's just speculating after talking to Kelly, Logan, and the oilrig foreman." Christian started to tell Devan of the broadcasts, but Morgan turned on the telly and played the two recordings of the previous two night's news broadcasts.

Devan stared at the telly for a moment, then she jumped to her feet. "That dirty, rotten, no-good . . ."

"Chancer. Gobshite. Fecking eejit," Christian supplied.

"Has Sean seen this?"

"Aye," Padrick said. "Don't fash. He and the officials are busy, controlling the media narrative."

"Same as MacLeod and the Scottish officials," Morgan added.

"I've got to stop that . . . that bastard, Rick. What's he doing in Scotland anyway?" Devan fumed.

"Says he's on special assignment." Padrick gasped as he tried to set his cup down.

"You need to lie down, rest. Let the salve work its magic," Christian said as he inclined his head toward the stairs. "Don't even think about protesting, or I'll—"

"I'll go, but the salve's helping already." Padrick winced as he got to his feet.

Christian ducked under his father's good shoulder and gently helped him up the stairs and back into the guest room where Padrick had slept the night before. Erin and Devan followed. Once he was settled, Christian ushered the ladies out.

"Devan and I can use a bit of a rest as well," Christian said. "We'll be back down before suppertime."

Devan started to protest, but Christian interlaced his fingers with hers and squeezed. "A couple hours, that's all."

"Right," Erin said, then turned to Devan. "Thank you for coming to our rescue. I don't know—" She choked up and looked away.

Devan gently pulled away from Christian and gathered Erin in her embrace. "I'm just glad Cuillen was with me." Devan loosened her hug and stepped back. "I really should talk with Cuillen. I've still not completely deciphered the prophecy. And I need to deal with Rick."

"Tonight. After you rest." Christian guided Devan down to the room he had slept in last night. He closed the bedroom door behind them.

He wove his fingers in Devan's hair, held her mouth to his, and lost himself in her sweetness. *More, more. Don't ever stop. She's mine. As much as I am hers.*

Her hands skated over his chest as she pushed the shirt from his shoulders. Her weather-roughened fingertips scraped down his stomach to the snap of his jeans.

He broke the kiss and covered her hands with his. "Let me just hold you for a bit longer." His voice shook and he paused to bring it under control. "God, I was so scared I'd lost you."

"I need you." Devan lifted her hands to his face, rubbed his stubble, and brought her lips to his in a soft, sweet meeting.

It was as though a gaping hole inside him waited to be filled. And it could only be filled by Devan. His Yank.

The tension inside him grew to an ache. With his pulse thundering, his heart pounding, he loved her. And together they soared.

When he caught his breath, he whispered, "*Beidh grá agam duit anois agus go deo. Coinníonn tú mo chroí.*"

"What did you say? It sounded beautiful."

He nuzzled her throat, then gazed into her sleepy eyes. "I shall love you now and forever. You hold my heart."

A soft blush flushed Devan's pale skin as she smiled. "And you hold mine. How did you learn so much Gaelic anyway? I thought it is spoken mainly in the west of Ireland?"

"That's true, but I picked it up fairly quickly in primary. And since there weren't too many of the sisters who understood it, I could say whatever I wanted, swear whenever I needed, without anyone harping on me. It was like my own secret language. For an orphaned lad, owning that one thing was precious, vital even."

"Now you'll need to teach me the Gaelic."

"Later." He kissed her rosy cheeks, then trailed his mouth down her body until she cried out for more. And he accepted the challenge.

# Fifty Five

Devan took a long shower. She let the hot water soothe her worries over Padrick's injury and all the needless dragon and rider deaths. As she soaped herself, she realized Liam still had the dragonhead cross necklace Christian had given her. *Does it hold some sort of magic? Maybe the giving of an object freely, releases whatever magic it is imbued with. Something to think about.*

She finished bathing and was drying off when she heard REED's tenor voice.

*"Devan, can ye hear me? 'Tis REED, compeer to Graeme."*

*"Yes, REED. Sorry I didn't get back to you right away. Is everyone okay? Did the Irish dragons and riders find you?"*

*"Aye. Golden BRIANNA was magnificent. She kept the Campbell dragons from flaming us. Alas, she and the others returned to Éire."* The dragon paused. *"Graeme asked me to relay that he and Liam explained the loss of magic at the skerry to the MacLean chieftain. He 'tis blaming himself for Liam's mental state. Liam's exile 'tis finished. His family will return here on the morrow. Graeme and I will stay here one more day to see his sister and the bairns settled. Then we are homeward bound."* Devan heard the wistful tone in REED's voice.

*"That's wonderful news about Liam. The MacLeod is setting up a clan gathering for all dragons and their riders, so I'll see you tomorrow at noon. Can you ask Graeme to bring a batch of Liam's special poultice tomorrow? I've an injured dragon here that I believe will benefit greatly from the concoction."*

*"Aye. I look forward to seeing ye again."*

*"Me too. Safe flight."* Devan broke the connection.

She found a change of clothes laid out on the bed and began dressing.

*"Ring Wearer. Where are ye? I have missed ye terribly. Are ye angry with me?"* GRAYSON's melancholy voice fluttered in Devan's mind as she finished dressing.

*"GRAYSON, dear one. I'm still in Scotland with DECLAN and ROARKE. Did BRIANNA not bespeak you? I'm not angry. Why would you think that?"*

*"Aye, golden BRIANNA said she located ye. That ye were lost for days. 'Twas my fault. I called for ye to come back to Éire for the hatchlings, and ye did no' arrive. Do ye know about them?"* GRAYSON thoughts were jumbled.

*"No. Tell me all about their hatching."*

*"ANNE and STRUAN. They are strange. Pure white with red eyes. Healer Timothy calls them albos."*

Devan laughed aloud but contained the humor in her voice. *"Do you mean albinos?"*

*"Aye."*

*"But are they all right?"* Devan ran her fingers through her freshly washed hair. *"What was wrong with their hatching?"*

*"Clan Leader Sean believes they could no' break their shells. They are tiny. I can see through their wings."*

*"They will grow, not to worry. How are you faring? Have you been practicing your communications with other dragons?"*

*"I am fine now that I have returned to Loughcrew. I do no' like it in Beaghmore,"* GRAYSON's tone hardened on the last sentence.

*"Do the dragons not talk with you?"*

*"The dragons are no' the problem. My dam's rider is no' nice. I understand why black DECLAN's rider does no' live there."*

*"Well . . . you can't always choose your family. Not like a dragon chooses his or her compeer."*

*"I suppose. When will ye return?"*

*"I'm needed in Scotland for a bit longer. But you can bespeak me any time you've a need. And you know DOCHAS and ROARKE will talk with you as well."*

*"Even if I am lonely?"* GRAYSON's melancholy leaked through.

*"Especially then. But you know who might also be lonely and in need of a friend? Niall."* Devan thought of Timothy's young grandson who had bonded with GRAYSON over each of them being bullied.

*"Oh, aye. Niall and I bespeak every day. Often more than once."*

*"Wonderful. The two of you are perfect together. Tell him to give you an extra nuzzle from me. And I'll be back to Éire soon."*

*"Safe flight, Ring Wearer."*

When she finally made it downstairs, Morgan and Christian sat in front of the television. The evening news was beginning. *Good. Let's see what Rick's up to tonight. He excels at pissing off government officials.*

Rick stood inside a television studio, in front of a map of the highlands. His perfectly coiffed hair and his ultra-bright veneered smile couldn't hide the smarmy asshole Devan was glad to be rid of. On cue, Rick pulled back his shoulders and plastered his I'm-smarter-than-you condescending look on his face.

"As I've been reporting over the last several days, there's something mysterious going on that the Irish and British governments aren't telling their citizens. And this investigative reporter won't settle for the brush-off. It's your right to know if the government is exposing its citizens to harm by experimenting with flying beasts, referred to as dragons. Are the whistleblowers being silenced?" Rick pointed a finger at a spot on the map.

"Two days ago, I received calls from several concerned citizens reportedly seeing fire in the sky and near gale force winds buffeting the heather just before that blizzard from the west swept through the area northeast of Ullapool. When I inquired with the local officials, I was told the phenomena was probably due to a lightning storm, nothing more.

"Today I went out to speak to the witnesses and to see for myself if there was evidence of any lightning strike. Two of the witnesses, Mr. John Scone and a Mrs. MacPherson, showed me the area below where they saw the fire in the sky. I saw several broad swatches of burnt grasses where the snow had melted. Something caused it, but there wasn't a single tree in the area that had been charred."

Rick turned back to the camera. "If my science hasn't failed me, lightning usually strikes the tallest object in the area. So why, if the official word is a lightning strike, weren't any of the trees in the forest hit? And why the sweeping burnt patches only on the low-lying grass?" The backdrop changed to an animated image of an evil-looking dragon swooping down over a medieval village, flames burning everything in the dragon's path. "My research—"

Devan yanked the remote from Morgan's hand and turned the television off. "That arrogant bastard wouldn't know the first thing about research. Certainly he knows nothing about dragons." She stormed to the entryway. "He gives honest journalists and researchers a bad name. And since he's put out a reward for information about my whereabouts, I think we should go collect. I want him gone, preferably back to America with his devil's tail tucked between his legs." She looked back at Christian. "Are you coming?"

"Damn right I am." Christian grinned and turned to Morgan. "Do you know where the broadcast station is?"

Morgan nodded. "I better drive you there. You can't show up on the back of a dragon, even if their magic keeps them hidden. Besides, I'll be able to keep you two out of trouble." He grabbed his jacket and a set of keys.

"I shall come along," Cuillen said. "That boyo dinnae heed me at all. We must ensure he will no' interfere in tomorrow's gathering."

Morgan groaned.

"Perfect," Devan grinned maliciously. "And I have an idea. I'll explain on the drive over."

As Morgan drove to the station on the outskirts of Ullapool, Devan laid out her plan.

"What happens if Rick's not at the station by the time we arrive?" Morgan asked as his fingers played over the steering wheel.

"Not to worry," Devan said. "Once he's got a story in his head, he'll forgo just about anything to see it through. Believe me, I've been the one who's been forgotten. No, he'll be there. Probably barking orders and chastising everyone for not working fast enough."

When Morgan parked the well-used Land Rover, Devan confirmed everyone knew the plan.

Devan, followed by Christian and Morgan, stormed into the television studio and halted at a glass-walled room.

Inside, Rick stood in front of a blue screen while a man working an expensive-looking camera zoomed in on him. Rick's face was in profile as he gestured toward the screen. When he turned his head toward the camera, he spotted Devan and grinned lasciviously.

Outraged, Devan yanked open the door and stalked in. "You call yourself an investigative reporter? You're a—"

"Calm down, sweetheart." Rick gestured to the cameraman to stop recording. "We've got an audience. Don't cause a scene now."

Morgan stayed the cameraman's hand, so the confrontation would be recorded.

"I've been searching for you. Where have you been?" Rick turned and scooped up some papers from the small table near the screen.

"I've been getting on with my life. Meeting new people, making friends," Devan said. "Without you."

"But you're my fiancée."

"No, I'm not. We had this out months ago. Our relationship ended. Badly. And even if you believe otherwise, I'm telling you here and now, we are over. Finished. Just go back to San Francisco."

"I'm working on a story. Maybe the biggest of my life. No way am I leaving now."

"Right. Your government cover-up story involving Ireland and Scotland and some flying beasts." Devan laughed. "I'm surprised. All the time we were together, I believed you were a real reporter. I just didn't realize you worked for *The National Enquirer*."

"I do not," Rick fumed. "You've never understood."

"I understand all right. You're a deceitful, lazy hack. Listening to an oilrig foreman who wants to blame anyone besides himself for the deaths of his men. Or believing a criminal like Kelly Dunkirk over the gardaí report. Do you even care who that jackass assaulted? Oh, right, it was a so-called trumped-up charge." Devan was on a roll now. "I'll tell you, since you couldn't be bothered to actually investigate." She used air quotes on the last word. "Your best pal Kelly assaulted me. He followed me and a friend of mine for days while we were on a sightseeing trip throughout Ireland. Kelly stole my father's cufflinks. He assaulted me, twice, as a matter of fact. Put me in the hospital both times. And he did all those things on the orders of his boss, Logan Walsh. A lowlife racketeer. But don't take my word for it—investigate.

"You couldn't even find me yourself. Had to use your clout and this platform to offer a reward. You're a joke. After I wouldn't bow to your greatness at that bistro in San Francisco, you broke into my parents' home. Thankfully, breaking and entering is just one more thing you suck at. But you did manage to get a look at my Irish citizenship petition, didn't you?"

Rick sputtered, but Devan wasn't finished.

"It gave you a starting point, that's for sure. Without your B and E, you'd still be twiddling your thumbs trying to find me. Pathetic."

Rick's face contorted with rage.

"And now you're claiming the beasts are dragons. You're delusional. Next, you'll be claiming there's a faerie standing right beside me."

Cuillen took his cue and appeared beside Devan.

*I hope Cuillen doesn't show up on camera as he claimed. Or I'll be the one looking the fool.*

The Faerie Prince tipped his jaunty cap and winked at Rick.

The rage disappeared as Rick stumbled back and raised his arms in front of himself. "Stay back. Get away from me, you . . . you . . . little man."

Devan looked around her, pretending innocence. "Who are you talking to? What little man? There's only myself and Christian here, and he easily tops six feet."

"Not him." Rick flapped his hands toward Devan's right side. "That man next to your hip. He calls himself Cuillen. Says he's a

Faerie Prince. I've already had one run-in with him. On the Isle of Skye. You don't see him?"

Devan looked down, then back at Rick. "There's no one there. How long have you been hallucinating? Are you on drugs? Do your bosses know about your propensity to lie?" *So far, so good. My plan seems to be working.*

Rick narrowed his eyes. "Bitch! You set me up. Even after all I've done for you. I'll get you for this. You'll be ruined. No university will hire you. I'll make sure of it. No one messes with Rick Hunter."

Cuillen disappeared, then reappeared on top of one of the large can lights.

Rick lunged for her, his hands extended as though to throttle her.

Christian stepped in front of Rick to block his attack, and snarled, "You won't be touching Devan. Ever. Again." Christian glanced at her. He didn't raise his voice, but the intensity of his last two words darkened his eyes.

"You can have the bitch. Good riddance. You're as crazy as that Faerie Prince." Rick backed away from the threat Christian posed.

Cuillen danced and made faces to draw Rick's attention.

Rick shrieked curses and ran from the glass-walled room.

Devan curled into Christian's embrace, pretending to be scared. Then loud enough for the microphone to pick up, she said, "I'm sorry it took me so long to realize Rick would go to any lengths to make a name for himself. Even concoct ludicrous stories and drag good people into lying for him, just to get a bit of notoriety. Now he's brought the citizens of Ireland and Scotland into his little games. I pray he gets some help. Really, dragons?" She shook her head, then had to keep her gaze averted as Christian led her past the cameraman.

Once outside, she burst out laughing. *God, it feels good to laugh again.*

Morgan strolled out of the building, smiling. "That's the most fun I've had in quite some time."

"That couldn't have gone any better. Especially with it all caught on camera. Please tell me the cameraman didn't stop filming." Devan turned to Morgan.

"He recorded it all. Said the news producer saw the whole thing, except for Cuillen of course, and he plans on airing it later tonight. I heard Rick screaming for his assistant to get him on the next plane out. He didn't care where it went, just as long as he was away from this backward country. Neither the cameraman nor the producer were sorry to see the last of Rick Hunter." Morgan unlocked the vehicle.

Once they were all inside, Cuillen materialized. "That 'twill set the boyo straight."

Morgan started the Rover and had just exited the parking lot when a wizened-looking faerie appeared on the dash. Morgan slammed on the brakes and jerked the wheel. The Rover came to a stop diagonally across the roadway.

"Christ Almighty. Who the bloody ifrinn are you?" Morgan glanced around, then maneuvered the vehicle back to the parking lot. His hands shook as he turned off the motor.

"'Tis me da," Cuillen said. "Dagda."

"Dagda?" Devan leaned forward to get a better look at him. "But you're Irish? What are you doing in Scotland?"

"Irish. Scottish." Dagda waved his hands as if the lands he named were inconsequential. "Borders don't contain me, the Celtic Faerie King. Father of the Tuatha dé Danann. I rule the Otherworld." He crossed his arms, then spoke to Cuillen. "What are you doing, playing parlor games? This is the exact opposite of not meddling in the affairs of humans. I see you have found the lass. Your duty is done. I command you to go home."

"I cannae. I willnae." Cuillen stood hipshot in the passenger seat facing Dagda. "That parlor game, as ye called it, kept that Yank eejit from telling the world of the magic."

Devan cleared her throat. "Dagda, I really need Cuillen—and yourself, of course—to help with the clan gathering tomorrow. From all that I've been able to piece together, the magic's been disappearing for a while. And it won't be restored overnight. I don't even expect the clan rivalries to stop that fast, but now I know it's my destiny to see Scotland whole and to keep the magic from extinction. I won't fail. But I also recognize I can't do this alone. Will you help me?"

"Remember what I told ye that eve in yer rath?" Cuillen gentled his tone, and Dagda nodded. "The gathering 'tis set. Noon, atop Dunadd. We are all linked. All survive or all die."

"Then it appears our fate is set as well. I shall see you on the morrow. For the magic of the lands must be restored." Dagda snapped his fingers and disappeared.

The drive back to the MacKay compound was quiet. Devan cuddled into Christian, laid her head against his chest, and heard the steady beating of his heart. When his arms came around her, the fears of the last few days vanished.

That night, over a delicious supper, Devan told of her harrowing time on the skerry and her realization of Liam being magic-starved. She left nothing out, not even her fear of failing.

*"Do no' fash,"* DOCHAS bespoke. *"Ye have done all that is within yer power, and more. Ye will prevail. It is our purpose."*

In the early morning hours, Devan awoke to a niggling feeling that she was missing something important. Something she had heard months ago. *What was it? Maybe about Padrick?* She racked her brain but still couldn't think straight. Knowing she wouldn't get back to sleep, she rose, left Christian wrapped in the covers, and went in search of a computer. She'd do a bit of research. She had an idea of what she might say at the clan gathering but wanted to refine it. She found Erin in the kitchen brewing some tea.

"Ah, couldn't sleep either?" Erin got another cup ready.

"I'm still puzzling out the prophecy. My mind's too active to sleep. Besides, I wondered if you have a computer I could use? I need to look up a few things."

"Sure. Computer's in the office." Erin poured the tea. "Follow me."

When Devan was settled in front of the computer screen, waiting for it to boot up, she stared at Erin, unblinking. *Do I dare tell her? Would I want to know?*

"What?" Erin said, then sipped her tea.

"It's . . . well." Devan's cheeks warmed. She looked away for a moment, then decided that perhaps this would be the only time she'd get a chance to say what was on her mind. "Padrick's still in love with you, you know. And I can see that you still love him."

"I can't deny that. But we're both committed to our dragons and our clans. We're in two different countries. I gave up any life I might have had in Ireland when I left. Besides, I've committed to co-leading with Morgan. My feelings can't be more important than my oath to a whole clan, or to my dragon."

"I realize that, and it's exactly right to feel that way. Just don't close your heart to Padrick. He's been wronged enough." *Bingo. Yes, that's what Ronan said—wronged. So Christian's The Seer and Padrick's The Wronged. That makes Erin The Exiled. And that makes sense. She exiled herself from Ireland.* Devan sipped her tea, trying to hide her excitement at how easily the puzzle came together after all. She considered Erin.

"And your son needs you both. Christian may be a grown man, but he's only now learning what family is all about. That when it works, it's the greatest gift." Devan tightened her fingers around the warm cup, the thought of her parents speared her with a sudden pang of longing. She pushed her melancholy deep into a corner of her heart and focused on the three adults who were now so important in her life, and how she could help them as they struggled with their relationships to each other.

"It took Christian over six months to let down his guard with Padrick and think of him as his father. And he's just met you. Then in a blink of an eye, Padrick risked his own life to save you. I believe that was the moment Christian realized, after being alone most of his life, he could lose you both and be alone again."

Before Erin could respond, the computer screen flickered. Distracted, Devan quickly lost herself in her research.

Erin reflected on what had just happened between herself and Devan—her son's soul mate. That the two were meant to be together was obvious by their deep love and obvious commitment to each other. But, as Erin studied the young woman—her striking features highlighted by the artificial glow of the computer screen—she realized she didn't know Devan any more than she knew her son.

She turned Devan's words over in her mind. *She's got courage, that's for sure. I'd never have had the confidence to speak my mind to someone I barely knew.* Like acid on an old wound, Devan's words had focused the guilt and regret Erin carried like a shroud around her heart.

The young woman who sat absorbed in her task—one she didn't volunteer for, yet assumed so readily—had cut through to the very heart of Erin's long-festering wound. *I didn't have the courage to fight for what I truly wanted—Padrick and the family we could've had. Bowing to Kiely's threats was easier. No, not easier, just more familiar. The actions of the naïve, Catholic girl I was back then. But I'm not that person anymore. And maybe Devan's insights will be the key for me to righting the wrongs I committed so long ago. I owe it to Padrick and Christian . . . no, to myself . . . to at least try.*

Erin felt the first vestiges of hope stir within her battered spirit and her admiration for Devan grew. *There's real depth to this young woman. Now I understand why she's the one to take the lead in healing Scotland and restoring the magic.*

# Fifty Six

The remains of Dunadd Fort rose out of Kilmartin Glen as though a giant boulder had been dropped from the heavens. Its prominence ever more profound due to everything around it being so flat. During the flight southwest, Devan had noted hundreds of ancient monuments ranging from stone circles and standing stones to megalithic tombs. Yet none were more impressive than the one they flew over now.

At Cuillen's direction, Devan requested DOCHAS, ROARKE, DECLAN, and TEAGAN to circle Dunadd Fort's rocky crag. The other MacKay dragons, with their riders, landed amongst the grassy landscape, well away from the road and buildings.

"There," Cuillen pointed to the terrace just below the ruined rock walls of an ancient citadel. "See the footprint where long-ago kings were crowned? 'Tis the Inaugural Stone, where ye must stand tae be heard by all."

Devan didn't understand how she would be seen, let alone heard, by the hundreds of Alba dragons and riders from so high above the valley floor, but nodded. She guided her dragon to land near the base of the hill.

"I'll stay here to await Sean and the rest of the Tuatha Dragon Clan emissaries," Padrick said.

Devan had called the Irish clan leader earlier that morning to request he, Aisling, and Michael, as province leaders, attend this meeting. She'd also insisted Sean bring GRAYSON because she believed the drake's deformity was another manifestation of the waning magic. If she was correct, then Ireland could ultimately be as severely affected as Scotland.

*Could Kiely's abhorrent behavior affect the magic? What about negative emotions?* Devan shivered, though the day was warming. *One problem at a time. The prophecy says I'm to heal a fractured nation first. Concentrate on that for today.*

Devan, Christian, and Cuillen approached a well-defined section of the rock wall and began to wind their way up the rocky defile. They entered the first ring of ancient rocks, then walked past outcrops of tall stones and navigated slippery flagstones to the second ring of rock defenses. The higher they went, the more ruinous the walls. They climbed to the top where Devan could easily use her imagination to visualize where a glorious, fortified citadel once stood—proud and imposing.

"Can you feel the magic? This place nearly vibrates with it." Devan spread her arms and twirled in place. "This is perfect. The energy here is rejuvenating."

"But 'tis no' where ye need be," Cuillen said, his arms crossed.

Devan sighed but allowed herself to be led back down to the terrace just below the summit. A visitor's sign next to the flat rock told of the concrete replica of the footprint that covered the rock slab to preserve it.

Dagda appeared. "When you stand here, my magic will project your voice."

Devan shook her head. "I won't betray the ancient kings by standing in the Inauguration Stone footprint, even a replica. Instead, I'll address everyone from the citadel. There is plenty of room for the clan members to roam freely and not feel threatened by an outsider. For I am not their ruler, and I won't presume that honor."

"You are wise in your assessment of the humans." Dagda stroked his chin. "I shall extend my magic to encompass the entire glen. You will be heard, yet all dragons and riders will be shielded from without."

"Thank you." Devan, followed by Christian and the two faeries, made her way back to the top. "Yes. This feels right." As she gazed out at the puffy cloud-filled sky, she watched as dozens upon dozens of dragons flew toward Dunadd. "And so it begins," she whispered to herself.

The glen filled with restless clusters of dragons and riders, all bedecked in their colorful clan tartans. Each clan arranged themselves in a pie-shaped wedge, with the clan chieftain in front, riders scattered behind, and their dragons spread out at the rear. Whenever a clan assembled next to a rival clan, open space separated them.

The Tuatha Dragon Clan spiraled down to land beside the MacKay clan, and Devan was happy to see Sean had indeed brought GRAYSON. Next, she saw the MacLean clan land. She waved to Graeme and Liam to get their attention, then beckoned them to join her.

When they arrived, she hugged them. Christian's stony expression reminded her of what he had told her last night—that he had envisioned Liam's attack. Christian wasn't convinced the man wasn't still a threat. Devan rushed to introduce them to Christian and the two faeries, hoping to allay his worry.

Last to land was the MacLeod clan. Devan recognized the chieftain as he slid from his dragon. He climbed to the citadel, alone.

MacLeod shook her hand, then nodded to everyone else. "It's your gathering, Ms. Fraser. We best get started before any skirmishes break out. I'll introduce you." He shuffled toward the edge and began speaking.

Devan, in a sudden bout of nerves, clutched Christian's hand.

He squeezed her fingers, pressed a light kiss on her lips, then whispered, "I'm so proud of you, a ghra. Remember, you were chosen as outlined in the Keltoí Prophecy. Use your strengths. And I'll be right here with you." Reluctantly, he released her hand.

Devan joined the MacLeod leader. He nodded to her, then stepped away.

"Dragons and riders of Alba," Devan spoke aloud to the riders, as well as telepathically to the dragons. "I've asked to speak with you all today because . . . well, as your chieftains know, the magic is waning."

Denials and shouts of rancor were heard. Dragons grumbled.

Suddenly, Liam and Graeme strode forward to stand at her side. And Christian wrapped a comforting arm around her waist.

"It's true," Liam shouted, then lowered his voice when he realized his words echoed through the glen. "I've experienced it firsthand."

"Is that what happened to your ugly mug?" Someone yelled.

"No. That was my fault. Six months ago I was exiled to a skerry for a horrible action that caused the death of one of my clan mates and his dragon. It was an accident, but The MacLean was right in punishing me." Liam stared at his uncle for a moment. "While on the skerry, I found out the standing stones there no longer held any magic. I had to send KENNETH, alone, to other places for the magic rejuvenating flights. And because I wasn't allowed to leave the skerry, I became magic-starved.

"I also found an ancient prophecy and deluded myself into thinking I was to play a part in it. That I would be the one to restore the magic. During those six months, I went radgy. More than radgy. When Devan and her dragon were forced to land on the skerry, I attacked her."

"Don't," Devan whispered as she rested a hand on Liam's arm.

He smiled, then continued. "I attacked Devan, and her dragon protected her."

"The Irish dragon flamed you? That's an act of war. Attack!" One of the men yelled.

Shouts and war cries erupted as dozens of riders raced for the citadel. Other riders found rivals and began throwing punches.

"Cease!" Cuillen waved his hands in the air and muttered the same incantation from yesterday.

Every person was halted, suspended in mid-action. The only ones able to move were those atop the citadel.

"Can they still hear me?" Liam asked the two faeries.

"Aye," Cuillen said. "But speak quick. These eejits are trying me patience. I've a mind tae—"

"You'll do nothing to harm any of them," Devan said, then turned to Liam. "Why'd you tell them all that? It was bound to stir them up. Maybe even cause some to come after you."

"I made a promise to myself the day you forgave me, even though you didn't fully trust me. I wouldn't lie anymore, even if I must face stiff consequences for my actions," Liam said to her. He removed the dragonhead cross pendant and gave it back to her. He smiled. "Thank you for loaning it to me. Even though it wasn't your talisman, it provided me with its own form of magic."

Christian took the pendant from her hand and placed it back where it belonged. He lightly kissed her neck and whispered, "A ghra, you are amazing. It's no wonder I love you."

Liam spoke to the crowd. "You're listening, but you're not hearing me. The flaming was my fault. I was magic-starved, and I attacked first. You all must understand, if this can happen to me, it can happen to anyone."

Devan raised her hands as if pleading for silence. "Give me a chance." She turned to Cuillen. "Can you release them, without letting them complete their intended actions? I don't like restricting anyone's freedoms."

Cuillen shrugged. "I do no' ken."

"I can," Dagda said. He spread his hands and intoned, "All shall be as before. None shall enact violence."

When Devan looked down, all the riders were back in their clan groupings, gazing around them with bewildered expressions on their faces. She inclined her head at Dagda for thanks.

"You can battle each other, but the magic is still waning, so you'll just lose the war. And in losing, the dragons will go extinct. Is that what you want?" When no one answered, she started down from the top. And the others followed her.

She reached the bottom of the trail and halted. She pulled the scroll from her sleeve, unrolled it, and read aloud. When she finished, a hush came over the crowd. Even the dragons were silent.

"According to the Keltoí Prophecy, it's my task to restore the magic." She paused to get her thoughts in order. "By now you all know I can bespeak and hear all dragons, but before I partnered with DOCHAS, I was a researcher. I was trained to look at all the data and come to rational conclusions based on evidence and facts."

"First," Devan held up one finger, "we know from Liam's experience, and from Sutherland's youngest son's corroboration of his father's neglect, that without consistent magic rejuvenating flights with their compeers, riders become unhinged. I suspect that was also the case with the Campbell chieftain. And over time, the progression gets worse. Until riders direct their dragons to flame others. Dragons and riders died yesterday."

"Second," Devan added another finger, "in the clan structure as it stands now, you and your dragon don't trust others, let alone rival clans. These negative emotions and all the clan skirmishes must have an effect on the magic. Yet just as the fracturing of the clans didn't happen overnight, it will take time for trust to be sowed."

Murmurs rose from the crowd, and fearing another wave of discord, Devan hurried on.

"Irish dragons can bespeak each other. Until recently, no Scottish dragon did. That is a trust issue. In time, I believe your dragons will build that trust and bespeak other dragons." She pointed to her ring on her raised fingers. "Another possibility is the lack of a talisman. All Tuatha dragonriders wear a pendant that matches my ring. Each of you should have one to bond you together as Alba dragonriders. Did not your forefathers come together as Scotsmen and declare their intolerance of English domination in 1320?" She began to recite the words. "Because while a hundred of us remain alive . . ."

The dragonriders united, and with raised voices, completed the Declaration of Arbroath.

Devan smiled briefly. "Will you dishonor what your forefathers fought for?"

"Never," the riders thundered.

"Then hear me now." Devan added urgency to her tone. "If you do nothing to change your ways, and the magic wanes enough that the dragons are no longer hidden, English leaders will see this as a security breach and bring the full weight of their political offices down on Scotland. You've probably seen the news over the last few nights. Both Irish and Scottish dragon clan leaders have managed to sway government officials on the best way to control the narrative. And I've neutralized the investigative reporter, for now."

Laughter and insults to Rick's integrity could be heard.

"But make no mistake, more dragon sightings won't bode well for keeping the Scottish clans from falling under England's thumb."

Gasps and inventive oaths rose from the riders.

*Perfect. Appeal to their stubborn Scottish pride. But don't let them get too riled up.* She strode to where the Irish dragons and riders were and knelt to hug GRAYSON.

"This is GRAYSON. He was born without wings. I believe, due to the fact his dam's rider was trying to stage a coup of the Tuatha Dragon Clan. The magic—a living entity—waned just enough to produce a drake. With time and perseverance, GRAYSON has adapted to become one of the most valuable members of our clan." She scratched his eye ridges, then stood.

"Scotland is not alone. Ireland is also affected." She glanced toward Dagda and Cuillen, who nodded. "As are the faerie folk. If both our territories are afflicted, then the rest of the Celtic nations probably are as well. There may be other reasons for the magic disappearing. We must root out all the causes."

Devan climbed the terraced hilltop. This time she stopped on the second tier and placed her foot in the carved footprint. She gazed out across the grassy glen, her vision full of dragons and their riders all looking to her.

"Today is a new beginning. Maybe the deaths suffered yesterday were a necessity, a catalyst to start the healing of Alba—the fractured nation the Keltoí Prophecy spoke of." She paused. Her heart leapt as she looked at Christian standing with Padrick and Erin. DOCHAS nuzzled GRAYSON as ROARKE looked on. Near the Fraser clan, Devan spotted Graeme and Liam and a pretty woman standing between them. Liam had an arm around the woman, who must be his wife, Merida.

*I finally am where I belong. I have a family. I love, and I am loved.* Devan wiped at the sudden tears that formed. "So I call on you now to gather together. Renew old alliances and forge new friendships. For tomorrow, we begin the task of helping our Celtic brethren. And together, we will stop the deterioration and restore the lost magic."

Devan clenched her fist and pressed it against her chest. "*Neart san aontacht. Crógacht inár gcroí.* Strength in unity. Valor in our hearts. Who will stand with me?"

*An Deireadh*

# Riders and Their Dragons

Irish Rider/ DRAGON/ Color

Devan / DOCHAS / Midnight Blue w/Silver wings
Christian / ROARKE / Forest Green w/Sea Foam Green wings
*Padrick / DECLAN / Black
**Sean / FIONN / Red
Aisling / BRIANNA / Gold
Kiely / TULLIA / Plum
Ronan / CALHOUN / Pearl White
*Michael / SEAMUS / Adobe Orange
Matthew / KIERAN / Brown
Aiden / SEBASTIAN / Pale Blue
Daniel / LORCAN / Taupe
Ryan / QUINN / Teal
Maggie / FIANNA / Buttercup Yellow
Shea / REGAN/ Maroon
GRAYSON / Gray
MALACHY / Copper (Dragonet born to FIANNA and KIERAN)
ROISIN / Oatmeal (Dragonet born to FIANNA and KIERAN)
STRUAN / Albino (Hatchling born to REGAN and LORCAN)
ANNE / Albino (Hatchling born to REGAN and LORCAN)

** = Tuatha Clan Leader
* = Province Leader

Scottish Rider/ DRAGON/ Color

Liam / KENNETH / Yellow
Graeme / REED / Rust
Erin / TEAGAN / Moss Green
Morgan / BOYD / Smoky Gray
Noreen / RHONA / Mauve

# Irish Clan Location Map

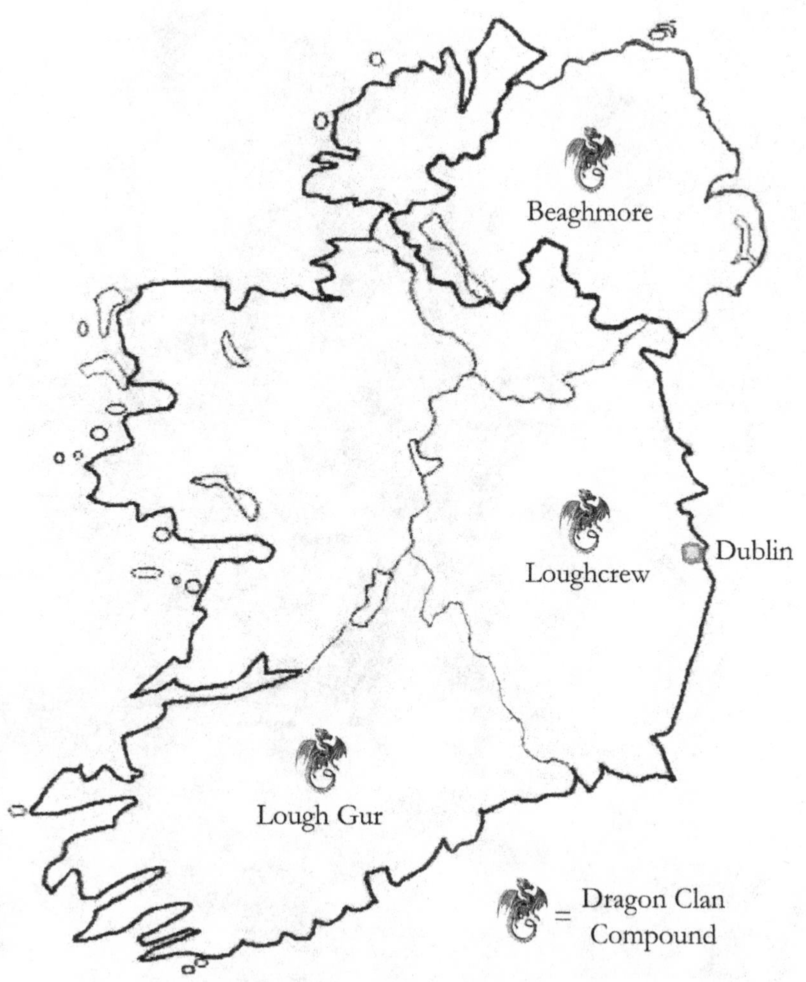

# Scottish Clan & Location Map

| | |
|---|---|
| 1 = Lochbuie on Isle of Mull | 2 = Exile Skerry |
| 3 = MacKay Clan Compound | 4 = Faerie Glen on Isle of Skye |
| 5 = Cothiemuir Wood | 6 = Dunadd Fort at Kilmartin Glen |

# Glossary

*A Ghra*: My Love / ahh graw
*A Storin*: My Treasure
*Agus mé, tú*: And I, you
Alba: Scotland
*An Deireadh*: The End
*At dheis Dé raibh a anum*: May his soul be in God's right hand
Bairn: Baby or small child
*Beidh grá agam duit anois agus go deo*: I shall love you now and forever
Bespoke: Telepathic communication between dragon and rider
*Biochas*: Virtue
Biscuits: Cookies
Bloody: Expletive attached to all manner of things
Blootered: Very drunk
*Bodhrán*: An Irish frame drum / bow-ran
Bollocks: Bullshit or messed-up
Boot: Trunk of vehicle
Bothy: Small, one-room cottage
Boyo: Variation on the word boy
Bugger it: General purpose expletive used to express displeasure
*Céilí* -or- *Céilidh*: Party / kay-lee
Chancer: Con man or trickster
Compeer: Partner
*Coinníonn tú mo chroí*: You hold my heart
Crisps: Chips
Cuppa: Cup of tea
*Cumhacht*: Power
*Dilseacht*: Loyalty / deel-shockt
Dochas: Hope / doe-haas
*Draíocht*: Magic
Eejit: Idiot
Éire: Ireland / AIR-a -or- Era
*Eitílt shábháilte*: Safe flight

*Eolas draíochta*: Magical knowledge
*Fáil*: Destiny / fall
Fash: Worry
Feck: Swear word
Gaol: Jail
*Gaothchothrom agus eitilt sábháilte*: Fair winds and a safe flight
Garda: Police (singular) / Gar-da
Gardaí: Police (plural) / Gar-d-i
*Geall*: Promise / Gy-al
*Glóir go Alba*: Glory to Scotland
Gloaming: Twilight
Gobshite: Asshole
Gobsmacked: Stunned
Havering: Talking
*Iarr ar an tuar Keltoí*: Seek the Celtic prophecy
Ifrinn: Hell
*Is breá liom tú I gcónaí*: I shall love you always
*Is breá liom tú, mo chroí*: I shall love you, my heart
Jumper: Sweater
Ken: Know
Knackered: Tired
Lift: Elevator
Loch / Lough: Lake
Maither: Mother
*Mí ádh*: Bad luck
*Mianach*: Mine
*Mo Caras*: My clan, my family
*Mo Chara*: Friend
*Mo Chroí*: My heart / Muh kree
Nae: No (Scottish) / Nay
*Neart san aontacht. Crógacht inár gcroí*: Strength in unity. Valor in our hearts
Nigh: No (Irish) / Ni
*Ni neart go cur le cheile*: There is no strength without unity

*Onóir*: Honor
Publican: Bartender
Quay: Pier / Key
Radge: Crazy
Rath: Underground faerie fort or home
Rubbish: Trash
Rucksack: Backpack
*Saoirse*: Liberty or Freedom / sear-sha
*Sgian Dubh*: Ceremonial Scottish blade / skeen-do
Shite: Swear word
Skerry: Small reef or rocky island
Slagging: Making fun of
*Sláinte:* Cheers / sloynta or sloyn-cha
Snap: Photograph
Tae: To
*Taoiseach*: Prime Minister
Telly: Television
Torch: Flashlight
Tuatha: A tribe or family group, like a clan / Too-aha dai
Whist: Be quiet

## Acknowledgements

First and foremost, I am honored and humbled by the care and nurturing, yet tough love of my critique group. They helped me cut the excess, develop believable characters, and learn this craft. They are fantastic writers all. And thanks to my diligent copy editor. Any remaining errors are mine.

Of course, I would not have met these people without joining the California Writers Club Tri-Valley Branch. A special thanks for the close friendships cultivated with some of the best human beings I have had the pleasure of sharing my writing journey with.

Thanks to my friends and family who put up with me living in my story world, I appreciate your support.

To my beta readers: I hope you enjoy the finished product.

A special shout out to the wonderful people I met in my wanderings through Ireland and Scotland. I thank you for your interest in me and what I was there to accomplish. Sláinte.

## Praise for other Novels

*The Keepers of Éire*:
"A wonderfully, intricately layered journey in the tradition of Anne McCaffrey's *Dragonriders of Pern.*"—Bella Online

*Reluctant Paladin*:
"Compelling characters in an imaginative setting with lots of excitement and adventure. I loved every page!"—Penny Warner, author of *The Code Buster Club* series

# About the Author

Jordan Bernal is the international award-winning author of *The Keepers of Éire, a* dragon fantasy that encourages readers to let their imaginations take flight. Her enduring love of fantasy, especially dragons, inspired her to write and publish through her independent press, Dragon Wing Publishing. In 2017, Jordan released a YA edition of *The Keepers of Éire* and published her middle-grade, anti-bullying spin off novel, *Reluctant Paladin.*

She grew up in the heart of Silicon Valley: San Jose, CA. She spent most of her career in the high-tech industry as a product coordinator/technical writer and earned her bachelor of science degree in business entrepreneurship. Jordan is a member of California Writers Club Tri-Valley Branch and credits her growth as a writer to her critique group, open mic nights, and various writing classes she has attended. She is also an active volunteer and presenter at the San Francisco Writers Conference.

Jordan lives in the Tri-Valley region of Northern California. She enjoys reading, photography, and spending time with Roarke, her Pomeranian.

For more information on Jordan's current projects, visit http://www.jordanbernal.com.